NEMESIS

A Novel of Old California

NEMESIS

A Novel of Old California

JOE YOGERST

Blank Slate Press | St. Louis, MO

Blank Slate Press | Saint Louis, MO 63116
Copyright © 2018 Joe Yogerst
All rights reserved.

For information, contact:
Blank Slate Press
An imprint of Amphorae Publishing Group
a woman- and veteran-owned business
4168 Hartford Street, Saint Louis, MO 63116

Manufactured in the United States of America
Set in Didot and Adobe Garamond Pro
Interior designed by Kristina Blank Makansi
Cover Design by Kristina Blank Makansi
Maps drawn by Shannon Yogerst

Library of Congress Control Number: 2018945419
ISBN: 9781943075508

To Julia, Chelsea and Shannon, who know
what it's like to live with a writer.

• La Jolla

Mission San Diego •

Mission Valley

San Diego River

• County Hospital and Poor Farm

⬛ Old Town

New ⬛ Town

• Golden Hill

• Ocean Beach

Dutch Flats

⬛ National City

San

Roseville •

Diego

Coronado

Sunset Cliffs

Ballast Point

Bay

• Point Loma Lighthouse

San Diego 1888

N

W   E

S

San Ysidro •

Mexico

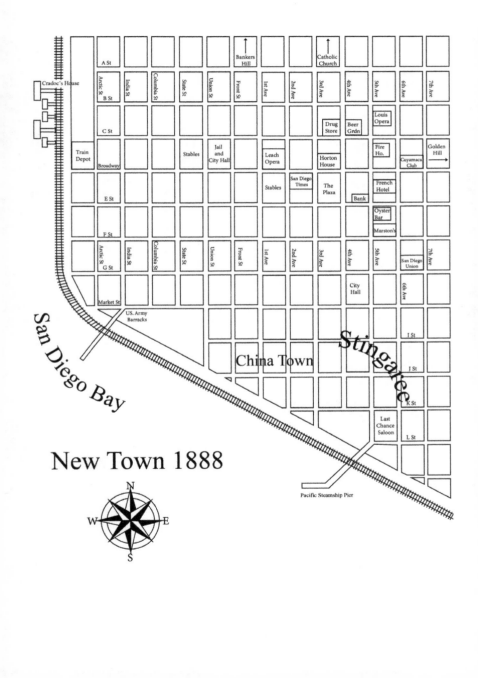

1

April 1888

AT THE TOP OF THE RIDGE he reined in, let his horse catch a breath while he took in the view. Blue sky, fresh breeze, ocean smooth as glass. The kind of day that could make you forget what you had set out to do. Which in his case was kill a man.

He slipped a telescope from his saddlebag and extended the brass. The Cliff House, a rambling wooden manse near the spot where the San Diego River trickled into the sea, came into view. An American flag with thirty-eight stars fluttered from a pole in a forecourt spangled with the buckboards and horses of those gathered inside for Saturday night cards and crumpet. Among the assembled transport was the dark-red brougham of Zebulon Archer, the first among those marked for death.

Assuming he could actually go through with it. In all his days, in all his scrapes, including the rare occasions on which he had fired a weapon in anger, he had never actually killed anyone. Wounded and lamed a couple, for sure. But never sent a man to the grave. And if by some chance he had killed someone in one those dustups, he could have justifiably claimed self-defense in every instance for the simple fact that the other bastard had been the first to draw his six-shooter, knife, or in one memorable case, a harpoon (moral of that story: never taunt a drunken whaler).

Yet he now found himself on the verge of taking the life of a man he barely knew. And not by quick and easy means. Zebulon Archer was going to suffer, experience something akin to the physical and mental anguish he had inflicted upon others. And suffer *now* rather than in some nebulous place after death. No matter what the Good Book said, nobody could guarantee that Satan would have his due with this sinner. That left earthly retribution as the only sure-fire remedy and he the only person with the motive, means, and opportunity to exact it.

So why the doubt? Why were his hands trembling and his guts about to heave? How was it that on the day of reckoning—an event pictured countless times in his mind—he was suddenly overcome with fear?

It certainly wasn't fear of getting caught. He was too clever, way too careful. Every detail of his plan had been mulled over, every possibility considered. He had studied Archer's movements, calculated his strengths and shortcomings, determined the man's vulnerabilities. He'd undertaken practice runs to ensure the feasibility of his plan in the real world, rather than just the hypothetical setting of his own mind. That's not to say everything would go as planned; life did have a way of dealing you jokers now and again. On any given day, anything could happen. Yet in the same breath, he was reasonably sure that he could dispatch the man and disappear without being seen.

It wasn't fear of his opponent. Archer might be larger than himself, but he was also older and much less agile, and not one to carry a reasonable weapon. Back in the day, the man always had a shotgun at arm's reach. But in recent years, thinking himself an upstanding member of the community and immune to the sort of trouble that requires such firepower, Archer had retired his twelve-gauge in favor of a derringer concealed inside his overcoat. But that poor excuse for a sidearm would never come into play, because Archer would never get a chance to retrieve it. That's how swift and sudden the attack would be.

Neither did he fear divine reprisal. He believed in heaven and hell, knew right from wrong, and figured that murder in most cases was not morally acceptable. But the Bible did make exceptions—for warfare and righteous retribution. And the killing of this man most definitely fell into the latter category. In modern times, the law had assumed responsibility for avenging egregious acts. But there were instances when the law found itself unable or unwilling to act, or hampered by an inability to prove guilt beyond a shadow of a doubt. That left the door open for individuals such as himself to exact punishment without offending the Almighty.

When you got to the bottom of it, his fear derived from just one thing—how taking the life of another human being would change him. How could it not? Was anything more earth-shattering than killing someone with your own hands and doing so on purpose? He'd seen it go both ways. Men who didn't seem the least bit troubled by bloodshed, as if killing were just another bump in the road. And men who were never the same, who could not come to terms with the abolition of human life even in cases (like war) where society condoned their action. Having never taken this step before, he had no way of predicting how his own soul would go.

Watching the sun disappear and dusk settle on the land, he tried to muster his courage. If he could not bring himself to end Zebulon Archer's life tonight, he would never be able to slay the others. And someone had to make them pay.

Dark enough now to conceal his approach, he nudged his horse down the slope and across the chaparral of the coastal escarpment. He knew the terrain well, not just from scouting it over the past few months, but from all the way back to his youth, when this lonely stretch of shore had provided an adventurous escape from schoolwork and household chores. Even in the dusky light, he easily navigated the trail that led down to Ocean Beach. Dismounting and leading his horse across the surf-splashed sand, he stole right up behind Cliff House without anyone noticing.

Through the big picture windows, he could see half a dozen men and an equal number of sporting ladies arrayed around a table in the parlor. Laughing, drinking, flirting, making wagers. And there was Zebulon Archer, alternately puffing on a stogie and sipping whiskey from a brown jug, oblivious to the fact this would be his last night on earth.

†

Around nine o'clock, Archer pushed back from his chair at the poker table. Making his way through swinging doors into the kitchen, he brushed past a young blonde working the scullery and onto the back porch. Down the steps he went, headed for a row of latrines behind the big house, clutching his little brown jug. As was common along the California coast, the night had taken on a damp chill. Archer almost turned back for his overcoat, but his bladder urged him onwards. Quick piss and he'd be back at the table.

Taking one last sip of whiskey, Archer carefully placed his jug on the ground and stepped into the nearest jake. Unlatching his trousers, he answered nature's call. He was in a grand mood, merrily humming as he relieved himself, calculating in his mind what sums he would ask of the banker, the judge, and the deputy mayor arrayed around the table tonight. Much later, of course, after the poker petered out and the gents had their turn upstairs with the ladies hired to provide "light entertainment" for the evening. It wasn't out-and-out bribery, merely how business was conducted these days. Booze, gambling, and quim in return for venture capital ... and an understanding that anything that happened at Cliff House on Saturday night never got spoken of again.

The leak completed, Archer shook his member and tucked it back inside his trousers. He nudged the latrine door open with an elbow and stepped outside, leaning over to retrieve his whiskey.

"What the hell," Archer grumbled. The jug was missing. A long evening of drink had left him more than a little tipsy, yet not enough to forget where he'd placed his beloved hooch. He had most definitely brought his drink along for the piss. Had to be here somewhere....

Squatting down on his haunches, Archer felt around in the dark. He heard footsteps and looked around. "Careful!" he shouted thinking the person might accidentally kick the jug.

When the person didn't answer, Archer looked up. "Who's that?" he asked as something hard clipped his left ear. Someone had taken a swing at Archer with his own jug.

More surprised than wounded, Archer scrambled back to his feet. "You sonofabitch!" he barked, charging at a shadowy figure.

The attacker took another swing. Archer lifted an arm to deflect the blow, but the move came a moment too late. The jug found solid purchase this time, slamming against the side of Archer's head and knocking him sideways. His legs wobbly, Archer managed to snatch a momentary grip on the outhouse door before blacking out.

When he came to, he was being dragged along the ground by a horse, his ankles bound and his arms trailing behind like a raggedy doll. He could taste blood in his mouth, and the side of his skull hurt like hell. Even in his muzzy state, without the faintest idea what his assailant's motives might be, Archer sensed mortal danger. He reached for the pocket where he kept his derringer, only to remember that he'd left his overcoat back at the house. He tried to bend forward and grab the rope wrapped around his ankles, but age and girth thwarted the effort.

Twisting his body sideways, Archer frantically reached out for the blur of sagebrush and manzanita whizzing past his face. But he could not achieve a firm enough grip to free himself or slow the horse's progress. When all else failed, Archer began to shout. Petition his companions, his peons, his whores—whoever might be within hearing distance— to rescue him from the phantom attacker. But it was all for naught. The sound of the surf muffled even his loudest appeals.

The dragging eventually stopped on a patch of smooth sandstone. Archer figured they were somewhere on the cliffs that stretched south from Ocean Beach towards the tip of Point Loma. He still had no inkling of his assailant's intent, but no desire to hang around and find out. Archer rolled over, tried to rise to his feet. He managed to prop himself up on his knees when a boot to the side of the head sent him sprawling to the ground again.

In silence and with measured speed, the attacker flipped Archer onto his stomach, drove a knee into the man's back, and tethered his arms in the same manner as his feet.

"What do you want?" Archer cried out.

But the attacker saw no need to respond. He was busy with other tasks, disconnecting the towline from the saddle, making sure it was still tight around Archer's ankles, and then disappearing into the dark.

"What do you want?" Archer's shouted again, louder this time. And once again his plea provoked nothing more than silence.

He could hear the attacker fussing over something in the distance and then coming back, his boots clacking on the clifftop.

"I've got money!" Archer pleaded, his panic rising.

Lifting him by the armpits, the attacker dragged Archer across the sandstone shelf to the edge of the precipice.

"Tell me what you want! Just let me go!"

His head hanging over the rim, Archer could taste the salt on his lips, feel the spray in his eyes, hear the waves crashing on the rocks below.

"I'll give you anything! *Anything* you want! Just tell me!"

And finally the attacker spoke, whispering "Sam Ah Choy" into Archer's ear.

Archer exuded a startled gasp. He knew the attacker's voice. And in the same breath realized the motive—revenge for something that happened so long ago he could barely recall the details.

"It was an accident!" Archer shouted as the attacker pushed him over the edge of the hundred-foot-high cliff. He braced for a crash landing that would surely end his life. But it never came. Instead, Archer felt himself being slowly lowered down the sandstone face to a point where the top of his head hovered about a foot above the rocky shore.

Dangling upside down in midair, moaning from the pain and panic, Archer was fully aware of his predicament, but unable to escape. Above the sound of the surf, he could hear his assailant ride off and leave him to fate. A wolf moon peaked over the crest of Point Loma. The tide would soon rise to its highest level of the month. The cove would flood and so would Archer's lungs. His death would not be slow, and it would not be easy. But even Zebulon Archer knew it was just.

2

NOISE ROUSED NICK PINDER from a deep sleep. He dragged the pillow over his head, and tried to ignore the disruption, but the infernal racket persisted. Some sort of ringing from downstairs. And then he remembered: *the telephone.* But who would be calling so early on a Sunday morning?

Throwing back the quilt, he lurched across the floor in the dark, stumbled through the bedroom door and down a flight of stairs to the ground floor of his house on Golden Hill. The ring continued as Nick lit a lantern and sneered at the shrieking box. It was brand new, installed just a couple of days before, a Western Electric machine mounted on a wall in the hallway, one of only three hundred in the entire county.

Other than a test by the telephone company to make sure the device functioned properly, this was the first time Nick had heard a peep from the apparatus. And now in his half-sleep, he couldn't remember how to use the damn thing. *Listen through the wooden stick ... talk into the hole on the front of the box.* He reached for the handle, brought it close to his face, still not sure what he was supposed to doing. He heard a female voice in the earpiece, an operator at the telephone exchange in town. "Mr. Pinder?"

"That would be me," he said cautiously.

"One moment please …"

The female voice vanished, replaced by a baritone male. "Mr. Pinder, is that you?"

Nick immediately recognized the voice as Angus Reed, night watchman at the County Courthouse and, more importantly, one of several dozen people around San Diego who fed Nick with a steady stream of tidbits and gossip in return for beer and whiskey money. In a town with three daily papers and several weeklies—and reader allegiance that swayed like willows in the wind—it was a necessary investment. A single headline could sell thousands more papers. And nobody had a better network of informants than Nick.

"Sorry about the hour," Reed shouted from the other end, "but I got a bit a natter that might interest you."

"Not a problem," said Nick, trying to shake the sleep from his head. He had purchased the telephone—paid for with his own funds—for just such occasions. And Angus wouldn't be calling at this late hour and in such a lather without proper reason.

"Zeb Archer's had an accident," the watchman announced.

Nick exuded a heavy sigh. "Angus, I appreciate the effort. But I don't think that justifies waking me up in the middle of the night."

"Haines is pretty worked up."

"Who the hell is Haines?

"The foreman out at Cliff House. He wants to talk to the sheriff. Wants somebody to come out and fetch the body—"

Nick cut him off. "Did you say *body?*"

"Well yeah…."

"Archer is dead?"

"I suppose so…."

"Why didn't you say so, man? What killed him?"

"Some kind'a accident is all Haines would say."

Zebulon Archer dead—that certainly was news and more than enough to justify the early morning intrusion. Assuming nobody else had the scoop. "Angus, are you the only one who knows?" Nick asked quickly.

"Far as I can tell," the watchman answered.

But that didn't mean a damn thing. Everyone had their stoolies. Nick had to act fast. "Do you know Elliot Patterson?" he asked the watchman.

"That photographer fella?"

"Exactly! He keeps a room at the St. James Hotel. I need you to go there straight away. Explain about the accident. Tell him to get his gear together and make haste to Ocean Beach. Speed is essential."

Silence from the other end of the phone. "Is there a problem, Angus?" Nick asked.

"I'm not allowed to leave the courthouse while on duty."

Nick shook his head in disgust. Like that had ever stopped Angus before. This was nothing but a shakedown. "Will another dollar suffice?"

"Yes sir, Mr. Pinder, It certainly will."

"Then get a move on!" Nick shouted, hanging the wooden earpiece on a hook on the side of his telephone. *Mighty fine invention*, he thought to himself. *Having one at home should prove most useful.*

Back in the bedroom, in the flickering glow of a table lamp, Nick stared at the woman on the other side of the bed. Roz was a few years younger, in her late twenties, blessed with copper-colored hair that fell in waves against her back, porcelain skin dabbed with delicate freckles, and the bluest eyes Nick had ever seen. He never tired of admiring his wife, even at moments like this when he was rushing to leave.

Roused by the commotion, Roz rolled over and stared up at her husband. "What's wrong, darling?" she muttered in a faint brogue, far too early to hide the Irish in her voice.

"Zeb Archer is dead," Nick answered, stepping into a pair of woolen trousers. "Some kind of accident out at Ocean Beach." He felt no need to elaborate. There was a story to cover, and duty called, even in the middle of the night.

Feeling the early morning chill, Roz pulled the quilt over her bedgown as she sat up straight. She thought in silence a moment, then decided that for once she would stand her ground. "What about today?" she asked.

"What about it?" was Nick's curt response.

"Easter Sunday," she reminded him. About the only time each year she could drag him to Mass.

He sighed. "Can't you go on your own?"

"That's not the point!" Indeed it wasn't. Roz had helped organize the holiday service at St. Joseph's Catholic Church by personally designing and supervising the creation of a large decorative Easter Cross made from hundreds of white lilies, golden roses, and scarlet geraniums, many of them grown in her own garden. This was an important day in her life, and she wanted her husband to be part of the celebration, both sacred and secular.

"Can't this wait till *after* Mass?" she pleaded.

"Roz, don't start...." The edge had crept into his voice, the condescending tone she so detested.

The tension in their marriage had become more pronounced in recent months, not to the breaking point quite yet, but definitely headed in a negative direction. While Nick's attitude certainly played a part in the decline of their marital bliss, that paled in comparison to his ever-increasing work hours. Late nights and weekends on the job had become much more frequent. And now here he was again, rushing straight from their bed into the saddle on some "do-or-die" quest.

"I'm sure someone else will cover for you," Roz said calmly, checking her temper.

But Nick didn't give an inch. "This isn't a drunken sailor we're talking about. It's Zeb Archer. One of the richest and most powerful men in San Diego. And he's dead. Which makes this a *very* important story. Which is what I get paid to write. So we can have a house like this. So you can have nice things."

He always threw that back in her face, an unspoken assumption that Roz had insisted on having their own house rather than renting quarters in town, that she craved a higher station in life, when in reality Nick was the rabid social climber. But it was useless trying to reason with him at moments like this. For that matter, it was useless even if there wasn't an urgent deadline to meet.

Rather than argue until she was blue in the face, Roz decided to cut her losses. "Can you make it later?" she pleaded, lower lip held tight beneath her front teeth, staring out from behind the quilt with two dusky blue eyes. "There's another Mass at noon."

Nick could never resist that sulk of hers, and he felt like a shit for trying. Already he felt guilty for having snapped at her. "I'll try my best," he said, softening his stance. And when the look on her face told him that trying still wasn't good enough, he said, "I'll make it. I promise."

Running his fingers through strands of rumpled hair, Nick kissed her plump lips. He considered for a moment forgoing the whole business out at the shore, crawling back into bed with his wife. He took her face in his hands, transfixed by the enormity of her eyes. Then he clutched her tight, like he was hanging on for dear life. For just a moment, Roz thought he would stay. But then ambition got the better part of romance.

Patting her on the back—his way of saying that time had expired—Nick withdrew his embrace and charged out the door like a schoolboy let loose at the end of a long the day.

†

Nick had already roused their house girl. And by the time he got downstairs, Lupe had a lantern in one hand and the reins for Nick's horse in the other, giving him the sort of look a daughter might give a father rushing out in the middle of the night.

He told her not to worry, but knew she would. That was her way. Lupe had been with them since the previous December, after spending several months cooking and cleaning at the St. Joseph's rectory. Nick had convinced the Mexican girl to come and work for them rather than the priest. Roz had protested at first; she was perfectly capable of taking care of the household herself, especially if Nick wasn't going to let her work. But in much the same vein as their house on the prosperous eastern outskirts of San Diego, Nick had eventually got his way. And so Lupe came to live with them, giving Roz even more free time.

If nothing else, her Spanish continued to improve, because the girl could barely speak a word of English.

Nick took the reins and boosted himself into the saddle of his chestnut gelding and disappeared down the hill, making his way towards San Diego. It was a strange town, a mix of Wild West and rowdy seaport with a bit of Mexican border thrown in, the only place Nick had lived in his thirty-eight years. He'd been raised in the lighthouse at the end of Point Loma, and might have become a lightkeeper instead of a journalist if his father hadn't gone off to fight for the Union and never come back.

Riding through the eastern outskirts of town, Nick passed one of the vacant lots where migrants camped until they got their bearings, bought themselves a piece of land in the subdivisions springing up around San Diego, or moved on. Scores of tents, carts, and covered wagons were scattered helter-skelter across the barren allotment, cook fires burning down to their last embers, muffled voices drifting from the dark. Any other place they would have called it a squatter's camp. But in San Diego they didn't use such unsavory language. Might offend potential buyers and bring the whole house of cards tumbling down—the land boom that underpinned the local economy, making the rich men even richer and keeping most everyone else employed.

Not wanting to attract undue attention, Nick kept a slow and steady pace down Broadway, a muddy and manure-soaked avenue recently renamed by the city fathers to make it seem more grandiose. A couple of drunks scuffled on the bandstand in the middle of the main plaza, their fracas illuminated by the electric arc lamp that hovered high above the square. But that didn't trouble Nick one bit. It would have been strange if there *weren't* drunks in the plaza at this time of night. By contrast, the enormous Horton House hotel on the plaza's north side remained quiet as a church mouse, the doorman snoozing on the front steps and barely a light ablaze in the upstairs rooms. All of this boded well for Nick. His journalistic rivals were asleep or otherwise occupied.

The *San Diego Times* was lodged on the second floor of a stout brick building on the west side of the plaza with a balcony overlooking the square. Nick's boss, Clive Bennett, the founder, editor, and publisher of the paper, sometimes slept in a small room at the back of the office on nights when he couldn't be bothered to walk the ten or so blocks down to *Medusa*, his live-aboard steam yacht. This being a Saturday, Clive was no doubt wide awake and hard at work in the Stingaree, the town's notorious saloon and red light district, making new friends and influencing ladies in ways that even Nick's fertile mind could not imagine. So he rode right past the office, continuing his slow mosey down Broadway, the bay now within smelling distance. The pithy aromas wafting up from the water were as familiar as anything Nick had grown up with, and if he really thought about it, one of the few things that lingered from his youth.

Three blocks down from the plaza lay the County Courthouse, four stories mounted by a copula and a basement that housed the county jail and sheriff's office. Nick spotted his snitch poised against the white picket fence outside the halls of justice.

"Good morning, Mr. Pinder," crooned Angus. "Or should I be saying goodnight?"

"That's a toss-up," Nick answered, peering down from his horse. "You find Patterson?"

"Helped him load up his wagon. He's already on his way out to Ocean Beach."

Nick pointed his chin at the courthouse. "What about the law?"

"Archer's foreman called again. I had to tell 'em this time. Fatty Rice was doing graveyard, and he rode out lickety-split. Don't think you'll beat him."

"Doesn't matter," Nick mumbled to himself. Fatty was a pushover. The deputy wouldn't interfere with anything he might want to do at the shore.

Nick flipped two silver dollars to the watchman. "I cannot thank you enough," he told his courthouse spy. "Git!" he snapped, and his horse galloped off.

†

Making his way across Dutch Flats in the dark, it took Nick about half an hour to reach Ocean Beach. Lights blazed inside Cliff House, but there didn't appear to be a soul around. "Anybody home?" he shouted at the wide-open front door.

A teenage girl appeared, clad in an apron and work boots. Nick didn't recognize her. Most likely a short-term hire for the weekend real-estate sales. "Where's everyone?" he asked.

The girl looked off to the south. "Over yonder. Somewhere down the shore."

Swinging his horse around, Nick headed south along the coast, cutting through the chaparral behind the sea cliffs. Soon he could see lights glowing in the distance, a cluster of torches and lanterns at the edge of Devil's Cove, a horseshoe-shaped cauldron known for its swift and unforgiving tides. On the edge of the precipice, a group of men huddled in a tight circle, condensation rising from their conversation as they fought the morning chill.

Nick did a quick double take. Dead center in the pack stood Wendell Smith, the young reporter who had joined the *San Diego Times* just a couple of months earlier. His forearms resting on the pommel, Nick glared at the young reporter. *How in the hell did that ass sucker beat me to the scene?* Smith was inexperienced, but awful eager. Maybe *too* eager. Pen pressed to paper, Wendell was asking questions and taking notes. *He must have his own snitch. Maybe even Angus, that stinking two-timer.* Nick would find out, bet your bottom dollar. But for the time being, the death of Zebulon Archer outweighed all else.

At that precise moment, Wendell Smith was coming to terms with a similar surprise. Whatever chance he had of snagging the Archer story for himself—and the keen praise of their boss—had just vanished. Plain and simple, Nick had seniority. And the ear of the deputies, not merely because he bought them drinks on a regular basis, but also because they reckoned Nick was the only reporter in San Diego with *cojones* that could match their own. Nick dared to be different. He dared, because it got him better stories than any other paper in town and because of the image it created. The tough guy. The hard ass. Nick would go places, ask questions, write stories that no one else would touch. And he didn't seem to be afraid of anything. How could a lawman not respect that? Nope, the young reporter didn't stand a chance.

Nick and Wendell exchanged a glance, silent recognition that whatever happened to Archer was now Nick's show to orchestrate. Having established his primacy, Nick swung

down from his horse and approached a skinny fellow in a navy blue uniform with a tin star pinned to his chest. Deputy Fatty Rice.

"Mighty cold this morning," Nick declared. "Man could use a drink."

"And me being a man," said Fatty, "I would not decline."

Reaching into his overcoat, Nick offered a sterling silver flask to the deputy, who took a long swig and passed it back.

"I reckon you wanna see the body?" Fatty asked.

"You reckon right."

Fatty grabbed a lantern and led the way down the sandstone terraces that waves had carved along one side of the cove. Wendell followed like a bashful puppy, hanging back, keeping his thoughts to himself. Reaching the bottom, they ambled across a rocky beach only visible at low tide. Stones crunched beneath their feet as the three men made their way along the base of the cliff, slipping and sliding on the wet surface.

"Hope you got a cast-iron stomach," Fatty warned.

No joke this time. They could smell Archer's corpse long before they saw it—the stench of human death mixed with rotting kelp. The men pinched their noses as they got closer. On the verge of losing his stomach, Wendell gagged. But he kept it down, determined to salvage something from this middle-of-the-night escapade.

About a hundred yards along the beach, Fatty stopped and held up the lantern. In the faint glow, Archer's corpse hung upside down, suspended from the clifftop by a rope wrapped around his ankles. Crabs feasted on the exposed parts of Archer's body, but the animals scattered as the three men neared the corpse.

"Is this how you found him?" Nick asked.

"Pretty much," said Fatty.

"You think he did this to himself?"

Pushing back his bowler hat, the deputy scratched a temple. "Mighty strange way to kill yourself. Don't you think?"

"So you're calling it murder?"

"I ain't calling it nothing," Fatty answered. "That's not for me to say."

Once again, it didn't really matter. Suicide, homicide, or misadventure, the demise of Zebulon Archer translated into front-page news ... and another feather in Nick's already fat cap.

3

MARSHAL CRADOC BRADSHAW was not a happy man. Someone had disturbed him in the dead of night, dragged him out into the cold and damp. And now, arriving at the shore, matters appeared to be out of control.

A human body hung upside down from the cliffs like a great pelagic fish that someone had hauled from the sea. Elliot Patterson stood behind a massive Empire State photographic camera, holding up a sled of magnesium powder, ready for action. And about a dozen good-for-nothings—including one of his own deputies—were lining up to get their picture snapped with the slimy carcass. At the very least, they were showing flagrant disrespect for the dead. At worst, disturbing evidence of a possible crime.

Overnight the marine layer had settled along the coast, low clouds as far as the eye could see. It would burn off by noon, but for the time being, the slate gray sea seemed almost indistinguishable from the sky.

A silhouette on horseback against the muted dawn, Cradoc slowly rode around to the other side of the watery maelstrom. He wore a slouch hat, a pair of leather riding boots that had long seen better days, and a full-length duster that concealed his weapons—a sawed-off shotgun and a Colt single action army revolver left over from his stint with the U.S. Cavalry.

It was Fatty Rice who spotted the marshal and his dappled gray mare staring down at them from the palisade. "Crap," the deputy muttered with no small amount of disquiet.

Cradoc scrutinized the scene with a mordant scowl, shaking his head back and forth like he could not believe this foolishness. No ordinance or regulation banned one from poking, prodding, or otherwise disturbing a dead body. Yet at the same time, common decency should prevail.

Unlike the others, Nick Pinder wasn't the least bit rattled by the marshal's arrival. He had his banner headline story. Patterson had all the photos they needed. The rest was afterbirth, nothing but souvenirs for those gathered at Devil's Cove this morning. Still, he couldn't resist a jab at his old nemesis.

"Get the marshal in the picture!" he shouted at Patterson, loud enough for the lawman to hear.

Moments later, the two of them stood face to face on the clifftop. "You've outdone yourself this time," Cradoc hissed at the reporter.

"It's just a photograph," Nick responded. "No need to get your knickers in a twist."

"What's the widow Archer going to say about you hanging up her husband's dead body like that?"

Nick was mortified. "You think *I* did that?"

"No, I think one of your minions did it, upon your request."

Nick wagged a scolding finger. "You really should get your facts straight before making accusations."

Cradoc's gaze shot toward Fatty Rice, lagging behind and just reaching the top of the bluff. "It's true, Marshal. That's how we found him—hogtied and hanging upside down."

"Told ya," Nick said with a self-satisfied grin as he swaggered off, headed for his horse.

Fatty also tried to slip past the marshal, but his attempt failed miserably.

"Where do you think you're going?" Cradoc wailed.

"I ... I ... I thought maybe ... maybe I would fetch some grub down at the big house."

"Get your ass back here!" Cradoc snapped.

"Yes, Marshal," Fatty murmured.

Even at the best of times, the deputies remained uneasy around Bradshaw, wary of his quick temper and the intensity with which he went about his job of keeping the peace in San Diego. They knew he did not suffer fools. And most of all, he did not suffer Nick Pinder. These two had history, in spades. Anyone who'd been around more than a couple of years could recall the days when they were thick as thieves. Through a strange twist of fate, a woman had come between them. Twenty years of friendship vanished overnight. And they had let their animosity spill over into their professional lives, making encounters like this tense for everyone in the vicinity.

Fatty led the way around the top of the cliff to the spot where a spike protruded from the ocher-colored stone. Cradoc squatted down, examined the steel shaft. It looked like a million others used on railroad tracks all across the country. Fresh scratches on the head indicated it had recently been struck by another metal object, presumably a hammer or mallet, leading to the inevitable conclusion that the spike had been placed for the express purpose of suspending Archer from the top of this cliff.

But that revelation did not answer other basic questions. Had Archer anchored the spike himself, bound his own legs, and then jumped? Or had someone concocted an elaborate and bizarre scheme to murder him? The blatant use of rope and spike implied that whoever planned the death—be it Archer or someone else—wanted the body found rather than lost at sea. And if that be the case, you really had to ask yourself another question. "Why?" Cradoc muttered to himself.

"What's that, Marshal?" asked Fatty.

"Why go through all this trouble?"

"I don't know, sir."

"No, you wouldn't," Cradoc groused. Gazing up from the spike, he scanned the vegetation behind the palisade. He stood up, walked a few paces, squatted down again. A horse had dragged something about the size of a human body through the chaparral, tracks coming from the direction of Cliff House. A pair of boot prints paralleled the horse tracks. Boots without spurs. In Cradoc's mind, that pretty much settled things—someone else had been here. Archer had not dragged himself to Devil's Cove.

Descending to the bottom of the cliff, Cradoc and Fatty made their way along the rocky beach, the marshal's rowels clinking against the black and gray pebbles. The corpse stank to high heaven. And even the marshal, quite used to the scent of death, held a kerchief to his face to keep from gagging. Twisting the body around, Cradoc examined the deceased. The marshal had known Zeb Archer for more than thirty years, from Archer's days as a humble carpenter through his ascendance to "lumber king" of San Diego and recent forays into property developments like Ocean Beach. He knew what the man looked like. But given the bloated, bloody condition of the corpse—especially the crab-eaten face—you couldn't say for sure who this might be.

Sinking to his knees, Cradoc gazed into the dead man's mouth, wide open and fixed in rigor mortis. He could see the upper teeth, but the lower chops remained hidden behind a swollen lower lip.

"Fatty!"

"Yes, Marshal?"

"Hold the body so it doesn't sway."

"Me?" The deputy did not relish the prospect.

"Would you rather feel around inside his mouth?"

"No, sir!"

With Fatty reluctantly clutching the corpse, Cradoc peeled back the swollen lips far enough to examine the other teeth. Both of the lower canines were plated gold. And seeing as Archer was known for his double gold cuspids, this pretty much had to be him.

Before leaving what he now suspected to be a murder scene, Cradoc told the deputy in no uncertain terms to remain at the cove and guard Archer's corpse until the medical examiner's wagon arrived. *Nobody* should disturb the body again. No photographs, no reporters, no souvenir hunters, no scavengers, and most of all no Nicholas Pinder.

"And if I hear otherwise," Cradoc warned the jittery deputy, "you can kiss your eighty bucks a month goodbye."

†

Swinging back into the saddle, Cradoc set off across the coastal escarpment. Three distinct tracks marked the trail away from Devil's Cove—a body being dragged, a single set of horse hooves, and the spurless boots. The general direction was due north towards Cliff House. And that's exactly where the trail petered out, near a row of wooden latrines behind the oceanfront edifice.

Beside one of the jakes, the marshal found shards of broken pottery, some of them covered in blood, and the neck-end of a whiskey jug with the finger ring intact. He picked up a shard, brought it up to his nose. You could still smell the hooch—high-grade bourbon—indicating it had only recently been broken. Probably last night. As to whether or not the busted jug had anything to do with Archer's demise, who knew at this point? The marshal had learned long ago to never assume or discard anything, no matter how trivial it seems at first glance.

Stuffing the jug neck and a couple of the pottery shards into the pocket of his duster, Cradoc made his way up the back steps of Cliff House and along the wooden porch. Entering the kitchen, he came upon a teenage girl in an apron and work boots stooped over a metal tub filled with dirty dishes.

"Were you here last night?" he asked, voice curt, all business.

"Who wants to know?" she answered with an equal amount of attitude.

Cradoc pulled back his coat to reveal a star pinned to a white cotton shirt.

"*You're* a marshal?" she gasped.

He snorted. "I know it's hard to believe. Were you here last night?"

"Yep," was all she said, going back to the dirty dishes.

"Did you see or hear anything unusual?"

"Nope."

He couldn't tell if she was being rude or shy. Did the girl have something against lawmen? Did she have something to hide? Or was she naturally insolent? "You mind standing up?" he asked.

"Got a lot of work, mister."

"Your boss won't mind—he's dead."

"I know," she said solemnly, slowly rising to her feet. The floor-length apron did nothing for her appearance, but she wasn't bad looking. Blonde hair pulled back in a bun. Broad shoulders. Sun-browned face. Someone who spent a lot more time outdoors than a "proper lady." Cradoc figured her for a farm girl from somewhere back east.

"What's your name?"

"Emma," she said plainly.

"Emma what?"

"Emma Lee Dawes."

"Where you from, Emma Lee?"

"Mizzura."

"Well, Emma Lee Dawes from Missouri, do you have any recollection of Mr. Archer going out yonder to answer the call of nature last night and not coming back?"

She glanced at the door that led out to the latrines, and then looked back at him. "A lotta people went out there last night."

"You hear any sorta noise—a scream, a shout, something breaking?"

"I don't know. The ladies from town were playing piano, singing pretty loud."

"What exactly was going on here?"

"Same thing that goes on *every* Saturday. Mr. Archer invites friends around for cards."

"And a little bit of flesh?"

Emma Lee blushed. "I wouldn't know about that."

"Can you recall who was here last night—besides the whores?"

Her memory surprisingly sharp, she reeled off the names of the deputy mayor, a county judge, a well-known banker, a Belgian who ran a hot-air-balloon concession at Ocean Beach, as well as the foreman of the subdivision. On the surface, none were obvious candidates for foul play.

The marshal thought a moment. What else could he learn from this girl? "One more thing, miss. What did Mr. Archer drink at these Saturday night gatherings?"

Emma Lee answered without hesitation. "Whiskey. Straight from the jug."

"That jug look anything like this?" Cradoc pulled the broken neck from his pocket.

"It surely did."

She waited for an explanation as to why the sheriff would ask such an odd thing, but it never came. Cradoc's mind had already jumped to the next step. Out the kitchen window, he spotted a line of wooden poles and a solitary wire coming from the direction of town. There had to be a telephone somewhere in the building. Cradoc found the contraption mounted on the wall of an office off the main lobby. He cranked it to life, asking the operator to put him through to the county hospital in Mission Valley. He left a message for Dr. Joe LeFevre, the county medical examiner: Send a wagon to fetch Zebulon Archer's body from Devil's Cove and carry out a post-mortem examination to determine cause of death.

The mouthpiece clicked back into its cradle when Cradoc noticed a framed poster on the office wall, a larger version of advertisements that Archer had placed in the local papers. "LOOK OUT!" shouted the headline. "Very soon, grand developments will be announced at Ocean Beach, which will be rushed ahead as the leading, best, and most attractive suburb and seaside resort in San Diego." Further down, the poster extolled the shore's "picturesque caves, rocks, inlets, and whirlpools rivaling the Niagara Falls."

"Yeah, right," the marshal mumbled to himself. The only thing rivaling Niagara Falls was Archer's overblown ambition.

Exiting the office, he took a quick look-see around the massive building. Other than the girl from Missouri, the place appeared to be vacant. No horses or buggies outside. Nobody pacing the halls. Whoever was here last night for cards and other shenanigans had scattered like rats from a sinking ship. No, that just wouldn't do—half a dozen married, churchgoing community leaders caught with their pants down around their ankles, literal or otherwise.

Before the long ride back to town, the marshal decided to relieve himself in one of the jakes out back. Having completed his business, he kicked open the outhouse door—and found the kitchen girl lurking outside.

"Jesus!" he blurted out. "Can't a guy piss in peace?"

But it was water off a duck's back. "What about my job?" Emma Lee asked urgently.

"I suppose you ain't got one." A cruel observation, but the truth often hurts.

"You know where can I git another?"

The obvious place, where so many young girls like her ended up, was the Stingaree, the red-light district along the San Diego waterfront. Working for Ida Bailey or one of the other madams. They'd get her some decent clothes, gussy up her hair, put her to work straight away—on her back.

He didn't know why—Emma Lee Dawes seemed like a thousand young gals who'd floated in town over the past few years looking for fame and fortune or maybe just a good man—but Cradoc felt sorry for her. He climbed into the saddle and looked down at her.

"You go into town," he said. "A place called the Oyster Bar. Ask for Josie and tell her I sent you. Josie Earp'll set you up."

"Much obliged!" she yelled as he loped off.

But Cradoc didn't hear. He was deep in thought, trying to figure the best way to handle the next (and most dreaded) task of an already piss-poor day—telling Mrs. Archer that her husband was dead and most likely murdered.

4

A VETERAN OF FOUR decades in journalism, Clive Bennett was a weedy little man with a salt-and-pepper beard and the spurious eyes of a rascal. He was in his late fifties and twice divorced, a somewhat caustic man who moved through life in a perpetual haze of tobacco smoke and whiskey fumes. As owner, publisher, and editor of the *San Diego Times*, Clive boasted an unfettered dedication to selling papers at almost any cost. From his perspective, the end *always* justified the means. Shock and awe—that's what sold. What made you famous, made you money, gave you job security. But it had to be true. As much as Clive reveled in blood-and-guts journalism, he would not tolerate fake news. A lesson quickly imparted to a young Nicolas Pinder when he joined the paper in his teens. Nearly twenty years down the road, that lesson was now staring both of them in the face.

Since hiring Nick Pinder as a wayward teenager—having somehow seen a kernel of brilliance hidden inside the young man—Clive had taught his star reporter everything there was to know about the journalism trade and the art of writing. Including the trick of reading out loud as one composed a story. Didn't matter if he was writing longhand or pecking at a typewriter, reading the words out loud was a surefire way to establish pace and rhythm, eliminate unnecessary words, and weed out awkward phrases. Nick didn't even have to think about it anymore. No matter what he was writing—love letter, shopping list, or in this particular case, the lead story for tomorrow's paper—the words came out of his mouth as well as off the tips of his fingers.

"*Mr. Zebulon Archer, the San Diego lumber company owner and real estate developer, was found dead early this morning at Devil's Hole near the Cliff House in Ocean Beach.*"

"Too wordy," Nick muttered to himself, ripping the paper out of his typewriter, balling it up with a fist, inserting another piece behind the roller and starting again. "*San Diego lumber king Zebulon Archer was found dead this morning near Ocean Beach, the victim of an apparent homicide ...*"

"Much smoother," said Clive, watching over Nick's shoulder as the story took shape. "But you're jumping the gun."

"On *what?*" Nick asked defensively.

"Nothing important," Clive responded, the sarcasm even more pronounced in his British accent. "Just the cause of death. The victim does not appear to have been shot, stabbed, or otherwise violently dispatched. There is absolutely no evidence of foul play. Yet you claim Archer was murdered."

"What else could it be?" Nick shot back, trying his best to win an argument with a man who rarely ever backed down on anything.

"I would argue for suicide," said Wendell Smith, hovering near enough to eavesdrop—and add his own two cents to a front-page story that should have been his to write given the fact that he'd been first to the scene of the crime.

"And why is that, Mr. Smith?" the boss asked.

"There is a good argument to be made that Mr. Archer hurled himself into Devil's Cove in a fit of depression, because his subdivision was failing miserably."

Nick rolled his eyes. "Oh please, Wendell." The kid was like a fly buzzing around your head, insignificant yet highly irritating and in need of being squashed.

But Clive urged the young reporter to continue.

"We've all seen the notices. They're in the paper every day. A warning to those who purchased lots in Ocean Beach that their real-estate contracts are null and void if they don't settle their debts forthwith. I'm told the deceased was owed thousands of dollars."

But Nick wasn't buying. "Archer was still making money hand over fist from his lumber business. He was one of the most powerful men in San Diego. He had his run of the gin joints and gambling halls and local floosies. Does that sound like a candidate for suicide?"

"People off themselves for all sorts of reasons," Clive pointed out. "Until such time as the medical examiner reveals both the exact cause and type of death, I think it prudent not to speculate."

Nick huffed in disgust. Since when was Clive concerned with prudence? "I don't have to remind you—seeing as you're the one who taught me—that our primary task as a newspaper is to inform and enlighten the public. Our readers will want to know what killed Archer. And they'll want to know tomorrow. If we don't tell them, I fear they may seek the answer elsewhere."

Clive scowled at his ace reporter. "That doesn't mean we just make shit up."

"It's speculation, not fiction. An intelligent guess based on the facts at hand. No different than most scientific theories, which you seem to publish without question. An awful lot of people in this town loathed Archer for the precise reason that he was so rich and so powerful. He didn't attain his lofty station in life by being a swell guy. Archer wouldn't think twice about walking over someone—crushing you into the sod—if you got in his way."

"That proves nothing, least of all homicide." Clive pointed at the typewriter. "Rewrite it."

"Can I say *probably* murdered?"

"No!"

"We can always retract later if we're wrong."

"And eat humble pie? No thanks. I don't like the taste. Not to mention the waste of perfectly good newsprint."

"All right, all right!" said Nick, finally backing down. He snatched the pages, balled them up, and threw them in the trash, too. Under his breath, he mumbled, "We don't need murder to sell more papers this time."

Clive eyed him suspiciously. "What in blazes are you talking about now?"

From the back of the room stepped Elliot Patterson, a leather portfolio tucked beneath one arm. In all the hoopla over the story, Nick was the only one who had noticed the photographer's quiet arrival.

"Show him," said Nick with a flourish.

From the portfolio, Patterson removed a selection of photos which he artfully arranged on the publisher's desk. The staff crowded around, staring at the sepia-toned images. Several people gasped, appalled by the gruesome visage—a bloated corpse hanging upside down above the beach.

"Poor bugger," said Clive. "You're not selling these, are you, Patterson? Much too ghastly, even for you."

"What we've actually got in mind," said Nick, "is publishing one of these photographs on the front page. Tomorrow morning, as a matter of fact, adjacent to my story."

"You can't be serious." Wendell's eyebrows shot up, shocked by the very thought.

Nick snorted. "Sweet Jesus, Smith. Grow some balls."

"My father would be horrified."

"Well, your daddy ain't the editor of *this* paper, is he?"

"Quiet!" Clive barked. His eyes moved from photo to photo and then up to Nick. "Ethics aside, I don't know of a single paper on the West Coast with the wherewithal or know-how to render a photograph on newsprint."

"Patterson and I have been experimenting," Nick said, nodding toward the photographer. "And we believe the process is now perfected."

Thoroughly uncomfortable with any conversation that involved more than two people, Patterson cleared his throat. "It's called *halftone* reproduction. Basically, it's a form of engraving, very similar to line etching, the difference being that one can also reproduce the gray shades—the so-called 'halftones'—rather than just the solid black lines."

As evidence, Patterson produced a recent copy of *Harper's Weekly* with a black-and-white photograph of President Grover Cleveland on the cover.

Clive pulled the page within an inch of his specs and carefully studied the president. He had heard about the halftone process and the fact that New York publications were now able to reproduce photographs. But this was the first time he had seen one of the images up close. "Looks like a bunch of dots."

"That's exactly what it is," Patterson enthused. "Halftones comprise hundreds of tiny ink dots."

Clive still didn't look convinced. "We can do this?"

"I've been doing dry runs on a halftone machine that I purchased earlier this year. So, yeah, we can do it."

Clive's attention drifted back to the photographs arrayed across his desk, half a dozen eight-by-ten images of Archer's body suspended upside down from the cliff. Printed on proper photographic paper and blown up to this size, the images were truly horrendous. Much too shocking to thrust upon the general public, especially women and children who might happen to snatch a glance at the newspaper. But in halftone form, the fine details largely obscured, they just might be able to pull it off without a public outcry.

The editor had no doubt that publishing a photograph of the deceased Mr. Archer would boost sales, maybe even double or triple their normal circulation of roughly 5,000 copies. But he remained unconvinced that San Diego readers were ready for the image of a prominent man, newly dead with a face half-eaten by crabs, splashed across the front page.

"I don't know," said Clive, nervously pulling at his beard. "If we can successfully render one of these images in the actual paper, our doing so could be construed as even more scandalous than jumping the gun on whether it's murder or not."

"It may be more scandalous," Nick interjected, "but truth is truth, whether written or captured by a camera. And there is no disputing that these images show the truth. How our readers interpret that truth—whether or not they deem it appalling or outrageous or murder or suicide—is beyond our control."

Clive leaned back in his chair, deep in thought.

"We haven't got an awful lot of time," Nick said. If they were going to run a photo in tomorrow's *Times*, they had to start the reproduction process at once.

"I'm well aware of that." Clive scowled. He was quiet a moment more, then he turned and screamed, "Max!"

Moments later, a mutton-chopped German stuck his head through the door. Maximilian Wartheimer, master printer and composer for the *Times*.

"You know about this halftone malarkey?" asked Clive, holding one of the gruesome photos aloft.

"Ya, ya," said the German in his thick accent. "I been workin' wit Nick and Elliot."

Clive looked around at his chief reporter. "Am I the only bastard west of the Mississippi who didn't know about this?"

"'Fraid so," Nick said, trying to sound a wee bit contrite.

The publisher twisted his seat around toward the German. "Will it work?" he asked. "Can we do this without making fools of ourselves?"

"*Nicht ein problem*," Max said confidently.

Still pondering the pros and cons, Clive exuded a deep breath. He gazed at the photos one last time then dragged his gaze up to his staff, still huddled around his desk. "Then let's make some history."

5

WYATT EARP SAT ON A STOOL at the Oyster Bar casually perusing the Monday morning edition of the *San Diego Times* as he nursed a lukewarm cup of coffee. He had seen a lot of things in his thirty-five odd years on the planet, some of them quite shocking and beyond easy description. But in all his days, he had never seen anything like this—a photograph of a dead man in a newspaper. Definitely a first, at least for him.

He turned the paper upside down and sideways, studying the photograph from every conceivable direction, as if a different angle might bring more clarity to the gruesome visage. Truth be told, the dangling corpse could have been anybody. Zebulon Archer or someone else. Likewise, it was impossible to identify any of the human figures poised on either side of the dead man. But there was no doubting the overall effect of the image: a dramatic portrait of death in black and white.

Bringing death into the home—or in his case, into his Fifth Street restaurant and gambling establishment—in such brazen fashion would be hard for a lot of folks to swallow. The local clergy would certainly be up in arms. And God only knew what the mayor or the other civic do-gooders would say. It was bad enough that some high-muck-a-muck had died under suspicious circumstances, but to have it brandished about in public like this....

Hearing the clink of spurs, Wyatt looked around at a figure moving toward him. "You look like shit," he told the visitor.

Brushing back his disheveled hair, Cradoc Bradshaw tossed his hat onto the bar. "You'd look like shit, too, if you'd spent the last twenty-four hours attending to a stinking, bloated, crab-eaten corpse."

"I presume you are referring to this." Wyatt brandished the front page with the headline: THE MYSTERIOUS DEATH OF ZEBULON ARCHER. The controversial photo poised right below.

The marshal sighed. "I figured you as a friend," he grumbled.

"Friendship don't mean I can't read the paper."

"Then buy the *Union*," Cradoc suggested.

"The *Union* don't run pictures like this." He stabbed the ghastly image with an index finger.

"Sucked in by the freak show like everyone else."

"You telling me this ain't real?" Wyatt asked.

"No, it's genuine. But so are pinheads and Siamese twins."

Wyatt was about to wisecrack, but Cradoc cut him short. "What's a fellow gotta do to get a drink around here?"

"Creosote's fresh," Wyatt pointed out.

"I was thinking along the lines of something stronger."

Wyatt waved at the barman. "Sam! Send the good stuff!"

A bottle of premium tequila came sliding down the bar.

Cradoc caught it with an outstretched hand and took a quick sip straight from the neck.

"I prefer my patrons use a glass," Wyatt scolded.

"Who says I'm not drinking the *whole* thing?" Cradoc took another swig, offered the bottle to Wyatt.

As had long been his custom, Wyatt declined. While he was perfectly willing to vend hooch at his saloons, alcohol never passed his own lips. In all the years they'd been acquainted, going all the way back to their days in Kansas, Cradoc had never known his friend to imbibe. Although folks had told him that Wyatt had been one hell of a boozehound in his younger days.

"Well, what's the verdict?" Wyatt asked.

"Mighty fine tequila."

Wyatt rolled his eyes. "In one of *those* moods, are ya? Suit yourself. I'm sure the *Times* will eventually have all the facts a citizen might ever wanna know about the demise of Zebulon Archer."

"The *Times* can suck my ass. And so can Pinder."

All of a sudden, it was clear why the marshal had worked himself into a foul mood. "Please don't tell me you had another run-in with Nick?"

The reporter didn't have to do much for Cradoc to get a burr up his ass. His very presence at a crime scene—or anywhere else for that matter—was enough to spark the marshal's umbrage.

Cradoc looked around at his friend and number-one confidant. "I don't rightly know how Archer died. Not till Doc LeFevre takes a gander. But my educated guess is homicide."

Wyatt stabbed another bony finger at the newspaper. "Says here he plunged down a cliff."

"Plunge isn't what I'd call being tied upside down and left for the tide and the crabs. But I don't think that's what actually killed him."

"And what elicits such a contrary opinion?"

Reaching into a pocket of his duster, Cradoc produced the jug neck and bloody pottery shards. "I found these behind Cliff House. One of the kitchen staff told me that Archer almost always drank from a jug that matches these shards. There was also blood on the ground and fresh tracks leading south along the shore. Looks to me like Archer was dragged—either dead or alive—to Devil's Cove. And he sure as hell didn't drag himself."

"Any obvious suspects?" Wyatt asked.

The marshal shook his head. "Nobody that comes directly to mind. But Archer had a way of rubbing people the wrong way—lots of folks over many a year. He was one of the first gringos to settle in San Diego after we snatched it from the Mexicans. Opened the town's first carpentry shop. Helped people build their homes and businesses. But he could never keep his mouth shut. He was a Copperhead and very vocal about it. Archer campaigned to have California admitted as a slave state. Almost got himself arrested during the war as an agitator and Rebel sympathizer. My daddy came this close"—Cradoc held a thumb and index finger about an inch apart—"to throwing his Dixie ass in jail."

"Didn't seem to hurt his bottom line."

"Archer may have been white trash, but he wasn't ignorant. He was one of the first people to jump into bed with Alonzo Horton. Quite a trick when you consider that fact that Horton was an Abolitionist from way back."

"Politics does make strange bedfellows," Wyatt quipped.

"Not so much politics, but profits. Greed rather than governing was their primary motive."

"I don't see the connection."

"I was gone by then, at school back east, but Archer helped Horton get elected county supervisor and together with a couple of others, they pushed to have the county seat—and just about everything else of consequence—shifted from the Old Town in Mission Valley to where we are right now beside the bay. In the middle of the night, I should add. Sneaky bastards. In return, Horton granted Archer a monopoly on lumber sales in the New Town and tossed him prime construction contracts. The rest, as they say, is history."

"He sold me the timber to build this joint," Wyatt announced.

"Archer sold us the wood for our place, too. The house my daddy built before the war. But that doesn't mean we were bosom buddies. My father loathed him, and I grew up with a strong dislike."

"Does that make you a prime suspect?"

"I suppose it does," the marshal conceded. "Me and a hundred other folks."

Cradoc and Wyatt might have gabbed all day if Josie Earp hadn't blown in off the street and interrupted their discourse. Folding her parasol and removing a fancy silk hat, she sidled up to the boys at the bar.

Howdy, Cradoc," she said as she leaned in to give Wyatt a kiss on the cheek.

"Hello, Josie," Cradoc shot back, feeling himself blush. No matter how he tried, Cradoc melted whenever she walked into a room. Didn't seem to matter that he'd known her for years. Josephine Marcus Earp wasn't the most beautiful woman he had come across, but she was certainly the most exotic. Her being Jewish, as well as an actress and singer, added to the forbidden allure. Not to mention her raven hair and dark eyes, the free and flamboyant way in which she deported herself, and her friendly, flirtatious manner.

Wyatt wasn't the least bit offended by Cradoc's schoolboy crush. A lot of men drooled over his common-law wife, and he was downright proud of that fact. But he was equally confident that no man could ever wrest her away. At least, no fool who wanted to keep on breathing. There was more than a grain of truth to the rumor that another man's lust for Josie had sparked the bloody showdown between the Earps and Claytons in Tombstone.

"Watcha got?" Cradoc asked, nodding at the contents of her straw bag.

"A couple of new songs," she said cheerfully, placing a volume of sheet music on the bar. The two men glanced at the cover—*The Mikado* by Gilbert & Sullivan—and grunted their disapproval. But Josie, having been a stage canary of no small repute when she first met Wyatt, adored musical theatre and show tunes.

"And this!" she gushed, pulling an unfamiliar item from her shopping bag.

Cradoc and Wyatt stared at the small metal object, about the same size and shape as a can of beans. "What the heck is that?" asked Cradoc.

"One of Mr. Edison's musical cylinders. Fresh off a train from New Jersey."

Cradoc held it up to one ear. "I don't hear anything," he joked.

Josie rolled her eyes. "You play it on a phonograph machine."

"We ain't got one of those," Wyatt pointed out.

"Soon enough we will. I ordered one from the Sears catalog."

"How much is that gonna cost?" her husband grumbled. He was a firm believer that good drink, pretty women, and games of chance were the only things needed to attract customers to a saloon.

"It will pay for itself," she said and ran her fingers along the cylinder. As a lifelong entertainer, Josie had equally strong feelings about the allure of music. She held that a silent saloon was a boring saloon and that a boring establishment made far less money. Plain and simple, music was good for the bottom line. "What do *you* think?" she asked Cradoc, knowing he would never disagree with her.

"Who doesn't like music?" the marshal said philosophically.

Wyatt shot him a glance. "You got a quim between those legs instead of balls, *Miss* Bradshaw?"

"That reminds me," Cradoc mumbled, suddenly recalling why he'd swung past the Oyster. "There's a girl coming to see you. Emma something or 'nother. Can't remember her full name. She's been working the kitchen at Cliff House."

"How many of these stray cats are you gonna send me, Cradoc? We can't take 'em all, you know."

"It's either you or Ida," he reminded her. "She seems like a good girl, hard worker. Can't be much more than nineteen, maybe twenty. And she asked politely."

"You're such a softy." Josie smiled sympathetically and pinched the marshal on the cheek. Her eyes flicked towards Wyatt. "Why can't you be more like him?"

✝

Having finished his yak with the Earps, the marshal rode back down Broadway to his office in the basement of the County Courthouse. Jose Cota, the only Mexican among the peace officers currently in the county's employ, sat at the duty desk.

Cota was the best of several dozen deputies who patrolled the streets of San Diego. Seeing as none of them had law enforcement experience prior to their current employment, their primary responsibility was crowd control. Making sure the drunken sailors, pistol-packing cowboys, and tarted-up floozies stayed right where they belonged—in the saloons and cribs below Market Street. More serious crimes were the purview of the only marshal, Cradoc Bradshaw, who'd been hired specifically to deal with murder, armed robbery, and other mayhem the deputies were unable or unwilling to tackle.

"Coyne around?" Cradoc asked.

His chair propped against the wall behind the desk, Cota pointed his chin down the hallway. "In his office."

"You hear anything on the street about Archer?"

"Only that he was a total *cabrón*. People are glad he's dead."

"Any particular reason?"

Cota laughed cynically. "They think lumber will be cheaper now."

Cradoc shook his head. "They don't know his widow."

Cradoc rapped on the door jamb and stepped in to the boss's office. A robust man with short gray hair and a spade beard, Sheriff Joe Coyne was a former miner and ditch digger who had scratched his way up from the dregs of society to a position of no small power and prominence. He'd been San Diego's "top cop" for more than a dozen years, as much a part of the local power structure as business tycoon Alonzo Horton, Mayor Hunsaker, and railroad magnet Fabian Kendall.

"Just the man I wanted to see," Coyne declared. Biting off a wad of tobacco, the sheriff waited for Cradoc to take a seat before continuing. "What's your take on Zeb?"

"I'm not really sure," Cradoc lied. "Not till I get LeFevre's report."

"Since when do you not have an opinion on something?"

"I'd rather be sure before I say."

"Spit it out," said Coyne, knowing full well the marshal wasn't speaking his mind.

Cradoc let out a deep sigh. "It's my belief, based on what I found at Devil's Cove and later at Cliff House, that Archer did not take his own life or succumb to an accident."

"You got a shred of evidence to support that theory?"

"No, but I've got a shard." Cradoc set the broken ceramic pieces collected from the ground behind Cliff House on Coyne's desk.

The sheriff shrugged. "Archer could have dropped his own jug and cut himself trying to pick it up. A couple of bloody pottery pieces don't mean the man was murdered."

"I agree." Cradoc nodded. "Which is why I plan on reserving judgment until such time as we have conclusive proof."

The sheriff scratched his goatee. "Archer ain't exactly gonna be missed, is he? If he'd just stuck to lumber and not drifted into property development, it might have been different. But with him dead, there's more meat for the other big dogs."

"He's never been well-liked."

"How well did you know him?"

Cradoc shrugged. "He was around when I was young, but we always gave him a wide berth. Archer didn't really take kindly to kids or anyone else for that matter. There's a reason why he and the missus never had children, and I don't think it's cuz he was shooting blanks."

"Somebody mentioned that Archer and your daddy had a couple of run-ins."

"My father was the Union commander in San Diego, and Archer was the leading Copperhead, so there was bound to be some friction. But it was all bluster on Archer's part. The only thing Zeb was genuinely passionate about was making fistfuls of money."

"You think that's what got him killed. The competition wanted him gone?"

The marshal shook his head. "That's not how rich people operate. They drive you out of business, ruin you in other ways. Still you gotta figure that Archer—if the other movers and shakers really were ticked by his move into property— would have been a hard nut to crack without brute force."

"So you're saying it's possible?"

"*Anything* is possible when it comes to murder," Cradoc declared. "*Anyone* is capable of killing another human being. If not with their own hands, then certainly by proxy. There's a whole heap of fellas out there who would gut someone for a week's wage. Even someone as powerful as Archer."

✝

Dark had fallen by the time Cradoc finished at the jailhouse, and having been up since the crack of dawn, he was dog tired and ready to retire. He fetched his horse from the hitching post outside the jail and walked it across

Union Street to the courthouse stables, free livery being one of the few perks of a job that didn't come with many bonuses.

His steed squared away for the evening, the marshal turned to thoughts of food. Where did he feel like eating tonight? He made a move for the Chinese chophouse at Broadway and First, but changed his mind, veering off towards a cook wagon parked around the front of the courthouse. A permanent fixture outside the halls of justice, the wagon featured a kitchen and counter inside four plank walls and a shingle roof. Its regular customers included judges and jurors, lawyers and lawmen. Most patrons chose to eat outside, sitting on stools, benches, or rickety old chairs around half a dozen barrels that served as tables.

Not in a mood to chat with his fellow man after such a tiresome day, the marshal settled at an empty table well away from the other diners. A menu posted on a blackboard affixed to the side of the wagon advertised veal loaf as today's special. But they served all sorts of victuals: biscuits and gravy, smoked ham and fish, homemade bread and butter, various stews and soups, and out-of-this-world rhubarb pie.

The owner—a gregarious Hoosier with a handlebar mustache and mutton-chop sideburns—spied Cradoc through the open door and scooted down the stairs with a kettle. "Spot of coffee, Marshal?"

"I suppose so." Cradoc's voice betrayed his weariness.

"Long day?" the Hoosier asked, dispensing java into an enamel mug.

"Nothing a good meal can't cure."

"I could scratch you up a steak. Fry it with some onions and gravy."

But Cradoc had something a little different in mind, having missed breakfast this morning, "How 'bout flapjacks?"

"Your wish is my command," the Hoosier intoned and disappeared into the wagon.

The cakes arrived lickety-split, five of them piled on an enamel plate, with a side of homemade butter and a brand new can of maple syrup that had just come off a train from back east. In the old days, before the railroad, most everything came by water, either all the way around the Horn or across the Panama jungle from the Atlantic seaboard. It took months, sometimes even a year, for merchants to get their orders filled. But the train, together with a telegraph, had revolutionized life in San Diego. Now you could order a crate of tinned peaches, a hundred-pound sack of coffee—or genuine maple syrup—and have it on your doorstep in a couple of weeks.

Cradoc took his time eating the cakes, savoring each bite, gradually making his way around the edge of the stack, saving the best for last—the butter-soaked core—which he counted as one of the most delicious things on God's green earth.

Slapping a couple of quarters beside his empty plate, he heaved himself up and started down Broadway in the direction of home. Passing the new Santa Fe train depot, he turned north along the waterfront, dark and silent at this late hour, nothing but stray cats and a few twinkling lights in the distance—the fishing villages of Roseville and La Playa on the western side of the bay.

Several dozen wooden houses on stilts perched along this stretch of shore. One of them belonged to Cradoc. Technically speaking, all of those who lived in these maritime abodes were squatters. But given that the bay was public rather than private land and the general inertia with which most government bodies conduct their business, there was very little chance of the marshal or his neighbors receiving an eviction notice anytime soon.

Dead tired, Cradoc shuffled across a catwalk to his creaky waterfront dwelling. He hung his duster on a peg inside the front door, laid his shotgun on the kitchen table, lit a lantern, and headed for the bedroom. For a moment he considered falling straight into bed, but then summoned the energy to kick off his boots and unbuckle his Colt, which he placed atop a wooden bureau. Cradoc snatched a toothbrush, stabbed it into a jar of Colgate Dental Paste, and cleaned his teeth on the back porch, staring out at the water, thinking about nothing in particular and everything all at once.

Cradoc really didn't give a shit about Zebulon Archer. As a kid growing up in San Diego, he'd detested the man's often crude and always rude manner. And truth be told, he no longer relished the prospect of a good investigation. Didn't matter who'd been killed or the nature of the crime. Peacekeeping had become like any other job and he no more than a cog in a judicial assembly line that processed the dirty deeds of mankind. But what else could he do for a living? He'd already tried and failed at soldiering. And law enforcement was pretty much the only thing in his life at present.

He spat into the bay, took a fleeting glance at a sailing skiff perched at the far end of the porch—when's the last time he'd taken it out on the water?—and stumbled back inside. Come midnight, he was still wide awake, tossing and turning, mulling things over in his mind ... things like

Zebulon Archer and Nick Pinder and the fact that another month had slid by without any change in his personal fate or fortune. Rather than fight his non-somnolent state, Cradoc crawled back into his clothes and went out into the night, heeding the advice his father had offered so many years ago: Nothing like a long walk to calm a restless soul.

6

ON THE MORNING of Zebulon Archer's funeral, an obituary in the *Times* eulogized the deceased as a model citizen, loved by his wife, trusted and admired by his friends and colleagues. It detailed Archer's rise from itinerant Southern carpenter to West Coast lumber tycoon and budding seaside developer, a pillar of the business community who had dedicated his life to transforming San Diego from a one-horse town into a dynamic metropolis that would soon challenge San Francisco as the powerhouse of the Pacific. The article went on to say that his tragic death had shaken not only those close to Archer, but the very foundation of local society.

His funeral unfolded in the new Baptist Church at the confluence of Tenth and E streets on the east side of town, an imposing clapboard structure with a towering steeple that could be seen for miles around. The mourners constituted a veritable who's who of local business, government, and society, including Mayor Hunsaker, Sheriff Coyne, Fabian Kendall, and the aging Alonzo Horton—the father of modern San Diego and mastermind of nearly everything that now surrounded them on the arid flats beside the bay.

Also in attendance were Cradoc Bradshaw and Nick Pinder, although for far different reasons. Nick was busy creating tomorrow's front page, telling Wendell Smith which mourners to interview after the service and directing Elliot Patterson on the best angles for photographs. Nick clearly relished his pivotal role, knowing that most of the eyes in the congregation were on him rather than the casket. His only regret was that Mrs. Archer—given the appalling condition of her husband's face and the rather limited cosmetic talent of local undertakers—had opted for a closed coffin. What a photograph that would have made!

Cradoc hovered near the rear of the church, a detached observer. *What a load of hypocrites*, he thought to himself. There wasn't a person present—except maybe the widow— that actually regretted Archer's passing, himself included. In Cradoc's mind, the world was better off without the likes of Zebulon Archer and his greed and prejudice, bullying and backstabbing. On the other hand, upholding the law was his sworn duty. And whether he liked it or not, that duty included ascertaining the who, what, when, where, how, and why of Archer's untimely death.

About ten minutes into the funeral, Clive Bennett stumbled through the open doors at the back of the church and snuffed out his cigar in an empty collection tray.

"Class act, Clive," a voice murmured from the shadows.

Not the least bit mortified, the publisher turned around and smirked at the marshal. "The least of my sins."

Cradoc had always thought of Clive as a bit of a snake— manipulative, cunning, and at times downright sleazy. But he respected the man for knowing his job and doing it damn well. And although he would have been hard-pressed to admit it out loud, Cradoc was impressed by the way that Clive had transformed Nick from an aimless wastrel into a slick reporter and talented scribe.

"I have a morbid fascination with death," Clive declared. "But what brings you here, Marshal?"

"Simply paying my last respects."

"Come now, Cradoc. How long have we known each other? You never do anything that isn't somehow connected to solving a crime."

The marshal shrugged. "Believe what you want."

But he actually did have an ulterior motive. Cradoc had once read a book about a lawman who had fingered the killer at the burial of the deceased. The marshal had been to an awful lot of funerals and it hadn't yet worked for him. But who knew? Maybe someday he'd get lucky. But shit if he was going to relate any of that to Clive Bennett, who would likely scoff at the notion, or use it as the cornerstone of some trumped-up story that would land Cradoc in hot water with the folks who paid his salary. Better to keep his trap shut and cards close to his chest.

"Enjoy the funeral, Clive," he said with a wave of his hat, and then he slipped out the back door. Cradoc figured he'd seen enough. Besides, he had a more important place to be.

†

Wyatt was just riding up in front of the church. Clad in a spiffy pinstriped suit and a brand-new bowler, he was the picture of modern sartorial elegance.

"Aren't we the dandy," Cradoc teased.

"It wouldn't hurt to invest in some threads yourself. Certainly help you with the ladies."

"I don't need help with the ladies."

"Yeah, you gotta beat 'em off with a stick."

One of Wyatt's ongoing obsessions—and there were many—was playing matchmaker to whomever he deemed romantically deficient. First and foremost Marshal Cradoc Bradshaw, who wasn't so much unlucky with women as disinterested in the female gender. When they'd first met, both had been unattached and perpetually on the prowl. Not a single female between the Mississippi and the Rockies had been immune to their charms and small talk. It would have been nigh impossible to say which lad was the greater ladies' man back in the day. Yet in recent years, Cradoc had transformed into a wallflower, and Wyatt into a friend determined to save him from "heart failure," as the legendary lawman called it.

"I didn't ask you along to nag me," Cradoc grumbled as he crawled into his saddle.

"Just saying," Wyatt said innocently.

He wasn't the type to give up that easy on anything, but especially a cause as worthy as Cradoc. Sooner or later, he would succeed in his romantic endeavor, because the great and mighty Mr. Earp had never known the meaning of the word failure.

Rather than ride along the main road north out of San Diego, they decided to shortcut through Presidio Canyon. About half a mile up the gorge, they skirted around the edge of an earthen dam and reservoir that supplied much of San Diego's drinking water. Beyond the lake, the trail climbed steeply through sagebrush and cactus onto a broad mesa. Off to the west, they could see Hillcrest, another new subdivision developers were trying to foist upon the tide of migrants.

"Weren't you thinking of buying some acreage up here?" Cradoc asked.

"Already have. Two small lots. And you should do the same. They're dirt cheap. Even *you* can afford them."

"I've already got a home."

"That's not the point. We're talking investment here. The way prices are rising, those lots are already worth more than I plunked down. I'm thinking of building a couple of small houses, renting them out."

The marshal rolled his eyes "Who'd wanna live way out here?"

"That's the same thing you said about Coronado and La Jolla. And look what's happening there. You really should get in on this, Cradoc. Before it's too late."

"Like I said, I already got a home."

"Yeah, but you don't *own* it. You don't even rent. Eventually, they're gonna develop that stretch of waterfront too, and you'll be plum out of luck."

Cradoc had an answer for that, too. "I got money stashed away."

"You think banks are any better? This may come as a surprise to someone who's been in law enforcement the better part of a decade, but banks do get robbed on occasion."

"Not on my watch."

"You think every criminal on the face of this Earth knows that big, bad Cradoc Bradshaw is guarding San Diego? Someday someone is gonna turn up who doesn't know—or doesn't give a shit—who you are or what you've done in the past. And they just might decide to rob the bank where you stash your cash. What then, my friend? No home, no money, and no dignity, because you didn't listen to your old friend Wyatt Earp when he told you to buy land and build a house."

Cradoc hawked and spat, his way of telling Wyatt to piss off. "Sometimes I think money is the only reason you came to San Diego."

"Maybe it is," Wyatt said with a shrug.

There wasn't a man, woman, or child who didn't know why Wyatt and Josie had fled Tombstone. After the famous shootout with the Claytons and subsequent violence, Wyatt had become persona non grata in the Arizona Territory. Didn't matter how spurious the charges might have been. The remaining Claytons had enough allies in local government to ensure a noose around Wyatt's neck if he should ever set foot back in Arizona.

Mr. and Mrs. Earp could have moved anywhere. They could have gone to Kansas or Texas, where Wyatt had previously labored as a lawman, gambler, and saloon owner. Or maybe up to Frisco, Josie's hometown. They could have settled down in Colton, the bustling railroad junction near San Bernardino where one of Wyatt's brothers had got himself elected sheriff. But of all the places on the map, they chose San Diego. Economics had definitely figured into their decision; the grapevine whispered that between his three saloons, Wyatt easily cleared at least a thousand dollars per day. Yet there were lots of places out West where the Earps could have raked in that kind of money. What made San Diego special was the presence of one Cradoc Bradshaw, Wyatt's old sidekick from Kansas. With Josie around, the two of them couldn't light the town on fire like their younger days. But there were still plenty of good times to be had. And crimes to be solved. Even though Wyatt no longer wore a badge, the tug of an unsolved crime still pulled at him. Puzzles to be solved. Riddles to be answered. Something to keep the brain alive while you're shucking cards and pouring booze for the hoi polloi.

Soon, the trail plunged from the mesa into Mission Valley, carved by the San Diego River on its way from the Cuyamaca Mountains to the Pacific Ocean and named after the old Spanish mission that now lay in ruins. Tucked between pastures and wheat fields in the valley bottom, the County Hospital & Poor Farm featured a special operating room for amputations and doctors highly proficient in the draining of abscesses. Those who could not afford medical treatment worked off their debt on the adjoining poor farm, tending to apricots, figs, and peaches that the hospital hawked at no small profit to hotels and restaurants in town. Indigent women deemed unsuitable to work the orchards were pressed into service boiling the fruit into the preserves bottled and sold by the hospital. Upon hearing that the boys were headed out that way, Josie had instructed her husband to purchase two jars of apricot jam.

An Indian kid stationed in front of the administrative building took charge of the horses as Cradoc and Wyatt dismounted. Inside the clapboard structure, a uniformed matron greeted them with a message that Dr. LeFevre would meet them in the morgue. Having been here on numerous occasions, Cradoc did not have to be shown the way. The most direct route was via the North Ward and its gauntlet of coughing, hacking, and desperately wheezing patients. But the marshal preferred a more roundabout— and presumably much less hazardous—route past the staff dining room and around the *outside* of the sick ward.

The morgue stood at the northernmost end of the hospital grounds, conveniently tucked between the Old

Men's Quarters (where many of the morgue's occupants originated) and the hospital carpentry shop (where their coffins were manufactured). The windowless room was slap dark as they entered.

"This place got a light?" asked Wyatt, striking a match on the side of his boot.

The match flickered long enough for them to locate a wall switch that activated a single, overhead electric bulb. The room was larger than it looked from afar, the walls covered in white porcelain tiles and the air a good twenty degrees cooler than outside. The concrete floor sloped to a drain in the center of the room. Arrayed around this hole were three wooden tables, only one of them occupied at the present time.

Waiting for LeFevre to arrive, Cradoc found himself studying a diagram of the body's internal organs on the wall beside the front door. Wyatt, on the other hand—the living embodiment of curiosity got the cat—made a beeline for the sheet-covered corpse.

"Good Lord!" Earp blurted out.

Cradoc turned around to see him peering beneath the sheet. "Goddamn it, Wyatt. Have some respect."

"She don't look dead. Come and see."

Beneath the sheet lay a young female, possibly a teenager, but certainly no older than twenty-one or twenty-two. Red hair. Rosy cheeks. Voluptuous body. Indeed, she did not appear dead. Cradoc figured she looked like a princess in a fairytale—a gorgeous woman trapped in a deep and abiding slumber.

Wyatt (being Wyatt) could not resist the temptation to touch the corpse, not in any sort of carnal way, but out of the innate inquisitiveness that had always been such a part of his being. "No pulse," he said, fingering her wrist.

"What'd you expect?" asked Cradoc.

"But she don't look dead!" Wyatt repeated. "Don't feel it either."

"That's because she only recently passed," said a voice from behind.

Poised just inside the door was a man in a long, white medical coat, his hair and beard nearly as pale as his clothing. Dr. Joe LeFevre was many things to many people—superintendent of the county hospital, official county physician, and the only medical examiner within a hundred miles. However, he was not the coroner, that being an elected position that required far more time in court (answering questions and reading medical reports) than it did in the actual morgue.

"What killed her?" asked Wyatt, still clutching the dead girl's wrist.

"*Rickettsia typhi.*"

"My Latin's a little rusty."

"Typhus," LeFevre said simply.

The girl's hand hit the table like a lead weight, as Wyatt flinched and jumped away.

"Not to worry," the doctor said. "It's the endemic variety. Carried by rats and fleas. Quite common, really."

"That's reassuring," said Wyatt, wiping his hand on his pants, not the least bit reassured.

LeFevre had a cardboard file tucked beneath one arm, the autopsy report on Zebulon Archer, which he opened on one of the empty examination tables. He skimmed through the inventory of injuries. "Needless to say, the extent of bodily harm was quite considerable. This includes multiple bone fractures, abrasions, dislocations, contusions, and extensive muscle damage. Both arms broken in several spots, every single rib fractured, both shoulders and ankles dislocated, and massive blunt-force trauma to the skull that resulted in internal bleeding and most likely brain damage. Exactly what one might expect when falling from a great height. But several things make me think that most of these injuries did not occur during the victim's descent down the cliff."

Cradoc's ears perked up. "Like?"

"For one thing, there is little or no damage to the crown of the victim's skull. In other words, despite falling headfirst, Mr. Archer did not land on his head. And the catastrophic damage to the rest of the upper body is widespread rather than concentrated in a single point of impact. Which leads me to believe the victim's downward momentum was interrupted—most likely by the rope around his ankles."

"Then how'd he get all banged up?" asked Wyatt.

"We will perhaps never know for sure," LeFevre surmised, "but I believe most of the damage resulted from the victim being repeatedly battered against the adjacent cliff by the surf and incoming tide. Flung, so to speak, like a rag doll. Both of the ankles were badly bruised and abraded by the aforementioned rope. But what I find a trifle odd is the fact that neither one of the victim's ankles is dislocated. And neither is the spine."

"Why should they be?" asked Cradoc.

"The laws of physics," LeFevre quickly rejoined. "Archer weighed roughly two hundred and fifty pounds. And two hundred and fifty pounds of anything falling a hundred feet generates an awful lot of energy. That energy is diffused either by coming into contact with something solid—like the ground—or a massive wrenching effect on whatever is holding it back. In this case, that would be a rope. Both of Archer's ankles should have been yanked right out of their sockets, and I would have expected some sort of spinal dislocation."

Cradoc couldn't figure where LeFevre was getting at. "In plain English, Doc."

"I believe—and this is only a theory—that Mr. Archer was slowly and very gently lowered down the cliff. And only then did most of his injuries occur."

"Is that what killed him?" the marshal asked. "All that getting knocked around?"

"As a matter of fact, no," LeFevre declared. "Most of the aforementioned injuries were sustained pre-mortem. The actual cause of death was drowning. Both lungs were saturated with salt residue. I would estimate that Mr. Archer swallowed several gallons of seawater. An impossible feat when one is already dead."

"So Archer was alive—and possibly conscious—while he was getting bashed against the cliffs?"

"Alive for sure. As for how long the man was conscious, that's anyone's guess. But I think it's a reasonable assumption that Mr. Archer's demise was neither slow nor pain-free. Certainly not the means by which I hope to meet my maker one day."

Flipping the autopsy report around on the examination table, the marshal turned to the final page, the doctor's decision on the manner of death. "Homicide," Cradoc read out loud.

"Most definitely," said LeFevre. "As to whether or not it was cold-blooded murder, drunken folly—or assisted suicide, as some suggest—that is not for me to say. But there was another human being involved in this. Of that, I am most confident. The only other assistance I can offer is this—" The doctor removed a small object from the breast pocket of his lab coat and held it aloft. "I found this lodged in the victim's left ear canal. I'm not sure what it might be, perhaps jetsam or flotsam from the sea."

But the marshal recognized the item at once—a pottery chard of the same color and texture as the ones he'd discovered beside the Cliff House latrines. Cradoc immediately saw the crime unfold in his mind. Archer smashed over the head by a whiskey jug ... dragged along behind a horse ... trussed up and lowered into Devil's Cove ... battered against the cliff and eventually overcome by water. Someone had wanted Archer gone, and they had planned for him to die in this precise manner. Not just an ordinary passing, but a torturous and agonizing death of the sort that you wouldn't wish on your worst enemy.

Following their confab with LeFevre, Cradoc and his sidekick swung by the small hospital shop so Wyatt could purchase the apricot jam for Josie.

"Do you know the new editor over at the *Union*?" Cradoc asked as they moved back out into the sunshine.

"You already know I know him. You've seen him at the Oyster on more than one occasion."

"Can you introduce me?"

"Am I allowed to enquire as to why?"

Cradoc looked at him with wily eyes. "Don't see why Nick has to get all the good stories."

"You low-down dirty dog," Wyatt sniggered. "You're gonna leak the autopsy to the *Union*?"

"Not the whole damn thing. Just the salient points. Like the fact that Archer was most definitely killed by someone else."

Wyatt shook his head in wonderment. "God strike me down if I ever cross you."

7

NICK PINDER ACCOMPANIED Archer's funeral cortege to Mt. Hope Cemetery, a burial ground on the eastern outskirts of San Diego. Elliot Patterson tagging along of course, because suddenly photos had become a huge part of their front-page coverage. Nick figured it would take a while before the competition caught up with the *Times* and that, for the foreseeable future, they'd remain the only local newspaper with the technology to reproduce photographic images on newsprint. Nick and Patterson were determined to take full advantage of that while they could.

Rushing back to the office, Nick wrote his story on Archer's send-off and passed the pages to Clive for editing. By the time he finally ran it down to the print shop in the basement, Nick's stomach was rumbling like a freight train. He hadn't eaten all day. Rather than ride home and wait for Lupe to rustle up some grub, he called Roz and asked if she would join him for dinner at the Horton House restaurant. Getting that phone installed was definitely a smart decision.

Half an hour later, the smartly clad maître d' ushered them to a corner table in San Diego's most fashionable restaurant. In a jolly mood, Nick asked the waiter to surprise them with a new libation. The man returned with something called Beringer—red wine made from grapes harvested and crushed in the Napa Valley. Having never before sipped California wine, Nick eyed the bottle warily. But when the waiter assured him that all of the best eateries in San Francisco were now serving "native wines" along with their French selections, Nick's hesitation evaporated. Both he and Roz thought it a marvelous drink, a welcome addition to the local palate.

"We should see for ourselves," Roz suggested. "How they make such a marvelous drink from grapes."

"Perhaps we'll get a chance someday."

"How about sooner rather than later?"

Nick scrunched up his face. "You're suggesting we take a holiday now?"

"Why not?" was his wife's hopeful response. "I've never been to San Francisco, and everyone makes it sound absolutely lovely. They've got a real opera house and symphony orchestra. I'd love to see what the ladies are wearing up there, what's currently in fashion. Not to mention the fact that we never had a proper honeymoon."

But the proposal disconcerted her husband. "I don't see how I have the time," he said. "And even if I did, I wouldn't want to be away from San Diego just now. This Archer thing is getting bigger and bigger."

"He was buried today. It's over."

"But they haven't caught the perpetrator yet, or even identified who the killer might have been. I have a feeling about this one and want to be here to cover the story."

"That might take months," Roz pointed out. "And it may never happen, according to the reports I read in *your* newspaper. No evidence and all that."

"That's the point," Nick countered. "What if evidence comes to light and I'm not here? Worse still, what if they catch the culprit, and I'm gallivanting around Northern California? There'll be no one to write the story."

"What about this new fellow Clive just hired?"

"Wendell Smith? A rank amateur."

"And it's not like Clive can't write. He's the one who taught you."

"I'm better than him now. Much better. And he knows it."

Roz shook her head in disgust. "There's always some excuse."

"What's that supposed to mean?"

But she never got a chance to answer. The waiter appeared again, this time asking for their dinner orders. Although the sauté of green turtle sounded most inviting, Nick decided on the escalope of clams on toast a la Sicilienne. Roz ordered the spring lamb with mint sauce. They would share side dishes of fried parsnips, lima beans, and fresh spinach.

As the waiter scooted off to the kitchen, their conversation resumed. Lowering her voice to almost a whisper so none of the other diners would hear, Roz said, "I'm bored, Nick. Bored out of my mind. If now's not a great time to travel, I fully understand. But then let me relieve my boredom via some other means."

Nick knew exactly what she meant: Roz wanted to work again. Restart her seamstress business, make fancy frocks for the sour-faced matrons on Banker's Hill. "No way," he said curtly. "No wife of mine is going to work."

They'd discussed the matter on previous occasions, during which Nick had related his reasons for his ardent disapproval. After his father's death, he and his mother had been expelled from their lighthouse home in favor of a boarding house in Old Town. Having never learned a trade or any other marketable skill, his mother had earned her living as an independent "working girl." Even though it provided a way to survive, Nick had always been ashamed of his mother's vocation and had become set against the idea of women working any kind of job.

But Roz didn't see it that way. "The world is changing, Nick. Women have proper professions these days." She reeled off the names of three highly successful local business ladies. "Kate Sessions and her nursery. Clara Foltz and her law practice. Josie Earp and the Oyster."

"Josie doesn't own the place," Nick countered.

"Well, she damn well runs it," Roz huffed. When heads turned at the sound of a woman uttering a vulgarism, she lowered her voice again. "It's not like I'm going to be working in a saloon. I'll be making dresses for God's sake. Dealing with the 'manor born' and such."

"That's exactly what irks me."

"What? That I'll be hobnobbing with the town's elite? Are you too ashamed to release me from my own gilded cage?"

"Just the opposite," Nick said sincerely. "I'm proud of you. Who you are. What you are. And I don't …" He struggled to find the right words. "I don't want you working for those rich bitches. Don't want you playing maidservant to anyone again." A reference to her youth in Ireland and teenage years in Boston when Roz had been indentured to several wealthy women.

Once again, his wife begged to differ. "It's nothing like that, and you know it. The service I render is no different than an attorney, doctor, or other professional. This would be *my* business. *I* set the prices, and *I* set the deadlines. Not the other way around."

But Nick wouldn't budge from his stance. "The Archer stories are going to boost us onto a completely different plain financially and socially. Soon I'll have a nationwide reputation. Book offers. Lecture tours. The sky's the limit. If you can just hold out for a few more months."

Roz responded with a long sigh. "'It's different this time.' That's what you've been saying for years, Nick. But *I* have a skill, too. *I* can run a business. No amount of money is going to change the fact that we can never have children or that I'm going absolutely out of my mind. I need to be doing something rather than doing nothing."

Without another word, Roz placed her napkin on the table, pushed her chair back, stood, and walked away.

Nick sat immobilized, wondering if he should follow his wife, continue to explain his feelings, or just let her blow off steam from this latest eruption. But then the waiter arrived with their entrees. Having been taught by his mother to never waste food, Nick decided to eat what he could, rather than rush home.

†

Cradoc Bradshaw spent the rest of the week tracking down and judiciously quizzing those who had been with Zebulon Archer on the night of his death, including the bank manager, the county judge, the deputy mayor, and the Belgian hot-air balloon tender. All of the gents more or less spun the same tale: they were drinking and playing cards at the Cliff House on the Saturday night on which the incident took place. Archer had excused himself from the table around nine o'clock and never come back. No one in the parlor gave it a second thought, because over the course of the evening, it was normal to slip away from the card table and disappear upstairs with one of the shady ladies. All four gentlemen could pretty much vouch for each other. They had lingered downstairs and in full view of one another for at least another hour after Archer excused himself.

While the interviews yielded next to nothing in the way of new information about Archer's death, they were useful all the same. Just being with these men, alone in a room, and casually discussing what had transpired that evening, gave the marshal a chance to appraise them as possible suspects in the murder. Either all of them were lying or all were telling the truth about what had gone down that night. In the end, Cradoc concluded that none of the gentlemen had been a party to Archer's sudden mortality. Huge sigh of relief on his part—the last thing any lawman wants is hanging a murder charge on a prominent local personage. But if not them, who?

Cradoc spent another couple of days trying to identify and locate the strumpets present at Cliff House that evening. Not an easy task when you considered how many there were in San Diego—more than a thousand prostitutes by some estimates—and the fact that many of them didn't use their birth names. Other factors also loomed. Sporting ladies generally didn't talk to the law, even if they weren't suspected of anything. And if the whores at Cliff House were freelancers, forget it. He'd probably never find them.

Making his way down into the bowels of the Stingaree district, Cradoc went from joint to joint until he hit pay dirt—a house that employed all the ladies present at Cliff House that night, including the dead man's regular squeeze. It seemed that Archer, both a clever businessman and notorious tightwad, had negotiated a "package rate" with this particular house to supply flesh for all of his Saturday shindigs.

While the marshal felt somewhat chuffed that he'd been able to locate the ladies in question, they couldn't tell him anything more about Archer's disappearance and death than he already knew. Like the gentlemen they had serviced that evening, all the women could account for their whereabouts around the time that Archer went to answer the call of nature. Besides, it didn't seem to Cradoc that your average cathouse gal would go through all the trouble of dragging someone out to the cliffs when a simple stiletto to the heart would suffice. For all his trouble, the marshal found himself on the receiving end of plenty of bawdy offers and salacious innuendos, but little that might aid or abet his homicide investigation.

Cradoc's perusal of the physical evidence proved equally frustrating. Despite their role in hobbling Archer, the broken whiskey jug and the bloody pottery shards had thus far proved useless in distinguishing an assailant. The steel spike driven into the top of the cliff matched those used on the California Southern Railroad. Given that local railroad construction had started seven years previous (1881), more than a million spikes had been pounded into the hundred and forty odd miles of track between San Diego and Los Angeles and various spur lines. The rope used to suspend Archer was equally common—three-quarter-inch cordage of the type employed in the rigging of hundreds of sailing vessels that weighed anchor in San Diego Bay each year. Woven with a blend of low and high strength hemp fibers, this sort of rope was perfect for hoisting heavy canvas sails—or a portly human body.

The killer had no doubt handled all of these objects, a fact that frustrated Cradoc even more. He had recently come across an article from a British scientific journal called *Nature*, a story about how one could theoretically use "fingerprints" to identify criminals. It had been known for some years that the swirls of skin on everyone's fingertips were unique. But some Englishman in India—the inspector general of the Bengal prisons—had ascertained that whenever a person touches something, they leave an impression of those swirls on the surface of that object. An impression apparently engendered by the sweat and natural body oils that occur in the skin. However, it remained scientific theory rather than crime-fighting reality. To Cradoc's knowledge, no one had yet devised an easy way to collect, classify, and match these greasy smudges. And even if such a thing were soon invented, it would probably take years, maybe even decades, before the method reached San Diego.

8

JUST AFTER DAWN, THE KILLER wandered the streets of San Diego's small Chinatown, populated by more recent immigrants with little or no knowledge of what had transpired in the 1860s. In the same manner as whores, drunks, and sailors, the Chinese were confined to a squalid area south of Market Street. They could work as cooks, cleaners, or gardeners in the finer parts of town, but they could only own their own property or businesses down among the rabble. Despite its rough edges, the Asian enclave had always been one of his favorite parts of town, a mélange of sights, sounds, and smells so at odds with the world he normally inhabited.

Ambling down Third Street past Woo Chee Chong's store and the Taoist temple, he passed a Chinaman selling live crickets in tiny matchstick cages and a tiny, elderly woman squatting on the ground, sorting various types of eggs—ducks, chickens, seagulls, and God only knew what else—into baskets she would take from door to door on her daily rounds. Further along were stalls selling ginseng, dried lizards, and deer antlers—all sorts of things to fortify body, soul, and sexual organs—and cages filled with rattlesnakes, a delicacy in the Chinese community. The serpent still alive, its body would be slit open with a razor, the bile and other bodily fluids drained into a ceramic jar for fermentation into snake wine, the body shredded into thin strips for snake soup.

He had always admired the Chinese, their determination and work ethic. Most had been coolies back in the old country and then worked as virtual slaves on the Western railroads until they earned their grubstake. Those who had decided to remain on this side of the ocean had absorbed the American dream of working your way up from nothing. Despite the derogatory snipes of white Americans, most Chinese were upstanding citizens, and Chinese neighborhoods boasted little real crime. Gambling and prostitution for sure. But very little violence. And when blood was shed, they took care of it themselves. If someone got murdered in Chinatown, the elders would quickly discern the killer's identity and dispatch the culprit in some back alley. No need for courts, judges, or law enforcement. They cleaned up their own messes. In that regard, he figured everyone should be emulating the Chinese rather than disparaging their existence.

Loitering at the corner of Third and J streets, the killer glanced through the open windows of a Chinese teahouse. Not a white face in the crowd. Asians occupied each table, sipping hot tea and slurping gruel as they chatted amongst themselves in their strange tongue. Every face in the place looked around as he stepped through the front door and pulled back a chair at an empty table. It wasn't every day they saw a *gweilo* enter their realm, especially one they recognized. They knew him all right, from his public standing and high-profile job. But their interest proved fleeting. Heads turned away, and they went back to their own chatter. Most were men, railroad workers and abalone fishermen grabbing breakfast before work. But the number of females had steadily risen in recent times as "mail order" brides arrived from San Francisco or from across the wide ocean.

Removing a newspaper from beneath his arm, the killer spread it across the tabletop, gazing one more time at the audacious headline and photograph—the *San Diego Times* front page from the morning after the Archer killing. He allowed himself a thin smile. Things had fallen into place nicely, much better than anticipated. He'd formed expectations of how events would unfold after Archer's murder. But even the wisest sage wouldn't have predicted how the cards had been stacked in his favor. Stacked in the favor of celestial justice. After all, justice is what this was all about. Retribution for crimes against both himself and the entire town.

The crabs ... he could have never predicted that. The crabs attacking Archer's face, rendering the man almost unrecognizable. As if nature also craved vengeance for the evil acts the man had once committed. Death by drowning paled in comparison to animals ravaging a human body— now *that* was unusual. People would remember Archer as the man who had his face torn off by crabs.

Ready to order, the killer caught the eye of the teahouse owner. Recognizing his customer, a broad smile broke across the proprietor's face.

"Long time no see," the owner said.

"Too much work."

"So busy you can't eat?" The owner scolded as he wiped the tabletop with a grubby towel. "Maybe Chinese people make more trouble. Then you eat here more. Better for you, better for me."

The killer laughed at the owner's joke. "Maybe so," he answered. "I do love your grub."

Not one to start his day with mysterious meat chunks floating in a bowl of rice gruel, he took a rain check on the highly recommended congee and instead asked for fried eggs and pork bacon fresh from the Chinese abattoir just down the block. Given the culinary variety of Chinatown, he wasn't sure they would be chicken eggs. But no matter, at least the dish would *look* familiar.

As the owner trotted off to the kitchen to place his order, the killer lapsed back into contemplation, this time pondering Archer's generous eulogies. All that talk about random violence and senseless killing, the discourse on Archer's "magnanimous contributions" to the community. *Please.* Other than his wife, no one had cherished the living Archer. But in death, the lumber king had been elevated to the status of a great public figure. He had greatly underestimated the outpouring of sympathy from the local elite. They certainly circled the wagons when they felt threatened. This had irked him at first. But in the week since Archer's funeral, he had come to think of it as possibly a blessing in disguise. By placing Archer on a pedestal, the shock would be all that much greater once he exposed the man's villainous past. He would show everyone soon enough why there was nothing random or senseless about Archer's execution, show them the man deserved none of their sympathy or admiration.

If anything, people should be admiring how he so carefully planned and carried out the man's assassination and got away scot-free. If you believed what you read in the papers and heard on the street, nobody had a shred of evidence thus far that connected him to the murder. No witnesses, no evidence, no apparent motive. He had planned and carried out a perfect crime. He was proud of that fact, but unsure if he could do it again.

As he had feared beforehand, killing had changed him, or rather *was* changing him, because it seemed an ongoing process. He could recall the adrenalin rush of that night—subduing Archer, dragging him to the clifftop, and pushing him over the edge. The satisfaction he had derived from Archer's utter shock when the man realized who his assailant was, what his crime had been, and that death would soon be his fate.

But that initial thrill had faded into a deep remorse about taking the life of another human being, even one as wicked as Zebulon Archer. Although he still deemed the act justified, waves of regret continued to ebb through his soul, most often in the middle of the night. Waking up with a cold sweat, a certainty that you, too, are damned for eternity, and a notion that you can never tell anyone what happened, not even your closest confidants. Even if other people sympathized with his motives for killing Archer—and understood the reason he employed such a gruesome means to carry out the task—they would never look at him the same if they ever found out he was the one who actually did the deed. The only choice was living a lie, never fully confiding in anyone.

At this point, the killer wasn't sure if he could go through with eliminating the other three men on his list. He would definitely expose his motives for taking Archer's life, because otherwise the entire point was lost and the deed wasted. Yet beyond that ... If he could subdue his emotions in the manner of a soldier marching into battle or the hangman releasing the trap door, then accomplishing the remainder of his quest was possible. But if he continued to struggle with the morality of it all—and the disturbing finality of ending another person's life—there was no telling what might transpire. He didn't want his heart to grow so dark that death meant little or nothing. But in the same breath, justice would never prevail if he did not continue with his plan.

Finishing off the last of his breakfast, he casually glanced around the teahouse. Most of the men had departed, off to their jobs on the tracks and among the tide pools. And now the room was slowly filling with women and children. At a nearby table sat a young Chinese mother and her two children, a boy and girl clad in the thick woolen uniform and lace-up boots of the Chinese Mission School. As they waited for their breakfast to arrive, the mother combed her daughter's long black hair into ponytails, while the son read a book.

Dipping his head, the killer could just make out the title—*Buffalo Bill: His Adventures in the West*. A dime novel by the renowned Ned Buntline. Amazing how even the Chinese knew of Buffalo Bill Cody. Would they feel the same, would the kid still be reading this book, if they knew the truth about Buffalo Bill? That Cody had forged his fame and fortune from fallacious exploits, that he was a razzle-dazzle showman rather than a genuine paladin?

Soon they would have another hero. A *real* hero. Soon that Chinese boy would be reading about him.

9

ROZ PINDER HEARD A KNOCK and went to the front door. Peering through lace curtains, she saw a young man clad in a gray suit with a red bowtie and straw hat. Fresh face, pale complexion, and a rather foppish demeanor. Not someone who had spent a good deal of time outdoors or engaged in anything remotely perilous. He carried a leather valise and had obviously come by horse—the bay mare with an expensive saddle tied to their hitching post. But she didn't recognize him.

Still, he looked harmless, perhaps a traveling salesman or itinerant preacher, and Roz pulled back the door. "Can I help you?" she asked.

"You must be Mrs. Pinder," the man-boy said chipperly, tipping his hat. "I am *very* glad to finally make your acquaintance."

He extended a hand, but Roz did not immediately reciprocate. "And whom might you be?"

"Did I not say? Excuse me. Mr. Wendell Smith. I have the great honor of working alongside your husband at the *Times*."

So *this* was Wendell Smith. She certainly knew of his existence from her husband and others, but had not yet come across him in person. Roz offered a polite smile and shook his hand. "Pleased to meet you, Mr. Smith."

"Likewise, madam."

"And how can I be of service?"

Wendell looked slightly flummoxed, as if Roz should already know the reason for his visit. "Mr. Pinder asked me to meet with him here at midday."

News to her. But in typical fashion, Roz rolled with the flow. One thing she had learned during her marriage to Nick was to always expect the unexpected.

"Please do come in then."

Roz offered him a seat in the parlor and went straight away upstairs. Being a Saturday, she had only just returned from her weekly provision shopping in town and had not seen her husband since leaving him in bed, sound asleep, early this morning.

She found Nick in the bathroom, wearing the long-johns in which he slept, shaving in front of the bureau mirror and a basin of hot water. "Who in blazes was banging at the door?"

"Wendell Smith."

"He's a touch early."

"You knew he was coming?"

"Yes, we planned this yesterday."

Roz stood in the doorway, staring daggers at the back of Nick's head until he turned around. "Is there a problem, darling?" His tone was pure innocence.

"What made you assume that bringing your work home would meet with my approval?"

Wiping away the excess shaving cream from his face with a towel, Nick said, "I figured meeting up with

Wendell here was better than me going into the office on a Saturday."

"Well, you figured wrong!" she snapped. "Just because your body's at home doesn't mean your mind is, too!"

Nick responded with what he figured to be his best weapon—abject silence.

"You've got nothing more to say?"

"I can send Wendell back down the hill." But his words lacked conviction.

"That's quite all right," she said icily, retreating from the room.

Roz briefly flirted with the idea of ducking out the back door, saddling a horse, and simply riding off. But propriety got the best of her, and she moved back into the parlor. "Nick will be right down, Mr. Smith. Meanwhile, can I offer you a beverage? Coffee perhaps?"

"I'm really more of a tea drinker, Mrs. Pinder."

"If you don't mind Earl Grey."

"That would be lovely."

Waiting for the water to boil, Roz steamed with anger. What was she going to do with Nick? He wasn't just staying late at the office and roaming all over creation in search of stories. Now he was bringing the work home! Next thing you knew, he'd be writing in their bed at night. Something had to give—either his work or his home life. Because the former now dominated the latter.

She heard footsteps on the stairs—Nick on his way down—and dutifully prepared coffee for her husband and tea for his guest. Arranging everything on a tray, she retraced her steps to the parlor. As she had been taught many years before by her benefactor in Boston, Roz served the beverages in silence, making sure not to disturb the men, and then withdrew quietly, all the while loathing the entire situation.

✝

Nick sipped his coffee and considered the man on the other side of the table. There wasn't much he *didn't* despise when it came to Wendell Smith. Born of the elite. Ivy League educated. Dispatched to the "Wild West" by Daddy (a prominent New York publisher) to garner real-world experience and learn the newspaper business from the ground up before returning to join the family rag. Nick would have been the first to admit he could no longer handle all of the day-to-day writing on his own. The *Times* had grown too large in recent years for one reporter to produce every single word. But why hire a nancy boy? *I mean, look at him!* Straw hat! Bowtie! Walks likes he's got a stick up his ass! Not to mention that whiny, prep school voice.

Nick preferred to work alone and normally did. He had agreed to Wendell's assistance on the Archer case only after a considerable amount of pressure from Clive. He didn't know for certain, but Nick had always suspected that money had changed hands between Daddy Smith and Clive Bennett. Otherwise, how could you explain the employment of such a buffoon?

Clive could force them to cooperate on the Archer case, but Nick still decided how to divvy up the workload. Out of spite, he had relegated his unwelcome sidekick to research rather than writing, a dog's body to amass background information on Archer, interview various people who knew the deceased, and keep tabs on the ongoing police investigation, in particular, the movements of Cradoc Bradshaw. Nick would snag the byline on whatever stories might be produced and Wendell no more than a brief mention at the very end. That burned the young reporter, and Nick knew it. But that was the way of the world. Nick had waited his turn and so would Smith.

For his part, Wendell Smith found himself pondering Nick. Even after three months at the *Times*, he still couldn't decide if he admired or reviled Pinder. He was such a bastard, lashing out with obscenities if you disturbed his writing, ordering you around like a common servant, and not offering even perfunctory thanks when you completed whatever laborious task you had been dispatched to attend. How could anyone be that full of themselves?

Yet at the same time, Nick had unmistakable charm, the kind of charisma that could sweep both men and women off their feet. And that oozing confidence was more than hot air. He got things done. He worked harder and longer than anyone else at the paper. His reporting and writing were nothing short of brilliant. Perhaps he should be despised, but Nick was also someone to emulate—tricks of the trade that Wendell could duplicate when he returned to New York.

All things considered, it was best to keep on Nick's good side. But often that was easier said than done, their current meeting being a good case in point. Smith had burned the midnight oil creating a detailed summary of everything he had learned thus far about the Archer murder.

But Nick had something else in mind. "What's Cradoc been up to?" he asked, just as Wendell was about to read his summary out loud.

"No disrespect," Wendell said, "but my time might be better spent trying to identify and locate the actual killer, rather than following someone who is attempting to do the same."

Nick didn't bat an eye at Smith's insubordination. As a matter of fact, he was amazed it had taken the young reporter so long to raise an objection. "Wendell," he said with an edge in his voice, "I am the decider on this story. And as such, I have decided on a division of labor in which I search for the killer directly and you do so indirectly by keeping tabs on Marshal Bradshaw. To state things in metaphorical terms, think of this as a hunt. You can go straight after your quarry and hope you get lucky ... or you can fall in behind the bloodhounds and wait for the dogs to sniff out the prey. We are pursuing both strategies, and you happen to be the one tailing the bloodhounds. Perhaps you and the dogs will get there first, or maybe I will. In such a manner, we get the story no matter what happens. And we do not have to concern ourselves with Bradshaw deciding that another paper besides the *San Diego Times* deserves to get the news first. Is that clear enough, Wendell?"

"I suppose." Wendell didn't even try to suppress his sigh.

Having failed to convince Nick to let him undertake what he considered a more significant role in the Archer investigation, Smith read out loud from his notebook, a long and excruciatingly detailed summary of Marshal Bradshaw's movements over the previous week. All said and done, it appeared Cradoc had been working the case alone and wasn't even close to naming a suspect or making an arrest.

"So he has shit all," Nick mused.

"I do suppose you could term it that way."

"But neither do we."

"Not for lack of trying," the young reporter said defensively. "Other than intermittent sleep and occasionally eating, I haven't done anything but work on this story for the last fortnight!"

"Sleep'll get you every time," Nick responded. "I've always held that the key to successful journalism is an endless flow of coffee."

"Coffee?" asked Wendell, puzzled by the comment.

"Don't mind if I do," said Nick, holding out his empty cup. "You'll find both coffee and kettle in the kitchen. But before you go, pass the mail. You did bring the post, didn't you, Wendell?"

"It's in here," said the young reporter, passing his valise across the table to Nick. "Do you take sugar?"

"Black, thank you. And a word of advice: *Real* journalists drink coffee. You really should switch. Put some hair on that chest of yours."

Wendell huffed his disapproval and shuffled off to the kitchen.

✝

Nick emptied the contents of the valise onto the low table, at rough glance about three dozen letters. The vast majority appeared to be nothing but letters to the editor. Belly-aches and complaints, supplications and petitions, as well as the ramblings of local lunatics, which often made the best reading. As the lowest rung on the *Times* totem pole, Wendell perused each and every letter received from the public and chose at least a dozen to be published in every edition. Anything addressed to a specific person at the newspaper was automatically forwarded to the name on the envelope. In this particular batch, there were several addressed to Clive Bennett and other staffers, but merely one bearing Nick's name.

Nick examined the envelope, turning it over in his hands. Both the name and address were typed. That alone was enough to make it stand out from the others, all of them handwritten. Typing machines were now common in the workplace, but seldom used for personal correspondence. Also odd was the lack of a return name or address on either the front or back flap. Flipping it over again, Nick examined the postmark—mailed the previous day at the main post office in San Diego.

After tapping the envelope on the tabletop, Nick ripped open an end, blew into the void, and shook out the contents. Onto the table dropped a two-page letter also composed on a typing machine. In silence, he began to read.

Dear Mr. Pinder:

Forgive me for making first contact with you in such an impersonal manner, but it is not possible for me, at this point in time, to call upon you in person.

The purpose of this correspondence is two-fold: to introduce myself as a person of knowledge and to illuminate a recent event in our fine city.

I am privy to information about the death of Mr. Zebulon Archer that is not yet known to the general public....

Nick had grown weary of "insider tips" on Archer's puzzling death. The *Times* had received at least a hundred missives from would-be informants claiming they had seen the homicide take place or possessed indisputable evidence that would help him solve the case. Most of these letters were no doubt prompted by a thousand-dollar reward that Mrs. Archer had posted in return for information explaining her husband's passing. Thus far, no one had come close to claiming the bounty. Nick and

Wendell had chased down every tip, and each had been a frustrating dead end.

Now here was another letter writer claiming insider knowledge of Archer's death. And not just any old information this time.

It was I who dispatched Mr. Archer.

An assertion made with such boldness that it raised the hair on the back of Nick's neck. He quickly read on.

Given the innate skepticism of every good reporter, I suspect you will mistrust my claim. If that be the case, then let me tell you, Mr. Pinder, that I have indisputable proof. All the proof that you shall ever desire or require.

Let us start with the fact that I can relate aspects of the affair known only by the marshal's office and the county medical examiner at this point in time.

For instance, I can say with some certainty that Mr. Archer's demise did not come about as a result of falling from a high precipice as reported in the local press. He was overcome by seawater. On purpose, I might add, by none other than yours truly. I did not force his head beneath the water, but rather let nature, in the form of the incoming tide, run its own course through Mr. Archer's lungs.

From the days he had worked alongside Cradoc rather than against him, Nick knew the marshal routinely withheld details of a crime as a means of weeding out false confessions. Only the true perpetrator would know what really happened. This seemed to be just such a case—the fact that Archer had drowned, rather than fallen to his death as everyone presumed.

Wendell came trundling back into the parlor with a fresh cup of coffee.

Nick waved the letter in the air. "This fellow claims to have killed Archer."

"Another lunatic?"

"I don't think so. Not this time. Whoever penned this letter seems to know an awful lot about the crime that hasn't been revealed by the authorities."

"Such as…?"

Nick began again from the salutation, reading out loud. By the time he reached the passage about the intentional drowning, the young reporter was hunched over his shoulder, eyes glued to the document.

> . . . more proof can be found beside the row of latrines behind the Cliff House. Scattered about the ground are the broken pieces of a ceramic vessel used to immobilize the accused before conveying Mr. Archer to Devil's Cove.
>
> The question you are no doubt asking yourself at this precise moment is why I would take Mr. Archer's life. The simple answer is that no one else seemed willing to undertake a task that should have been accomplished long ago.

"What on Earth is he talking about?" Wendell asked.

Nick shook his head. "I have no idea." But soon enough they had their answer.

> As you are already aware, having been around in the "old days" yourself, Mr. Archer was a loyal son of the Confederacy as well as an outspoken critic of anything he found loathsome or vile. And that included just about any human being who was not of white, Anglo-Saxon, Protestant heritage. That, in and of itself, is not a crime. After all, one of the founding precepts of this great nation is freedom of speech.

However, Mr. Archer found it imperative to act upon his beliefs by striking out at those he saw as responsible for the demise and degradation of the American way of life. While he had a limited tolerance for those who occupied this land before his arrival — Indians and Mexicans — he held a particular disdain for recent immigrants from China.

In the spring of 1865, a group of Chinamen arrived in boats from northern California. Their initial activity was abalone harvesting and they very much kept to themselves on so-called "junk" sailing craft anchored in the bay. But it was perhaps inevitable that eventually the Chinamen would seek economic opportunities on land, too. And that is what raised the ire of Mr. Archer—competition in the form of a Chinamen by the name of "Sam" Ah Choy, who began selling lumber from the back of a handcart parked on the plaza in Old Town. At substantially reduced rates, I might add. Not only did this end Mr. Archer's monopoly on lumber sales in San Diego, but it inspired other Chinamen to test the waters of mainland commerce, and soon half a dozen handcarts could be seen around the plaza.

Mr. Archer was the leader of the small, but vocal minority who disapproved of this enterprise. These men took it upon themselves to "encourage" the Asians to abandon their terrestrial endeavors and return to the high seas where they belonged. When discourse failed to dislodge the flaxen-skinned migrants, Mr. Archer and his cohorts resorted to violence, including the surreptitious beating of several Chinamen.

This, too, failed to achieve Mr. Archer's aims. The Chinese did not take heed until "Sam" Ah Choy was discovered lifeless in the wetlands downriver from Old Town …

"Is any of this true?" asked Wendell, figuring quite rightly that Nick must have been around when these deeds transpired.

Nick looked up, squinting as if trying to recall something in the distant past. "I can't recall. I was pretty young at the time, six or seven." And then he picked up reading again, eager to reach the letter's climax.

Despite their suspicions to the contrary, the military commanders who administered the region at that time had no choice but to deem Mr. Choy's passing a death by misadventure. There was simply no proof to the contrary.

While a public inquiry into Mr. Choy's passing would have been the most righteous course of action, there were concerns amongst San Diego's civic and military authorities that local Confederate sympathizers might take up arms if one of their number were accused or arrested in connection with the death of a Chinaman. In other words, keeping the peace trumped the pursuit of justice, especially in the absence of indisputable proof.

However, as an eyewitness to the aforementioned incident, I am in a unique position to declare that Mr. Choy's demise was nothing short of murder. Having incapacitated his victim with the assistance of several like-minded ruffians, Mr. Archer held his head beneath the waters of the San Diego River until such time as Mr. Choy was no longer breathing.

"So Archer was a cold-blooded killer?" Wendell straightened and ran his hand through his otherwise perfectly groomed hair.

"So our correspondent claims."

"But why wait more than twenty years to exact revenge?" Wendell asked, stooping to see the rest of the letter.

Indeed, the letter writer, in his slow and methodical way, had not neglected that consideration.

One might ask why I did not alert the proper authorities immediately after the incident. For the simple reason that I was terrified of Mr. Archer and his allies, and quite rightly feared that something similar might befall myself and those close to me if I should utter a single word about the ghastly events that had passed before my very eyes.

I have always been discomfited by my lack of valor and ashamed that I was not able to step forward directly thereafter. Hopefully recent events, belated as they are, will serve to rectify at least a portion of my earlier inaction.

- Your Humble Servant

Nick sprang to his feet. "Any idea where Clive is this afternoon?"

"My guess is somewhere in the Stingaree, getting a leg up on Saturday night."

"Check the *Medusa* first—maybe he's still sleeping off last night's bender. If he's not there, start working your way up Fifth Street. I'll meet you at the office. We've gotta find him, fast."

10

LEFT WITHOUT A FATHER at the age of three
and having struggled through most of his life as a two-bit
miner and laborer, Joe Coyne was more than a might bit
proud of what he had accomplished since coming to San
Diego. In a dozen years as the county's chief law officer, he
had amassed a tidy sum. Not from his government salary,
mind you, but rather cash proffered by those who desired
a slightly different interpretation of the law than what was
officially on the books.

Make no mistake, Sheriff Coyne would not brook violence of any sort. And in his years at the helm, he had managed to rid San Diego of much of its Wild West reputation
(thanks in no small part to his hiring of Cradoc Bradshaw).
But victimless crime was another matter. Much of what
transpired in the Stingaree district was technically illegal.
Yet the vice trades—prostitution, opium, and gambling—
flourished in open view. Try as they may, local do-gooders
could not stem the ever-rising tide of sin. Primarily because members of the political and business establishment
were amongst the trade's best customers and partially

because the purveyors of vice contributed handsomely (and often) to Coyne's personal "retirement fund."

Coyne had used those funds to buy a piece of the rock—a house on Banker's Hill. And while his home may not be nearly as grand as those of the business and finance establishment, it was pretty damn good for a poor kid from Ohio who had ventured west at the age of fifteen with nary a penny in his hole-filled pockets. Yes, the man had done well for himself.

With a city charter on the horizon—and the built-in job security that would keep Coyne in office until whatever age he should deem to retire—there was no reason to continue busting his balls. The sheriff still rose at the crack of dawn. But unlike days gone by, he now took his time getting to the jailhouse, preferring instead to take breakfast on the front porch of his two-story clapboard home, a ritual he cherished to no small end. On mornings when it wasn't foggy or overcast, he would contemplate sunrise over the bay and the bustling waterfront town that had rendered him so much good fortune. He would listen to the birds and breathe in the sea breeze, and the Mexican maid would bring him toast and coffee. One by one, the newsies would deliver the daily papers to his doorstep, and Coyne would spread them out on his breakfast table. He relished the *Sun* for its malicious and often spurious gossip. He was more of a *Union* man when it came to political bent (thoroughly Republican). Yet the sheriff would be the first to agree that neither could hold a candle to the *Times* when it came to crime. Even Coyne had a grudging respect for Nick Pinder.

On this particular Sunday, Coyne grabbed the *Union* first, scanning a front-page article about an upcoming visit by Governor Waterman to San Diego. He read through some of the tittle-tattle in the *Sun*. Last but not least, he picked up the *Times* and just about choked on his toast. The banner headline screamed: VIGILANTE KILLER STALKS SAN DIEGO.

"What in God's name!" Coyne blurted out. He read on, expecting some trumped-up account of murder in the Stingaree, a crime of passion perhaps, two sailors fighting over a gal. What he got instead was the shock of his long and distinguished law enforcement career: A letter from an anonymous author confessing the murder of Zebulon Archer to avenge the death of a transient Chinaman twenty-odd years before. Whoever penned the letter had details about the crime withheld from the general public, details Coyne himself knew from the autopsy report. Pinder had also cited newspaper articles from 1865 about the drowning of a Chinese merchant by the name of Sam Ah Choy in the San Diego River, as well as the testimony of a local priest who had arranged the burial of the deceased pagan in a non-Christian plot.

The sheriff felt himself go faint. This simply could not be true! *Not in my town! Not on my watch!* Flinging the paper over the balcony and flipping over the breakfast table, he rushed back inside to get dressed.

†

An hour later, Coyne stood before his entire staff in the jailhouse. Not a single deputy was left on the streets, and those off duty had been roused from their beds. If the local rogues had known about the gathering, they could have had their way with the banks and mercantiles.

"By thunder!" Coyne demanded. "I want the bastard arrested straight away!"

"We don't know who he is," Fatty Rice reminded him.

"I'm not talking about the killer, you dolt. I'm talking about Pinder. I want him shackled and behind bars! Prosecuted to the full extent!"

"I don't believe he's broken any laws," Cradoc Bradshaw said from the back of the room.

But that just made Coyne even more steamed. "*You* of all people! Defending Pinder!"

"I'm not defending him. I'm just saying we don't have a valid reason to detain him. So why bother?"

"Why bother?" The sheriff's voice went up a full octave. "Because one of our most prominent citizens was just brutally murdered. And Pinder seems to be the only one with any clue who the killer might be."

Coyne spat out a huge glob of tobacco—straight onto the floor rather than into the lobby spittoon—shoved another wad in his cheek and glared at Cradoc. "You think it's true? That Archer drowned that Asian fella?"

"I don't remember his name. It was a long time ago, and I was pretty young. But there was a Chinese man found dead in the river. A lot of people—including my father—suspected that Archer had something to do with his death. But it was never proved and soon forgotten."

Given the motive stated in the letter, one had to assume that the author/killer must be Chinese, too. There weren't a lot of white folks, no matter how outraged, who would exact gruesome revenge for the killing of a yellow man. They would have to double check, but the marshal didn't think any of the Asians currently residing in and around San Diego had been around when the drowning described in the letter took place. Most of them had arrived in a later wave of Asian émigrés. As for the other Chinese who had come with Choy, they had fled San Diego shortly after his murder and never been seen nor heard from again.

Besides, the language just didn't seem right. Cradoc read a passage from the letter out loud. "That sound like a foreigner to you?" he asked Coyne.

"Nope. But I hear there's some pretty smart Chinamen."

"Yeah, but smart *and* fluent in English are not one and the same. This sort of writing requires formal education, not worldly wisdom. And there aren't an awful lot of Chinese in San Diego that fit that bill."

"Maybe he's not from these parts," Coyne mused. "They left San Diego, right? They wound up somewhere else? Maybe this Ah Choy fellow had kinfolk, you know sons or something, who got educated and pledged to avenge his death once they came of age."

"I'm not saying that's impossible," the marshal responded. "But my gut tells me the killer is a horse of a much different color than what most folks will likely assume."

The sheriff let out a deep and distressing sigh. "We gotta jump on this straight away. I don't wanna see it escalating into the biggest thing since indoor crappers. The sooner we catch whoever wrote this letter—and put a noose around his neck—the better for all concerned."

The marshal knew exactly what the boss meant. Rather than the general public, Coyne's "all concerned" were the local powerbrokers, a handful of men who had made a fortune from San Diego's land rush and didn't want anything to upset their juicy apple cart. If would-be migrants perceived San Diego as the wild and wooly frontier rather than the tranquil seaside oasis portrayed in the railroad station posters, they might stop coming. And that would spell financial disaster for those who had staked their futures on the sale of sunshine and sod.

Like the sheriff and nearly everyone else in town, Cradoc's financial well-being was largely dependent on extenuation of the real-estate boom. If the bubble burst, he might be out of a job, along with hundreds or possibly thousands of others. Truth be told, he would have loved to see the house of cards come tumbling down and San Diego revert to its sleepy old ways. Going back to the past would suit him just fine. If the murder of Zebulon Archer proved the spark for such a collapse, so be it. Not his concern.

On the other hand, catching Archer's killer *was* his concern. And even if the marshal wasn't driven by the righteous indignation or intellectual curiosity that had spurred him in past, there was his sense of duty. "We'll get him," he pledged on his way out the door.

"How can you be so sure?" asked Coyne.

"Because the bastard wouldn't have wrote that damn letter if he didn't wanna be found."

†

By dusk on Sunday, the *Times* had broken its all-time sales record, more than ten thousand papers sold, roughly one copy for every white adult male in San Diego. None of the other newspapers had ever come close to that total. And while that may have paled in comparison to the daily figures of the leading New York or San Francisco papers, it was unprecedented for the bottom half of the Golden State.

The newsroom had broken into spontaneous celebration, everyone having a jolly old time on Clive's dime. The publisher of the *Times* had never been miserly when it came to rewarding his charges. It encouraged them to work even harder. And even if it didn't, Clive enjoyed any excuse to throw a party.

Although it was the Lord's Day and the town much more sedate than the previous evening, word spread of the merriment. The newsroom flooded with freeloaders looking for a good time, including writers and editors from the other papers, who were all at once envious and awed by Pinder's journalistic coup. But the crowd had grown to encompass all manner of citizenry—attorneys and merchants, soldiers and ship captains, and politicos of every persuasion, including those who just a few hours prior had advocated swift (and unofficial) retribution against the town's flaxen-skinned inhabitants. Clive Bennett would later claim this merriment, rather than sagacious law enforcement, had averted a lynching spree.

By eight o'clock that evening, the celebration had spilled onto the plaza outside. When yet another case of hooch arrived by buckboard—this time courtesy of Nick Pinder—a loud cheer went up from the drunken throng. It had been years since San Diego had witnessed such a delirious response to a news event, going back to the end of the war when word reached town that North and South had finally brokered peace.

But the moment was about to be shattered. Because making his way across the plaza, up the stairs, and into the newsroom was Cradoc Bradshaw. "I need the letter," he said flatly, addressing both Nick and Clive, sitting with a dozen others around the copy desk.

"It's in the paper," Nick said flippantly.

"The *original*," said Cradoc with an even harder edge.

The revelry continued around the periphery of the newsroom. But those nearby fell silent, an expectant air charged with the possibility of violence.

"Relax," said Nick with a crooked smile, well oiled by now and slurring his words. "You're not going to learn a damn thing from that original that you haven't already read in the *Times*. We published it word for word."

"I'll make my own judgment," Cradoc said curtly.

Bennett spoke up. "Marshal, you simply cannot prance in here and make demands."

"Archer's killer is still at large," Cradoc reminded him. "The quicker we apprehend him, the better for everyone, including the ladies and gentlemen in this room."

"You're not going to find anything new," Nick repeated, lifting a drink to his lips.

"I don't want to argue with you, Nick. Just hand over the letter."

By now every eye in the newsroom had fallen on the two of them, watching the showdown between the former allies turned adversaries, wondering who would yield first. The marshal was taking a big chance trying to bully Nick in front of this bunch, the entire press corps and many of the town's leading politicians and business owners. And Nick wasn't backing down. If anything, he was enjoying the confrontation, because it cast even more attention his way. And he wasn't going to let anyone, least of all Cradoc Bradshaw, spoil his big night.

"Take a load off, Cradoc!" Nick patted the back of an empty chair like it was the head of a large, friendly dog. "Wendell! A glass for my old friend! Better yet—a bottle!" Turning back to the marshal, he said, "Shall we debate the case, swap theories? Like old times."

A shadow of indecision fell across the marshal's face. A slight twist of the lips, an extra blink of the eyes. Enough for Nick (but no one else) to realize that Cradoc might actually be considering his offer.

But the marshal's hesitation vanished as quickly as it had appeared. "It's too late," he spat back, kicking the empty chair with a boot.

"Don't be so bloody melodramatic. Here's your letter," said Nick, removing an envelope from his jacket. Emboldened by his journalist triumph and surrounded by his own people, Nick wasn't the least bit intimidated by Bradshaw's bravado. "If you wish to scrutinize it further, be my guest."

He flicked it sideways across the copy desk. The envelope hit Cradoc square in the chest and dropped to the floor like a dead bird. The marshal glared back, clenched his fists, but otherwise checked his temper.

A bystander retrieved the letter, passed it to the marshal. And Cradoc retreated without further comment. He had what he'd come for—the original dispatch. His challenge now was advancing the investigation beyond mere words on paper.

11

THE FOLLOWING MORNING, Cradoc Bradshaw sat at one of the window tables in the Oyster Bar, staring at the woman behind the counter. Josie Earp, wooden clipboard in hand, taking the booze inventory. They had made a fair amount the previous evening on take-out sales to people headed for the big shindig at the *Times*, and Josie was trying to figure what needed re-stocking.

The marshal noticed Josie staring at him in the huge Brunswick mirror behind the bar. He diverted his eyes, but too late. "Quit looking at me that way, Cradoc Bradshaw."

"*What* way?" was his feeble response.

"Those puppy dog eyes." She whirled around and faced him across the counter. "I *am* flattered. But it's not right."

"I was just thinking," he said defensively. "Staring at nothing."

But Josie's look said she didn't believe him. "Come here," she said, beckoning with a long finger.

"Why?" Cradoc asked nervously.

"I'm not gonna bite. Get your butt over here." Josie snatched a bottle from behind the bar. She uncorked it, filled a shot glass and shoved it across the mahogany counter.

"It's awful early," he muttered. "Even for me."

"Drink it!" Josie commanded.

He sniffed the tequila and downed it in a single gulp, feeling the burn as it trickled down his throat. The gratis drink foreshadowed something. But what?

Josie pursed her lips. "She's working out fine, you know."

"Who?" asked Cradoc, no idea what she meant.

"That gal you sent over. The one from Missouri. Emma Lee Dawes. I set her up with a job at the Tivoli—washing dishes, sweeping the floor. She's a hard worker. And a fast learner. Precious few like her these days."

"And there's a reason you're telling me this?"

Josie shrugged. "Just passing time till Wyatt arrives. Take it any way you like."

Cradoc knew this was most definitely *not* passing time. His gawking had set her mind to running. He could fairly well see the mental dominos falling inside Josie's head, gradually making their way around to him. He knew exactly what she was thinking: *You need to stop staring at my fine behind and get yourself a woman.*

"—tragic life," Josie was saying about the girl. "Her husband was killed in some kind of riverboat accident on the Mississippi right before she came out West."

Cradoc decided to float along, humor Josie till she finished her say. "She don't look old enough to be married."

"She's not as young as she looks. And she cleans up mighty fine."

"Just saw her that once, at Cliff House."

"You should see her now," said Josie, batting her eyes as Cradoc. "I could set you up, you know."

He couldn't take it any longer. "Josie!" he whined, a plea for her to just let it go.

"Cradoc!" she wailed in return, mocking him like an older sister might.

"Am I interrupting something?" asked a burly voice from behind, Wyatt coming through the swinging doors at the front of the saloon. "I can come back later if you two aren't done with whatever it is you're doing."

Josie waved away his concern. "Just the marshal staring at my ass again."

Wyatt came up beside him, foam on the tips of his handlebar mustache from a just-finished shave. He looked even more dapper than usual, an expensive tweed suit over a neatly pressed white shirt with Oxford collar. He did not appear to be armed, but the marshal knew better. Wyatt wore a shoulder holster beneath his suit jacket and nearly always had a smaller weapon hitched beneath a pant cuff. As the proprietor of three drinking and gambling establishments in San Diego, concealed weapons were among his indispensable business tools. And there was always the off chance that his long and controversial past might eventually catch up—somebody that Earp had locked up, shot down, punched out, or otherwise crossed during his many years as a lawman looking for payback. You never knew when some assbite might jerk a gun on you.

"I was explaining about Emma Lee," Josie told her husband.

Wyatt sucked on his teeth in mock despair. "Cradoc's gonna think she's too young."

"That's *exactly* what he thought."

"You did tell him that she's been hitched, already primed for the sack and all?"

"I did, dear. But that didn't seem to matter."

"I'm still here." Cradoc waved his hat at them.

But the Earps continued to chat amongst themselves like the marshal wasn't anywhere in the vicinity. Slipping behind the bar, Wyatt reached down to grope Josie's rear. "And did you inform the marshal that Miss Dawes also has a pretty firm caboose?"

"More or less. I suggested he take a wander down Tivoli way and look for himself."

Cradoc shook his head in disgust. "You two are *sooooooooo* funny. I didn't come here this morning to get sermonized about my love life."

"Then where's the goldarned letter?" asked Wyatt, getting down to business.

The marshal removed the document from his duster and placed it on the bar. Two pages, double-spaced, neatly typed in blue ink. All capital letters. No return address or any other indication of who might have penned and posted the correspondence.

"You think it's bona fide?" asked Wyatt, staring at the missive upside down from the other side of the bar.

That same question had spun through Cradoc's mind a thousand times since taking possession of the letter from Nick the previous evening. "Whoever wrote this letter knows things about the incident that only a handful of souls—namely you, me, Coyne, and Doc LeFevre—were privy to."

"People talk," Wyatt pointed out. "Can't keep things covered up forever."

"Idle gossip is one thing; someone claiming to be the perpetrator of the crime quite another. And if you weren't the killer, why set yourself up for a date with a noose?"

Wyatt's mustache twitched. He leaned in for a closer look. "Never seen nothing like it."

The marshal had already examined the envelope for clues. Affixed to the upper left-hand corner was a two-cent green postage stamp with George Washington in profile. Nothing the least bit unusual about that. Franked at the general post office in the middle of San Diego, the one next to Ervin's Grocery Store, on the day before delivery. Nothing unusual about that either.

Hundreds, maybe even thousands, of folks posted letters in San Diego on a daily basis. Scattered around town were street boxes into which you could slip a letter at any time of day. Hotels and boarding houses collected mail from their guests, as did the local military posts and other government agencies. Any number of ways the author could have posted his communiqué without being detected. So the key to his or her identity must lay somewhere else. Perhaps in the words rather than the paper on which they were so eloquently rendered. Or perhaps in the mechanism by which those words were produced—a typing machine.

†

Marston's Emporium stood down the block from the Oyster Bar at the corner of Fifth and C streets, a stout brick building with big picture windows displaying the latest dry goods available inside. Awaiting their scheduled arrival, owner George Marston had stationed himself just inside the front door, pocket watch in hand and a frown on his face. "Gentlemen," he said curtly. "I was beginning to think you had forgot our appointment."

For God's sake, they were only two minutes late. But the marshal felt obliged to apologize. Marston was doing him a favor by opening up before regular business hours, and he didn't want to come across as cavalier. "Sorry, George," he muttered.

"Quite all right," said Marston in a tone that said it was most definitely *not* acceptable.

With a natty suit and slicked-down hair (parted straight down the middle), Marston was the epitome of progressive modern American. He didn't drink, didn't whore, didn't have any appreciable sense of humor. And one evening per week, he offered an upstairs room free of charge for meetings of the Women's Christian Temperance Union. Unlike the majority of his colleagues and customers, Marston truly seemed to believe that clean living and hard work engendered success. As proof, he could offer his own biography—proprietor of the town's finest emporium, as well as a member of the town council and chamber of commerce. If you could somehow ignore his puritan ways and prickly manner, George wasn't a bad fellow.

Marston cleared his throat. "And what can I do for you at this early hour?"

"We'd appreciate a quick look at your typing machines," Cradoc explained.

"Are you interested in lease or purchase?"

"Frankly, neither." The marshal whipped out the letter from the would-be killer. "We're hoping you can tell us what sort of machine this was made on."

Pulling the cover page close to his face, Marston scrutinized the typeface, grunting now and again when he came across something of interest. "I presume this is the missive which Mr. Pinder wrote about in the *Times*?"

"It surely is," said Cradoc. "Can you tell us what kind of machine made it?"

"We can certainly try, Marshal."

Marston led them through the main showroom filled with all sorts of household bric-a-brac to a room set aside for commercial office supplies—ledger books, stationery, writing implements, cash registers, and typewriters of various shapes and sizes.

"At present," said Marston, "there are about twenty different typing machines available to the general public. I would imagine this font fits one of those."

Reaching beneath the counter, Marston retrieved a loose-leaf book, each page dedicated to a description and sample typeface of every typing machine currently in stock. In alphabetical order, of course, because the proprietor insisted upon order in all aspects of life and business.

"A very simple font," Marston mumbled to himself. "Clean lines ... sans serif."

Cradoc glanced at Wyatt who frowned and shrugged his shoulders. "*Sans* what?" the marshal asked.

"Serifs are the small lines or feet attached to the terminal ends of each letter." He showed his visitors an example in the book. "Your letter does not possess such feet. Thus, it is sans—or without—serif."

"How much are these contraptions?" asked Wyatt, tinkering with the keys on a typing machine perched on the counter.

Marston segued right into huckster mode. "You have a good eye, Mr. Earp. That's our new Remington. All the latest bells and whistles, including a shift key to move back and forth between lower and upper case. Used by governments, firms, and individuals throughout the nation. A superior typing machine if there ever was one. Normally goes for a hundred dollars, but I'm willing to knock ten off the price for you."

"That the same Remington that makes guns?"

"Indeed it is, sir. Although the typing machines are now manufactured by a different company, you'll find that the precise workmanship and engineering that goes into Remington weaponry is featured on this fine specimen."

"You think Josie might like one of these?" Wyatt asked the marshal.

But Cradoc didn't respond. He was methodically plowing through Marston's catalog, trying to match the font on the mysterious letter with those in the book. Caligraph ... Columbia ... Hammond ... Remington ... Yost. He eyed Marston with manifest disappointment. "It's not here. How can that be?"

"If a given font does not exist in the book," Marston said, "then I'm afraid it's not from one of the brands we currently vend."

The marshal looked at Wyatt and then back at Marston. "Then how did the killer make this letter? Where did he get the typing machine?"

"*That* I cannot tell you," Marston answered.

"Does anyone else in San Diego sell these contraptions?"

"Of course," said the proprietor. "But no one boasts a larger selection at more reasonable prices. And nobody sells anything that's not already in this book. Nobody trumps Marston."

The marshal exuded a deep sigh. "This fella didn't make his own typing machine. There has to be another explanation."

"Perhaps I can offer one." Marston slipped out from behind the counter and started off across the store again. Cradoc and Wyatt tailed him up a flight of stairs and down a second-floor hallway to an office occupied by a company clerk and a row of wooden filing cabinets.

"Mr. Thomas," asked Marston, "would you be kind enough to point me in the direction of our business records from the late Seventies."

Thomas yanked open the drawer. "Any document in particular, Mr. Marston?"

"Anything typewritten will do."

Rifling through the file, the clerk passed Marston a random receipt. "The letter please," he commanded Cradoc.

Marston laid the two pages side-by-side on the clerk's desk, eyes flashing back and forth between the fonts. Suddenly, a smile rose across his face. "Gentlemen, I think we've got a winner! Both of these documents were created on a Sholes & Glidden. The typing machine upon which Mark Twain composed *Tom Sawyer*. Well, not composed per se. His handwritten manuscript was apparently typed on a Sholes for submission to Mr. Twain's publisher. But I digress. See for yourself."

Cradoc and Wyatt studied the adjoining documents. Indeed, the typefaces looked identical. All capital letters. No little feet.

"Where's the machine that made this receipt?" asked the marshal.

"Alas, it is no longer with us," Marston informed. "Sholes was the very first typing apparatus we sold and used in our own office. A lovely piece of workmanship housed in a hand-painted, lacquered box. But it was large and un-trustworthy compared to the machines that appeared later.

And rather immoderate when it came to price—when you added the cost of shipping from the factory in New York, you were looking at no less than one hundred and sixty dollars. Yet in my humble opinion, its most glaring drawback was the foot treadle."

Marston reached across and slapped a long steel handle on the clerk's typing machine. The carriage shot sideways and halted with a loud bang. "The Sholes didn't have a hand return. You had to use a foot pedal to move the carriage back to the left and start typing another line. An act that requires no small amount of dexterity and a great deal of time to master. We were glad to see it go, weren't we, Mr. Thomas?" The clerk nodded.

"How many did you sell?" Cradoc wanted to know.

Marston scratched his temple, trying to remember. "Around a dozen, I seem to recall. Mr. Kendall purchased a couple for his railroad offices. The mayor bought one for city hall. And I believe the county got one on which to render official court documents."

"And the newspapers," Thomas reminded him.

"Ah yes! Three different papers were amongst the first to purchase a typing machine in San Diego—for obvious reasons."

"Anyone else?" asked Cradoc.

"Not that I can recall. But …" Marston waved a hand at his beloved files. "Somewhere in this room is a record of all purchases. I can send you a list, if that will help. Typed, of course, on a much more modern machine."

Cradoc nodded. "If it's not too much trouble."

"What happened to your own Sholes?" Wyatt asked.

Marston deferred to his clerk who looked up at Wyatt. "I believe," said Mr. Thomas, "it was donated to charity.

One of the local churches. But off the top of my head I can't remember which one."

"That's right." Marston nodded. "I remember now. They wanted it for the rectory or some such thing. The machine was more or less worthless by then. Sitting around collecting dust. Amazing isn't it? How quickly things change these days? Hard to keep up, really. The march of machines! Someday mankind itself will be obsolete. All of us!"

12

ROZ REACHED AROUND expecting to find Nick asleep beside her, but all she found were crumpled sheets. And they weren't even warm. But he wasn't far away. She could hear his voice through the open bedroom door, somewhere downstairs.

Retrieving a silk dressing gown from a hook behind the door, Roz moved out onto the second-floor landing. Nick stood at the bottom of the stairs, speaking into the telephone, having an animated conversation.

"Even by Western standards, this was a highly unusual killing," Nick was saying. "The means alone is enough to make it noteworthy beyond San Diego. It's not every day that you come across murder via incoming tide. There's also the revenge motive, prompted by the victim's own sinister past. And first and foremost, a letter from Mr. Archer's assassin. It truly is unprecedented, not just in these parts, but all of California and the West...."

Rolling her eyes, Roz perched herself on the top step, hoping that her husband would soon finish the conversation. They did have somewhere to be—a matinee at the Leach Opera House. And not just *any* performance. The incomparable Lillie Langtry making a rare appearance in San Diego, starring for two days only in a drama called *A Wife's Peril.* An ironic topic, given the fact that Langtry's own marriage had recently come unraveled. After years of estrangement—and untold indiscretions—Jersey Lil had recently finalized her divorce from Irish landowner Edward Langtry. Nothing like a scandal to fuel attention. Demand for tickets to her San Diego appearances had been so intense that the opera house management had shifted the entire orchestra to one side of the stage in order to accommodate more seats. Nick had purchased the tickets as a means to make up for missing so many evenings and weekends over the past few months.

"That's a very generous offer," Nick continued. "No, I haven't sold the story to anyone else in Los Angeles. It'll be your exclusive."

So that's what he's up to, Roz thought to herself. He's selling the bloody Archer story to another publication. She wasn't going to carp about anything that would convey more money into the household. But employing their telephone as a business tool was another thing altogether. It had seemed like such a brilliant idea at first—getting themselves a telephone at home. One of the first domestic lines in San Diego. Something to brag to their friends and neighbors about. But now Roz wondered if they had been too hasty. The bloody thing had become, in very short order, another way for Nick to blur the line between home and work.

"Tomorrow?" Nick blurted out. "You want to run my story tomorrow? That means I'd have to write and somehow dispatch the story today ... I fully understand that news has a limited shelf life. But today, sir? That's a tall order ... I'd have to go into town, the telegraph office. Yes, Mr. Otis—an extra twenty dollars would certainly sweeten the pot."

What? Roz thought to herself. *Did Nick just say what I thought he said? Has he lost his bloody mind?*

She sprang to her feet, ready to confront her husband. But then she heard the door slam. She could hear his boots along the front porch. Roz raced back into the bedroom and parted the curtains in time to see Nick galloping down the path on his chestnut steed. As the tears began to roll down her cheeks, she slumped onto the bed. She had never thought of herself as much of a weeper, but it seemed to come easy these days. Too much pent-up emotion. Almost constant frustration. A growing notion that she was wasting—or had already squandered—the best years of her life.

You had to shake your head in wonderment and maybe even laugh. Things were so different in the early days of their marriage. Nick rushing home from the office to be with her. Candlelit dinners and holding hands in the plaza. Nick flinging open the bedroom windows, the sea breeze flowing through their darkened bedroom, as they made love until dawn. Nick's intensity frightened her a bit. But gradually, she had surrendered unconditionally to his passion. Roz became warm and secure within their union. It began to define her life. She wanted—she needed—no one else but Nick.

Now that seemed like such a long time ago. Like another life in a different place. What had gone wrong? Why had Nick retreated so far into himself? Were their courtship and newlywed days nothing more than an aberration? Was he showing his true colors now rather than before?

As a Roman Catholic of good standing, Roz did not believe in divorce. "In sickness and health" still meant something to her. And there was the upside to consider. There weren't a lot of women who could say their husband had never raised a hand against them. Nick didn't drink much, and he certainly did not gamble. As far as Roz could tell, there were no other women in his life. If work remained his only vice, perhaps she had no right to complain. On the other hand, it still rankled. How a relationship could be so remarkable, so fresh, so scintillating and then so utterly broken, with no notion of how to patch things and a partner who didn't seem to want to try. For the first time, Roz flirted with the notion that she could perhaps live *without* Nick.

Damned if she was going to let him ruin another day. If Nick had other things on his mind, so be it. She would attend the theater on her own. With that, she picked herself off the bed and moved across the hall into the bathroom.

It took Roz a good hour to compose herself. She wiped the tears away and took a bath. Sitting at her vanity, she brushed the knots from her long red hair, parted it straight down the middle and pulled it into a tight bun at the crown of her head with a few short, curly bangs covering her forehead. Next, she considered her freshly scrubbed face, still lusciously moist and pale despite her years beneath the Western sun. She could not go out without at least a touch of make-up—a hint of arrowroot powder on her cheeks and bit of color on the ample waves that comprised her lips. Pulling back and considering the full effect, Roz liked what she saw in the mirror.

Everything except her rather ample breasts. They were assets at present—if one could actually call them assets—

because contemporary fashion dictated that the ideal woman have plenteous bosoms above an hourglass waist. She laughed out loud at a thought from the past. Cradoc had often told her to throw away her corsets because her body was naturally perfect. She smiled at the memory of something that had happened on a long-ago afternoon, Cradoc deftly "undoing" her corset with a buck knife before making love on his balcony in broad daylight—a most radical act for an Irish Catholic lass.

Catching herself in a moment of weakness, Roz blocked the thought from her mind. Why was she even thinking about Cradoc Bradshaw, dredging up the past?

She moved from the vanity to the bedroom wardrobe. The racks inside slouched beneath the weight of clothes she had made for herself since coming out West. The outfits never failed to remind her of the career she had relinquished in order to marry Nick. Back in the day, she had been a damn good seamstress and dressmaker, earned her living that way after arriving in San Diego. Roz had made a name—and a tidy sum—designing and sewing frocks for the wealthy matrons of Banker's Hill and the big haciendas. Many of her customers had pleaded with her to keep working after marriage. But Roz had demurred with what, at the time, seemed like a perfectly legitimate excuse. She needed the time to devote herself to becoming a proper wife and mother, although in the intervening years she had become neither. It was a painful realization that if she had stuck with it, her fashions would now be on sale in all of the best stores in San Diego and possibly other cities.

Having completed her makeup, Roz slipped into a pair of black stockings and gartered them above the knees.

Next, she donned knee-length cotton drawers and a silk chemise. Her corset of choice was an equipoise, braced by stiff cotton rather than whalebone and therefore much less likely to restrict her breathing or movement. She could actually bend over and slip into her own riding boots rather than begging Lupe's assistance. Over this, she secured a corset cover and a bustle around her waist. Last but not least came one of her favorite creations—a scarlet riding habit and black waist-length, jet-bead jacket. Reaching into the wardrobe, she snatched a black lady's top hat with trailing veil and looked at herself in the mirror again. *Not bad if I may say so myself.*

She had already asked Lupe to accompany her to the play. The girl might not understand much of what Miss Langtry would say—in a British rather than American accent. But at least she would get the gist, and Roz could fill in the gaps with a whisper now and again into Lupe's ear. After a quick lunch, they started down the hill on the buckboard.

Clattering past the migrant camps and churches around the eastern edge of town, Roz found herself pondering Cradoc again. One couldn't help but think what life would have been like with him rather than Nick ... if Cradoc hadn't gone away when he did ... or if he had returned sooner.

Her liaison with Cradoc had been an entirely different sort of relationship than the one she later forged with Nick. Both of them young and not a care in the world. Concepts like marriage and family the last things on their mind. She had only recently escaped the yoke of her working-class Irish Catholic upbringing and was basking in the glow of liberation. She and Cradoc had made love, for sure.

But they were really more like friends who relished one another's company rather than a modern-day Romeo and Juliet. Roz had never told Cradoc she loved him, and he had never uttered those words to her. Neither had there been any discussion of a mutual future. In retrospect, that had probably been a grave mistake. But a moot point given what happened later.

Roz never intended to go straight from his bed into that of another. Nick and Cradoc were about as close as two men could be. And if not for Cradoc, she would never have met Nick. She especially enjoyed his humor, and eventually she counted Nick amongst her inner circle. And he was always the perfect gentleman. Not even a hint of romantic interest in Roz until long after Cradoc led a posse south of the border and failed to return.

Nick had pledged to look after Roz in his absence—nothing more than any good friend would offer. And he remained true to his word, calling on Roz every few days to see if she needed anything, every so often inviting her for tea or lunch with other friends and acquaintances. Everything strictly on the up and up.

Four weeks later, survivors of the posse trickled back from Mexico with tales of a bloody skirmish and great loss of life. Among those missing was Cradoc Bradshaw. In her grief, Roz turned to Nick. And before she knew it, she had fallen in love with the man, both his unbridled passion for her and the zeal with which he went about his quest for journalistic success. Roz eventually convinced herself that she could spend the rest of her life with Nick, and in no time at all, he asked for her hand, and they were married.

There was no way for them to know that Cradoc had survived—largely, it seems, on the strength of his longing

for Roz. And equally, there was no way to foresee how
betrayed he would feel upon his miraculous return to San
Diego.

13

ON A MUGGY MORNING in late May, Cradoc Bradshaw sat at his desk trying to decide whether or not to release from custody (without charges) a local transient who had stolen a cow. The man was not of sound mind or body, and the marshal would normally have let him off with just a warning. If not for one complication: the animal in question belonged to Mayor Hunsaker. Still, it was a no brainer. The marshal would get a load of shit when the mayor discovered the cow thief had been liberated. But that was a small price to pay for doing the right thing.

Cradoc heard footsteps and looked up to see a nattily dressed young man descend into the jail, straw hat pressed against his chest.

"You need some help?" asked Cradoc, thinking the guy looked like the type who might have been ripped off in a card game, not so much by deception as his own folly, and had come to report the transgression.

"I'm Wendell Smith," the fellow announced with no lack of self-importance. And when the marshal replied with nothing more than a blank stare, he added, "Wendell Smith from the *Times*. You requested a sample from one of our typing machines. The old Sholes & Glidden, I do believe."

Cradoc sat up straight in his chair. "Took you goddamn long enough. I asked for that a week ago. I was on the verge of getting a warrant."

"I'm awfully sorry," Wendell replied. "But Mr. Bennett has been weighing the legality of your request and its implication upon our First Amendment rights."

"You've gotta be kidding," the marshal shot back. But he could tell by Smith's sober bearing that it was no joke. For whatever reason—maybe for the pure pleasure of jerking the marshal's chain—Bennett was dragging his feet. "You tell Clive that we consulted with the county attorney and a local judge, and that both of them assured us that our request for the typing samples is well within the law."

"But not necessarily the Constitution," Wendell countered. "Freedom of the press and all that. Mr. Bennett considers the request a distinct intrusion."

Cradoc could have launched into a lecture on how obtaining a typing sample and suppressing speech were not one and the same thing. But on this particular morning, he felt no need to explain himself to Wendell Smith or anyone else. "Where the hell is it?" he barked.

"Where's what?" asked a confused Smith.

"The goddamn sample. Isn't that why you're here?"

"Ah, yes ..." Wendell fumbled around inside his jacket and produced an envelope, which he passed across the desk to the marshal.

Cradoc removed a single sheet of paper from inside. Typed about halfway down was a single sentence that began with the words *"Forgive me for making contact with you in such an impersonal manner ..."*

He looked up at the young reporter. "I asked for the alphabet, not a reproduction of the killer's letter."

"I thought an actual line from the felon's prose might be a tad more appropriate," Wendell replied. "I presume, Marshal, given the fact that you are still collecting samples, that you have not yet located the machine upon which the killer composed the original letter?"

A thinly veiled yet clever attempt to glean a quote for publication. But Cradoc didn't take the bait. This assbite reporter and everyone else in town could speculate all they wished. But he was not about to explain himself or his actions in an ongoing investigation. Still, the young reporter persisted.

"Is there precedence for this—solving a crime via type identification?"

You had to give the kid credit for trying. Maybe that's the only way to get ahead at an outfit like the *Times*. Curry favor with someone who despised your newsroom rival and who just might, out of spite, slip you the sort of information that allowed you to write a story that vaulted you ahead of that rival. Certainly, an enticing proposition—using this Wendell Smith fellow to screw Nick. But the marshal could see no other benefit. By way of deflection, he turned the tables on Smith. "I don't recall ever seeing your byline in the *Times*."

The remark was meant to ruffle Wendell's well-groomed feathers. And indeed it did. "I assure you, Marshal, it's there," the young reporter said defensively. "Nearly every day and almost always on the front page."

"Beneath Pinder's, of course."

"Not always. I'm a journalist in my own right."

And ambitious, too. Either that, or terribly ill-informed

on the demeanor of the local marshal. "How long have you been in town?" Cradoc asked.

"Nearly five months."

"And during those five months, has no one bothered to inform you that I do not fraternize with members of the press, do not grant special access, do not pay for tips, do not divulge confidential information in return for *anything*?"

"Yes, they have, Marshal. I'm well aware of your repute. And the fact that you leaked Archer's autopsy report to our biggest rival."

The marshal glared. "That wasn't me."

"Maybe and maybe not," Wendell retorted. "But if you should ever get the urge, I wanted you to know, sir, that I can lend a sympathetic ear. And who knows? You might need something from *me* at some point in future."

Cradoc didn't like this Smith fellow one bit. Way too clever for his own good. Way too self-important. The marshal's grim stare told the young reporter to get a move on.

"Keep me in mind," said Wendell, bowing ever so slightly as he backed away from the desk.

†

The young reporter having departed, Cradoc wrenched open his desk drawer and withdrew a cardboard folder containing both the original letter and samples he'd collected from the owners of the various Sholes & Glidden typing machines that still existed in San Diego.

Wendell's question had been remarkably prescient. As far as Cradoc knew, no one had ever solved a crime by matching words and typing machine. But that didn't mean it couldn't happen. George Marston had already planted the seed in his mind by casually mentioning that no two typing machines produced exactly the same imprint on paper. Immediately grasping the significance, Cradoc asked why that was so. Marston replied with a long and overly complicated discourse on the intricacies of the modern typing machine. The twenty-six characters at the end of the "typebars"—the metal letterheads that strike the carbon sheet against the paper page—were marginally different on each machine. Although produced of the same molds, usage of the machines over a period of time endowed the letterheads with tiny cracks, uneven wear, and slightly varied pitches. Differences too small for the naked eye to detect, but quite obvious when comparing documents from two machines beneath a magnifying glass.

Thus, it was theoretically possible to link the Archer correspondence to a single typewriter. Assuming the marshal could locate that particular machine. With that in mind, Marston had provided a list of the two dozen Sholes his emporium had sold in the late 1870s, their serial numbers rendered on a small brass plaque on the underside of the frame. Upon receiving the list, Cradoc had petitioned the various owners to provide an alphabetical sample of the typeface. If the original owners were no longer in possession of said machine, they were required to tender details on how they had disposed of their Sholes.

The sample from Wendell Smith was the fourteenth the marshal had received thus far. Removing the original letter from the binder, Cradoc placed it on the desktop beside the *Times* sample. Reaching for a magnifying glass, he began to compare.

"Dammit to hell," Cradoc mumbled to himself.

"Another miss?" asked a familiar voice.

Cradoc gazed up into the face of Joe Coyne, chomping on a wad of chew that made his cheek bulge. The marshal had been so involved in examining the typefaces that he hadn't noticed the boss emerge from his office.

The sheriff had deep reservations about Cradoc's typewriter theory. Even if such comparisons could be used to finger a suspect, he doubted that such unorthodox evidence would hold up in a court of law. Then again, Cradoc had solved cases in the past through fairly irregular means. As long as it didn't interfere with what Coyne considered the main thrust of the murder investigation, the sheriff didn't mind his number-one detective going off on this tangent.

"'Fraid so." Cradoc leaned back in his chair with a heavy sigh. "And this is one of the samples I was counting on to shed some light."

"Who's it from?"

"The *Times*."

Coyne rolled his eyes to high heaven. "You think somebody over there killed Archer? That takes the cake!"

"If you're going to ridicule my theories, maybe I shouldn't even discuss them."

"You're telling me that Nick Pinder killed someone for no other reason than to get himself a good story?"

"No ... I'm suggesting that maybe Nick took advantage of the fact that somebody else killed Archer by inventing an imaginary letter written by an imaginary killer—and *that* is how he got himself such a goddamn good story."

"Even that's a stretch."

"Not as much as you think," Cradoc responded. "I could easily type a letter, mail it to myself, and claim that somebody else sent it. Anybody can."

"Fair enough," said Coyne. "But you just said yourself that the original letter wasn't done on the machine at the *Times*."

"Not the one this sample came from. But Marston sold twenty-three of these machines in total. Nick could have composed the letter on any of them. Or got somebody else to write and post it. He could have paid someone."

"And you think Pinder is capable of such deceit?"

"Not just capable, but damn good at it. When we were kids, Nick made up stories all the time. My dad used to take us out on patrol around the county, and we'd sit around the campfire at night and spin yarns. Nick was always the best. Better than my dad or any of the troopers. He'd make up the wildest tales about goblins and ghosts. Scared the shit out of me."

Coyne noticed that a certain fondness had crept into the marshal's voice. He could see it in the man's eyes, too. Nostalgia for things long gone, a sentimental side that Cradoc showed none too often. A small chink in the man's considerable mental armor.

"And when we were teenagers," Cradoc continued. "Nick conjured the most incredible stories to impress girls. He even had his own theory about how to lie successfully, what he called the Ninety Percent Rule. Always tell ninety percent of the truth. And spin that ninety percent in such a way that nobody ever suspects the bogus ten percent that lies beneath. Worked every time! With his mother, with our teachers, with the various girls he lured into kissing in the reeds beside the river. It was unreal—his talent for obfuscation."

"Telling stories as a kid," Coyne felt obliged to point out, "is one helluva lot different than writing lies as a grown man. Especially when it comes to something as serious as murder."

"Point taken. But what's ninety percent of the truth in this case? Nick receives a letter in the post—a confession from someone claiming to have killed Zebulon Archer. He really did get a letter. The letter really did make those claims. That's your ninety percent. The critical ten percent is that Nick knows who wrote the letter. Not the genuine killer, but Nick himself or someone in his hire."

"Then how do you account for the particulars of the crime that Nick nor anyone else in the local press had access to?"

Cradoc had an answer for that, too. "You and I and everyone else know that Nick can find out anything he wants in this town if he spreads enough cash around. He's got informants *everywhere* including more than a couple in this jailhouse. And he's cultivating new sources all the time. It wouldn't have been hard for him to acquire details of Archer's autopsy."

"All fine and dandy," said Coyne, who had just about heard enough of this nonsense. "And certainly not beyond the realm of possibility. But it's beside the point. Establishing the letter as a fraud does not reveal who killed Archer."

"Neither does prosecuting animal thieves."

The sheriff shrugged off the dig. "Nothing I could do about that. The mayor shouts, we jump. Even for something as trivial as an old milk cow. But other distractions"— Coyne cocked his head toward the typing samples on the marshal's desk—"I can do something about. Especially if they start to interfere with or distract from our primary objective."

"What's that supposed to mean?" Cradoc asked gruffly.

"I fully appreciate that you and Nick have a past that neither of you is willing or able to come to terms with. I can't fault you for that. But I can fault you for letting that past blind you to the bigger picture. Nick may or may not have written that goddamn letter himself. But last time I checked, it wasn't illegal for a journalist to deceive the public. Immoral, perhaps. But *not* illegal. I did not employ you—at considerable expense, I might add—to expose reprobate journalists. I hired you to catch felons, quell violence, and restore order to the streets."

Cradoc stabbed a finger at the documents on his desk. "My gut tells me this will give us the answer."

"And mine tells me it *won't*," said Coyne. "And seeing as I'm the boss, my innards take precedent. Now I can order you to cease and desist with this typing machine crap, or you can take it upon yourself to let it fade away. Don't matter to me as long as you get back on track and find Archer's killer, rather than trying to nail Nick for something that is most definitely not a crime."

"And what would you have me do instead?"

"What you were doing before. What you do best. Snooping and sniffing around. Talking to people. Making 'em nervous. Spreading seeds of doom amongst those who might help us solve this crime."

"I've already questioned anyone in San Diego with even the slightest reason to kill, mutilate, or look sideways at Zeb Archer. All of them have rock-solid alibis."

"Ah, but you haven't looked everywhere," Coyne reminded.

The marshal knew exactly what he meant. "You're suggesting I head up north?"

"It's not me who's suggesting. Try the mayor and the city council—the people who pay our wages."

"None of whom gave a shit about Archer's killer until that infernal letter arrived. Can't have some Chinese fella murdering white folks."

"Don't mock me," said Coyne.

"Then be reasonable! You know just as well as me that a Chinaman didn't kill Archer and that sending me to Frisco won't accomplish a damn thing."

"I won't disagree. But it's getting to the point where it no longer matters what you and I think or what the actual truth might be. Just like that goldarned cow this morning, we are often at the whim of Hunsaker, Horton, and the other people who run the show. That, my friend, is the bottom line. And like I've told you on more than one occasion, we either learn to live with it—or get out of town."

14

CLIVE BENNETT CHUGGED the rest of his beer and slammed his mug on the picnic table. "I don't want to say I told you so, but—"

"Yes, Clive. You told me so." Clive had taken at least partial credit for everything else that he had achieved as a journalist, might as well take some credit for this, too. And you couldn't dispute the fact that Nick would have never considered selling the Archer story beyond San Diego if not for the editor's urging.

"And how many rags have you snagged thus far?"

"A couple dozen. Mostly in California. But a fair number back east too—New York, Chicago, Boston, Philly."

It was that slack time between lunch and dinner when half the population was taking a siesta and the other half well on their way to inebriation. You had to wonder how anyone got any work done. On the other hand, the mid-afternoon intermission offered a welcome respite from the relentless hammering, sawing, and other construction noise that reverberated across San Diego for much of the day. The "sound of progress" as developers called it.

On this particular afternoon, Nick and Clive had grabbed a table at Mayrhofer's Beer Garden and were already onto their second pint of pilsner. Overcast skies and muggy air heralded a monsoon blowing up from Mexico with a likelihood of heavy rains starting that very evening. Having already put tomorrow's paper to bed and nothing else of any news value happening around town, they had decided to grab a brew or two before the showers arrived. But only after ditching Wendell Smith, who would have put even more of a damper on things than the impending squall. The boy didn't drink, didn't seem to know snatch from a hole in the ground, and couldn't tell a joke to save his life. If ever you needed proof that elite Eastern prep schools didn't actually "prep" you for anything approaching real life, the unfledged Mr. Smith was it.

Clive was just getting started on what would no doubt be a lengthy evening of carousing around town, but Nick was going home to dinner with Roz for the third straight night, part of his ongoing mea culpa.

"Like flies to shit," had been Clive's prediction. The big eastern papers were all over the Archer story. Not because they found it especially gruesome or the victim particularly newsworthy, but simply because it differed from all of the other blood-soaked tales coming out of the Wild West. Knowing that novelty always sells, Clive had advised Nick to pump up the story's eccentricities. Not that they needed exaggerating. The Archer affair oozed oddity from the get-go. Definitely not your everyday slaying or slayer.

Nick had begun by soliciting the story by telephone to newspaper editors around California, a feat made possible by the recent completion of long-distance lines north along the coast. But seeing as transcontinental telephone service did not yet exist, he had reverted to the telegraph for contacting more distant newspapers. He didn't even have to rewrite. He could essentially sell the same words again and again—like money for nothing. The easiest greenbacks Nick had ever made.

And now Clive counseled him again. "Once you've got a foot in the door with all these other rags, you've got to bloody well leverage that for all it's worth. Keep milking those contacts. *Determination*—that's what it's all about. That's not to say you don't need a modicum of skill in this business. But time and time again, I've seen tenacity trump talent. You've gotta be that bloody little dog that grabs hold and never lets go."

"Yeah, but what happens when the bone is clean?" Nick retorted. "I've pretty much written everything there is to write about Archer, unless there's another break in the case. And that looks highly unlikely at this point in time." The local rumor mill predicted the assassin would probably never be identified, let alone apprehended.

"Forget Archer," Clive advised. "There are plenty of other stories. Now that you've got a foot in the door with these big shot papers, I wager you can sell them all sorts of things. Anything unique that transpires around here. And not just hard news, but features, too. Interviews with well-known people who happen to be passing through—politicians, thespians, knights of commerce. You establish yourself as a go-to man for anything that happens in San Diego or even Southern California."

"They'll always send their own reporter for big stories," Nick suggested.

"Not necessarily. Not if you can save them money on train tickets and hotel bills by giving them what they need by telegraph or telephone. Same as you did with Archer. And that's especially true of the papers back East. They simply don't have the resources or time to dispatch someone to the other side of the continent at the drop of a hat. You, however, can become their eyes and ears in these parts."

Assuming one actually had news that people in other places wanted to read about. That was the challenge for Nick. It wasn't every day that something as compelling as the Archer case crossed your desk, which is why the story had sold so easily outside San Diego and why it would be so difficult to replicate.

But no question, Nick wanted more. Not so much the money gained from spreading his story around—although the extra cash was nice—but the satisfaction that came from having so many more people read and praise your words. He wasn't famous yet, not beyond San Diego. But Clive assured his protégée that he was indeed trodding the right path.

That knowledge did nothing to quell Nick's impatience. "Do you think there's enough for a book?" he asked. Because that's what he really desired—his name emblazoned on the front of a hard-backed tome. Published in New York or Boston, of course, and distributed nationwide for all and sundry to read. Nick had already done the research. Several publishers—like the Old Sleuth Library and the celebrated Frank Tousey—specialized in crime. The James Gang and other outlaws starred in their dime novels. And Nick reckoned that Zebulon Archer's demise made an equally compelling story. He could already picture the cover in his mind—the title and his byline above one of Elliot Patterson's gruesome black-and-white photos of the corpse. If that didn't sell, *nothing* would.

But the boss quickly shot him down. "One murder does not a book make," Clive explained. "Not unless the victim is someone of Lincoln's stature. Not to mention the fact that it's a tad bit difficult to pen a true-crime saga when one has no idea who the killer might be. Such books are all about the villains, not the victims. And we don't have one. At least not until our mysterious letter writer is captured or killed. Or murders someone else."

The remark took Nick by surprise. Most people assumed that Archer's was a one-off murder, an act of revenge not likely to be repeated. Clive's opinion ran contrary to that. "You honestly believe he might kill again?" Nick asked.

"I wouldn't bet money on it," said Clive, downing the dregs of his latest beer with one hand and summoning a waiter with the other. "On the other hand, against all odds and whatever clichés might be tossed about, lightning does occasionally strike twice on the same spot. We just might get lucky."

The waiter arrived, asked if they wanted another round. But Nick didn't answer. He was lost in thought, chewing over what had just been said, trying to figure out a way to keep his career soaring—and wondering how he could *make* more luck, rather than wait for it to happen.

†

As the storm rolled into San Diego that evening, Cradoc Bradshaw fled into the Oyster Bar with hundreds of others trying to evade the dreadful weather. With every inch of his fiber fixed on the Archer case—and how it was making his life hell—the marshal might as well have been alone. They weren't even close to identifying (let alone apprehending) a suspect. And they probably never would be, given the amount of time (more than six weeks) that had elapsed since the crime and the fact that clues like the broken whiskey jug had not lived up to their initial promise. The killer remained a phantom, someone who came and went without leaving more than a negligible trace. Other than the letter, of course, which the marshal still had his doubts about. Even if it proved genuine rather than a clever fake, nothing more could be deduced from the paper, type, or wording that revealed the killer's whereabouts or identity.

Even Cradoc realized the investigation had reached the point of diminishing returns. Way too much time and energy for zero payback thus far. Time to cut this one free, slap it on the ass, and let it trot off into the sunset. Dig your heels into more important things—crimes you can actually crack.

If Archer had been a humble sailor, cowpoke, or brown-skinned peon, the case would have been shelved long ago as unsolvable. Possibly as early as the day after the murder. But the victim figured among the dozen richest men in the county, and, as if that weren't enough to keep the fire burning, the dead man's widow—the eternally dowdy Mrs. Archer—had hired a private detective to look into the matter. The cocksucker had been snooping around town the last few days, talking to the same people and asking the same questions that Cradoc had in the weeks prior. An interloper earning his repute (and continued employment) not through the discovery of new evidence, upshots, or anything else that might have proved useful in solving the crime, but rather via snide remarks in the press about how local law enforcement didn't seem up to the task. The *Times*, much to its credit, had ignored the detective's self-serving gibes. On the other hand, the *Union*—owned by one of Archer's cronies—had taken up the cudgel against local law enforcement and gleefully reported the private detective's unbecoming remarks.

Cradoc could feel everything funneling down to him—the pressure and responsibility for apprehending the culprit and ultimately the blame if no one got arrested, convicted, or hanged. Having been confronted by similar situations in past, the marshal knew he was slowly but surely being hung out to dry, a scapegoat for Hunsaker and all the other duly elected.

With his own back against the wall, Coyne had suggested in all seriousness that they find some patsy to assume the blame. Not an innocent man, mind you, but some mudsill who deserved dire punishment, even if not for this particular transgression. Yet even in the dismal, disheartened state into which he had sunk in recent weeks, Cradoc could not let someone hang for something they didn't do. And that fate definitely awaited whoever killed Zebulon Archer—a tight noose and well-oiled trapdoor.

Perhaps he should have been more shocked that Coyne would suggest framing someone for the crime. But the marshal's cynicism had hit rock bottom. If this is how the local establishment chose to enforce the law, there wasn't much Cradoc or anybody else could do about it. He'd learned through bitter experience that you either hold your tongue and get on with the job or move on. As a young officer in the U.S. Army, he'd been saddled with a similar choice and eventually decided upon the latter. Cradoc had shifted into the civilian world, thinking it less prone to political whims and personal vagaries. But he had discovered, first in Kansas and now in California, that the military did not have a monopoly on idiots and assholes. Seemed like wherever you went, whatever you did, sons of bitches fucked up the job, and by extension, your life.

Cradoc might have sat there the rest of the evening, feeling sorry for himself and nursing the same lukewarm beer, if a familiar face hadn't stepped through the pantry door—the blonde from Cliff House, balancing a tray full of wet, recently washed mugs. Recognizing him in return, she broke into a wide smile.

As she transferred the mugs from tray to shelf, the marshal studied her face in the mirror behind the bar, trying to recall her name. And she seemed to read his mind. "Emma Lee Dawes," she told him without looking around. "In case you was wondering."

"Cradoc Bradshaw," he responded, tipping his unshaven chin.

There came an uneasy pause, neither one of them knowing what to say next.

"I thought you were working at the Tivoli," the marshal finally remarked.

"Was till yesterday," she responded. "But one of the gals here quit unexpected, and Mrs. Earp asked me up." Having finished the stacking, Emma Lee turned to face the marshal.

She looked considerably more polished than the first time they had met. Her blonde hair pulled back into a tight bun, her skin scrubbed, and wearing a simple calico work dress that complemented her womanly assets, the girl now presented a quite attractive facade. Cradoc found himself wondering if Emma Lee's transformation was her own doing or the work of Josie Earp, who had a knack for influencing and inspiring those around her.

"Thanks for hooking me up with Mrs. Earp," she said earnestly. "Otherwise I wouldn't be working or even standing here right now."

"I'm glad it panned out," he told her, smiling without knowing he was doing so. "You plan on staying in San Diego?"

"Long as there's work and a roof over my head, don't see no reason for moving along. Besides the fact that I got nowhere else to go."

"You don't pine for Missouri?"

The girl's eyes lit up. "You remembered?"

"Well, yeah," Cradoc said sheepishly. She seemed to think it a big deal when it was nothing more than his knack for retaining useless facts, especially those amassed during a criminal investigation.

"Can't say I miss it," she continued. "Mizzura's the past. This is now. And you can't beat the weather here. No-sir-ee. Don't care if I never see another winter."

Cradoc took another sip of beer, trying to think of something to say, keep the conversation going. "Where you staying?" he asked.

But Emma Lee didn't answer. She was looking past Cradoc at somebody coming up behind the marshal. "Gotta run," she said urgently. Snatching his mug—still half full of beer—she disappeared through the pantry door just as a thick hand came down on Cradoc's shoulder.

"Did I see what I think I saw?"

Cradoc looked up to see Wyatt, grinning like a fool.

"And what do you *think* you saw?"

"You flirtin' with a young, female employee of mine."

"Don't be an idiot," Cradoc said with an exaggerated eye roll.

"You were!"

"I was not!"

"So you say. But I know what I saw—you acting like an overgrown schoolboy, all puckered up and ready to go."

Cradoc shook his head in dismay. "Here we go again. Dr. Lovelorn."

Wyatt slid onto the stool beside his friend, his slicker sopping wet from the rain that continued to come down in sheets. "As a long-time connoisseur of the female gender— prior to my current nuptials, of course—I can confidently declare that Emma Lee Dawes is a damn fine specimen of womanhood. If I was not already entangled with a most luscious siren, I would not hesitate to worm myself into her world, so to speak. And I don't think that you, my closest friend and associate, should hesitate in this regard. "

"We were just talking."

"There's nothing on this earth that *don't* start with talk."

"She was thanking me for introducing her to Josie, that's all."

"Then why's your pecker a mile long?"

Cradoc glanced down at his lap before he could catch himself.

"Gotcha!" Wyatt slapped the bar and barked out a loud laugh.

The marshal sighed. "Can we please talk about something else?"

"Whatever's on your mind, Mr. Bradshaw."

"I'm going to San Francisco," Cardoc blurted.

Wyatt's eyebrows arched. "For what?"

"Talk to Chinese folks."

"You can't be serious?"

Cradoc sighed again. "Rather than have our elected

officials and the general public assume that local law enforcement has spent the last six weeks twiddling our collective thumbs, Coyne has decided to dispatch his one and only marshal to San Francisco to locate and interrogate the remnants or descendants of the Chinese that Archer and his buddies ran out of town more than twenty years ago."

"Another dead end," Wyatt quipped. "Put good money on it."

"The point of dispatching me," Cradoc explained, "is not solving the case, but covering Coyne's butt."

"Even if you don't find the killer?"

The marshal smirked. "In his feeble, greedy mind, the only thing standing between Joe Coyne and infinite job security is keeping up appearances. And the easiest means to accomplish that task is sending me to Frisco on a wild goose chase. Doesn't matter if I spend the entire time drinking and screwing my way up and down the Barbary Coast rather than finding the actual killer. Coyne assumes that everyone in San Diego—everyone who votes, that is— will think he made the effort, rubberstamp the city charter next year, and we'll have a proper police department with a proper police chief appointed by a proper police commission dominated by his political allies. Coyne will never have to run for election again. He'll be set for life. And as of this morning, he is convinced that none of this will transpire unless I venture north to San Francisco."

"And you're just gonna up and go?" Wyatt asked.

"I am not being given a choice."

"Then quit! I could use a man like you."

"You got plenty of bouncers already."

"I'm not talking muscle. I'm talking brains. A new

business venture I've been pondering for some time now—promoting big-time sporting events. Boxing, horse racing, and maybe even baseball. You'd be a full partner. Fifty-fifty split on the profits. Straight down the line."

"There's no money in baseball," Cradoc quipped.

But Wyatt didn't see things that way. "There is if you take bets and fix the games."

"I just don't see a lot of people laying money on a game that involves grown men trying to hit a little round object with a wooden stick."

"Then ignore my offer. Wallow in your self-pity. I don't give a damn."

Cradoc looked around at his friend, surprised by the sudden flush of emotion. "We're a tad bit touchy this evening."

"Because you're being a jackass. You're clearly unhappy with your job and have been for months. I give you an out—an opportunity that involves both profit and the great outdoors—and you turn your nose up like it's pig shit."

"I'm a lawman, Wyatt. Always have been, always will be."

"I made the switch!"

"Because you *had* to. Otherwise, you'd still be wearing a star rather than dickin' around with cards and whiskey."

Wyatt looked genuinely hurt. "That's what you think I do? That's what you think this is—running a joint like the Oyster? Dickin' around?"

"I didn't mean it that way."

"Sounded like it."

"I'm sorry," Cradoc told him. "In case you didn't notice, I'm a little touchy myself. And I don't need anyone else turning the screws." The marshal put a hand on Wyatt's shoulder. "I appreciate the offer. Really, I do. But I'm not ready to make that leap. Maybe at some point in the future, but not now."

The two friends stared at one another a long beat, chewing over everything that had just been said.

"You need to get yourself laid," Wyatt suggested, dead serious.

Cradoc rolled his eyes again. "Normally I would," he said sarcastically. "But I got things to do before I sail."

✝

Nick Pinder nudged his horse into an alley opposite the Oyster Bar, the rain falling steadily but not enough to impede his view of the saloon. Through the front windows, he could see Cradoc Bradshaw in deep conversation with Wyatt Earp.

Clive's advice about books was still whirling around in Nick's head. But he disagreed with the editor on one crucial point: they weren't just about killers; they were also about the heroes that tracked down and caught those villains. Wild Bill, Pat Garrett, Bat Masterson, and their own Mr. Earp were just as celebrated as the scoundrels they brought to justice. Bestselling books revolved around them, too. And Nick didn't see why his own would-be tome—even without a killer in custody—couldn't do the same. The perfect protagonist sat across the street from him at this very moment. The problem, of course, was that he and Cradoc had not exchanged a cordial word in years and likely wouldn't anytime soon. Not unless one of them took the initiative to mend the immense fence that now separated the two former friends.

Would Cradoc ever be able to let bygones be bygones? Nick had his doubts. But that didn't mean he shouldn't try.

Nick was about to slide off his horse and step into the bar when Cradoc pushed through the front door. The marshal considered the weather, buttoned up his duster, and pulled himself up onto a wet saddle. Nick presumed he was going home. But Cradoc jerked his horse around and headed in the opposite direction. Where the hell was he going in this weather, at this time of night?

Nick followed him down Fifth Street in the steady rain, hat pulled low and the collar of his slicker turned up to shield his face from both the weather and Cradoc's recognition.

It did not rain often in San Diego, but when it did, the water came down like a plague of toads, bringing with it flash floods, fallen trees, and drowned livestock. Northbound trains had stopped running that afternoon for fear that one of the trestles near Temecula would wash away. All steamship service along the California coast had been suspended because of unreasonably high seas. Both the San Diego and Tijuana rivers had become raging torrents.

The junction of Fifth and Market, normally the town's busiest crossroads, swirled with mud and horseshit. Even on horseback, it was tough going, the footing slippery and the mire higher than the animal's fetlocks. Stepping carefully, Nick and his mount continued to follow Cradoc into the Stingaree. In the blink of an eye, the smart saloons and hotels of the upper town gave way to dram shops, dive bars, and squalid flesh-peddling cribs.

Nick watched from a distance as the marshal rode up to the Pacific Coast Steamship Company ticket office at the bottom of Fifth. Still perched on his horse, Cradoc pounded on the front door, but no one came to answer. The marshal brought his horse around and hitched her amongst a dozen other nags arrayed beside a waterfront groggery so far down the social scale that not even the local soaplocks dared to drink there. They called it the First & Last Chance Saloon for good reason: the first place for sailors to whet their whistle upon reaching dry land and the last place to quench their thirst before setting sail again. Even on this tempestuous evening, the establishment brimmed with loud and obnoxious seamen who had chosen to ride out the storm ashore rather than in the dreary quarters on their ships in the bay.

Leaving his own mount around the other side of the saloon, Nick entered through a rear door. Hanging at the back of the room, he could see Cradoc and the barman talking. They chatted for around a quarter hour before the marshal tipped his hat and left.

Nick sprang toward the bar, flagged down the tender. "What were you and the marshal talking about?" he asked urgently.

The barman didn't offer anything more than a grin.

Nick rolled his eyes, slapped a dollar on the counter.

"He was asking about Frisco," the barman admitted. "Where to stay, where to eat, that sorta thing."

"He's going up north?"

"One would presume."

A dozen new questions shot through Nick's mind. *What's in San Francisco? Does this have anything to do with the Archer case? Should I be concerned? Should I follow? Am I going to miss something if I don't?*

Nick dashed out the front door and into the tempest, determined to continue his surreptitious pursuit. But

Cradoc and his horse had already vanished. Nick retrieved his own beast and trotted up Fifth Street, hoping to relocate the marshal and muster enough courage to offer an olive branch. But Cradoc had disappeared into the tempest, leaving Nick to wonder how long he might have to wait for another chance to renew their alliance.

15

LEAVING HIS HORSE BEHIND, the killer set off on foot along the railroad tracks that curled along the edge of San Diego Bay. The inclement weather made it impossible to see a hand stretched out in front of his face. But in his meticulous preparation, knowing that he would not be able to utilize a lantern or any other form of light no matter what the weather, he had counted and then recounted the number of footsteps along the tracks to reach his destination. Only with that number in his head did he feel safe venturing through the rain and dark on a night like this.

The tracks led him out of the built-up area and into a no man's land of mudflats and sagebrush on the southern fringe of San Diego. Soon the din of the Stingaree saloons gave way to other sounds—the clatter of raindrops smacking his hat and the crunch of his boots in the gravel between the ties. No longer buffered by trees or buildings, the wind grew fearsome, the rain nearly horizontal. Even with a good coat, the weather quickly soaked him to the bone. Shivering from the wet and cold, he thought about turning back, attempting this on another night. But it might be months before everything aligned just right again, all but the weather that is. So he steeled himself and pushed on to Chollas Creek, churning with vicious, muddy runoff from the mesas and canyons above town. Somehow he managed to keep his balance on the slippery wooden ties of the trestle that carried him across the raging watercourse.

Just beyond the wooden bridge, a structure loomed in the darkness—the Golden State Meat Packing Company. San Diego's only modern stockyard and slaughterhouse, and one of the largest manufactories on America's western coast. The brainchild of James G. Ingraham, or "Yankee Jim" as they called him in the old days, before he had much cash or clout, when he was no more than a lowly butcher rather than the proprietor of three haciendas and a collective herd of more than ten thousand head of cattle.

Yankee Jim's entrepreneurial ambitions had grown in proportion to San Diego's real-estate boom. In days gone by, he had simply raised the cattle before herding them into town for someone else to slaughter. With the arrival of the train three years prior, it became more timely and economical to drive the cattle to a new railhead near his haciendas and ship them into town.

That initial interface with mechanization had set the gears grinding inside Ingraham's head and proved the spark for a plan whereby he could make even bigger profits by slaughtering the animals and packing their meat. As a result, Yankee Jim had transformed into the main purveyor of beef and assorted products to most of the eateries, hotels, and butcher shops in San Diego, as well as commercial steamships and Kendall's railroad, the gold mines in Ensenada and Julian, visiting naval vessels and the permanent Army garrison. Ingraham put more food into local mouths than everyone else combined.

Livestock holding pens ringed the slaughterhouse, a massive wooden structure suspended on pilings so that effluent produced by the plant went straight into the bay. On any other night, the cattle would break into ceaseless bleating if a person appeared out of the dark. But cowed by the storm, they huddled in silence as the killer slipped between the slaughterhouse and their corrals. The night watchman, lodged in a wooden shack beside the main entrance, was equally oblivious. Between the rain and darkness—and the drowsiness that overcame the watchman around this time on *any* given night—the guard had no clue that someone approached. The killer easily slipped around the guardhouse undetected, made his way about a hundred yards further down the tracks to another entrance at the south end of the slaughterhouse.

Sliding back a heavy wooden door, the killer stepped inside the massive structure. About two hundred yards long and about fifty yards wide, it housed what Ingraham liked to call his "disassembly line." Based on the cutting-edge packinghouses of Chicago and Cincinnati, the line featured a series of workstations where stock was efficiently transformed from live animal into dressed meat. A narrow-gauge track with miniature flatcars moved the product from station to station. Further mechanizing the process, each station boasted a hoist and heavy steel shackle hooks to raise and lower the carcasses. The slaughterhouse was a marvel of modern engineering as well as a tribute to Ingraham's vision and genius. But it would also prove his end.

†

Yankee Jim Ingraham listened to the rain beat a steady rhythm against the metal roof of the Golden State Meat Packing Company. But he didn't let it interrupt his task of examining the books, figuring out more ways to slash costs and increase profit.

The storm had set him in a foul mood. Given its isolated location along the bay, about a mile south of the Pacific Coast Steamship wharf, the plant would likely be cut off from the rest of San Diego for days. They couldn't drive in more cattle, and they wouldn't be able to ship any product. Rather than having his workers standing around doing nothing—and accruing wages—Yankee Jim had furloughed almost his entire staff for the duration of the maelstrom. While he bemoaned what would surely be two or three days of lost production (and profit), at least he wouldn't have to pay anyone other than the watchmen.

Most men would have taken the opportunity to socialize, if not at the bars and brothels below Market, then perhaps the Cuyamaca Club and other respectable uptown establishments. But Ingraham, a loner by choice, always preferred his own company to that of others. A somewhat pious fellow, he had no discernable lust for the vices that plague so many other men. He was known to take a drink on occasion, but was certainly no drunkard. A widower for many a year, Ingraham now and again bedded some of the Indian women in his employ, but had never actually paid for carnal pleasure. His only genuine interest, now that his children were all grown, would seem to be the accumulation of even more wealth and power. And that's exactly how he had chosen to pass the storm—ensconced at his desk, poring over the books, ciphering ways to achieve even greater margins.

Figuring it downright impossible to reach his own north county home while the storm raged, Yankee Jim had booked a room at Horton House for the next three nights. That's where he would retire tonight once he finished perusing the company ledgers in his cabin-like office perched on stilts above the factory floor. From his desk, he could gaze down the entire length of the disassembly line, keeping tabs on the workers and marveling at his capitalistic brilliance.

Around nine o'clock, Yankee Jim closed the last of the ledgers and was just about to lock them in the office safe when he noticed someone loitering at one of the workstations on the factory floor. The place where sides of beef were seared with the Golden State brand before loading onto wagons or railcars. The fellow appeared to be stirring the hearth back to life with a branding iron, tiny sparks lofting through the factory's dim interior.

Stepping onto the balcony outside his office, Yankee Jim shouted down at the squatting figure. "Hey, bub!"

The person did not respond, did not look around, refused to acknowledge him in any way. Instead, he kept at the hearth, poking and prodding the coals, the tip of the branding iron glowing orange.

"You!" Ingraham called in a scratchy voice that went with his lanky frame. The tone of someone used to giving orders rather than taking them. More irritated than angry. And not the least bit alarmed. In his lair, the unidentified figure did not pose a threat.

Again, the person continued to stare at the fire, stirring the coals again.

Frustrated at the lack of response, Yankee Jim decided to confront the man. He briefly flirted with the idea of retrieving his sidearm from a holster slung over his office chair. But the situation didn't seem to call for firepower. Just some bum trying to avoid the storm, that's what he figured.

Ingraham made his way downstairs and across the factory floor. Nearing the hearth, he yelled, "Answer me, you cocksucker!" and clamped a hand on the man's shoulder.

Still clutching the branding iron, the intruder whirled around from his squatting position.

Yankee Jim recognized him at once. "What are *you* doing here?" he asked, baffled by the man's presence.

The intruder responded by stabbing Ingraham in the chest with the branding iron, a thrust so quick that Yankee Jim didn't have a chance to fend off the strike. The rod burned a "GS" through his gabardine waistcoat and the white linen shirt beneath. Reacting rather than thinking, Ingraham grabbed the business end of the iron and recoiled in pain as the scalding metal took the skin off his hands. He stumbled backward, away from the hearth, but too late to avoid another thrust. This time the hot iron struck the right side of his face, between his nose and thick sideburns. A third blow seared into his groin. Ingraham doubled over in pain, clutching at the crotch of his dark cassimere trousers.

As a coup de grâce, the intruder landed a powerful blow to the skull with the side of the branding iron. Ingraham crumpled to the slaughterhouse floor, still conscious but unable to muster any resistance. As the smell of burnt flesh rose through the building, Yankee Jim found himself curled in a ball on the brick floor, moaning from the pain of his multiple wounds, unable to strike back or defend himself.

Working with methodical haste, the intruder secured Ingraham's wrists with a pair of handcuffs. He reached up for a metal meat shank and hooked it onto the chain connecting the cuffs. Using the workstation crank, he hoisted Yankee Jim about three feet off the ground and moved a miniature flatcar into position beneath his feet. He lowered Ingraham onto the flatcar and rolled him about halfway down the slaughterhouse floor to the evisceration station.

The evisceration station served two distinct functions. Removal of any vital organs (i.e. brains, kidneys, hearts, intestines) that could be used as food products, and the reduction of the leftover animal fat into wax-like tallow. The rendering process was actually quite simple, perfected a thousand years or more before, and largely unchanged since medieval times: Dump raw animal fat into a cauldron and simmer for several days prior to straining and cooling. With the advent of electricity, tallow had lost much of its market in the United States. But animal-fat candles remained far more common in Mexico than Edison's remarkable bulbs. And that's where Yankee Jim shipped the bulk of the tallow produced at this plant.

Another hook, another hoist, and Ingraham's expensive black leather shoes were dangling above a vat of gelatinous bovine. This particular batch of tallow had been boiled, simmered, and strained just before the rains came. It had been left to cool in anticipation of cutting, crating, and shipping early the following week, by which time the storm would have passed and normal trading activities resumed. Fast to burn and slow to harden, its current consistency resembled quicksand. And it stank to high heaven. Not as pungent as pig fat, mind you, yet vile enough to wake the dead.

As Yankee Jim started to come around, he realized his predicament and began to twist and turn, trying to break free. To no avail, of course. The contraption holding him aloft could withstand the mass and muscle of a thousand-pound steer. No amount of struggle would set a human free.

"Why are you doing this?" Yankee Jim pleaded, looking his attacker in the eyes.

"Moosa Canyon," was the curt response.

That was enough to push Ingraham over the edge into total panic. "You're crazy!" he shouted.

"That may well be," the intruder said philosophically.

"Put me down!" Yankee Jim demanded. "Put me down *now* and we'll forget this whole thing." And when the attacker didn't respond, he tried something very uncharacteristic—humility. "I didn't mean to kill those folks. Didn't mean to harm 'em in any way."

"Wrong answer." With a crank of the wheel, the intruder lowered Ingraham's feet closer to the tallow.

"I didn't! Swear to God. I didn't mean to hurt 'em! They shot first! It was self-defense!"

"Wrong again." The intruder lowered him another notch, not quite touching the noxious yellow brew, but near enough for Ingraham to feel its lingering heat. "I want the truth, the whole truth, and nothing but."

Yankee Jim stared back in silence, thoroughly mystified as to why this man was doing this to him, what stake he had in events so long ago, or what connection to the people Ingraham had so grievously harmed.

The intruder lowered him another notch. "I'm waiting."

For the first time, Ingraham seemed to grasp the fact that he might actually die. "Stop!"

"Then say it!"

"We shot first! We killed 'em in cold blood!"

"The *whole* truth!"

"I shot the woman myself. But I didn't kill her kids. My men did. That's the Bible truth!"

Thinking he might now survive the ordeal, Yankee Jim exuded a deep sigh of relief. But his relief melted into an even deeper panic when his assailant cranked the handle again and his shoes cracked the tallow's thin upper crust.

"Have you lost your fucking mind?" Ingraham cried out. "You can't do this!

Without any hesitation, the man lowered him another notch, up to the knees this time. The fat still warm, yet not hot enough to scald him instantly.

Yankee Jim tried raising his legs from the yellow muck. But the effort proved useless, the energy wasted, the machine simply too efficient to overcome whatever strength he could still muster. And Ingraham knew it. "Help!" he screamed, trying to rouse the night watchman. "Help me!" But the rain beating on the metal roof, the wind whipping against the packinghouse walls, easily overwhelmed his petition.

The man lowered him further, to his waist this time, his body now half submerged in the cauldron. Yankee Jim began to whimper, tears forming in his eyes. "You have what you came for! Let me go!"

"And meet the same fate as the poor sods you shot? I think not, Mr. Ingraham."

"I won't! I won't come after you! I swear! I won't say a word. *To anyone!*"

Another notch and Ingraham sank up to his chin, gasping for air as the molten fat constricted his chest.

"God's sake, please!" he spat out. "I'll stand trial! I'll do my time!"

He wouldn't, of course. Not in a million years. Not with his kind of wealth and power. Like the first time around—when he and his men were implicated in the Moosa Canyon massacre—Yankee Jim would find a way to weasel out. Even if you could get him in a courtroom, he would refute this confession. Or claim that torture had been used to extract it. They wouldn't get past the initial hearing. The case would get tossed. The man would go free.

Almost as if he could see the plan taking shape in Ingraham's mind, the attacker turned the wheel again, and Yankee Jim's mouth and nose disappeared beneath the surface. He could no longer scream, no longer beg for mercy. What could still be seen of his face began to turn a gruesome shade of purple as the tallow clogged his throat and lungs. Moments later his thrashing stopped. And the second reckoning was over.

16

IT TOOK THREE DAYS for the storm to work its way through, but by the end of the week, the California coast sparkled again with blue sky and calm water. The tempest had wreaked havoc on maritime schedules, and the San Diego waterfront had reverted to hustle and bustle as crewmen and longshoremen rushed to get passengers and cargo aboard ships that had been laid up in the bay waiting for the wind and rain to pass.

Among those caught up in the frenzy was Cradoc Bradshaw, standing at the top of the Pacific Coast Steamship wharf with two saddlebags (the only "luggage" he owned) and a ticket tucked into the inside pocket of a fancy overcoat, borrowed from the sartorially adept Wyatt Earp so as not to look out of place amongst the wags of San Francisco.

The marshal had booked passage on a 300-foot ironclad steamer called the *Santa Rosa*, docked in deep water at the far end of the pier. Even though he had never before sailed on the ship, he knew the sleek, double-stacked profile from watching her cruise in and out of the bay from his back porch. Launched in Philadelphia in 1884, the *Santa*

Rosa was one of the more modern ships on the California coastal route, capable of making the 500 nautical-mile-run to San Francisco in less than three days with two hundred passengers.

The steamship company provided a narrow-gauge loco-motive with passenger car to transport customers and baggage to the end of the wharf. But Cradoc decided to walk, hoping the fresh air and sunshine would help him shake the cobwebs of yet another largely sleepless night. Yet the stroll proved easier said than done. Even at the best of times—with a great mound of coal running down the middle of the pier and stacks of lumber waiting to be carted ashore—the PCS wharf did not facilitate pedestrians. On this especially busy morning, the pier brimmed with freight wagons, don-key carts, buckboards, and passenger conveyance of every conceivable shape and size, from perambulators with crying infants to Wells Fargo stagecoaches.

Amongst the human boodle beside the *Santa Rosa* the marshal noticed a familiar face— Emma Lee Dawes. Wearing the same calico dress he had seen her in just a couple of days before at the Oyster Bar. Sans the white apron this time, but clutching a wicker picnic basket. She stood alone, casually glancing at the crowd as if looking for someone.

Cradoc did not presume that the object of her ardent searching might be himself. She must be on the lookout for one of Wyatt's high rollers departing San Diego after the storm. But the marshal had been raised by a mother who emphasized etiquette, and he could not board the ship without at least a casual salutation to the lass.

Emma Lee smiled as the marshal approached, rocking on her heels in a chirpy manner, obviously glad to see him.

"I was starting to wonder if this was the right ship," she told him, holding out the basket.

"That's for me?" asked the surprised marshal.

"Odds and ends from Mrs. Earp for your journey. Some sort of herb for seasickness—you're supposed to boil it into tea. Cotton balls for your ears in case the engine noise keeps you up at night. A bottle of tequila—we weren't sure they'd have it onboard. And a book for your reading pleasure. Mrs. Earp wanted me to tell you that she just got it on mail order from England and that you will be the first in town to read it, but please don't leave it behind in San Francisco, because Mr. Earp would very much like to read it, too."

Cradoc flipped up the basket lid. *A Study in Scarlet* by Arthur Conan Doyle. He had heard of neither the book nor the author. Still, Josie had never given him a read he hadn't enjoyed. The gift basket was totally unexpected, yet typical of the woman who had settled down with his best friend.

"Hope you don't mind," Emma Lee confessed, "but I read the first couple chapters while I was waiting."

The marshal almost blurted out, "You can read?" But he caught himself just in time. "Don't mind a bit. What'd you think?"

She perked up even more. "I love the main character, that Sherlock Holmes fellow. He's sort of like you, a detective and all. But an Englishman. Hope I get a chance to finish it after you and Mr. Earp are done."

"I'm sure that won't be a problem." This girl was full of surprises, definitely more to her than met the eye. He reached for the basket. "And thanks for bringing this down at the crack of dawn."

"Always been an early bird," she crooned. "Git the worm and all that."

There followed an awkward pause, neither one of them knowing what to say as the dockside crowd swirled around them. Not an awful lot of people made Cradoc nervous—made his tongue dry and hands clammy—but this girl appeared to be one of them. He obviously had a thing for her but wasn't quite sure what the nature of that thing might be. She was definitely a looker, and it had been quite a while since his last carnal liaison of any kind, and unlike so many women, she was easy on the ears as well as the eyes. But the marshal hardly knew her. And she worked for Josie and Wyatt. And should he really be courting someone so much younger than himself? Emma Lee seemed barely out of her teens. If afforded enough time, Cradoc probably could have summoned a hundred reasons why he should not smile, chat, or otherwise consort with the girl. Because whatever they got into would certainly end in tears for her and a nagging sense of guilt for him, a man with plenty of romantic baggage already.

"I should be boarding," Cradoc mumbled, assuming that would be the end of this latest encounter with the girl from Missouri.

But Emma Lee was having none of it. "I ain't never been on a steamship," she informed him. "At least, not one that runs on the ocean."

Propriety getting the best of Cradoc once again, he invited her onboard for a quick look-see. *What harm can it do?* he told himself as they mounted the gangway.

After checking in with the white-clad purser, Cradoc followed a uniformed porter to his accommodation. Emma

Lee tagged along behind, eyes flashing all around, taking in the big ship like a star-struck child.

Not the type who cherished sharing space, Cradoc had booked his own cabin on the berth deck and paid the single supplement out of his own pocket. The room was tiny—he could have easily touched both walls with outstretched fingertips—but well equipped in an efficient, modern way. Two small bunks, one above the other, plus a tiny wooden table and chair, a wall-mounted mirror, several conveniently placed clothing hooks, and a slender wardrobe outfitted with half a dozen wooden hangers. On the table rested a freshly washed towel emblazed with the PCS emblem—a red Maltese cross.

At a glance, the lodging looked a far sight above the *Orizaba*, the lumbering old side-wheeler that had preceded *Santa Rosa* on the weekly run between San Diego and points north, and the last ship that Cradoc had sailed on until today. No matter how small the digs, the marshal looked forward to the voyage, three blissful days at sea when it would be impossible for anyone to contact him about anything. The whole of San Diego could tumble into the ocean, and he wouldn't know the difference, not until they docked in Frisco. Cradoc couldn't recall the last time he'd had so much time to himself and his own thoughts. And it could not have come at a more opportune moment, given his state of mind and the flux that plagued his life of late.

The steamship porter, assuming by their comportment that Cradoc and Emma Lee were a couple, felt obliged to point out that both the men's and women's washrooms were located amidships. Emma Lee took the opportunity to excuse herself and disappeared down the hall.

"First seating or second, sir?" the porter asked Cradoc when she was out of earshot.

The marshal replied with a blank stare.

"For lunch and dinner, sir. First seating or second?"

"You need to know now?" Cradoc asked.

"It *is* customary, sir."

"I suppose first seating," he finally answered, for no other reason than maybe there was more grub if you ate early. "And one only. The young lady will be disembarking shortly."

The porter flashed a disconsolate look, as if to say: *Too bad.*

Yes, indeed, thought Cradoc. And suddenly she appeared in the doorway, smiling at him again with those big, farm-girl eyes and luscious lips.

Cradoc flipped the porter an Indian head for his trouble. The young man made a point of shutting the cabin door as he departed, leaving the marshal and his companion alone in the tiny room. There followed another pregnant pause, even more noticable than before.

"It's small," she said nervously. "But sorta cozy." And without gaining sanction from the cabin's actual occupant, Emma Lee plunked herself on the bottom bunk, testing the mattress with her fingertips. "Hope you like rock hard," she declared.

"It's only two nights," Cradoc responded. "Day after tomorrow, we'll be sailing through the Golden Gate."

"How long you gonna be gone?"

Cradoc shrugged. "It's kind of open-ended. I don't know how long it'll take to locate the people I'm supposed to be questioning—assuming they agree to meet with me, rather than run and hide."

The marshal had made telegraphic inquiries with the San Francisco police, who had put him onto the owner of a Barbary Coast saloon frequented by Asians. The proprietress had assured him that (for a price) she could hook him up with people of consequence in the Asian community who would subsequently (for a price) bring him into contact with remnants of the abalone fleet that had once fished off San Diego. It seemed a lengthy and somewhat tenuous line to hang your hopes on, and Cradoc had braced himself for nothing more than thin air at the end of his striving. But he had been commanded to venture northward, and being a good soldier, the marshal could not disobey a direct command from his superiors, no matter how blind, misguided, and self-serving their motives.

Emma Lee suddenly rose from the bunk, toe-to-toe with Cradoc in the cramped cabin, her eyes fixed on his lips. Absolutely no question in his mind what would or should or could happen next.

If not for the whistle that abruptly rattled the ship. Emma Lee flinched, and the moment passed. "What was that?" she yelped.

"First call for all those going ashore."

"Does that mean I have to leave?"

"Unless you'd care to spend the next three days aboard this ship."

"You bet I would!" she snapped back.

And Cradoc had no doubt it was true. To say the least, it would be highly intriguing—three days in this cabin with Emma Lee. But such was not to be, at least not on this trip.

Wending his way up to the weather deck of the *Santa Rosa*, the marshal watched the girl practically skip down the gangway and onto the wharf. As the steamer cast off, they waved to one another. She lingered at the end of the pier long after the ship had pulled away. Cradoc could still see her standing there, a tiny figure in a calico dress, as they rounded Dead Man's Point and slowly turned towards the mouth of San Diego Bay.

What did she want from him? Or more importantly, what did he want from her? A one-night stand, a casual fling, or something more substantial? Questions without answers. That seemed to be his entire life these days.

Rather than rack his brain over matters that could not be resolved, Cradoc settled into a deck chair. He opened the book Josie had bequeathed him and began to read. *"In the year 1878 I took my degree of Doctor of Medicine of the University of London, and proceeded to Netley to go through the course prescribed for surgeons in the army...."*

17

WITHOUT ANY FAMILY or anyone he might call a friend in San Diego, and with no apparent interest in courting any of the local females (for a single night or otherwise), Wendell Smith spent his free time alone. As such, he normally rose at the crack of dawn, dressed, and scurried out the door while most of the town still slumbered. After taking his breakfast in the all-day cafe on the ground floor of Horton House, he would amble across the plaza to the *Times*, arriving before any of the other staff.

Wendell savored the morning hours (and the empty newsroom) as a time to pen letters to his parents in the East, muse on the state of his own life, and ponder the details of whatever story he happened to be working on. What the young man may have lacked in raw literary talent and people skills, he more than made up for with a meticulousness that verged on obsession. Nick Pinder might be the master of broad brush strokes—and drawing quotes out of people who wouldn't normally give a journalist the time of day—but Wendell trumped him when it came to getting down the facts.

On this particular morning, the big storm finally having blown itself out, Wendell had penned about half the weekly letter to his beloved mother when a couple of ruffians tumbled through the front door. One of them tall, fat, and clean-shaven; the other short and lanky, with a full black beard. Both clad in full-length aprons stained with blood, guts, and yellowish goop. Butchers by the looks of it.

"We're looking for Mr. Pinder," said the short one, stepping up to the front counter.

"He's not yet arrived," the young reporter announced.

Somewhat flummoxed, the two men looked at one another and back at Wendell. "We'll wait." said the short one.

On a hunch, Wendell asked them to state their business.

Once again, the two men uneasily looked at one another and back at Wendell. And once again, the short one answered. "No disrespecting, but it's a private matter."

"Perhaps it's something I can help you with?"

"I reckon we should talk to Mr. Pinder."

"Suit yourself," said Wendell, directing the men to a wooden bench beside the front door where the messenger boys lingered between assignments.

"You go," the short one whispered to his companion. "Stand guard till I git back."

"Not till I git my share!" the big one sniveled, the first words he'd uttered since arriving at the *Times*.

"You'll get your blasted share!" the short one snapped back, nervously glancing at Wendell. "Now shut your trap and get a move on."

With his companion gone, the short one settled onto the messenger bench and removed an envelope from his back pocket, which he carefully laid upon his lap as if the most precious thing in his possession.

Wendell returned to his letter, but couldn't get his mind off the man in the bloody apron and his stark white envelope. A gaping hole pierced the envelope almost dead center, a jagged tear that could have been produced by a bullet, knife, arrow, or hundred other sharp objects. He reckoned that if the men had come to the office rather than Nick's house, it must have something to do with a story rather than a personal affair. And if that be the case, it might be a story that Wendell could just as easily write. And ransom. The big man had suggested cash would have to appear before the envelope changed hands.

Neatly folding the unfinished letter to his mother, Wendell slipped it into a desk drawer and looked across the newsroom at the visitor. "I can top his price," he said sharply, his words echoing off the newsroom walls.

Startled, the man looked up. "Huh?"

"Whatever Mr. Pinder is reimbursing you—I can top it."

"I don't know what you're talking about, fella." But his fidget betrayed a lie.

"My cash is just as good as his. And you'll have more of it. *Lots* more if the story is good enough." For the first time, Wendell could see a shift in the man's demeanor. Nothing spoken, mind you. More a physical thing. A glimmer in his eyes, a wrinkle in his brow. An ever-so-subtle opening to exploit.

"How much?" asked Wendell.

The man merely stared at him.

"How much!" he asked again, harder this time.

The man licked his lips. "Twenty dollars," he said slowly, knowing the amount outrageous.

God almighty, Wendell thought to himself. The man was either certifiably insane or sitting on a gold mine of information. Not a lot could be worth that much—only a bona fide political scandal or major crime.

"I'll give you twenty-five," Wendell blurted out before he could help himself.

"You don't even know what it is," the man pointed out quite correctly.

"I'm willing to take that chance."

The man's eyes fell to the envelope, resting easily on his lap. "Thirty," he muttered before looking up again.

"What?"

"Thirty dollars," the man repeated.

"That's outrageous!" Wendell shouted.

"That may be the truth, mister. But that's the price. Thirty bucks."

Double Wendell's weekly salary. Not that he needed the money—he got a monthly stipend from Daddy. But that was beside the point. In half a year with the *Times,* he had never paid more than five dollars for a news tip. This was six times that amount for something that could be utterly worthless. Still, whatever imbues a person with hunches and gut feelings continued to work overtime inside Wendell Smith. Like a gambler who's dead certain he's got the best hand at the table, he wasn't about to fold.

"I'll meet your price," he heard himself saying, almost like an out-of-body experience, "but not without some hint as to what this is all about. It's the same deal Mr. Pinder would give you. I know him well enough to know that he doesn't buy sight unseen."

The little man didn't respond at first, merely sat in silence, his eyes shifting between the envelope in his lap and Wendell on the other side of the counter, pondering the pros and cons. And when finally he spoke, they were words that would change Wendell's life. "He struck again," the man said calmly.

"Who?"

"Whoever it was that kilt Zeb Archer."

Wendell felt himself go flush. "How can you be certain?"

"I got the body, and I got the proof." The little man waved the envelope like a magic wand.

It took Wendell's brain about a second to process the implications. *Another murder. Another letter!* Here for his taking. Assuming, of course, it panned out. "Who did he kill?" was the first of many questions that came in quick succession.

"You wanted a hint, I gave you one. Anything else requires cash dollars."

Wendell dug into his trousers for a money clip and counted out twenty dollars, which he spread across the top of the counter in fan-like fashion.

"That's not enough," the short man remarked.

"That's all I've got on my person," Wendell said desperately.

The man shook his head and turned for the door.

"We can walk over to the bank."

"It ain't open yet."

"It will be soon!" Wendell blurted out. "Surely, that's not a problem."

"Only if Mr. Pinder shows." By now the man knew the worth of his information, knew he had the young reporter over a barrel.

Squeezing his face between both hands, Wendell thought hard and fast. *Crap!* Where could he get money on short notice? And then it came to him—Clive! He didn't know if the publisher was asleep in the back of the office, snoozing on his yacht, or strung out at some cathouse. But it was worth a shot. "Don't move!" he told the butcher. "I'll be right back."

He crept down the hallway to Clive's room and pushed open the door enough to see the boss slumbered on his daybed, snoring like a locomotive. Reaching through the crack, Wendell quietly grabbed a jacket hanging from a peg beside the door. Tucked into the inside pocket, Clive's wallet contained more than enough cash to seal the deal.

After receiving the bulk of his payment, the man surrendered the envelope, "Nicholas Pinder Esq." typed neatly on the front. Wendell took a deep gulp. Not only was he pinching Nick's story, but also waylaying his private correspondence. That wasn't illegal, as such, but certainly underhanded and highly unethical.

Whatever guilt Wendell bore vanished upon opening the envelope. The single sheet of paper inside, folded in thirds, bore three punctures down the middle of the page. But that did not obstruct the message, neatly typed and single-spaced:

Dear Mr. Pinder:

In lieu of anyone else choosing to take responsibility, it has once again become my duty and obligation to render justice…

†

With the butcher in tow, Wendell rushed to the hotel where Elliot Patterson bunked. The photographer did not answer his door. The night clerk, roused from a drowsy slump behind the front desk, had no idea where Patterson might be, whether the photographer had gone out early or simply not spent the night in his own abode.

It would have been nice to have a photograph to accompany the story, but it by no means quashed Wendell's plan. He set off for his rendezvous with destiny, the cantankerous little man leading the way, both of them plodding along on horseback through the mud-covered and mostly empty streets and finally out through the sagebrush on the southern edge of town. The breezy bayside flats were still pockmarked with puddles, but the water in Chollas Creek had fallen measurably in the last few hours, most of its muddy runoff flushed into the bay.

By now, Wendell had spoken enough with the short man to learn his name (William Hornblend) and the extraordinary turn of events that had brought them together on this sunny day in May. Hornblend and his hefty companion made tallow at the Golden State Meat Packing Company. Their job required them to strain and pour off the animal fat left to congeal in the tallow vat. Reaching the factory on this particular morning, Hornblend and his companion had stumbled upon their boss dead in the cauldron and an envelope affixed to a hook above the corpse. Rather than alert the law, the tallowmen had decided to announce their windfall to Nick Pinder in hopes of scoring a cash bounty.

Arriving at the slaughterhouse, Wendell and the little man came upon a good number of horses tied up outside. Other workers had arrived. One of the mounts, a big chestnut gelding, looked vaguely familiar. But Wendell was too caught up in the moment—and the momentum of seeking the story—to worry about where he might have seen the horse before. Rather than poised at their own workstations inside the factory, everyone had gathered around something on the far side of the massive structure, a section that Hornblend identified as the tallow cooking and cutting area.

Pushing and shoving, they made their way toward the front of the throng, where Wendell came face-to-face with the most horrific thing he had seen in his twenty-three years, something that made his head swoon and pushed his stomach to the verge of vomit. Not the fact that Yankee Jim Ingraham was submerged up to his eyeballs in gelatinous animal fat nor the decomposition starting to disfigure the victim's face. The horrid corpse was nothing compared to the wily eyes of Nick Pinder staring back at him from the other side of the cauldron.

All of the breath suddenly sucked out of his chest, Wendell felt like he'd been clobbered with a two-by-four. *How in Sam Hill did Nick get here first?* Had the other tallowman, worried about getting his rightful share of the bounty, gone to Nick's house instead of back to the factory? Had there been another informant?

And not only that, Elliot Patterson was also there, setting up his Empire State camera, getting ready to snap photos for the story. *His* story. Wendell's scoop. Not anyone else's. Nick wasn't going to poach it. Not this time. There would be no repeat of Devil's Cove.

Mustering his bravado, Wendell moved right up to Nick and said, "We need to talk."

"Damn right we do," Nick spat back.

Casually they slipped to the back of the crowd and to a quiet corner of the factory floor, where no one could overhear.

Smith fired the first volley. "This is my story!"

"You know how it works, Wendell. Whoever gets there first."

"I paid that Hornblend fellow thirty dollars!"

"Then I suggest you ask for your money back."

"You don't even know what this is all about."

Nick took a step closer. "It's not your fucking story! And the sooner that sinks into that silver-spoon brain of yours, the better for both of us."

Yet Wendell wouldn't back down. "They came to *me*, not you." A blatant lie on Smith's part, but how would Nick know?

"Should'a got here faster," Nick said arrogantly, turning to leave.

But Wendell called him back. "You can have the body, but I've got this." He removed the envelope from his coat and held it aloft.

Nick tried not to look impressed. "And what might that be?" he asked, his voice dripping with derision.

"A letter from the killer," Wendell said boldly, his confidence building with every word. He hadn't realized it till now, but the story was nothing but a run-of-the-mill murder without the correspondence to connect the dots. "The killer left it on the hook above the cauldron."

"I wasn't born yesterday," Nick snapped back, insinuating that it might be fake.

"It's on the same sort of paper, written in what appears to be the same typing, and with very similar language and content to the first letter. It could be a clever copy ... or the genuine article. But either way, it trumps your corpse. "

"Lemme see," said Nick, pointing his chin at the envelope as he stepped closer.

"Not unless you agree."

"To what?"

Wendell had to think fast. What could he gain from this? What's the most he could salvage from Nick having arrived first at the scene of the crime? "A double byline," he said. "We share the claim."

"I'm not sharing shit with you," barked Nick, lunging for the envelope.

Wendell quickly slipped it into a coat pocket. If Nick wanted the letter, he was going to have to fight for it. While Pinder would no doubt triumph in any fisticuffs, the brawl would play out in front of dozens of people. Workers who would be able to bear witness of the assault to Clive Bennett, the law courts, and most importantly Cradoc Bradshaw—who would die for a chance to toss Nick behind bars—even for something as trifling as the assault and battery of a fellow journalist.

"I'm offering you a fair and square deal," Wendell told his counterpart. "Otherwise, you can read the details in tomorrow's paper. In *my* front-page story about the letter. You know as well as I do which one the public will be drooling over. Not the gory details of a cattle baron's death—fascinating as they might be—but the fact that Ingraham and Archer share an assassin."

"You son of a bitch," Nick hissed.

"Nothing more than you would do under the same circumstances," Smith reminded him. For the first time in their months of working together, Wendell had Nick by the balls, and both of them knew it.

18

CLIVE BENNETT CAVORTED around the room like a demented leprechaun, flashing an evil grin and waving his arms in the air. "This is incredible! The biggest scoop I have come across in thirty years of journalism. This tops everything I've covered before—the Civil War, the Golden Spike. Hell, even Lincoln's assassination. Well, perhaps not Lincoln. I was there, you know. In Ford's Theater that very night. But this …" He waved the killer's latest letter with a flourish. "This is absolutely, entirely, and utterly remarkable."

The editor's elation echoed through the building, loud enough for the print staff in the basement to hear. Thinking that an angry reader had stormed the newsroom, the printers had surged upstairs, ink-stained fists at the ready, expecting a brawl, only to be confronted by nothing more than the boss pumping his arms in the air as he danced a joyous jig around the room. Clive had always been a volatile character, but no one could recall him being *this* excited.

"Calm down, Mr. Bennett," Wendell Smith implored. "You're going to have a coronary."

"Let him have his fun," said Nick, who sat in a corner of the room, basking in his own satisfaction. Despite the deal he'd forged with Wendell, Nick knew full well that he would eventually come to dominate the coverage. They might be sharing a byline tomorrow, but from there on out, Nick would feature as the primary writer.

Even though he would also gain from Ingraham's murder, Wendell couldn't understand their elation, an office full of people acting as if they had just struck gold. Unable to keep his tongue, Wendell finally spoke out. "Need I remind you, a man is dead."

"We're not gloating over his demise," said Clive, sweating from his dance and now leaning with one hand against the desk. "We're simply delighted for ourselves. Don't you realize what we've got here? We've won the bloody derby, man! This may be the single most important newspaper event in San Diego history. We're no longer dealing with a single, paltry local murder, but a story that'll surely make headlines around the world."

"I wouldn't go that far," Nick interjected, in fact hoping the story would do just that.

"I'm dead serious," Clive said, catching his breath and putting on a sober face. "You think this story sold before? Wait until the public gets a load of Act Two. By the end of next week, they'll have heard of the *San Diego Times* not just in England and France and all of the other great modern civilizations, but also in the most distant corners of the globe, all the way from Cathay to the Dark Continent."

Even Nick—with all of his hopes and dreams—thought Clive was putting the horse well before the cart. They hadn't written the damn story yet. Hadn't even penned the first word.

Slipping behind his desk, Clive yanked open a drawer and removed a box of cigars. Lighting up, he stared out the window, deep in thought. "We need a name," he suddenly declared.

"And how do we get that?" asked Nick, not catching on.

Clive whirled around. "Not his *real* name, you dolt. A nom de plume. An alias. Something dramatic that catches the public's imagination."

Nick scoffed at the very thought. "The story is astounding enough already. We don't need a cheap moniker."

"Quite the contrary," said Clive. "A beguiling epitaph can help sell even more papers, earn even more fame, garner even more fortune."

"How about the San Diego Slasher?" said Wendell, trying to weasel his way into the conversation and the decision-making process. "Or the Bayside Beast?"

"I'm as partial to alliteration as the next fellow," said Clive. "But it must bear some connection to reality. Our bloke doesn't slash. And only one of his kills has been along the bay. But you're getting the hang of it, Wendell. Keep 'em coming."

"This is ridiculous," Nick muttered. "We don't have to call him anything."

But Clive adamantly disagreed. "If *we* don't, somebody else will. Most likely one of the other local rags. We either name him ourselves, or it's out of our hands. Besides, all of the great criminals of our day and age have nicknames— Billy the Kid, Dynamite Dick, Black Jack Ketchum."

Nick grimaced. "Those are all so vulgar."

"Then how about something classical?" Wendell suggested, taking full advantage of a rare opportunity to side with the boss against Nick.

"Not a bad thought, but what?" asked Clive.

Wendell thought a moment and said, "Hades—Lord of the Underworld?"

But the boss shook his head in disagreement. "Hades was the gatekeeper, a simple public servant, not the one who consigned you to Hell. Wasn't really evil, was he? Not to mention the fact that a lot of our readers, the more religiously inclined, would balk at our using a word they consider an expletive."

Clive darted from the office, his two minions following him across the newsroom and down the hall to the editor's private quarters in the rear.

"Where is it?" Clive mumbled, sifting through the hundreds of books stacked on the floor, tables, and shelves around the room. "Ah, here!" He snatched a volume on ancient mythology, thumbing through the section that listed the myriad deities, and thinking out loud as he scanned the names. "Apollo? He was a bit of a gadfly. Dionysus? A worthless pretty boy. Good old Hermes—patron of thieves and liars. But we're not dealing with perjury or bank robbery. We're talking brutal murder and revenge."

Clive suddenly looked up. "I've got it! *Nemesis!* Whose heavenly portfolio, amongst other things, included retribution and vengeance. 'The one from whom there is no escape,'" the editor quoted from memory. "That fits our bloke to a tee!"

But Nick shot him down again. "The only problem being that Nemesis was very much a female."

"You're testing my patience, boy."

Nick shrugged. "Simply pointing out a fact."

"Which I find both helpful and irrelevant for the simple reason that 'nemesis' has evolved into a generic term for anyone—male, female, or otherwise—who seeks justice or revenge. Besides," Clive said flippantly. "Who's to say our own vigilante is not of the fairer sex."

"Give me a break, Clive. A woman couldn't possibly have committed these murders."

"Balderdash! Nobody has been caught. Nobody has been named. Nobody has been identified. Which makes Nemesis an even more fitting appellation."

"I find it most appropriate," said Wendell, butting in again. "And certainly a name our readers will latch on to. As dramatic as we are likely to find."

"My point exactly," said Clive. "Nemesis it is!"

Nick could have argued the point till hell froze over, but he knew it a lost cause. Once Clive made up his mind, there was no going back. They could have their silly name. It was still *his* story, *his* crime, and very much *his* killer. And anybody who tried to snatch it away should be prepared for the fight of their life.

Making his way to the newsroom phone, Nick had the exchange operator ring home so that he could inform his wife about all that had transpired this morning.

Roz seemed blasé at first, but Nick lured her with boundless enthusiasm. He spoke to her like a boy telling his mother about a perfect grade in school. And Roz responded like a mother, opening her heart like she hadn't done in months, letting all the anger and frustration wash away in the wake of a long-overdue outpouring of (honest) emotion from her husband. It reminded her of when they had first met, with Roz swept up in the tide of his passion.

True, it was passion for work that had prompted the outburst, but Nick's yearning to share the triumph with his wife also transcended the telephone line, as if everything he attained was on her behalf.

Nick wouldn't let her have a word in edgewise until he had finished a long and rambling dissertation on the course of the morning's events. He paused, almost out of breath.

And Roz whispered into the phone, "Darling, I'm proud of you."

Fueled by his wife's accolade, and with Wendell sitting next to him at the typing machine, Nick composed the story in less than an hour. Being largely self-taught, Nick wrote in a peculiar manner. Before committing word to page, he would stare into the middle distance, a sentence forming in his head, and then recite the line out loud as he typed the words. Stare at the air a little more, declaim the next line, and so on until the story ended.

Nick had never been indisposed to drama, especially at Clive's urging, so he portrayed the newly christened "Nemesis" as a vengeful grim reaper roaming the county in pursuit of justice. A shrewd criminal who carefully plotted every move and meticulously covered his tracks to avoid detection. But Nick also added sympathetic touches. The killer, whoever he might be, seemed to truly believe his bloody deeds filled a void of justice left by loopholes in law and courts. Perhaps his mind was errant and his methods brutal, but his heart was in the right place.

Clive gave the story one last read, changing a word here and there, adding the punctuation that Nick always had a habit of ignoring when he wrote in such a flurry. Finally finished with the text, the publisher added Wendell's name to the byline and had Smith deliver it to the basement for typesetting, along with the latest letter, published verbatim on page two.

Yet Clive wasn't quite satisfied. Something seemed to be missing from their coverage, but he couldn't put his finger on what that might be. He spun around in his chair, staring out the window again. It was dark by now, the plaza lit by the towering arc lamp and light streaming from Horton House, people coming and going from various evening affairs. *What in God's name are we forgetting?* Clive asked himself. Then it came to him—a visual. Not of Yankee Jim's corpse, mind you. One of Elliot Patterson's photographs had already been chosen for the front page. What Clive actually had in mind was a picture of the killer.

And the fact that no such image existed wasn't about to thwart him. "Wendell!" he screamed across the newsroom.

The young reporter came trotting up, still out of breath from his jaunt to the basement. "Yes, Mr. Bennett?"

"Do you know where the Canary House is?"

Wendell went flush.

"Do you or don't you?" barked Clive.

"Yes, sir. I know its location."

"Good. Because I want you to run down there— and by 'run' I do mean go as fast as your scrawny legs will carry you—and fetch a girl named Ada. Big redhead. Bring her back here pronto. You got that?"

Wendell seemed flabbergasted by the request. "Not that I would know, sir, never having frequented that establishment myself, but isn't one supposed to go *there*?"

Clive scrunched up his face. "I don't want to fuck her, you fool. I want her to draw us something. She's a very fine artist, I'll have you know."

Wendell wasn't about to ask how his boss had discovered the redhead's artistic bent. So he hurried down to the Stingaree and returned with the voluptuous Miss Ada, who sat in Clive's office with charcoal and drawing paper. As they watched, she rendered a picture of a Grim Reaper looming over bayside San Diego with the name "Nemesis" inscribed across the bottom of his cassock. Far more than one of Patterson's crime scene photos, the sketch seemed to embody the threat facing their waterfront burg.

Calling everyone into the newsroom, Clive held the caricature aloft for all to admire. Wendell was predictably outraged by its crassness. Nick seemed strangely disinterested. But everyone else heartily approved. Clive was a big believer in democracy, as long as it coincided with his own convictions, and he was certain the ghoulish illustration—in combination with the story, letter, and photo—would push circulation over the fifteen thousand mark for the first time in the paper's history. The *Times* had caught a big one, and they were going to ride it for all its worth.

Dismissing the staff and closing his office door, Clive decided the time was also ripe to take Ada for a ride.

19

CRADOC BRADSHAW SAILED back into San Diego Bay aboard the *Santa Rosa* the first week in June, chomping at the bit after three days at sea and the knowledge (via telegram from Wyatt Earp) that another prominent citizen had been murdered—apparently by the same fiend.

As expected, his journey to San Francisco had been a wild goose chase. He had located several dozen members of the Chinese group that had passed through San Diego more than twenty years before. The few he could cajole into talking became belligerent at the first mention of Sam Ah Choy, and those who recalled the name Zebulon Archer did so with no small amount of malice. Cradoc soon became convinced that most of the Chinese he spoke with would have killed Archer if given half a chance. Yet every last one of them had air-tight alibis reinforced by family, friends, employers, or the marshal's own perusal of steamship and railroad passenger manifests. The trip north had been nothing but a waste of time.

Charging down the gangplank, Cradoc exchanged a warm handshake with Wyatt. "This for real?"

"Far as I can tell," Wyatt told him, handing over a copy of the *Times* with the headline "NEMESIS STRIKES AGAIN!"

"Nemesis?" the marshal spat out.

"The *Times* has apparently given our boy a name. You know Clive's penchant for grandstanding."

"How do we even know it's the same killer?"

Wyatt snorted. "'Cuz it says so in the paper."

Cradoc quickly scanned the main story—Yankee Jim's death in a vat of animal fat, the message from the killer left on a meat hook, revenge for some long-ago transgression. And in an adjoining box, the letter reproduced verbatim with "Your Humble Servant" at the end. He would read it later, in a quiet place where he could study every phrase and nuance, determine for himself if the missive had indeed been authored by the same person as the Archer creed.

As the two of them moved up the pier, dodging handcarts and mule trains, a thousand questions rushed through Cradoc's mind. They came out like pellets from a cockeyed shotgun—in no particular order and aimed just about everywhere.

"Where's the body?" he asked.

"Six feet under."

"They buried him already! *Who* let that happen?"

"Nobody around to stop it."

"What the hell was Coyne doing?"

"Twiddling his thumbs per usual."

"Please tell me Doc LeFevre got a look at the corpse before it went into the ground."

This time Wyatt had good news. "It's my understanding that he *was* able to perform a postmortem. They apparently had one hell of a time getting Yankee Jim out of the tallow. It was almost rock-solid by the time they found him. Doc had to stoke a fire and melt the goddamn stuff to extract the corpse."

"What a way to go." Cradoc suppressed a shudder.

"We bought most of our meat from Ingraham," Wyatt lamented, wondering where the hell he was going to get his prime rib now.

"So did my mother. Long before he married that Spanish gal and got his mitts on her family's hacienda, he was the town butcher. She wasn't a bad looker, so it wasn't hard to see why Yankee Jim took after her. But the other way around, that was always a mystery. Nobody could figure why she took up with him. Except maybe as a way to rebel against her parents."

"Happens all the time."

"Just look at you and Josie."

Wyatt chose to ignore Cradoc's taunt. By now they were on dry land beyond the waterfront, walking up lower Fifth Street through the heart of the Stingaree. A good hour before noon, the saloons were already overflowing and the ladies of the night plying their trade in broad daylight.

Wyatt ran his thumb and forefinger over his ample mustache. "Did Archer and Ingraham run together in the old days?"

"Not that I recall. Both of them had shops in Old Town about a block apart. And they must have known each other—it was such a small place in those days and not a lot of white folks. Other than that, I can't see a connection. I don't remember Ingraham having a political bent one way or the other, even during the war. He was a typical tight-fisted New Englander, profit his primary motivation."

"You make that sound like a bad thing."

Cradoc huffed. "It is if you're a cheat. His scales were fixed. You ask for three pounds of beef, he'd give you two and a half. Most people wouldn't know the difference. But my mother did. Once she cottoned on, she weighed everything at home on her own scales. And if she'd been shorted, she would stomp back to the butcher shop and demand a refund. Needless to say, he soon stopped cheatin' us. But his reputation lingered. He didn't seem to give a shit whether anyone knew or not. He was the only game in town. You wanted fresh meat, you either had to buy it from him or kill it yourself."

"That's one way to get rich," quipped Wyatt.

"One way to get yourself killed, too. What in Sam Hill was he doing at the slaughterhouse in the middle of a storm?"

"He was apparently there to batten down the hatches and send everyone home. Ingraham booked himself a hotel room and went back to the factory to catch up on paperwork. At least, that's what he told the desk clerk at Horton House."

"The killer must have been stalking him," Cradoc figured. "Tracking his movements the day the storm blew in, because otherwise he wouldn't have known Ingraham was at the slaughterhouse that night."

"So whoever killed him," said Wyatt, picking up the marshal's thread, "is someone who blends in. Someone who didn't pose a threat or raise alarms. Someone that Ingraham could have passed on the street without giving a second thought."

"Anyone come to mind?"

Wyatt smiled. "Besides you and me?"

✝

Cradoc went home to shave, bathe, and change his clothes after the long voyage. In lieu of having his own telephone, the marshal had asked Wyatt to call both Doc LeFevre and Joe Coyne, have them meet him at the jailhouse in an hour's time. Before leaving home, Cradoc finally sat down and read the stories in the *Times* about the latest killing.

He noticed the main story had a double byline—Nick Pinder and Wendell Smith—and chuckled, wondering how that strange marriage had come about. Certainly not Nick's idea. *But I digress*, he thought to himself. The story presented a fairly straightforward account of how two packinghouse employees had discovered Yankee Jim Ingraham's body in a vat of tallow on the morning after the big storm cleared out. Nothing earth shaking in any of those disclosures.

But the letter from the alleged killer, reproduced inside of a thick black border on page two of the *Times*, was a far different matter. Addressed once again to Nick, it contained the same sort of logic used to justify the earlier assassination of Zeb Archer.

Dear Mr. Pinder:

In lieu of anyone else choosing to take responsibility, it has once again become my duty and obligation to render justice in the name of the public good.

As you have no doubt discovered by this juncture, given the means by which this correspondence was delivered into your care, the subject of my latest work is Mr. James P. Ingraham, also known as Yankee Jim. As owner and proprietor of the Golden State Meat Packing Company, as

*well as three cattle haciendas in the northern portion of
our county, he was a person of no small standing in our
community.*

*By virtue of his wealth and social standing, Mr.
Ingraham felt himself above and beyond the law. This is
not unusual for a man of his station, and certainly not a
crime unto itself. But when used in concert with actions
that harm fellow citizens, such notions of entitlement are
cause for alarm—and punishment.*

*As you might recall, the incident to which I refer
transpired in the spring of 1878, when Mr. Ingraham
got wind of squatters in Moosa Canyon, most of which
fell within the boundary of his hacienda lands. Riding
out himself to investigate, Mr. Ingraham came across
Mrs. Elizabeth Going, an indigent widow, and seven
members of her family, including her elderly father, a
grown cousin, and her five children. They had constructed
a rudimentary lean-to for shelter and had begun tilling
the land in order to feed themselves.*

*Mr. Ingraham was well within his rights as a property
owner when he requested the Goings immediately vacate
his land. And it is well documented that Mrs. Going
replied by drawing a shotgun and driving him away.
Rather than employ legal means to solve the matter, Mr.
Ingraham chose to take matters into his own hands by
organizing a "posse" of his own wranglers and returning
to Moosa Canyon.*

*A scuffle ensued, during which Elizabeth Going,
her grown cousin, and youngest child were slain in
cold blood. Mr. Ingraham claimed self-defense, and a
subsequent public inquest relinquished him and his men
of any criminal culpability in the matter. As was the case*

with Mr. Archer, justice was corrupted to serve the needs of the rich and powerful— those who float near the top of our society rather than dwell in disease, depression, and abject poverty near the bottom.

As before, I do not relish the role of judge, jury, and executioner. But we are often helpless when it comes to determining our destiny, and as such, it has fallen to me to avenge those who cannot avenge themselves.

Last but not least, the burden of proof. Did I dispatch Mr. Ingraham? Or was it someone else? A copycat, a fake, a phony of some sort? The proof is in the brand we choose to use.

–Your Humble Servant

Cradoc calmly folded up the newspaper, shoved it into the pocket of his duster, and strode into town.

†

They convened in Coyne's office with the door closed. Cradoc asked Jose Cota to remain outside, posted in the hallway so that nobody could sidle up to the door for a listen. Frankly, he no longer trusted most of his own deputies not to leak tidbits to the local press. Until they figured out if they had a multiple killer on their hands— and how they were going to handle the case—the fewer people who knew the better.

The assembly did not get off to a smooth start.

Coyne and Cradoc were present, as was Doc LeFevre, who had ridden all the way from Mission Valley with the only copy of the Ingraham autopsy, which nobody but the doctor had been privy too thus far. It was the fourth person in the room was the issue.

"So, what can I do you for, Mr. Earp?" asked Coyne, assuming his presence must have something to do with a completely different matter than the Ingraham murder.

"I asked him to sit in," Cradoc explained.

Coyne spat out a huge wad of chew. "I don't know if we can do that."

"Why not?"

"No disrespecting," the sheriff told Wyatt, "but I don't know if the mayor and city council would take kindly to me having a wanted man on the payroll. Even more so when the crime for which he's wanted is homicide."

"You know those are trumped-up charges," Cradoc reminded the boss.

"No matter. The warrant still exists."

"Come on, Joe! Other than you and me, there isn't another lawman within a hundred miles with Wyatt's experience and insight. We need all the help we can get."

"I don't know ..." said Coyne. At least he was hedging.

Wyatt cleared his throat. "I'm not asking for recompense."

"And it's not like we have to deputize him," LeFevre said, tossing in his two cents.

Chomping on a new wad of tobacco, looking thoroughly ambivalent, it took Coyne a minute or two to make up his mind. "If this comes back around to bite me—"

"I'll take full responsibility," Cradoc assured him.

"Fine. As long as—"

"It was my idea. You didn't know."

Satisfied, Coyne sighed. "Alright, then. Let's get down to business."

Cradoc flashed Wyatt a grin. This would be the first time they had worked a case together in years, since Earp had left Kansas in search of new opportunities in the Arizona Territory. And while it may not have been official, it was as close as they were going to get in renewing what had once been a formidable law-enforcement partnership.

"What do you know about Moosa Canyon?" Coyne asked Cradoc, since the marshal hadn't been around then.

"Not an awful lot. Don't even know when it happened."

"Seventy-eight," said LeFevre. "Or thereabouts."

"I was in Dodge then," Cradoc said. "I don't even remember hearing about it."

"The gist is well covered in the latest letter," LeFevre explained, tipping his chin at a copy of the *Times* on the sheriff's desk. "Ingraham and his men confronted squatters on one of his haciendas. Things turned violent, and several of the interlopers were shot and killed."

The kind of thing that happened all the time in the West, but rarely got prosecuted because of conflicting testimony from the various sides involved.

"Did it ever go to trial?" asked Cradoc.

Coyne spoke up. "Yes and no. Ingraham was indicted for murder by a grand jury. But his attorney managed to get the charges dismissed on a technicality. One of the grand jury members was not an American citizen, but a recent arrival from Europe and therefore ineligible to serve."

"In other words, he got away scot-free."

"So it would seem. Until our letter-writing assassin showed up again last week." The sheriff shook his head in dismay. "Someone killing people like this ... spread out over days or weeks ... highly planned and premeditated." He shook his head. "That does beat all."

"But not without precedent," Wyatt declared. "There was an episode in Texas a few years back. Fella they called the Austin Annihilator. He killed six or seven servant girls over a two-year span. He'd sneak into their rooms, drag 'em out of bed, and kill 'em with an axe after having his way with them."

Leave it to Earp to conjure some obscure connection. But that's exactly why Cradoc wanted him onboard. He was like a walking, talking encyclopedia with a brain that seemed to retain everything to which it had ever been exposed.

"Anyone caught?" asked Coyne.

"Nope. Several men got arrested, including the husband of one of the victims. But there was never enough evidence to convict anyone. The killings stopped like that!" Wyatt snapped his fingers. "But they were never solved."

"Also that Packer fella," LeFevre declared. "The one in Colorado. The miner who killed five other diggers."

"Didn't he eat 'em?" asked Wyatt.

"So they say. He claimed they were already dead or near dead from frostbite, and cannibalism the only way he could survive winter in the Rockies. That swayed the jury enough to convict him of manslaughter rather than murder."

"Hate to rain on your parade," Cradoc interjected, "but neither of those cases resembles our situation. We're dealing with something completely different, maybe even unique. Acts of revenge carried out by a killer not personally affected by the supposed transgressions."

Wyatt asked a good hypothetical: "You think there's any connection whatsoever between Sam Ah Choy and Moosa Canyon?"

"The incidents happened more than a dozen years apart in totally different parts of San Diego County," Coyne explained. "One revolved around Chinamen and the other around white squatters. So I doubt it."

"Anything hinky in the autopsy?" asked Cradoc.

LeFevre shook his head. "I haven't come across even a faint similarity between the two homicides. Other than the letters, which are not my domain, and the fact that both victims were dispatched by rather bizarre means."

"Didn't they both drown?"

"Not exactly," LeFevre answered. "Drowning is caused by a massive and sustained fluid influx into the lungs. That's what happened to Mr. Archer. On the other hand, Mr. Ingraham suffocated to death. A massive blockage of the throat and nasal passages by animal fat. It wasn't liquefied enough to seep into his lungs and cause drowning. Rather, it cut off his air as effectively as if a cushion or pillow had been pressed against his face."

LeFevre explained how Yankee Jim's hands had been clasped tight behind his back with a pair of handcuffs, causing bruising and lacerations to both wrists, no doubt inflicted during efforts to break free.

From his black leather medical bag, LeFevre produced those very handcuffs, broken in two during the autopsy process, the keyhole and links still clogged with waxy tallow. He passed the cuffs across the table to Cradoc, who could tell at once they were of the same variety used by San Diego law enforcement, himself and Sheriff Coyne included.

LeFevre read on: "Mr. Ingraham also sustained rather ample contusions to the upper back from what appears to have been a pole, rod, or stick wielded with no small amount of force. Last but not least, he was branded three times."

The other three men suddenly looked up. "Come again?" asked Coyne.

"The corpse had three freshly rendered brands—the left side of the face about halfway between mouth and ear, as well as the chest and groin."

"What sorta brand?" asked Wyatt.

"By all appearance, one of the victim's own rods. The letters 'GS'—as in Golden State. The exact mark applied to his sides of beef."

"Wait a goddamn minute," said Cradoc, reaching for the newspaper. Stabbing a finger at a passage in the would-be killer's letter, he read out loud. "The proof is in the brand we choose to use."

"He's claiming ownership," said Wyatt, immediately picking up on the thread.

Coyne looked from Wyatt to Cradoc. "Of Ingraham's body?"

"No, the crime." Cradoc jumped up from his seat.

"Where the hell are you going?" barked Coyne.

Hand on the doorknob, the marshal glanced around. "To get the original letter." Seeing the alarm rise on Coyne's face, he added, "I won't make a scene. Swear to God!"

"Yeah right," the sheriff retorted. "Fool me once, it's my own fault. Fool me twice … uh …" He couldn't remember the rest of the phrase. "You know what I goddamn mean. Get your ass back in that chair."

But Cradoc continued to plead his case. "The only way to verify beyond a shadow of a doubt that the writer committed both crimes is comparing the typeface on both letters. And we don't have the second one in our possession yet."

"We sure as shit do," Coyne revealed. "Which I would have mentioned if I could'a got a word in edgeways." He pulled open his desk drawer and withdrew a now dog-eared and extensively finger-marked envelope with a hole through the middle. "Nick sent it over after the story came out. With a little note saying he was surrendering the letter as a quote-unquote 'public service' to the people of San Diego."

Typical Nick Pinder bullshit, Cradoc thought to himself. But no matter. The marshal had what he needed. He fetched his magnifying glass and scooted back into the sheriff's office.

Wyatt, LeFevre, and Coyne circled around as Cradoc placed the missives side by side and examined them. The paper used for both letters was indistinguishable: thick stock of the type one might purchase in a fancy stationery store; slightly beige in color rather than stark white; and exactly the same size. More importantly, the type also matched, both letters composed on the same sort of machine.

"Sholes & Glidden," Cradoc mumbled to himself, looking up at his companions. "On second thought, I think this is what the killer means by 'proof is in the brand'—the brand of typing machine rather than the cattle branding iron. His clever way of claiming ownership of both murders."

But the ultimate test was determining whether the letters had been typed on the exact same machine. During one of his countless perusals of the Archer letter, the marshal had noticed a tiny fissure in the left leg of every "M." Now he ran the magnifying glass down the Ingraham letter looking for a similar flaw. There it was! An identical cleft!

No doubt about that now, the same man had taken both lives. Yet they were still far from knowing who that killer might be.

20

WHILE CRADOC BRADSHAW struggled to identify the killer, Nick Pinder basked in the glow of his expanded notoriety. The day after his latest coup, San Diego's other daily papers published the shocking revelation that the same assassin had dispatched Ingraham and Archer. With no source of their own, they resorted to quoting directly from the *Times* in some cases almost word for word. Beyond that, the other rags were stymied on how to cover the story other than the same interviews with the victim's slaughterhouse and hacienda workers that Wendell Smith—yet again relegated to the bridesmaid role—had already penned for the *Times*.

As Clive Bennett predicted, reporters from the *Union* and *Sun* began to pester Nick in a desperate bid for fresh copy. Nick took these interview requests to the boss and asked permission to speak with the other papers. Clive didn't hesitate to grant his blessing, gloating over the competition groveling at their doorstep, one of the ultimate triumphs of journalism. The local weeklies soon followed. Journalists also arrived by train from Los Angeles to quiz Nick and file their own stories on the heinous events unfolding down the coast. Who was this Nemesis? What were his motives? Would he strike again? Why did the killer communicate only with Nick? Did Nick feel threatened in any way?

Soon it became impossible to open a newspaper anywhere in California without coming across a story about Nemesis and Nick's extraordinary correspondence with the killer.

This presented Clive with an unforeseen dilemma: the other San Diego papers outsold the *Times* on days when interviews with Nick appeared. This was not part of his battle plan. They were stealing his glory! Not to mention the additional money in his pocket that came with increased circulation. In response, Clive banned interviews with competing media and instructed Nick to concentrate on producing more copy of his own. In the meantime, Clive instructed Wendell to interview Nick for the *Times*. He had absolutely nothing new to say about the murders. Nick simply rehashed the same old details. But it was another Clive Bennett masterstroke. Circulation shot up again. Indeed, the public seemed to have an insatiable appetite for both Nick and Nemesis.

†

Exhausted by all the attention and burning the midnight oil for days on end, Nick decided to do something he had not done in months, perhaps more than a year. He took a day's leave from work and slept in.

He had discovered a few weeks prior, quite by accident, that one could render a telephone incapable of accepting incoming calls by simply disconnecting the wire that ran into the wooden telephone box from the pole outside. He had done so last night before turning in. Anyone who needed to contact him for work or otherwise would have to ride out from town. Nick knew that if a real emergency arose, Clive would dispatch someone to fetch him. Roz had been both surprised and thoroughly pleased by Nick's gesture. And she hadn't seen anything yet.

Nick lounged in bed through much of the morning, sorting through copies of *Collier's Once A Week, Scribner's* monthly, *Murray's Magazine,* and other periodicals accumulated on his bedside table. Reading material intended to catch him up on global affairs—which he had sorely neglected in the wake of the Nemesis murders—and stimulate story ideas. Prospectors had found gold amid the jungles of British Guyana. The Brazilians had finally abolished slavery, the last nation in the Americas to officially end the odious institution. Prince Wilhelm, who had a disfigured and largely useless left arm due to childhood palsy, was about to be crowned the new Kaiser of the German Empire. Alexander Graham Bell, inventor of the machine that Nick had cleverly disconnected in the downstairs hallway, had launched a brand-new venture—a learned club called the National Geographic Society dedicated to the "increase and diffusion" of worldly knowledge. This included the creation of an eponymous magazine, and Nick made a mental note to subscribe to the new publication.

Fascinating as all of that might be, none of these stories sparked ideas that Nick might spin into a San Diego angle.

On the other hand, something in a recent edition of *Harper's Weekly* proved much more fertile—the photograph of a massive canal under construction across the Isthmus of Panama, along the very route that the conquistador Vasco Núñez de Balboa had followed whilst discovering the Pacific Ocean nearly four hundred years before. A French company was endeavoring to build the canal. Although thousands of workers had succumbed to dreaded tropical disease, they were pushing ahead with the gargantuan project. If ever completed, the engineering marvel would cut the sailing time between San Diego and New York by more than half. Now *that* he could repackage as a story for the *Times*.

Roz came into the bedroom around ten and announced that breakfast was being served. By the time Nick shaved and dressed, Roz and Lupe had pulled the kitchen table and two chairs out back, placing them on a patch of grass that caught the morning sun. And there they ate together, husband and wife, for what seemed like the first time in ages. Eggs fried over easy, strips of bacon, fresh tortillas, and coffee. A feast prepared by the ever-remarkable Lupe, who had transformed into not just a good cook in the short time she had been in service to the Pinders, but also a demonstrative addition to the household, warm and loving like the daughter that Nick and Roz could never have.

From their perch on the lawn, they could look across to the other homes on Golden Hill, including the blood-red monstrosity recently erected by the writer, artist and actor Jesse Shepard, a house he dubbed "Villa Montezuma" in his typical over-the-top fashion. Beyond lay the bay, stretching off to the south towards the dark mesas of Mexico and the Coronado Islands. It was a marvelous summer day, the fog already well out to sea, the bay sparkling, and just enough of a breeze to take the edge off the heat. A picture of how things might have been between Nick and Roz if their time together had taken a different tack, if Nick hadn't let work and writing consume his life. In his mind, it wasn't too late. For Nick, this glorious June day marked the start of a campaign to win back his wife's heart and mind.

At about half past one, a goods wagon pulled by two mules came trundling up the path from town. Onboard sat a burly gringo in a beaver hat and a Mexican sidekick hunched beneath a sombrero and serape. They removed a wooden crate from the flatbed and hefted it into the living room. Wielding a crowbar, the big gringo ruptured the crate. Inside, protected by straw stuffing, was a brand-new Model VS 2 sewing machine. Known for its wondrous vibrating shuttle, the Singer rested in its own rosewood case on a five-drawer sewing table with treadle base and foot pedal, the very machine that Roz had ogled in the window of Marston's Emporium months earlier. She was shocked that Nick had taken notice, and even more surprised that he had remembered so long after.

Nick had purchased the contraption with money earned from selling the Nemesis story to out-of-town papers. His way of apologizing for letting his writing overshadow his wife. And a not-so-subtle insinuation that perhaps she should take up sewing again, if not for profit, certainly for recreation and her own sartorial satisfaction.

As Roz cleared the protective straw away from the machine, Nick slipped into the kitchen and returned with two glasses and a bottle of champagne. Not the cheap stuff, but a bottle of demi-sec from Reims. Making sure not to douse the sewing machine, he popped the cork, and they toasted twice. Once to Singer and once to their marriage. Roz couldn't recall the last time she had seen her husband so cheerful, far removed from the remoteness in which he had languished for months.

Before Roz knew it, they had polished off the bottle, and Nick began to undress her, right in the parlor. And when she protested—they could hear Lupe rummaging around in the kitchen—he took Roz by the hand and pulled her upstairs. Stripping her naked, he swung her around into a sitting position on the bed and stepped back to consider the artistry. "You truly are divine," he crooned.

Roz replied with a blush, crossing her arms in an involuntary reflex. They made love just once. But it was long and good and slow, more finesse than fervor. Afterward, they lay sprawled on the bed, drenched in sweat, at peace with the world and themselves. Nick nodded off—she could feel the change in the velocity of his breathing—and Roz clutched him tightly in her arms, wanting to believe their union had finally turned a corner and would always be such. Like back in the days when she had truly been the most important thing in Nick's life. Yet Roz knew in her heart of hearts that it most likely wouldn't last. In another day or a week or a couple of months, Nick would fade away again. That other side of his life would reclaim him, as it had a dozen times before.

How do you keep someone's undivided attention? Could passion last for more than a fleeting moment? Roz couldn't answer either question. As she lay there, she found herself thinking that perhaps that was the nature of things— relationships that ran in seasons, at times fresh and crisp like the first days of summer, at other times dark and cold like winter.

Curling up against her sleeping husband, she would relish the warmth while it lasted.

21

CRADOC WAS EATING at his usual late-night haunt, the cook wagon outside the County Courthouse, when he spotted her at one of the other tables, sitting alone as she read a book in the dim light of a lantern. Emma Lee Dawes. Her face flickering in the light. Her eyes tracking back and forth across the pages.

"Good evening, ma'am," he said hovering over her table. And when she looked up from the book, he tipped his hat.

"Marshal," she said, surprised to see him. "You're up awful late."

"So are you."

"I'm a night owl from way back. Never get to bed before midnight, even when I got nothing to do."

"I seem to recall you're an early bird, too."

Emma Lee shrugged. "I've never been a big sleeper. But it don't seem to harm me." She flashed a wide smile. "You eatin' or just passing through?"

"Waiting for my order."

"I'm waiting for mine, too." Her eyes flared with an idea. "We could eat together."

"I don't wanna impose," he said politely, when in fact he did.

"Wouldn't ask if I didn't want the company."

So Cradoc pulled up a chair. "What are you reading?"

She held up the cover—*Alice's Adventures in Wonderland* by Lewis Carroll. "Mrs. Earp says it's brand new. Not many folks have read it yet."

Cradoc pursed his lips, nodding approval, astonished to catch her with yet another new book. "Any good?" he asked.

"It's a mite hard to read at times. An awful lot of words I don't understand. But the story's a hoot." She sat up straight on her stool, excited to tell him. "It's about this English gal—her name's Alice—who follows a white rabbit down this hole to a place called Wonderland, where most of the people are made from poker cards. Well, I guess they're not cards. More like cards that come alive. There's also this little mouse that falls asleep all the time and this crazy fella with lots of hats." Then suddenly she stopped. "I'm boring you."

"Not at all," he said. And he was telling the truth. Far from being bored, he was intrigued by her passion. Such a change from the jaded souls he normally came across. "You seem to like books more than most folks."

"Never thought about it, but I guess so," she answered with a smile.

"You pick that up on your own?"

"My grandparents were big readers. Back in Mizzura."

Cradoc wanted to ask an obvious follow-up question. But she seemed to read his mind.

"They're the ones who raised me. Ma died giving birth to me, and Daddy ran off. I never knew him."

"Sorry to hear that," Cradoc told her.

"It weren't a bad thing, getting raised by my grand-parents. They taught me how to read and all."

"Are they still around?"

"No. They died six, seven years ago." Enough time had passed that sadness no longer figured in the revelation. No big deal. Just a statement of fact.

"So you've been on your own?"

"Since I was thirteen," she confessed.

"Holy smokes," he said. "How did you get by?"

Emma Lee wondered if she should tell him or not. The whole truth, that is, rather than the abridged version most people got. Rather than snuff out the spark she could feel growing between them, she decided on the latter course. If this thing between her and the marshal transformed into something more than just friendship, she could always tell him later.

"It weren't easy," she said. "I did a lot of things ... stealing, cheating, lying." Emma Lee looked him straight in the eyes.

The marshal waited for her to mention her marriage. And when she pointedly didn't, he decided to just let it go. Probably too painful to talk about.

"You do anything you can to survive," she added.

Cradoc nodded, thinking about his own brush with mortality. "I know what you mean."

Her eyes widened, incredulous. "You've been down and out?"

"Just once, but it was pretty bad. A few years back, I got shipwrecked down the Mexican coast. Almost drowned." On the spur of the moment, Cradoc decided to redact his own survival story. She didn't need to know all the nitty-gritty. "To make a long story short, I was stranded for six months on a desert island. Nothing to eat but crabs, lizards, and bird eggs. No fresh water, so you had to suck on cactuses."

"Oh my Lord," she said, both of her hands on her face, her mouth in a perfect O. "How did you escape?"

"I eventually built a driftwood raft and floated back to the mainland. And I've never told anyone this—" Cradoc lowered his voice, looked around to make sure nobody else was listening. "I stole a horse. Rode it all the way back to San Diego."

Emma Lee was astonished. The marshal really did know what she meant by *anything* to survive. Still, she wasn't about to confess her deepest, darkest secret. At least not yet, and maybe never. "I talk way too much for my own good," she blurted out.

"I don't mind."

"Stop pulling my leg."

"I'm dead serious. You're always so …" Cradoc searched for the word. "Always so *enthusiastic* about whatever it is you're doing or talking about. Most people couldn't care less about what they're telling you. You're a breath of fresh air."

Emma Lee's eyes glimmered with appreciation. "No one's ever told me *that* before—that I'm a breath of fresh air."

Then the food arrived. A heaping plate of meat, carrots, and potatoes for him, a dish of pie for her.

"That's all you're having?" Cradoc pointed at the pie.

"I already ate dinner—at the Oyster. I get it free, you know, cuz I work there. But I just love the pie at this place, especially the strawberry with rhubarb."

"So do I," he mumbled through a mouthful of brisket. "Best pie in town."

They ate in silence a while, the marshal polishing off his huge plate of grub, while Emma Lee slowly put away the pie, savoring every bite.

"You live around here?" she asked, breaking the silence.

Cradoc raised his chin towards the waterfront. "About five minutes that'a way."

"I didn't think there was anything west of here but the train station. And water."

"There's a row of old fishing shacks. You've gotta walk across a wooden catwalk to reach 'em."

Her eyes widened again. "You live in a fishing shack?"

"I've added things here and there, made it a proper home."

"I can't imagine." She shook her head in amazement.

"Yeah, it's one of those things you kinda gotta see."

"Then why don't you show me," she said like it was no big deal.

When, in fact, it was a very big deal. At least to Cradoc. Had the girl just invited herself to his home? And if so, what was her intention? It might be nothing more than innocent curiosity. On the other hand ... *Put that out of your mind!* he scolded himself. No sense getting your hopes up when they could easily be dashed.

"Well, I ... I ... I don't ..." He stammered like a blithering fool.

Calm and collected, Emma Lee smiled back. "You don't *what*?" she asked, gazing at him with those big green eyes.

"It's late," he reminded her, still trying to act nonchalant. "I thought you might be tired."

"I'm the night owl, remember?"

It might be the look in her eyes or the tone in her voice, but Cradoc figured her intent was more than innocent curiosity. Not twenty minutes later—after Cradoc had paid both of their cook wagon bills—they stood on the back porch of his house, looking out over San Diego Bay.

She nodded toward the harbor mouth. "What are them lights over there?"

"A couple of fishing villages called Roseville and La Playa. They were the only settlements on the bay when I was a kid. The fishermen used to haul their catch into town in the foulest-smelling carts you could ever imagine. I don't know how my mother got close enough to buy anything, but we used to have fish at least once a week."

"I didn't know you grew up here."

"Yeah, I spent my first seventeen years in San Diego, before my parents shipped me off to military school in the East."

"Was it different then?"

Cradoc rolled his eyes. "Oh God, yes. What they now call Old Town was the *only* town in those days. Nobody lived where we are now. It was still called Punta de los Muertos—Dead Man's Point. The only thing here besides sagebrush and jackrabbits was the military post where my father worked. That was the first thing the Americans built when they took San Diego from the Mexicans, a fort right next to the bay so the garrison could be re-supplied by sea if the Mexicans ever counterattacked. Riding down here every single day wore on my father. But he wanted my mother and me to have a town life, a normal existence."

"Why'd they call it Dead Man's Point?"

"I don't know for sure, but the legend is that the Spaniard explorers who discovered the bay lost a number of men to scurvy and other ailments. Right along here, in the soft mud beside the shore, is where those unfortunate souls were buried."

Emma Lee shivered. "You're making my flesh crawl."

Cradoc laughed—typical female. Squeamish about death and anything related. "This ain't New Orleans. The dead don't come back to life."

"That's not what I been hearing."

"Don't believe the rubbish you hear at the Oyster."

"I'm talking about the newspapers," she countered. "Did you see that drawing in the *Times*? That Nemesis fella. He looks like some kinda monster! Not to mention the fact that nobody's seen him or even knows who he might be. Doesn't that sound like a ghost to you? Could be one of those dead Spaniards out for revenge cuz we stole their land."

Not a theory Cradoc was likely to pursue. But likewise, he didn't want to put her off. She might up and leave.

"I honestly don't know what to believe anymore," he told her, close to the truth. "In all my time as a lawman, this is the most frustrating case I have ever come across. The murders were in different locations and by different means. Other than the fact that they had lived in San Diego for many years, the victims didn't seem to have much in common. We've talked to hundreds of people who may or may not have seen or heard something that could help us identify the killer. And we don't have anything but a vague description of someone who may or may not have been the perpetrator. So maybe you're right. Maybe it is a ghost."

The girl looked up at him now with wide eyes. "I like the way you talk," she said softly.

And he was starting to like just about everything about her. She wasn't half bad looking. But her spunk, her confidence, her entire demeanor, intrigued him far more than her beauty or body. And he didn't think Emma Lee was nearly as innocent as she let on. Some gals were like that—felt like they had to act all coy, because society dictated that females should not speak their mind or take the initiative with a man. But not Emma Lee. Nothing the least bit coy about her. Matter of fact, Cradoc found himself wondering who was prey and predator amongst the two of them.

The conversation lapsed into a silence filled with anticipation. Both of them knowing what should happen next, yet both hesitating, waiting for the other to make the first move.

"Whattaya reckon?" Emma Lee asked nervously. Then she looked up at him and ran her tongue over her lips.

Almost in unison, as if on some instinctual cue, they leaned into one another, lips touching lips, struggling out of their clothes with a fury that matched their passion, not an ounce of hesitation on her part. It was easy enough removing her simple cotton frock. But undoing a corset in the dark—*that* was another matter. Still, you find a way, especially at times like this. And soon enough, she was minus everything but her socks, which Emma Lee refused to discard with the excuse that her feet were cold. They made love right there in the open air, Emma Lee leaning against the wooden railing, Cradoc gently working his way up inside of her. The palms of her hands flat against the railing, she used the wooden beam for leverage to move herself up and down against him. Moaning ever so slightly at first, barely more than a whimper, and then progressively louder as their passion increased.

After they both finished, they slumped in one another's arms, still breathing heavily.

"Wouldn't mind a little heat," she said.

Cradoc led her inside, fed wood into the pot-bellied stove, and stoked a fire to life. As flickering light filled the room, he got his first good look at Emma Lee's body. One of those women who actually look better undressed, she was a tad plump, but it suited her. Everything in the right proportions, like the cherubs he'd seen in paintings in the houses of rich people in the East. At some point during their lovemaking, her blonde hair had come undone, and now it tumbled down her back to just above her heart-shaped butt. She didn't seem to have an ounce of shame, unclothed in front of a man she barely knew—a man doing his best to shield his own nakedness behind the kitchen table.

They were soon in the bedroom, Emma Lee pulling him down, wrapping her legs tight around his waist, running her hands through his curly hair. Cradoc didn't think he could recover so quickly. But with her hand around his cock, gently moving along the shaft, it wasn't long before he was hard again. She took her lips slowly down his chest and over his stomach. And for the first time in years, Cradoc lost himself completely in an act of love.

Later in the evening, Emma Lee snoozing quietly beside him, waves lapping against the wooden pylons beneath his house, Cradoc lay wide-awake. The girl had proved a much better lover than Cradoc would ever have expected. Granted, she had been married a spell, which meant she wasn't a complete greenhorn when it came to carnal knowledge. Still you had to wonder: *How did she get so damn good?* But what really surprised him was his own behavior. He could not recall another time in the past five years when he'd made love to a woman without wishing it was Roz.

22

RATHER THAN WALK the four blocks east along Broadway, Nick decided to make a bigger splash arriving by carriage at the Cuyamaca Club, where he had been summoned to meet with one of San Diego's most prominent and powerful citizens. Strolling across the plaza, he approached one of the horse-drawn cabs parked in front of Horton House.

"You *do* know it's just down there," said the somewhat flabbergasted buggy driver when Nick announced where he wanted to be taken. You could actually see the club entrance from where they were standing.

"I'm quite aware of its location," Nick snapped back. "Do you want my custom or not?"

With his surly passenger in the back, the driver did a U-turn and sauntered up Broadway. He made another U-turn and pulled up at the wooden boardwalk fronting the venerable club. Nick paid him the exact fare and not a penny more.

The building was nothing to write home about, a two-story clapboard structure that didn't look all that much different from a large house, which is exactly what it had been until the current occupants assumed ownership. The inside is what counted. Or rather the idea of what lay beyond the front doors—the county's first and thus far only private club for gentlemen, founded the year prior as a place of social intercourse between those with a vested interest in San Diego's growth and development. Heavy emphasis on the latter, seeing as land developers comprised a good deal of the club's initial membership.

Stepping inside, Nick found a lectern where visitors announced themselves upon arrival. As a bald-headed valet scanned the guest list, Nick looked past him into the main lounge with its silk drapes and bolstered leather armchairs. A thin veil of smoke hung across the room. And even at a distance, you could detect the aroma of fine Havanas, rather than the stogies that stank up lesser establishments. There was, of course, not a female in sight, and not a single person of color. Nor, Nick suspected, anyone lacking an Anglo-Saxon heritage and surname.

Nick was relieved to discover his name on the guest list. The valet requested he follow him, and they wove their way through the room to a table in the back, where Nick's host awaited.

Fabian Kendall was a gregarious New Englander and one of the few serious rivals to Alonzo Horton's stature as San Diego's most powerful man. Kendall and his brothers had purchased the Rancho de la Nacional after the war and transformed the south bay hacienda into a budding agricultural oasis called National City. That alone would have made him eminent in local circles. But Kendall also brought the railroad to town, connecting San Diego with Los Angeles in 1885. And now he was on the verge of launching a political career, his eyes and considerable fortune cast firmly on the congressional seat held by Civil War hero William Vandever.

With his spade beard and mutton-cup whiskers, Kendall looked like a thousand other men one might see around town. The thing that set him apart—besides his hundred-dollar suits—were striking blue eyes framed by thick brows. The sort of eyes that radiate dominance, which is exactly what Kendall was doing as he rose to shake Nick's hand.

"Welcome!" he said, looking his guest straight in the eye. "I hope I haven't taken you away from anything important?"

"Not at all," said Nick. "Slow news day."

"Then will you join me in drink?"

"It would be an honor," Nick answered, playing along with the protocol.

A month ago, they wouldn't have let him in the front door at the Cuyamaca. But now here he was sitting with one of the town's most important personages in the most exclusive club in all of Southern California. As much as he appreciated the recognition of men like Kendall, the irony did not escape him. Nick was no different than he'd been a few days prior. He looked the same, thought the same, talked the same, walked the same. But suddenly the world saw him with much different eyes. One of Clive Bennett's journalistic credos was spinning other people's misfortunes into golden opportunities for oneself. And here was tangible proof. Nick would not be hobnobbing at the Cuyamaca if Zeb Archer and Yankee Jim had not been murdered by dramatic and mysterious means.

A certain part of Nick craved the limelight, while another part of him shunned stepping out from the shadows in which he had dwelt for most of his life. Deep down inside, he was still the street kid, son of a woman who had sold her body to support them after her lighthouse keeper husband had perished in the war. He'd always thought of the rich and powerful as natural foes—hypocrites and carpetbaggers, rather than clubby drinking buddies. Was it possible to solicit their approval and utterly detest them in the same breath? He was about to find out.

"Name your poison," Kendall demanded, a waiter hovering over their table.

Nick wasn't quite sure what movers and shakers slid down their gullet. He tried to think of something sophisticated. And when he asked for sherry, his host exploded with a belly laugh.

"This isn't the garden club," Kendall chided.

"Then whatever you're having," Nick responded, awkwardly shifting in his chair. Not five minutes inside the inner sanctum, and he had already embarrassed himself.

Kendall told the waiter to bring "the usual" (whatever that might be) then turned his attention back to Nick. "Those are some stories you've been writing, about that Nemesis fellow."

"Lucky break," said Nick, feigning modesty, drawing the other man into even more effusive praise.

"Lucky my ass!" Kendall spat back. "That's what I call good old-fashioned journalism. Of the sort we don't see enough of in these parts." And Kendall would know. Because in addition to being the primary force behind the railroad coming to San Diego—and one of those who had expedited the demise of Old Town and the subsequent rise of Horton's New Town along the bay—Kendall had also helped establish the *San Diego Union*, the only serious rival to the *Times* amongst the town's half-dozen daily and weekly newspapers.

Much like the club in which they now sat, the *Union* supported the local establishment. Although it pretended to be independent and speak for all the citizenry, its editorial line and underlying journalistic thrust was readily apparent—anything good for the local business barons and big developers was good for San Diego. The *Times*, on the other hand, had always been the upstart. The paper of the working class, the downtrodden, and recent immigrants. A journal that wasn't afraid to poke fun at the rich and powerful, including Fabian Kendall.

The waiter reappeared with a pair of crystal tumblers and a bottle of something called Laphroaig. The two men clinked glasses and downed their amber nectar in a single swig. Kendall snatched the bottle and quickly poured another round. "Whattaya think?" he asked.

Nick held up his glass. "Best bourbon I've ever tasted."

"That's because it's *not* bourbon. It's a Scottish single malt. I keep my own case behind the bar for special occasions." Assuming, quite rightly, that Nick had no idea how to say the name, Kendall now pronounced it in slow motion. "La froyg—that's how one should say it. The perfect drink for San Diego."

"How's that?" asked Nick, taking the bait.

"In the language of my Gaelic forefathers, the name means 'beautiful hollow by the broad bay.' A perfect description of our fair city, don't you think?" But the man didn't give Nick time to answer. Kendall had not summoned him to engage in idle banter. There had to be an underlying motive, and moments later it emerged. "Like I was saying before, lucky or not, it's quite a caper you've came across."

"Much obliged." Nick wondered where this was heading.

"Between you and me," said Kendall, lowering his voice, "you know who this Nemesis fellow is, correct?"

"Haven't a clue," Nick answered. Had the man not read his stories?

Kendall seemed befuddled. "How can that be?"

"Because he's never revealed it—to me or anyone else that I'm aware of. As was said in the articles that ran alongside the letters, the first was delivered by regular post and the second left at the scene of the crime. In both cases, the author did not offer any indication of who he really is."

"Honest to God?" Kendall genuinely seemed to think Nick privy to the killer's true self.

"Trust me, Mr. Kendall, if we knew the identity of the killer, we would have published his name in the *Times* as both a public service and news coup."

"Not necessarily."

Now it was Nick's turned to look mystified. "What possible reason could we have for concealing his name?"

"Several come to mind," Kendall declared. "Being a newspaperman myself, I can envision a circumstance in which one withholds certain facts in order to—how shall I say?—sprinkle them through future stories."

"What are you suggesting?" asked Nick.

"That Clive Bennett knows full well, perhaps even better than the buffoon who edits my own rag, how to finagle a story for all it's worth."

"I assure you that Mr. Bennett would never do such a thing." Although Nick had to admit it wasn't a half bad idea.

"And why would we do that?"

The railroad tycoon shrugged. "Maybe the killer is a

friend, acquaintance, or even a family member. Maybe you agree with his motives for dispatching Archer and Ingraham."

Nick sat up straight in his chair. "Mr. Kendall, please. How can you even suggest such a thing?"

"History, my dear fellow," Kendall retorted. "Your paper, your editor, and even yourself have never been especially gracious to the powers that be in this town. I seem to recall that you took Archer to task several years ago for what you termed 'profiteering' on lumber sales. And the *Times* adamantly campaigned for Yankee Jim's conviction in that Moosa Canyon flap."

"That doesn't mean we would sanction their murders or conceal their killer. First and foremost, it just wouldn't be right. But more importantly—and I'm sure you can understand this as a businessman—it would in no way profit myself or the *Times*. As a matter of fact, we'd sell far more papers if we actually could publish the killer's name."

"So you're telling the God's honest truth? You have no idea who penned those letters and presumably murdered Archer and Ingraham?"

"Not in the faintest," Nick said bluntly.

Having settled that point, at least for now, Kendall steered their conversation onto other popular topics of the day. Not surprisingly, the man was an ardent Republican and had much to say about his party's upcoming National Convention, scheduled for three weeks hence in Chicago. Kendall would be attending himself, traveling back by train, his first venture into the political limelight and perhaps not his last, according to the local grapevine. Kendall's candidate of choice amongst the fourteen men vying for a chance to reach the White House was Senator

Sherman of Ohio. "Although Harrison will give him a good run for his money," he surmised.

Kendall thought a moment, pulling at his dark brown goatee. "May I be so bold as to suggest something radical?" he suggested.

"And what might that be?" Nick figured it must be something to do with free trade, protectionism, or one of the other ongoing Republican themes.

"What would you think about coming to work for me?"

Nick just about choked on his single malt. "Did I hear you right?"

"Dump that rag you work for and write for the only *real* paper in San Diego. I'll double the pittance Bennett is paying you. And to sweeten the pot, I'll throw in this." Kendall raised his hands to signify the Cuyamaca Club. "One word from me, and this plunder is yours."

"I don't know what to say, Mr. Kendall." Nick really didn't, astonished by the offer and its implication. Never in his wildest dreams did he imagine his meeting with Kendall would pan out in such a way.

Kendall's lips curled into a wily smile. "Say yes. That's all I need to hear."

"Because of the Nemesis stories?" Nick asked incredulously.

"You're now a household name. And household names sell papers no matter what they write. Frankly speaking, you working for me translates into more money in my pocket. And that's what it's all about."

Nick wasn't naïve enough to think his decisions were merely a matter of dollars and cents—and membership in the Cuyamaca Club. He knew enough people at the *Union* to know how things went down behind the scenes. Kendall had a well-honed repute for meddling in the newsroom, getting his editor and writers to angle stories to his own financial and political advantage. That's not to say that Clive Bennett didn't have his own agenda. Nick's current boss most certainly did. But power and wealth weren't Clive's primary motivations. After thirty-odd years in the newspaper business, Clive actually relished the process of collecting and disseminating news. He loved the rush you got from a hot story. And he truly did view the Fourth Estate as a pillar of society, something to be nurtured for the benefit of mankind, rather than milked for all it was worth. Clive had instilled these same values in Nick. And although it was mightily tempting—an opportunity that would perhaps never come his way again—there was no way that Nick would compromise his values for a duplicitous codfish like Kendall.

But how to tell the man such without insulting him? *That* was the challenge. Burning bridges never got you anywhere. At some point in future, Nick might change his mind, decide that helping the rich get richer was his true calling in life, rather than trying to save the world.

"Mr. Kendall, I've been at the *Times* an awful long time…."

"And your loyalty is most commendable," Kendall responded. "Something I value in my own employees. But there comes a time when a man must think of his future, break his ties with the past, and march onto a new field of battle. Where would my brothers and I be today if we'd stayed in the New Hampshire hamlet where we grew up? If I had not persuaded Eastern banks to finance construction of my railroad? I beg of you to think along those same lines."

"Sir, I just don't know ..." Nick couldn't help but think there was another, clandestine motive for Kendall's offer. He had never hidden his feelings about the owner of their biggest journalistic rival. Everyone knew that Nick detested the railroad tycoon. Why would he want someone like that on his staff? It had to be more than profit. And there remained only one other thing that would interest a man like Kendall—power. In this case, controlling the flow of information to your advantage.

"Sir, can I ask you something?"

"I'm an open book," Kendall answered, failing to grasp the irony.

"If I was to come work for you, how would we handle the Nemesis case?"

"As you know, we are a more serious publication than the *Times*."

"Yes, but what exactly does that mean in terms of how the story gets covered?"

Kendall didn't beat around the bush. "I don't believe in idolizing a wanton killer."

"That's what you think we've been doing?"

"To a certain extent, yes. Christening him with a name from Greek mythology and such. Deplorable sensationalism."

Nick was quick with his response. "But that's what sells more papers. And isn't that your motive for recruiting me?"

Kendall didn't have a quick comeback this time. "There are other considerations," he said cryptically, without elaborating on what any of those considerations might be. He flashed a chilly smile, those blue eyes bearing down on Nick. "There is certainly no need to decide on my offer post haste. Mull it over for a couple of days. And discuss with that lovely wife of yours. In the meantime, have another drink on me."

Pushing back from the table, Kendall stood. "Take your time. As much as I would love to linger, other business awaits."

Nick stood to shake hands and watched as Kendall made his way across the room, stopping here and there to greet other luminaries before disappearing out the front door.

Sinking back into his seat, Nick told himself that he should cherish the moment, soak it up now, because he probably wouldn't be drinking again at the Cuyamaca Club for quite some time. No way was he going to jump ship. Much like today's news, he was no more than a fleeting curiosity to someone like Kendall, who would move on to the next sideshow as soon as Nick was no longer of any value to him. Pity really ... to be saddled with morals, ethics, and a narrow purpose rather than continually grasping for all you could take. But that was his lot in life, one he would gladly accept without complaints. After one more drink.

"I'll have another one of these *froggy* things," Nick told the waiter. "On Mr. Kendall's tab."

23

LIKE JUST ABOUT EVERYONE else in San Diego, Cradoc Bradshaw had taken to calling their anonymous assassin "Nemesis." Partly it was laziness, lack of anything else to call the brute. But if asked, the marshal might have admitted that he sort of liked the nom de plume that Clive Bennett had conjured for the killer. Sure it was cheesy, but it also rolled off the tongue. Uttering one word was a whole lot easier than spewing "the guy who killed Archer and Ingraham" every time the case got mentioned. And people certainly knew who you were talking about from the get-go. Until such time as they knew his true identity, Cradoc was content to use the over-the-top alias.

The marshal spent the weeks after his return from San Francisco trying to establish a link, no matter how tenuous, between the killer and his latest victim. As part of that quest, he spoke with Ingraham's family and friends, ranch hands, and meat factory employees. Much like Archer, Yankee Jim had his enemies and detractors. Rivals in the cattle and food business, especially the small-time butchers he was slowly driving to extinction with his automated cow-cleaving. Yet no one stuck out as having the motive, means, and opportunity to kill the man.

The prospect of fingering a suspect became even more remote when you figured in the letters and the killer's elegantly stated motivations. Other than the fact that Archer and Ingraham had got away with murder at some point in their past, there were no readily apparent connections between the long-ago incidents. Chinese immigrants and white squatters. Politics and property rights. Death by drowning and death by gunplay. Victims who had not known each other. And completely different means of dispatching the two men that Nemesis had murdered.

By the time he reached the bottom of the list of people that he wanted to question about Yankee Jim's demise, Cradoc had come to the conclusion that the deadly letter writer either had some sort of Robin Hood complex or discovered a connection between Archer and Ingraham not yet obvious to the marshal or anyone else in law enforcement.

Plumb out of leads—and under pressure from Joe Coyne, who was under pressure from the mayor—the marshal began to work his way down a list of secondary contacts, people with only a marginal connection to the homicides. Cradoc knew it was grasping at straws, but that's all he had left at this juncture.

One lingering item was asking Father Figueroa about the comment in the *Times* after the first murder—the fact that he'd helped arrange the burial of Sam Ah Choy on a plot of unconsecrated land adjacent to the Christian cemetery in Old Town. That's not how Cradoc remembered things. He recalled his own father saying words over the dead Asian's grave. The priest certainly could have been amongst the onlookers. Several people had wandered up from town for the service behind the old Spanish presidio, most of them just curious gawkers. If the padre had been there, perhaps he could recall something small or seemingly insignificant that might shed fresh light on the Archer case. And if not, no big deal. One more thing to check off a list growing shorter by the day as the leads and loose ends fizzled out.

†

Standing on the top rung of a wooden stepladder, Roz Pinder used a measuring tape to figure the width and height of the windows in Father Figueroa's bedroom in the church rectory. Nick certainly didn't intend a return to professional fashion when he gave her the Singer sewing machine, but he could hardly complain about Roz making new curtains for the priest's house. After all, stitching remained an essential part of her past and how Roz had come to her current station in life.

Fresh off the boat from Ireland, her parents had apprenticed Roz to a prominent Boston dressmaker, who put her to work as a lowly seamstress. But the girl discovered, dabbling around the workshop in her spare time, that she had a talent for design. The dressmaker, without the least bit of shame, pilfered the designs and called them her own. As a thirteen-year-old migrant worker, Roz tolerated the theft of her creativity. By the time she was sixteen, Roz had determined that she would no longer stand for it.

Spotting an employment notice in one of the Boston papers, Roz had clandestinely written to the headmistress of a California school advertising for a seamstress to make its uniforms. She secured the job, used every penny she had to buy passage to the West Coast, and arrived in San Diego without so much as a dollar in her pocketbook. But the job and her new life were everything she had dreamed about in that dreary Boston workshop.

Kate Sessions, headmistress at the Russ School, encouraged Roz to use her spare time creating fancy frocks for the town's wealthy matrons. Her couture became an overnight success, earning Roz more money than she had ever thought possible, as well as an entrée into local society. In less than a year, Roz's risky decision to flee from Boston to San Diego had catapulted her from indentured servant to woman of independent means and modest notoriety. All on the basis of her skill with a needle and thread.

Much like riding a horse—or making love—you never forgot how to sew. But as she was learning today, it *was* possible to get rusty. Having finished measuring the bedroom windows, Roz moved into the kitchen and then a fairly large front room that doubled as a parlor and parish meeting hall. Last but not least she ventured into Father Figueroa's office, where she pushed aside a small wooden table with a typing machine in order to reach the window. Standing on a stepladder, reaching up to measure the top of the window frame, she noticed a familiar face approaching on horseback—Cradoc Bradshaw.

Moments later, she heard a knock at the front door. Wrapping the measuring tape around her neck, she hopped down from the ladder and went to greet him. Roz couldn't wait to see the look on his face when she pulled open the door rather than Figueroa.

And sure enough, he flinched. "What are *you* doing here?"

"I'm a good Catholic girl," she teased.

"Besides *that*—"

"I'm making new curtains for the rectory."

Cradoc snorted. "How'd you get roped into that?"

"It was my idea," she declared proudly. "My own little project." As well as a means of exerting her independence. Not fully, mind you, but enough to make her feel like she wasn't totally dependent on Nick. Although she wasn't about to admit that to Cradoc.

"Nick finally letting you work?" he asked.

"I won't be getting paid. It's volunteer. My way of giving back to the parish."

"Work is work," he mused. "Whether you're getting paid or not."

"Nick gave me a new sewing machine, and I have to do something with it. Might as well be for the glory of God."

Roz hadn't seen Cradoc since the ugly incident at the *Times*, when he had crashed the celebration after the first Nemesis letter. He had looked haggard that night, and discontented. But now Roz thought she saw a certain gleam, not just in his eyes, but Cradoc's whole manner. A spark she hadn't seen in years. She wondered if it could be the Nemesis case, the energy that comes with taking on a new investigation, or something else in his life. Perhaps a woman? She was about to inquire, but never got that far.

Cradoc looked into the room. "Is the padre around?"

"I'm afraid he's in Old Town. His regular Wednesday rounds to minister to people who can't make it to church for the sacraments. Is there anything I can help you with?"

The marshal sucked his teeth. "Nothing that you're going to agree to," he said sarcastically.

She knew him well enough to know that he was only *half* kidding. Still, this was a vast improvement over the grimness he normally displayed around her. She wondered if he had finally gotten over everything that had happened in the past, all of the drama from what now seemed like so long ago. Did time really heal all wounds? And if so, what was his magical curative?

But again, this wasn't the time or place to ask. It's not why she was here, and not why Cradoc had made the ride up the hill from the jailhouse. "If you don't mind me asking, why did you want to see the Father?"

"Nothing earth-shattering," he answered. "Something he said in the paper that I wanted to double check. Something that may or may not have some minor bearing on the Nemesis case. Most likely not."

"How's the investigation going?"

"You read the papers. You know as much as I do."

"You expect me to believe that?" Roz responded.

"It's true this time."

"So you really have *no* idea who the killer might be?"

"Not a damn clue. Two months down the line from the first murder, and we aren't any closer to making an arrest or even naming a suspect than the morning they found Archer's body dangling from that cliff."

"Can I quote you on that?" Roz quipped.

Cradoc smiled. "Like I'd be saying anything if I thought you were gonna blab it all back to Nick."

Given their history, it was an incredibly generous thing for him to say. "You still trust me that much?" she asked.

"Stuff like this—for sure," he said without batting an eye. Implying, of course, there were other ways in which he *did not* trust his former lover.

An awkward moment of silence followed, all of that past hovering between them, all of that baggage. And then Roz spoke up. "Would you like to leave a note for Father Figueroa?"

"Naw, I'll come back some other time. It's not that urgent." He flashed a warm smile before turning to leave. "You were damn good," he said without further elaboration.

"At what?" she said, not quite sure what he was getting at.

"Making dresses for all those rich gals. You were the best in town."

"I don't know about that," Roz said, blushing a bit.

"No, you really were. You should take it up again. I hear women saying all the time how they wish you were still making dresses."

"Do you?"

"Well, maybe not *all* the time. It's not like I'm going to tea every day on Banker's Hill. But often enough. You wouldn't have any problem getting back into the saddle."

Cradoc tipped his hat and crawled back onto his horse. Roz watched him disappear around a corner and returned to her task.

She carried out the last of the measurements for the office curtains and moved the typewriter back into place beneath the window. It was an old machine, nothing like the slick new typing devices that Nick and the others used at the *Times*. Yet it was quite striking in appearance, decorated with diminutive paintings, floral patterns, and gold-leaf motifs. A small nameplate on the black metal façade read "Sholes & Glidden." Didn't mean a thing to Roz. But then again, typing was not amongst her many skills.

24

LIKE SO MANY AMERICAN towns and cities, San Diego pulled out all the stops on the Fourth of July. Clive Bennett made the most of the 1888 holiday with a rollicking party on the premises of the *Times* to which he had invited all of his most loyal advertisers and many of the big wigs of local commerce and government. Alonzo Horton was throwing his own shindig across the plaza in the garden of the grand hotel that bore his name. And it seemed like most of the rest of the citizenry had somehow squeezed themselves into the dusty open space that San Diego claimed as its town square, the bandstand in the middle of the plaza protruding from the swirling, shouting, swaying sea of humanity.

Cradoc Bradshaw had planned a much different Fourth of July than the vast majority of San Diegans. Spurning the Independence Day Parade and the boisterous parties, he had removed the tarp from his skiff, lowered it into the water for the first time in years, and asked Emma Lee to join him in a day of sailing.

She had readily agreed, and around nine o'clock in the morning, Cradoc and Emma Lee hopped aboard with picnic lunch and sundry beverage, as well as towels and an umbrella to shield the lady from the unrelenting California sun. It was, after all, high summer. The marine layer that hovered above the coast through most of May and June had vanished, leaving glorious sunshine and temperatures expected to reach well into the eighties.

Feeling rusty beneath the mast, Cradoc decided on a practice spin around the near shore before cruising into deeper water. At just under twenty feet, the skiff represented the outer limit of what the marshal could handle in a moderate breeze. Yet by no means was it easy going. Cradoc went through several erratic tacks before he got the hang of working the main, the jib, and the tiller in concert.

Snuggled up in the stern beneath the umbrella and a colorful Mexican blanket, her back against the gunwale, Emma Lee watched him battle both wind and boat. She was beside herself, couldn't stop laughing when the boom came around and whacked Cradoc in the back of the head, and then again when he almost ran them aground on the mudflats along the north side of the bay.

"Have you done this before?" she asked sassily.

"Wouldn't know it, would ya? It's hard to grow up in these parts without learning a little about boats. But that doesn't make you a master and commander."

"Did your daddy teach you?"

Cradoc normally wouldn't go down that road. But today he thought *what the hell.*

This was a good test of how far he had managed to wean himself off the past. "Nick taught me," he said flatly.

"Nick, the newspaper fella?"

"That would be him."

"So you and him really were friends?"

"Once upon a time...."

"I didn't believe Mrs. Earp when she told me. Not the way you two are now."

"Yeah, we were friends," Cradoc sighed. "And he's the one who taught me how to work one of these damn things. He used to live up there." Cradoc pointed to the lighthouse atop Point Loma. "His daddy was the lighthouse keeper, and my father commanded the U.S. Army garrison. They knew each other through work, and Nick and I were tossed together when we were barely out of diapers. When we got old enough to go to school, Nick lived with us in town during the week and went back home for the weekends. Sailing is how he got back and forth."

It was strange hearing himself talk about growing up with Nick after so many years of shunning that part of his life. Even odder was pulling it off with no trace of emotion. Maybe he had finally gotten over the events that had split them apart. And maybe this woman at the front of the skiff had expedited his healing. She was babbling on about her own past now, something or other about Missouri.

"We don't have a lot of these kinda boats back home. Least, not on the river. Keelboats and flatboats for sure. Barges and paddlewheelers, too. But not much with sails. I don't know if it's a lack of wind or what. Never really thought about it until I got out here. It's a whole different way to travel. So smooth and quiet."

"Didn't your husband make his living on the river?"

She flashed him a funny sort of look, and Cradoc thought maybe he shouldn't have mentioned her dead spouse. Other than the fact that she had once been hitched, and her husband had accidentally died—prompting her move to the West Coast—he didn't know an awful lot about Emma Lee's marital history. Not being the type to meddle when it came to personal matters, Cradoc had not previously broached the subject. Still, if he was willing to divulge a smattering of his own past, perhaps it was only fair that Emma Lee should do the same.

"He worked a couple of the big paddlewheelers, like the *Natchez.*"

That didn't seem too painful for her to answer, so Cradoc continued. "What was his job?"

"He was what you might call a jack of all trades."

"Did you ever get a chance to travel with him on the Mississippi?" She looked at him sort of cockeyed again. And Cradoc backtracked. "Sorry, I didn't mean to pry. Sometimes I don't know when to keep my mouth shut. But I do find myself wanting to know everything there is about you."

"You do?" she asked, surprised by his frank admission.

"Well yeah. You know what it's like when you … fancy someone."

They had made love several dozen times, but this was the first time that either had said anything remotely affectionate to the other.

Emma Lee's face broke into a warm smile, her eyes going a little bit watery as she considered the implications of what her lover had just confessed. She tossed aside the blanket and crawled to the stern, her face hovering just inches away from his own, staring into his eyes. They came together in the deepest kiss they had yet shared … and the boat shot sideways as Cradoc released his grip on the tiller.

Scrambling to bring the vessel under control, Cradoc once again found himself the butt of her amusement. She doubled over laughing at his distress. "My granny always said that men can't do two things at once."

"Your granny was dead right," he answered, ducking just in time to avoid the boom as it swung around from starboard.

Cradoc decided to concentrate on skippering the boat, lest they end up beached along the bay rather than the romantic rendezvous spot he had in mind. Soon they were cruising past the village of La Playa, the waterfront alive with the local fisherfolk in a smaller version of the same Fourth of July revelry going on in San Diego. Ballast Point and its whaling ghost town loomed dead ahead, and suddenly they were out in the open ocean. Off to the south, Cradoc pointed at the red-tiled dome of the new Hotel Del Coronado and the Coronado Islands in Mexican waters below that invisible line called the international border.

At the foot of Point Loma stood a brand-new lighthouse that had recently taken the place of the one above where Nick had grown up. The new beacon soared higher, boasted far superior technology, and would be less encumbered by fog. While it might be more efficient at saving lives and ships, it would never replace the earlier light station in local hearts and minds. Cradoc wasn't the only one who mourned the loss of the old gal. Many of the old-timers considered the quaint whitewashed structure one of San Diego's most endearing symbols.

Cradoc cleared the rocky shoals and kelp beds off the tip of Point Loma and forced the skiff into a sharp right turn, tacking back and forth in a northerly direction until they reached a secluded cove with a sliver of sandy shore. "This is it!" he said and tossed the anchor overboard. Then a thought occurred. "Do you know how to swim?"

"As good as a dog," she answered. Emma Lee glanced warily at the expanse of water between skiff and shore. "Why do you wanna know?" she asked suspiciously.

"I thought we'd swim over to the beach."

"I didn't bring a bathing costume."

"Who says you need one?" Cradoc said teasingly, removing his shirt and flinging it onto the deck.

"But how are we going to … " It suddenly dawned on her what her lover had in mind. "I'm not stripping naked in broad daylight!"

"I've already seen your birthday suit," he reminded her, delighted that for once he had surprised her with salacious insinuation rather than the other way round.

"It's not *you* I'm worried about," she shot back.

"Look around," said Cradoc, sweeping his arm across the uninhabited shoreline. "We're alone."

"You don't know that!"

"Trust me, I do. You can only reach this cove by boat." He kicked one boot off, and then the other, undid his silver buckle and dropped his drawers. "You coming or not?" he asked, standing at the bow in his red long-john bottoms.

She looked him up and down, obviously liking what she saw. She licked her lips, took a deep breath. "Turn around."

"What?" He couldn't believe his ears.

"Turn around!" she repeated.

"How many times have I seen you naked?"

"Don't matter. Either you turn around while I get undressed or you wet that little willy by yourself."

Feeling little willy get hard, Cradoc readily complied, staring at the water, the beach, and the chaparral-covered slopes of Point Loma while she removed her clothes.

"Don't turn around!" she said from behind.

"I'm not!"

Moments later, he heard her shuffling along the wooden deck on her way to the bow.

"Drop your long-johns," she ordered from just over his shoulder.

The marshal did exactly as he was told, pulling the underwear down and around his ankles until he stood buck naked on the deck of a boat bobbing up and down in the ocean. A lady next to him, naked herself. Who would have thought? Not even Wyatt.

Suddenly he was flying off the bow and into the water. The little witch had pushed him! His head sinking beneath the surface, Cradoc took in a huge gulp of seawater and came up coughing. Emma Lee floated nearby, having made the transition from boat to water without Cradoc snatching even a fleeting glimpse of her disrobed body. While he found her modesty confusing given all that had already passed between them, he also found it charming. She surprised him in so many ways.

They slowly made their way towards shore, Cradoc swimming proper strokes and Emma Lee dog paddling, tumbling through the waves as they neared the beach. He took her by the hand and pulled her onto dry sand. It was only then that he noticed her socks— sopping wet on both feet.

"I told you my feet get cold," she said timidly.

Cradoc wanted to say they'd get even colder wrapped in damp wool. He didn't buy that her feet were chilly; had to be another reason. Maybe she had webbed feet or crooked toes or another malady brought about by birth or childhood accident. But if she didn't want to say, he wasn't going to force the issue.

On the cusp of surf and sand they fell into a deep kiss. Cradoc pushed the wet hair off her face, caught her eyes and said, "You're beautiful, you know that?"

She actually blushed. "Nobody's told me that in a *long* time."

"Then I'll say it again. Everything about you is stunning."

They made love on the beach, the surf splashing up and over their bodies, the sun glistening off their skin, oblivious to anything but each other, like they were the only two people in the world. Bringing each other to the brink and then backing off, starting over again and again, no concept of space or time.

Emma Lee flipped him around and crawled on top, her legs astride his thighs. Using her hand she slipped him inside. Bracing herself with outstretched arms against the sand, she began to move up and down on his manhood, a slow progression from ecstasy into something that nobody had yet invented a name for, a state of bliss so acute it was almost torture. Cradoc tried holding it as long as he could, clenching his fists, actually gritting his teeth in an attempt to stretch the rapture as long as possible. And when he heard Emma Lee shudder and scream, Cradoc finally let himself go, a spasm that ran through his entire body and deep into hers.

Slumped against his chest, Emma Lee lay quiet for the longest time, sobbing softly. He didn't want to ask why—if it was happiness or sadness that had prompted the tears, a statement on the present or the past.

Cradoc went back to the boat, stuffed supplies into a waterproof goatskin bag, and swam back to shore. They enjoyed a picnic lunch on the sand, drank more grog than perhaps prudent, made love again, and stayed way too late for Cradoc to attempt passage back into the bay. He made a fire, and they curled up to sleep on the strand, cozy beneath the Mexican blanket and wrapped in one another's arms.

25

GETTING BACK INTO THE SWING of work after the holiday, Cradoc Bradshaw confronted the unsavory task of clearing out a bunch of Indians squatting in Switzer Canyon, about a mile north of town. Normally a deputy or two would have assisted the eviction. But Wyatt Earp, no doubt trying to avoid something that his wife wanted him to do, had suggested they ride up together.

They hadn't talked about Nemesis in some time, and for good reason. It had been almost six weeks since the second murder and conventional wisdom was now drifting towards an assumption the killer would not be heard from again, either scared off by all the hoopla, quietly eliminated by means of natural or accidental death, or incarcerated for a different crime and currently doing time.

Everyone had their opinion, including Wyatt. "I think he just saw the light."

The marshal laughed. "And what light would that be? The sunshine coming out of your backside?"

"The light of God, you godforsaken heretic. I think the fella saw the error of his evil ways and has repented.

Melted back into the general populous from whence he came."

"And you base this judgment on…?"

"The moralizing that underlies his reasons for killing. Straight from the Good Book. Eye for an eye and all that crap. The fella must be a Bible thumper to frame murder in such an ethical manner. I believe a good man can only kill so much before it starts to rot his soul. Why do you think I quit peacekeeping?"

"Because saloons are much more lucrative?"

"Go ahead and mock. But it's a far sight better than anybody else's theory about why our assassin has vanished."

"He doesn't even exist!" Cradoc shot back. "That's what I keep telling you and everyone else. Nick made him up. He took two entirely different and unrelated murders and concocted the 'story of the century' by creating an imaginary assassin."

"That flies in the face of your own evidence."

"What evidence? There's no proof this killer exists other than those damned letters. And you know as well as I, they could have been faked."

"They were made on the same typing machine. You said so yourself. And it's not one of the ones currently used at the *Times*."

"Yeah, but there's still half a dozen missing machines. Nick could have easily squirreled one away at home or in the office. Places we can't search because we could never get a warrant because we don't have probable cause."

Wyatt was willing to admit the Archer letter could easily have been a phony. After all, it had surfaced days after the crime, giving the author plenty of time to create and deliver a forgery. "But what about the second?" he mused out loud. "How in the hell did Nick manage that slight of hand?"

"He's got informants everywhere. He could have heard about the murder, arrived at the slaughterhouse before anyone else, planted the letter on that hook and skedaddled. Or he could have paid off fellas who brought in the letter to the *Times*. There's any number of logical explanations."

"Logical, but not likely," Wyatt countered. "You're talking conspiracy theories now. And not even especially plausible ones."

"And your 'divine intervention' is plausible?"

"More than any of yours!"

By now they were within eyesight of the Indian encampment, a cluster of huts fashioned from branches, driftwood, and whatever else the natives could scrounge from the surrounding terrain. Cradoc wasn't even sure who owned this land in the mesa country above San Diego. But they had filed a court complaint that had worked its way through the legal system and onto his desk—an eviction notice he was compelled to enforce.

Spying two white men on horseback coming up the canyon, the Indian kids alerted their elders, and a greeting party had formed by the time Cradoc and Wyatt reached the camp. They were Kumeyaay, three or four families by the looks of it. Filthy and dirt poor, as were most of the Indians around San Diego. They had their own land, tiny reservations scattered at the far corners of the county. But a lot of them drifted into town looking for work. Manual labor mostly—digging ditches, shoveling manure, that sort of thing. And while the local merchants and developers were more than glad to hire them for next to nothing, a lot of those same folks didn't want Indians living anywhere nearby, as if they could somehow magically disappear once the workday ended.

The marshal spoke with the elders in Spanish, the only language they had in common. But he got his message across: they had until dusk the following day to move elsewhere. Didn't matter that this particular patch of chaparral was currently unused, basically useless, and well out of sight. Whoever owned this sod didn't like Indians and wanted them gone.

They didn't put up a fuss. The Kumeyaay never did. They were harmless, which is why they were still around (unlike so many other tribes) and why they got pushed around so much. The great paradox of the American Indian: Adapt to the white man's ways or die. Cradoc felt like a heel. But it *was* his job. And if he declined, Coyne would dispatch someone else from the jailhouse to run them off the land, probably by much less gentle means, like burning down their huts or roughing up the elders.

It was a quiet ride back into town, Wyatt chewing over whatever was preying on his mind. In his roundabout way, it finally came out. "I've been burned a couple of times on card dealers," he mused. "Fellas that ran off with the bank. Nowadays, I always do a background check on anyone who wants to deal at any of my establishments."

"And what's this got to do with Indians or anything else on the planet?"

Wyatt's mustache twitched. "Emma Lee wants to be a faro dealer."

"She told me."

"Like anyone else, I checked her out. It's not like I could exclude just her."

Cradoc eyes narrowed. "I wouldn't expect you to," he said warily, wondering where Wyatt was going with this.

"I got the results back this morning. A telegram from St Louis."

"And?"

"All her ducks don't line up."

The marshal pulled his horse up. "What are you having such a goddamn hard time telling me?"

"There's a warrant for her arrest in Mississippi."

"For what?" Cradoc asked harshly.

Wyatt licked his lips, took a huge gulp. "Murder."

A thick silence formed between them, the old friends staring at one another.

"I wouldn't normally pry into the background of those you choose to fuck, but in this case, it very much is my business. She asked to deal faro at the Oyster. It would have been remiss of me *not* to check her out. And as your friend, I feel obligated to inform you of the findings. "

"It won't change how I feel about her," Cradoc growled.

"I imagine it won't," said Wyatt, thinking about his own situation, an outstanding warrant for his arrest in the Arizona Territory for the very same crime. "But the fact remains that she is wanted for murder. Giving her the benefit of the doubt, I have requested further explanation of the circumstances, which I will be more than glad to share—with you and only you—when it arrives."

Cradoc had to resist an overwhelming temptation to go for his gun. Wyatt would have beat him easy, and even if he could have drawn quicker, killing his best friend wouldn't solve a thing. "To hell with you," the marshal hissed. He jerked on the reins to turn his horse around, and tore off down the canyon.

26

NO MORE THAN two dozen faithful were in attendance at the Wednesday evening novena, most of them gray-haired widows of Irish or German extraction. Standard for this particular church, the only Roman Catholic house of worship in New Town, which unlike the old San Diego was dominated by Protestants and their various denominations.

Without wealthy patrons, the church had lapsed into a rather scruffy affair, a clapboard structure perpetually in need of fresh paint and new roof shingles. Situated amid the lumberyards and stables on the northwestern edge of town rather than the grandiose "Church Row" on the east side—and lacking a telltale steeple—St. Joseph's Church would have been easy to mistake for a boarding house or commercial establishment rather than a house of God.

The padre leading the service was similarly cursed. A once-energetic young clergyman, Father Figueroa had passed into middle age as a shadow of his former self, gradually broken down by the daily grind of managing a meager parish and the disappointment of being virtually ignored by the archbishop in Los Angeles. If drink had been his only trespass, the Gates of Heaven would no doubt have awaited this cleric. But over the years he had fallen into a much deeper abyss.

The novena drawing to a close, the padre thought he saw a familiar face at the back of the church, lingering in the shadows beside the rear doors. But when he looked again, the man had disappeared. Perhaps it was just his imagination ... or the paranoia that had come to infest him since last winter, when the priest had forged an unholy alliance with the person in question.

Spooked by the sighting—real or not—Figueroa hurried through the rest of the novena and watched the faithful shuffle out into the night. Suddenly the church was empty, no movement but the flicker of the votive candles, no sound except a scurry of rats beneath the floorboards. And that distressed him even more. Ducking into the sacristy behind the altar, he quickly exchanged his sacred vestments for a simple black cassock.

Moving through the sacristy door, Figueroa scanned the weed-filled yard between the church and the rectory. He looked right and left, and then right again, before deciding the coast was clear. Like a field mouse trying to avoid a hawk, he shot across the yard and into the priest house. Locking the door behind him, the padre fetched a lantern from the kitchen counter and methodically went from window to window, making sure they were all closed and locked before making his way to the bedroom at the back of the structure. He could now finish what he had started before the novena.

Entering the bedroom, Figueroa's lantern illuminated a young girl on the bed, her mouth gagged, her hands and feet bound to the bedposts, her body unclothed. She was

Mexican, past puberty, but perhaps not yet a teenager. The priest didn't really care what her age might be. All he knew is that she was young and virginal prior to coming to work for him as the rectory cook and cleaner.

Upon seeing the priest, she flinched and began to scream, her cries muffled by the gag. She pulled at the ties, trying her best to escape, but to little effect.

Feeling himself go hard, Father Figueroa lifted his cassock and crawled atop the girl, entering with a thrust that made her eyes bulge and her scream even louder. He had already cum inside her once, before the novena, and now set about doing it again, maybe even a third time if he could keep himself awake long enough tonight.

He thought he heard a knock at the front door, someone calling his name. Must be one of his damn parishioners—they were always pestering him for something. But it didn't last long, and Figueroa resumed sliding in and out of the young Mexican girl, nothing but the sound of bedsprings and her piteous moans as the priest labored his way to another climax. He really wished he could kiss her on the mouth. But there was no way he would take that chance again, not after one of his former "lovers" nearly tore his lower lip off with her teeth. For much the same reason, he would never let them near his manhood. He would have to content himself with intercourse. Although that did not preclude him from pretending the girl's lips (rather than her quim) were wrapped around his penis.

Without warning, the bedroom door burst open, kicked so hard it went flying off its hinges and into the adjoining wall.

Figueroa looked around, anger in his eyes, vexed that someone would interrupt his bliss. He didn't recognize the man at first, the one standing in the doorway with a bandana covering the lower half of his face.

"You son of a bitch!" was all Nemesis had to say for the padre to recognize his voice—and shift the priest from annoyance into total and absolute fear.

Extracting himself from the girl and rolling off the far side of the bed, Figueroa pulled the black cassock down to cover his genitalia. "This isn't what it looks like," he pleaded.

But it could not be anything other than the violation of a child—and the breach of an agreement that Nemesis had forged with Figueroa some months back, after discovering the priest's penchant for young flesh. For years, the padre had been luring young girls from Mexico, many of them orphans, with a promise of eternal salvation and three meals a day in return for taking care of the rectory ... and his reprehensible cravings.

Last winter, Nemesis had caught him in the act of defiling a previous housekeeper. But the priest had been quick on his feet, begging him to keep the secret in return for information about other citizens of San Diego, knowledge of heinous acts that had reached Figueroa via the confessional. When the visitor at first refused—disgusted by the depravity and determined to bring the priest to justice—Figueroa responded with a tantalizing sample of what he had to offer, murder and mayhem of such a degree that Nemesis could not ignore it.

So they made a deal—silence in return for the lowdown on other people's mortal sins and a pledge by Figueroa to refrain from young flesh.

But on the bed lay indisputable proof that the padre had contravened their pact. The girl was gagged and crying, straining at the cords that held her down. Gazing at the intruder with huge dark eyes, she silently begged for intervention, imploring him to end her misery. Having seen enough, Nemesis extracted a gun from the holster beneath his overcoat and took a menacing step toward Figueroa.

"We had an arrangement," the priest implored.

"And you broke it."

"I can tell you more! Much more!"

No doubt, Figueroa could spew more names, far more wrongdoings. But his fury ebbing, Nemesis had passed the point of no return, the ability to negotiate with such a beast. The priest could no longer be trusted—to keep his hands off children or keep the killer's own dark secrets. Among all the people of San Diego, only Figueroa knew his true identity. No one but the priest could end his quest before its projected finish. And that would just not do.

Raising the pistol, Nemesis moved around the bottom end of the bed.

Figueroa back-peddled into a corner of the bedroom, begging for mercy, pleading for one more chance to make things right, trying to strike another unholy bargain. The priest dropped to his knees, hands clasped, bawling like a coward, shivering with fear.

Nemesis thumbed back the hammer of his weapon, placed the barrel flush against Figueroa's forehead. The priest was praying now, talking to his god, eyes closed as he prepared to meet his fate—eternal damnation.

When a moment passed and nothing happened, the priest opened his eyes. Nemesis still hovered over him but the killer now seemed to be of two minds as to how to proceed.

As the barrel came away from his face, Figueroa's eyes went wide, filled with relief and the notion that he would not perish tonight. But he had badly misread the visitor's intent.

"I'm not going to shoot you," the killer declared. "You don't deserve to die that fast." And he smashed the gun into the side of Figueroa's head. Not once or twice, but several dozen times, until the padre's face was a bloody pulp and his heart no longer beating, his brain spewed across the room, the bed, and the young Mexican girl.

Shaking with adrenaline, spittle dripping from the side of his mouth, Nemesis glanced around at her. Horrified by his rage and no doubt thinking she was next, the girl resumed her frantic screams. And only then did Nemesis realize what he had done. He had broken one of his own rules of engagement, dispatched a man he had no intention of killing—*someone not on his list*—in a manner he would find most reprehensible when he took a moment to reflect.

Worst of all, he had lost control. Let emotion overwhelm his better judgment. Put himself in a position where someone besides this malevolent priest might identify him.

Thinking about how to cover his tracks, Nemesis wiped the gun on Figueroa's cassock and slipped it back into his holster. He'd burn or bury his own blood-soaked clothes before first light. The girl posed a much different problem. But what could he do? She was innocent, not part of his vengeful design.

Snatching a blanket from a bedroom chest, Nemesis covered her nakedness. He momentarily disappeared from the bedroom and returned with a mug of water from the kitchen.

As he sat on the edge of the bed and offered a drink, the girl tried to squirm away.

"No voy a dañarle," he told her. I'm not going to hurt you.

Nemesis stroked her hair like you would a troubled horse, speaking to her in her native tongue, gazing at her with compassionate eyes, trying to calm the girl, get her to believe that he meant her no harm. When she finally stopped whimpering, he removed the gag from her mouth, put the mug to her lips. She drank half the water in a single gulp, had to catch her breath before drinking again.

"No voy a dañarle," he assured her again. Nobody would harm her now. The bad man was dead.

"Dejeme ir!" she pleaded. Let me go!

It broke his heart, but he couldn't. They had to find her this way. Had to know what evil had been done to her. Know the reason for the priest's death. He gave her a last sip of water and reluctantly replaced the gag.

"Estarán aquí pronto." Somebody will be here soon.

With that, he retreated from the room, down the hallway and into the rectory office, where Nemesis went about the task that had originally brought him to the rectory so late on a Wednesday night—composing and typing the last of his letters addressed to Nick Pinder.

27

DEEP BLUE LIGHT CREPT through the windows, the first stirrings of a new day. Carefully releasing himself from Emma Lee's grasp, Cradoc rolled over on his side and stared at her. She lay sound asleep, nostrils flaring with each breath, eyelids fluttering with some untold dream, at peace with both the world around her and the man she had come to know so well over the past few months.

What the hell am I going to do with her? the marshal asked himself in the dark.

Cradoc didn't want to do anything. He liked things just the way they were, that interlude when everything about a woman is new and exciting. He enjoyed her mind, the natural curiosity she seemed to have about nearly everything in life, and her determination to become more erudite by reading books or simply asking questions. He cherished her effervescent personality, the way she could brighten up a room just by walking into it and make him smile even when she found him in the foulest temper. And of course, he relished their sensual moments, her ability to pleasure him in ways he had never even known about.

There was absolutely no reason to upset the boat … other than the fact that she had apparently murdered someone. No further information had arrived from Wyatt's investigator in St Louis. And until such time as it did, Cradoc would not confront her. Maybe even then, he would keep things to himself.

Leaving her to sleep, he quietly arose and dressed. In the kitchen, stoking the potbelly stove to life so he could brew some coffee, he heard footsteps approaching on the catwalk outside and then a knock on the front door. "Bradshaw!" someone yelled from the other side of the wood.

Cradoc immediately recognized the voice as Joe Coyne. Stumbling through the dark, he jerked open the door. "What in the Dickens are you doing out at this hour?"

"Looking for you," the sheriff replied, spitting a wad of tobacco into the bay. "Figueroa is dead. Most likely murdered."

"The priest?"

"None other. Someone attacked him at the rectory, beat him to a bloody stump. You'd hardly know it was him. A young Mexican girl was found with his body."

"Found how?"

"In his bed. Disrobed beneath a blanket. As much as this pains me to say given the faith of my birth, one is left with the rather unsavory conclusion that Figueroa was buggering her."

"Sounds like self-defense. You don't need me."

"The girl didn't kill him. She was bound hand and foot. And gagged, too. There's no way she could have done it herself."

"Christ almighty," Cradoc mumbled. "Hold on. Let me throw on some clothes."

†

St Joseph's Church was just up from the waterfront, no more than a 10-minute walk from Cradoc's abode. Fatty Rice was stationed at the rectory door, a couple of other deputies posted around the churchyard. An hour from dawn, the sky remained dark. No curious onlookers or odious reporters. The town had not yet been aroused to the homicide.

The scene in the bedroom was enough to make you retch. Blood and brain matter was scattered about—across the plaster walls, the wooden floor, and even the ceiling, covering the bedside table, window curtains, and bedding—except for a spread-eagle form on the mattress, where the Mexican girl had been tied down.

Figueroa's body slumped in a corner, curled into a fetal position and clad in an ankle-length black cassock, the face swollen to twice normal size and cleaved by dozens of gashes, any of which could have been the fatal blow.

"Obviously a blunt object," Coyne mused out loud. "What do you figure?"

"I've seen these kinds of wounds before," Cradoc answered. He removed his own Colt, held it up to the dead man's face. "He was hit like this ...." He demonstrated the downward hacking motion. "Again and again and again. The cylinder smashed his cheek. The butt caused the deep cuts along the side of his head. No doubt about it—pistol whipped."

And that, in itself, provided a clue to the crime. Plugging somebody with a six-shooter was no big deal. Just aim and pull the trigger. On the other hand, pistol whipping (like knife fighting) was a much more personal way of killing someone. An act of passion or hate rather than cold-hearted need. Whoever dispatched the priest had despised the man to the point where it wasn't just necessary to kill him but to utterly destroy him in the process.

"Who would do such a thing?" Coyne exclaimed.

"Someone who didn't like what he was getting up to."

"But a priest, for God's sake?"

Cradoc flicked his eyes towards the bed, the bloody outline of the young girl. "Sooner or later we're all sinners."

Coyne shook his head in disgust. He might have been a fallen Catholic, but he was Catholic all the same. And Irish to boot. You just didn't murder a priest, no matter what transgressions the padre may have committed.

The marshal was already running a scenario through his mind. "So somebody barges in on the padre and his young victim, beats him to death, but leaves without releasing the girl. Is it only me who finds that odd?"

"No," Coyne muttered.

The marshal thought a moment. "Anything stolen?"

"Not that I can tell. The collection box had money in it. Not a lot, mind you. But this ain't exactly a rich parish. The gold chalice is still in the church and it doesn't look like anything's been taken."

Thinking out loud, Cradoc continued. "If the killer knew the girl, he would have released her. He wouldn't have left her like this for strangers to find. Don't you think?"

"One supposes."

"But that eliminates the most obvious motive for some-one coming here and killing the priest. Leaving us with shit-all in terms of motive."

"You don't think it was ..." The sheriff's voice trailed off.

"What? That this is the work of our letter-writing friend?" Like some kind of curse, neither one of them wanted to say the name Nemesis out loud. Cradoc shook his head. "I wouldn't totally discount the possibility. But it doesn't have the right feel."

The sheriff begged to differ. "The brutal murder of a well-known person with a sizable skeleton in his closet— sounds like our friend to me."

But Cradoc noticed several disparities. "This looks spur of the moment rather than meticulously planned. That's not his modus operandi. Not to mention the fact there's a witness, somebody who might be able to identify the killer. Which reminds me—where's the girl?"

"I had Cota take her up to my place for safekeeping. Doc LeFevre is on his way to take a look at her. She's in a bad way, barely able to talk."

"Cota get any kind of take on the killer?"

"Nothing more than the fact that he was white—not Mexican or Indian. He was wearing a bandana, so she didn't get a good look at his face."

"It's a start," said Cradoc, scanning the room, looking for anything that might reveal how the crime played out. He noticed bloody boot prints on the floor between the bed and wall, figured that might be important, until closer inspection determined they were overlapping prints from several different shoes—most likely from his own deputies gawking at the corpse. God, they never learned.

Out on the front porch, he confronted Fatty Rice. The marshal nearly scolded the deputy for spoiling yet *another* crime scene, but figured it was a lost cause. Instead, he asked Fatty how they'd found out about the killing.

"Telephone," the deputy told him. Fatty had actually taken the call. Male voice. No discernible accent. And very sparse with his words: a single sentence informing that Father Figueroa was dead inside the priest house.

Cradoc moved back inside, down the hall, and into the rectory office, where he found a telephone perched on the wall. Cranking the machine to life, he summoned the graveyard shift operator at the central switchboard. "Miss, this is Marshal Bradshaw ... Yes, *the* Marshall Bradshaw ... A telephone call was made to the jailhouse about two hours ago. I need to know where that call was made, where it came from. Do you have any way to tell?"

As a matter of fact, she did. The call came from the instrument in Cradoc's hand at that very moment. The rectory telephone. Figueroa's killer had reported the crime himself. Talk about ballsy. That meant the killer had been in the very office where Cradoc was now standing. The marshal found a lantern, struck a match, held it up to examine the room. Desk ... bookshelf ... typewriter ... Wait. *What?*

He moved the flickering light back toward the typing machine. Taking a step closer, the marshal just about pissed himself. A nameplate glistened in the light— Sholes & Glidden. "Son of a bitch," he whispered. Cradoc ran a finger across the carriage wondering if the killer's fingers had touched the keys. Placing the lantern to one side, he flipped the typewriter upside down, found the serial number. Indeed, it was one of the missing Sholes, a machine from George Marston's list. Whether it was *the* machine, the one that Nemesis used, there was only one way to find out.

The marshal scrounged around the office for a piece of paper. And when he couldn't find anything blank, he used the back of an old Sunday sermon the priest had most likely typed himself. Cradoc rendered each and every letter, working his way through the entire alphabet. Even in the dim light he could see they were lacking "little feet." It was the correct font. But that didn't prove a damn thing.

Folding the paper neatly in three, the marshal tucked it inside his duster and slipped out the front door. He thought about going to see the girl, the one who'd been defiled by Figueroa. But that could wait. This was far more important.

Walking at a brisk pace, his heart pounding so hard his chest was heaving, Cradoc made his way to the jailhouse. Sitting at his desk, he placed one of the original Nemesis letters and the rectory sample side-by-side, carefully compared them with a magnifying glass. It wasn't until Cradoc reached the letter "E" that he knew for sure. Both versions tilted slightly to the left at precisely the same angle. And not only that, they bore similar nicks and scratches. And then he examined the letter M. He sat back and let out a soft whistle. Without a doubt, the rectory typewriter matched the Nemesis correspondence.

28

CRADOC MADE STRAIGHT for the Oyster Bar. A "CLOSED" sign hung in the window and the doors were bolted. The only person he could see through the big front windows was a Mexican kid mopping the floor behind the counter. He stood for a moment on the boardwalk, wondering if he dared wake the Earps an hour before dawn. And having convinced himself that he should, the marshal turned heel and made for Burns Boarding House on Third Street.

Eliza Burns, the proprietress, was just getting breakfast together in the dining room. Cradoc tipped his hat to her as he cruised through the foyer and upstairs to the second floor, where the Earps rented a suite of rooms. His pounding was met by Josie in a silk kimono, book in hand, not a trace of sleep in her big, dark eyes. No need to ask: she had evidently been awake for hours, reading.

"Cradoc!" she blurted out, unable to contain her surprise. He rarely visited their quarters, and certainly not as such an early hour.

"Is Wyatt awake?"

"I wouldn't think so, but do come in. I'm sure he'll be delighted to see you," she said, half sarcastically. Wyatt did cherish his shut-eye.

Cradoc waited in the parlor while Josie ducked into the adjacent bedroom. "Honey," he could hear her say. "You have a visitor."

After a suitable amount of grumbling, Wyatt appeared at the bedroom door, clad in a faded red union suit, scratching an itch in his crotch that didn't seem to want to go away. "This better be good," he groused and wiped the sleep from his eyes with his other hand.

With Wyatt still in his skivvies, they grabbed coffee in the boarding house kitchen and sat at the dining room table, lit by a single kerosene lamp. Cradoc gave him the short form: Father Figueroa pistol-whipped to death in the process of molesting a young Mexican girl who apparently witnessed the crime ... the killer using the priest's own telephone to alert the jailhouse. "And get a load of this—" He reached inside his coat and withdrew two neatly folded sheets of paper and spread them on the table.

Wyatt immediately recognized the document on the left as a Nemesis letter. The document on the right bore a typed rendition of the Roman alphabet in the same font as the Nemesis correspondence.

"Yeah, so?" asked Wyatt, not immediately catching on.

The marshal stabbed a finger on the letter. "*This* is Nemesis." And moved his hand across to the alphabet. "*This* is the Sholes & Glidden typewriter in the rectory at St Joseph's."

Wyatt's eyebrows arched. "Are you sure?"

"The Es are an exact match and so are the tiny fissures in the left leg of the letter M. As are several other letters.

I'll get a second opinion from Marston, but I'm ninety-nine percent certain that each and every Nemesis letter was typed on the rectory machine."

"You don't think ..." Wyatt's voice trailed off.

"That Figueroa was Nemesis?" Cradoc shook his head. Back in the day, when he'd been involved with Roz, she had taken him to Mass on several occasions at St Joseph's. Many other times, the marshal had seen Figueroa around town. The padre was slight of build and meek of manner, didn't seem to have the physical strength or mental fortitude to carry out kills of the Nemesis variety, let alone ordinary homicide. "I'm not saying it's impossible. Just highly unlikely."

"If he was shaggin' some Mexican kid, the old padre was already well on his way to Hades. So why not brutal murder, too?"

Cradoc begged to differ. "There's a huge leap from fornication—no matter how deviant and disgusting—to cold-blooded murder."

"Eye for an eye—straight from the Bible. Isn't that what Nemesis is all about? And Figueroa had the typewriter, for God's sake. That's enough to convict him right there."

"Then who killed *him*? And why?" asked Cradoc.

Wyatt shrugged. "I don't know. Maybe some upstanding citizen who discovered his secret identity and—taking a page from the good book of Nemesis—decided to take matters into his own hands. Did the girl get a look at the priest killer?"

"Apparently not. She told Jose Cota the fella had a bandana around his face. And get this—she described the killer as '*el hombre quién mata a diablos*'."

"The man who kills devils? Now *that* sounds like Nemesis."

"For sure. But it still doesn't add up. Figueroa's murder looks like a messy, spontaneous beating rather than a carefully planned ambush."

Wyatt cottoned on at once. "So if Nemesis did kill the priest—"

"I'm not saying Nemesis didn't do it. I'm just saying it wasn't premeditated. Something went wrong. The killer was thrown off his game. This very well could be the mistake we've been waiting for."

The marshal had expected Wyatt to be more ecstatic. This was huge news, the biggest break they'd had in the Nemesis case. But his old friend seemed either unconvinced or less than thrilled. After a moment of silence, Cradoc finally asked, "You don't agree?"

"It's not that."

"Then what's eatin' you?"

"I got another cable ... from my source in St Louis."

Cradoc didn't say a word, just gave him a look.

"I'm not sure this is the best time," Wyatt cautioned.

"Just tell me, for God's sake. Who'd she kill?"

Wyatt blew a gust of air between his lips. "Her husband."

Dumbstruck by the revelation, it took Cradoc a few moments to respond. "No mistake?"

"Not according to my source. The details seem to be fairly well known. She knifed him in a riverboat cabin while he was sleeping." Wyatt ran a finger across his neck. "Took all his money and jumped ship in Vicksburg."

"When did all this happen?" Must have been years ago, Cradoc was thinking.

Wyatt tugged at the end of his mustache before answering. "Right before she came to San Diego."

29

THE POSTMAN CALLED on the Pinder home in the late morning on a government mule laden with heavy leather mailbags. In an effort to make his rounds a tad bit faster, residents of outlying areas had been asked to construct a receptacle of some sort where the road passed their property.

Lupe always kept an eye out for the postman and went to fetch the mail from a tin bucket that Nick had nailed to a fence post about a hundred yards down the path from the house. Retrieving the most recent batch, Lupe took it around the back of the house to Roz, fussing over some recently planted carrots in the vegetable garden.

Leaning back on her haunches, Roz used a sleeve to wipe the sweat from her brow and examined the only letter delivered that day. Nick's name and address neatly typed in a font that she recognized, she knew the sender at once. Her first impulse was tossing the letter into the kitchen stove and swearing Lupe to secrecy. Whatever that envelope contained would no doubt derail the progress that she and Nick had made in their relationship over the past few weeks. If Nick did not read the contents, never knew of its arrival, the better for both of them.

But if the letter really was what Roz assumed it to be—another missive from the killer—there would be consequences even if she burned it. Nemesis would find another means of reaching out to her husband. Not to mention the drama if Nick ever discovered that she had purposely destroyed such a crucial correspondence.

Brushing the soil from her apron, Roz asked Lupe to saddle up a horse while she changed into riding clothes. Nick would have to make the decision himself, whether or not to initiate contact again with this maniac. He must be the gatekeeper, not her.

†

Nick and Clive were hovering over page proofs in the newsroom when Roz suddenly appeared at the front desk.

"You miss another lunch date?" Clive chided Nick.

"I don't think so," Nick answered, going to greet his wife. "What a pleasant surprise," he beamed. But her grim expression told him that something wasn't right. "What is it?"

"Can I speak to you and Clive alone?" she asked.

In the privacy of the editor's office, Roz removed the letter from up a sleeve and passed it to her husband. Nick's eyebrows arched in immediate recognition. He had to suppress a smile, struggling to contain his own glee.

Clive also recognized the envelope. "Did he kill again?" he asked hopefully.

"I wouldn't know," Roz said sourly, resigned to another change in their fate. "It's still sealed."

"Well, bloody well open it!" the boss shouted, sliding an ivory-handled letter opener across his desk.

Nick slit the envelope and shook out the contents: A single sheet of the same high-grade stationery that Nemesis had used for his previous letters. Nick took a deep breath, began to read out loud:

Dear Mr. Pinder:

I hope this finds you well. Some time has passed since our last correspondence, but I wanted to assure you that I have not 'run for the hills' as one of your competitors in San Diego journalism has so crudely suggested. Rather, I have been biding my time and waiting for an opportune moment to continue my work.

Nick looked up at Clive and then around at Roz. Nemesis was *not* finished; he would strike again.

In the meantime, I thought it might be useful to more fully articulate my motives and intentions via a completely different means. I would like to propose a dialogue in which you ask the questions and I furnish the answers. Please feel free to publish the queries, at your convenience, in the newspaper. I will gladly render the answers and post them back to you in short order . . .

Clive smacked the desk with the flat of his hand. "Bloody brilliant! Why didn't I think of that?"

"Can we make tomorrow's paper?" Nick asked quickly.

"Let's double check downstairs."

Roz couldn't believe her ears. "You're not seriously going to consider this?" She normally refrained from offering advice on her husband's career. In the end, Nick always did what he wanted, almost always contrary to what she recommended. But this was different.

"Why wouldn't we?" Clive said, truly mystified.

"You were already treading on thin ice publishing his previous letters. But this definitely crosses a line into something that most people—including most of your readers—would find morally reprehensible."

"But still not illegal," Clive pointed out.

"You know as well as I that something can be fully legal and utterly immoral all at once. I need mention nothing more than slavery."

"*Slavery?* Oh please—" Nick blurted and immediately regretted it. Because he now saw something in her eyes that had never been there before, a loathing so strong he had to avert his own gaze.

"Perhaps you're blind to the resemblance, but I'm certainly not. Human bondage and this perverse thing you call journalism both profit from the suffering of others."

"Nobody suffers from publishing these stories."

"How do you know?" she shot back. "How do you know that Nemesis wouldn't have become discouraged and vanished after the first killing if you hadn't paid him so much attention, given him a platform to spout his deranged rhetoric? Yankee Jim might still be alive, and God only knows how many people in the future. And don't get me started on the fact that Nemesis is dangerous—and could be deadly—even to those such as yourselves who feel immune to his fury."

"The bloke wouldn't touch a hair on Nick's head," Clive countered. "One never kills the messenger."

"That's absolute rubbish!" Roz howled. "There are plenty of other people the killer could exploit if something happened to Nick." And then she turned to her husband. "So don't think yourself so damn exceptional. You're just like any other tool—easily disposable, easily replaceable."

"No disrespect, dear. But I agree with Clive. I don't find Nemesis a threat, at least not to me."

There was something eerie—or totally foolhardy—in his confidence. Roz took him by the shoulders, gazed straight into his eyes, and said, "Listen to me! For once in your life *think* instead of just diving in. I love you. I don't want to see you hurt. And instinct tells me this is going to end badly. From the bottom of my heart, discontinue your dealings with this madman. And please, *please*, don't raise it another notch."

"Darling, I fully understand your feelings, but—"

Roz could tell by his tone that Nick clearly did not understand, that her words and emotion were not enough to dissuade him from the foolhardy path he seemed determined to follow. "Then bloody well get yourself killed or thrown in jail!" she shrieked. "*I've* had enough!" Slamming Clive's door with enough force to make the walls quiver, Roz fled across the newsroom and out onto the street before anyone could see her cry.

Nick stared at the back of the door, wondering if he had finally gone too far, pushed his wife beyond the point of no return.

"She'll get over it," said Clive, lighting a cigar. "She always does."

But Nick had doubts this time.

30

WYATT HAD SET ASIDE a few small rooms at the back of the Oyster Bar for high rollers, private salons where they could eat, drink, relax, and maybe even snooze between turns at the faro and poker tables. On this particular night, he had reserved one of them for a much different purpose—poring over Nick's question-and-answer interview with the killer and comparing the content with all the other evidence thus far gathered in the Nemesis affair.

Only the leads on the investigation—Bradshaw, Coyne, and Earp—had been invited to the conclave, and in order to keep whatever they might discover from leaking to the press or public, they had decided to assemble at a location away from the courts or jailhouse. Frankly, they no longer trusted anyone outside their own small inner circle from trying to make a buck off the Nemesis case. Most of the deputies would gladly pocket a little coin in return for divulging salacious details of their investigation to the other Nick Pinders of the world.

Cradoc breezed in around eight o'clock, grabbed a drink at the bar, and joined Wyatt in the back room. "Coyne's gonna be little late," the marshal announced, taking a seat on the opposite side of the table from his long-time friend.

"Late for suds and grub? Oh my!" said Wyatt with mock despair.

"Kendall wanted an update on the investigation. And he wanted it *now*."

"When are y'all gonna stop kissing his ass?" Wyatt asked. "He's not even an elected official."

"Yeah, but he's got all the duly elected in his pocket. And giving him the lowdown on a regular basis keeps at least one of the local papers off our back."

Wyatt took a long, slow sip from his coffee mug, all the while staring at Cradoc.

"And there's a reason you're eyeballing me?" the marshal asked.

"As long as it's just the two of us …"

"What?"

"There's something I've been meaning to get off my chest."

Cradoc sighed, rolled his eyes. "*Not* Emma Lee again."

"Far from it," Wyatt answered.

"What else would make you so goddamn brassy when it comes to my business?"

Wyatt hesitated, wondering if he should even broach the topic. "Now don't take this wrong …"

"Just spit it out!"

"I've been wondering for a while now …"

"What?"

"How do I phrase this delicately …?" Wyatt blew air through his lips as a sign of surrender, looked his friend straight in the face and asked, "Are you Nemesis?"

Flabbergasted by the very suggestion, Cradoc didn't know how to respond at first. And Wyatt construed that silence as possibly an admission of guilt. "I knew it ... I knew it ... I just knew it!" Wyatt yelped, pounding a fist into the palm of his hand.

"Have you lost your friggin' mind?" Cradoc finally asked.

"You're not denying it."

"Because I can't believe you would even think such an outlandish thing."

"Come on, Cradoc. You're all about justice. That's why you left the Army—because the big bugs in Washington wouldn't accept your findings in the Custer investigation. They wanted to portray him as a great American hero who died for his country fighting the savages rather than a reckless commander who got his troops slaughtered. You and me ... we didn't hesitate going above and beyond the law to take down bad guys in Dodge City because we figured the end result justified our means. And you're the one who told me about how many times you and Nick purposely stepped outside the law to catch criminals during your bosom buddy days."

Cradoc scoffed at the notion. "You really think Nick and I are in cahoots again? No more bad blood, no more hard feelings. Everything that happened just water under the bridge. And that we somehow concocted this grand scheme—that revolves around an imaginary killer named Nemesis—to catch fellas who had somehow evaded justice for evil deeds done long ago."

Wyatt leaned forward. "It's not *that* far-fetched. Given your history. Both you and Nick."

"Coming from the mouth of a man who's wanted—

dead or alive—in the Arizona Territory because of his own vigilantism."

"Of course! I'm right there with you, brother. I'm just sore you two didn't let me in on the conspiracy."

"There is no goddamn conspiracy!" Cradoc shot back.

"You can tell me, Cradoc. You know I can keep a secret."

"If I was going rogue, don't you think you're the first person I tell? That you're the one I'd conspire with rather than Nick?"

Wyatt shook his head. "I don't know … you and Nick. I think you still got a hard-on for one another you're just not willing to admit. Not only to me, but also to yourselves."

Cradoc was in the middle of flinging his beer mug at Wyatt when the door swung open and Joe Coyne came rushing into the room. Wyatt ducked quick enough to evade the flying mug, which smashed into the wall behind him.

"Did I miss something?" asked Coyne, turning to stare at the spot where the mug hit the wall.

"Just horsing around," Wyatt said quickly, brushing the broken glass off his shoulders.

Coyne looked to the marshal for confirmation.

Cradoc shrugged and flashed a tight smile. "Boys will be boys."

†

Joe Coyne was not above reproach when it came to leveraging his position at the jailhouse for extra cash. But the sheriff was also aware that any short-term financial gain was far outweighed by the prospect of losing his job if the case remained unsolved—and especially if the killer kept dispatching prominent citizens. And while they may have had their "operational" differences over the nuts and bolts of solving the crime, he knew Cradoc still valued the sheriff's perspective. Coyne may have grown overweight, over cautious, and avaricious after so many years with a badge, but his logic was still faultless and his intuition invaluable.

The ground rules for this evening of brainstorming were simple: no idea would be discounted no matter how rash or seemingly irrelevant. They would pool their hunches, rack their brains, and hopefully—by midnight or even dawn if that's what it took—discover some clue, some link that had been previously overlooked, even the thinnest shred of evidence that could lead them to the killer.

Their first task was re-examining what just about everyone around town was now calling the "Nemesis Manifesto"—the killer's carefully crafted answers to the questions put forth by the *Times*. Several days after its publication, the shock had by now worn off. It was not so much what Nemesis had to say—much of it the ramblings of a lunatic, albeit a very well-educated lunatic—but the fact that the newspaper had entered into a back-and-forth dialogue with an assassin who was still on the loose, and apparently bent on killing again. There had been a swift backlash from local political and religious leaders. But whatever downside that might engender was offset by the fact the *Times* had set yet another circulation record. Unseemly as it might be, the people of San Diego just couldn't get enough. And as Clive had predicted, there wasn't a damn thing the authorities could do about it.

Cradoc had already determined that the manifesto had been rendered by the same typing machine as the killer's previous missives. Franked at the main post office in San

Diego on the 23rd of July, the envelope bore no return address, handwriting or other markings that might have disclosed even a miniscule hint as what the killer's identity might be.

Between the newspaper version and the original letter delivered (once again) by Wendell Smith, Cradoc had read the transcript at least a dozen times and in the process put together a loose profile of the killer based on his opinions, themes, and vocabulary during the question and answer session. Knowing that he was perfectly capable of missing something that might be vital, the marshal had suggested they go through the answers one more time, line by line, in the hope that Wyatt or Coyne might notice something he had missed.

"This son of a bitch is all over the map," the marshal declared as they got down to business. "He talks about religion, he talks about politics, he talks about what's inside his own head. You can't tell if he's the messiah, a savant, or merely your standard-issue nut case."

"Maybe all three rolled into one," said Wyatt, tossing in his two cents.

It was difficult to assess the killer's language as belonging to one particular group or another. After the Archer killing, nearly everyone (but Cradoc) had assumed the felon was Chinese. Yet in retrospect, it was now clear that his speech was almost devoid of ethnic or regional mannerisms. Every phrase could pass for the standard English spoken anywhere in the thirty-eight states.

Yet there had been a definite evolution in his tone. In the first correspondence with Nick, the killer's manner had been deadly earnest, almost bland. He had stuck to the matter at hand—the murder of Zebulon Archer and his motives for doing such. And while not exactly curt, the writing in that initial missive was Spartan, nothing more than the bare bones.

After the murder of Yankee Jim, the killer seemed more confident and relaxed. More like a seasoned professional—both at murder and composition. Here and there he dared to be brazen. And the meticulous side of his personality came into full bloom. Even more intriguing were his analogies, the examples used to justify his behavior. The interview—if one could call it such, given the fact that it had been done remotely—was another thing altogether, more like a philosophical lecture rendered by someone who considered themselves one of the great minds of our time.

Cradoc read a passage out loud:

"Those who so vehemently condemn my actions hail from government and law enforcement—the institutions most responsible for the lack of justice I strive to remedy. I haven't heard one ordinary citizen demand that I be stopped. Quite the contrary. For whatever reason—their own sense of justice or revenge or simply bloodlust—they condone every step that I've made thus far ... There must be rules and regulations to maintain order in society. But likewise, there must be an alternative means to contend with evil that is protected, condoned, or even spawned by the powers that be. Lacking any other options, I am that alternative means."

"Maybe he's a teacher," Wyatt offered. "Someone from one of the local schools. It's not like your general populous is going to reflect in such a sophisticated manner."

"Or it's all bullshit," Cradoc countered. "I've come across more than one drunken bum with an ability to shovel this sort of intellectual crap."

"Point taken. But our man is no dolt," said Wyatt, reiterating his original point. "You've gotta give him that. He's committed two murders without giving us so much as a whiff as to who he might be."

"He's bright all right," said Joe Coyne, finally joining the conversation. "Not so much because of what he says, but what he does. This fella is like no criminal I've ever come across before. He hasn't made even a paltry mistake. And I have the suspicion that what we know about him thus far is exactly what he wants us to know."

Hands clasped behind his head, Cradoc let out a long breath. "Other than his smarts, which we sort of already suspected, does the interview get us anywhere closer to identifying this fella?"

Wyatt took in a deep breath and then exhaled slowly. "Not really. But I'm starting to suspect the whole affair is a lot more personal than our killer is letting on." Reaching across the table for the transcript, Wyatt recited one particular passage: *"Like any man, I fear the hangman's rope. But even more so I fear defeat—which is what capture would mean to me—defeat of my ideals and all the careful planning and hard work that I have put into this quest since its inception.* He doesn't mind getting caught or even hanging as long as he kills everyone he has set out to destroy. For someone to be that determined...."

Cradoc picked up the drift. "It has to be *very* personal. I fully agree. There has to be something else. Something he's not telling us. Another way to connect the victims other than the fact they both caused the death of innocent people."

Josie Earp entered with a platter of food—grilled steaks, baked sweet potatoes, lima beans, and bread—which she placed in the middle of the table amongst all their notes and documents. Wyatt and Coyne tore through their grub like famished animals; Cradoc poked at his plate with a fork, mulling over every detail of the case with every bite.

Next, they turned their attention to the victims and what could be deduced from their circumstances. Both were white, male, and roughly the same age (in their fifties). Yet beyond community picnics and other general gatherings, the two victims had moved in different social circles. Archer was part of the establishment, the Cuyamaca Club crowd; Yankee Jim had largely kept to family and friends on the haciendas of North County. Archer had been a Baptist, Ingraham not much of anything when it came to religion. Likewise, their politics diverged: Archer a Confederate sympathizer and dedicated Democrat; Ingraham a Republican from way back and most definitely a Union man.

Yet the victims did have two things in common: both had benefited from the demise of Old Town and the controversial shift to New Town. And both had taken human life and somehow avoided punishment for those transgressions.

"We know from our own investigating," said Cradoc, "that the criminal acts Nemesis ascribes to his victims did take place. Both Archer and Ingraham got away with murder. So he can claim a certain righteousness."

"But seriously," said Coyne, pushing his empty plate aside and shoving a wad of chew into his cheek. "How virtuous can this fella be? A bonafide moralist doesn't run around drowning and suffocating people. Doesn't that make him just as evil?"

"A lot of folks say the same about the death penalty," Wyatt pointed out. "That hanging contradicts the Good

Book—'Thou Shalt Not Kill'—every bit as much as the crime that sent that person to the gallows. Especially for things like horse theft or rustling."

"We don't hang animal thieves around here," Coyne said defensively.

"They do in Texas!" Wyatt spat back. "You look the wrong way at some joker down there and you'll find yourself strung up."

"What if he really does have a deep sense of justice," Cradoc mused, "and doesn't see a moral contradiction between his own actions and the actions of those he's killed?"

"Then I'd say he's certifiably insane," Coyne declared.

"Or incredibly empathic and compassionate," the marshal retorted. "With a compelling need to protect those who cannot protect themselves."

"And then blab about it to the whole goldarn world," Wyatt added.

"That's one of the things I just don't get," said Coyne. "If justice is your only motive, just kill the bastards with as little fuss as possible rather than splashing it all over the papers."

"Because he's clearly got *other* motivations," Cradoc added. "He craves attention or affection. Not just from those around him but the entire community."

"Isn't there a name for that?" asked Wyatt.

"Megalomaniac," Cradoc said.

"I was thinking more like *politician*."

And they all laughed, a bit of mirth in amongst the earnestness.

"But like a politician," Cradoc continued, "perhaps his jabbering to Nick is a means to seek approval for his thoughts and deeds."

"You're assuming that Nemesis has a conscience," the sheriff observed.

"We don't have any reason to think he doesn't," Cradoc suggested. "He could easily be of two minds about what he does. The men I've been forced to shoot in the line of duty—I knew it was a just and righteous action. But that didn't mean I felt great about it or that I didn't want to hear other people tell me it was the right thing to do."

"You had the law on your side," Wyatt declared. "In each and every one of those cases."

"In his warped mind, Nemesis also thinks the law is on his side. A higher law. As well as public opinion."

Coyne scratched his scalp, confused about something. "So what you're saying is that by talking to Nick, Nemesis is asking the public to approve his crimes?"

"I'd bet good money on it," Cradoc answered. "Every reader becomes a part of the jury. And so far, given the overwhelmingly positive reaction by our fellow citizens, the jury is tipped in his favor. Public opinion reconfirms the virtue of his deeds, no matter how misguided or gruesome."

After several minutes of further reflection, Coyne suggested they take a short break. "I don't know about you two, but my bladder's about to burst." Pushing back from the table, the sheriff headed for the john at the back of the Oyster.

"Gotta check on the faro tables," said Wyatt, slipping out of the room behind Coyne.

Left alone, Cradoc continued to contemplate the case. *Had there been anything like this in the annals of American crime?* Multiple murder was nothing new—like the fellow in Texas who killed all those maids and the cannibal miner of the Colorado Rockies. But those affairs were nothing like what they now faced in San Diego. The Austin Axe Murderer had been a sexual predator; Alfred Packer had dispatched other prospectors in order to seize their claims and then devoured them as a matter of survival.

Nemesis was a horse of a far different color. The notion that kept coming back to Cradoc was the French Revolution. Or rather what happened right after the king was deposed—the Reign of Terror—murder as a means of transforming society into whatever happens to be your ideal of a better place to live. *Isn't that exactly what we have here?* Nemesis wasn't some common criminal with base motives. He was more like a modern Robespierre, the primary force behind France's national cleansing via the guillotine. Cradoc had always been struck by a line recited during one of his history courses at West Point, words that Robespierre had used to justify his bloodshed: *La terreur n'est autre chose que la justice prompte, sévère, inflexible.* "Terror is nothing other than prompt, severe, inflexible justice." And that pretty much defined San Diego's reign of terror—the prompt, severe, and inflexible justice meted out by Nemesis.

Robespierre would probably have endured as the head of the revolutionary government—and not lost his own head—if he had known when to quit. Given what had sparked the revolution, he surely would have got away with eliminating the French aristocracy. But when he turned to executing ordinary people for seemingly minor crimes (like food theft), the rabble turned against him. *Will Nemesis repeat that mistake? Take things one step too far?* If the killer quit right now, if he never struck again, the law would never catch him. He could live amongst the good citizens of San Diego until the day he died, and no one would ever be the wiser. No matter how dreadful the thought, Cradoc found himself hoping that Nemesis would take another victim, or at least attempt such, because that was probably the only way they were ever going to catch the bastard.

The door burst open, and Cradoc looked up, expecting to see Wyatt or Coyne returning to their summit. But what he got instead was Emma Lee charging into the room with an empty serving tray and a look of absolute shock on her face.

"I didn't know *you* was here," she blurted.

"Me and Wyatt and Sheriff Coyne. We've been going over things."

Emma Lee scooped a couple of dirty plates onto her tray. "You haven't been around much lately," she said without looking him in the face.

The marshal shrugged. "Been kinda busy."

"Too busy for me?" she said bluntly. That was her way; get right to the point.

Cradoc struggled to respond. "You know what it's like."

"No, I don't. Why don't you tell me?"

"Emma Lee …" he pleaded, hoping she would let him off the hook.

But she wouldn't. "Is there somethin' we need to discuss?"

Like why did you stab your husband? And why didn't you tell me you killed him? Two questions that Cradoc sorely would love to ask but could not bring himself to utter even now that he had the perfect chance.

"I'm a grown woman. I can take it," she told him.

Cradoc continued down the coward's road instead of manning up. "I don't know what you mean."

"Like maybe you don't wanna see me no more?" She had stopped the clearing up and was staring down at him with accusatory eyes.

Truth be told, he *did* want to keep seeing her. Splitting those luscious thighs, kissing those moist lips, and generally just hanging out with the most low-maintenance gal he had ever had the pleasure to know. The caveat being that she had murdered someone or been accused of doing so. The only way Cradoc could continue to keep her company was putting on blinders. Because delving into her past would stir up things that he just didn't want to deal with at the present time. Not with everything else happening in his life—the killer, the case, Nick Pinder, and all that crap. So Cradoc decided on the easy way out.

"How 'bout tonight?" he asked.

Emma Lee broke into a huge grin. Instantaneous joy. One of the reasons he liked this girl so much and could maybe even love her.

"Come around my place when you're done," he told her.

She cleared the rest of the table and turned around to leave as Wyatt ambled back into the room. "Excuse me, Mr. Earp," she said merrily, slipping between the boss and the door post.

Soon as she was gone, Wyatt narrowed his eyes at Cradoc. "You didn't tell her *again?*"

Cradoc cringed. He didn't want to talk about it.

"Goddamit, Cradoc. You can't keep stringing her along. She's not the kind of gal who's gonna read your mind and skedaddle on her own."

"I will," Cradoc said weakly.

"Yeah … right in the middle of when you're fucking her tonight. Put the girl out of her misery, Cradoc. It's the right and proper thing to do."

31

CRADOC BRADSHAW WOKE well before dawn, Emma Lee cradled in his arms and still sound asleep. He placed his cheek against her chest, listening to her gentle breathing, taking in her distinct aroma, a blend of powder and a little bit of perfume and the sweat from their long and furious lovemaking. A smell Cradoc had come to know so well in the last few months and that was now ingrained in his brain as eau de Emma Lee.

He rolled onto his back, stared at the ceiling, listening to the lap of waves off the wooden pilings beneath his house, and wondered what the hell he should do with this girl. Did he love her or not? And did it really matter in the greater scheme of things? Because one way or another he had to get to the bottom of what Wyatt had told him, the goings-on in Vicksburg. Not as a lawman, although that certainly factored into his conundrum, but as a human being. How does a guy lay with a woman night after night, how does a fellow come to trust his lover implicitly, knowing that she slit the throat of the last man who did so?

Ah, but let us not forget the word "alleged." Because no

matter what Wyatt had learned from his source in St Louis, and no matter what the warrant for her arrest might state, Emma Lee was still presumed innocent in the eyes of the law. Cradoc knew as well as anyone that facts can often be wrong, people falsely accused and later exonerated.

But still....

It made sense on so many levels. Why she'd come out West. Why she didn't talk much about her past. Why she was already a veteran (and *very* experienced) lover rather than an eager neophyte. There was no getting around the fact that Cradoc had not been her first. Emma Lee had been with at least one man before, presumably her husband, and perhaps even more.

Tossing the covers back, Cradoc crept out of bed, making sure not to wake her. Buck naked, he relieved himself off the back porch. He fetched some water from his cistern, stoked a fire in the potbelly stove in the kitchen, and put on some coffee to boil. Ambling back into the bedroom, he looked around and found the trousers he'd worn the night before and took another long look at his sleeping beauty.

He didn't have to blab, didn't have to say a goddamn thing. Nobody other than Wyatt would ever know. Wyatt would not condemn him. Not with all the skeletons the notorious Mr. Earp had in his own closet. They could all live happily ever after. No, Cradoc didn't have to say a thing.

But still....

I'm not like that, he thought to himself, sitting at the kitchen table, sipping his fresh cup of coffee and staring out at the bay. The rising sun hit the crest of Point Loma before anything else, reflecting off a small whitewashed object that he knew to be the old lighthouse. Where Nick had lived as a kid. Where Cradoc had spent so much time as a boy. Those really were innocent times. None of the bullshit they now faced on a daily basis. No life-changing, earth-shattering decisions like the one preying on Cradoc's mind at the moment.

And all of a sudden, there she was: Emma Lee standing in the bedroom doorway. A sheet wrapped around her voluptuous contours, not from modesty, but rather the morning chill. Looking at him with those big green eyes, inviting him back to bed without having to say, making Cradoc hard without even touching, the energy pulsing through his body.

He almost got up, nearly answered her silent, sensuous beck and call, before deciding on the spur of the moment to get it off his chest. "What happened in Vicksburg?" was all he said.

Emma Lee stared at him a long beat before answering. "Whattaya mean?"

Just by the way she said it, Cradoc knew it was true. She had killed someone. She had wielded that knife. "Come and sit," he said lightly, almost a whisper.

"Why?" she asked, her suspicion roused.

"Come and sit first," he repeated.

And she did. Pulling back a chair on the opposite side of the table, she wrapped the sheet even tighter around herself, arms across her ample bosom.

"You wanna be a faro dealer," Cradoc stated.

Emma Lee nodded. "Yes."

"And you are aware that Wyatt does a background check on all new dealers to make sure they're not thieves, cheats, or scam artists?"

"No, I didn't know."

He could see her panic rise. She had to know now. Had to know that Wyatt—and by extension Cradoc—had uncovered her secret.

"He cabled a fella in St Louis, asked him to look into your background. Wyatt does that for everyone—not just you." Cradoc waited for her to respond. And when she didn't, he continued. "The fella came across a warrant for your arrest in the state of Mississippi."

"Does it matter?"

Cradoc shrugged. "I've spent the last two hours pondering that very question."

A single tear rolled down her cheek. "It must ... or you wouldn't have asked."

There was a long silence between them, Cradoc staring into her eyes, wishing that he had kept his tongue and he was back in the bedroom working his way inside her again.

Another tear and another after that, and soon more than Cradoc could count. Rather than break down in front of her lover, Emma Lee fled. Tripping over the bottom of the sheet as she went, nearly falling as she disappeared into the bedroom.

Cradoc found her belly down on the bed, face buried in a pillow, balling like a little kid. He didn't know what to do, how to handle this aggrieved soul, this woman he had just wounded, perhaps beyond repair.

"Emma Lee," he said, but she didn't look around. He called her name again, to no effect.

"Can't you just trust me?" she finally asked.

He took a deep breath, didn't answer right away. And to the girl, that *was* his answer. She glared around at him, something awful in her eyes now. If not hate, then pretty close. "I didn't wanna spoil what we have."

"How would telling me the truth spoil things?"

"Cuz the truth ain't always what it seems."

She threw the sheet back, started to dress, but kept talking. "You asked how I survived after my grandparents died. Well, I didn't. Not really. Not in any sense you might call human. Until this riverboat gambler fella came along. He cleaned me up, fed me, gave me pretty clothes—and taught me how to pleasure him. There's no way I was going back to living like an animal again. So I did what he said. And it was fine for a while. We got married and all that. But he changed." She took a deep breath, struggling to continue. "My husband started to lose *way* more than he won at the tables. And he decided to pay off his debts by letting the winners have a go with me."

"That's why you killed him?"

She flashed him the hardest glare of all. "No. That is not why I stabbed him through the middle of the heart until he was good and dead. *This is!*"

Emma Lee whipped off her socks, the first time he had seen her naked feet. And Cradoc felt himself gasp. Half her toes were missing or mangled, and both feet were covered in circular scars made by the business end of a cigar or cigarette.

"My God," he blurted, reaching to embrace her.

But she was having none of his affection now. Emma Lee scooped up her shoes from the floor and brushed past him, barefoot as she fled out the front door.

32

CRADOC SCRIBBLED A QUICK note to Joe Coyne—he was taking the day off for unspecified "personal reasons"—and left it square in the middle of the sheriff's desk. The last time he had skipped work was July 4th, when he'd sailed Emma Lee out to that beach on the far side of Point Loma. That was only a few weeks back, but now seemed like an eternity. For the time being, the investigation into Father Figueroa's murder and the ongoing turmoil with Nemesis could wait. Cradoc had something much more pressing to deal with.

Fetching his horse from the livery, the marshal trotted over to the Oyster Bar. He looped his reins around the hitching post, took a deep breath, and mounted the boardwalk. He could see Josie Earp through the big plate-glass windows, engaged in serious elbow grease as she wiped down the counter.

As Cradoc pushed through the swinging doors, Josie looked up long enough to recognize his mug and went back to her polishing. "I'm here to see Emma Lee," he announced as he reached the bar.

"And a hearty good morning to you, too," Josie said.

Cradoc blushed. "Sorry … good morning. I didn't mean to be rude."

"You never *mean* it."

He let the comment pass, tried to get back on track for what he'd come to do. "Is Emma Lee around?"

"No," Josie said curtly.

"Any idea where she is?"

"Why? So you can have her arrested and sent for trial?"

The response took Cradoc by surprised. "So you know what she did?"

"Of course. Wyatt tells me everything. But I don't necessarily agree with my husband. Especially on this. Which you would have known if you had bothered to ask."

"You're mad at *me*? She murdered her husband for chrissake. I'm supposed to blow that off like it's no big deal?"

Josie finally looked up from her polishing. "If women wrote the laws instead of men, it would have been justifiable homicide rather than cold-blooded murder. Or maybe even self-defense. A man mutilates my body, burns me with cigarettes, you better believe I'm gonna stop him from doing it again."

"I get that," Cradoc tried to explain. "But I'm a lawman."

"Then why not arrest Wyatt? Ship him back to the Arizona Territory?"

The marshal shook his head in dismay. "You make it sound like I'm the one who's done something wrong."

"You have!" Josie snapped at him. "And you know that, too. Otherwise you wouldn't be here right now with your tail between your legs asking about the poor girl."

The marshal stared back in silence. What was he supposed to say to that? Other than admitting the truth.

He took a deep breath. "I loused up, you're right. I should have never said anything ... should have given her the benefit of the doubt. But now I wanna fix it."

"You're a little late."

"Why's that?"

"Because she gave notice, packed her things and left."

Cradoc felt himself go flush. A dozen questions shot through his mind at once. But only one word came out: "Any idea where she might have gone?"

"She didn't say, and I didn't feel inclined to ask."

"For God's sake, Josie. I've gotta find her. Tell her that I don't care what happened back east. Tell her that I—" He couldn't quite get out the two words that came next. "Tell Emma Lee how I feel about her, what she means to me."

Josie gave him a look, an I-told-you-so scowl she flashed whenever someone did something incredibly stupid and was frantically trying to reverse course. But it also presaged her helping you extract your ass from whatever sling you had managed to place it in.

She flung her apron on the counter, grabbed Cradoc by the arm like a naughty little boy and frog-marched him toward the front door. "You check the train station and the wharf," she said urgently. "I'll try a couple of boarding houses and hotels where she might have gone."

†

As Josie and the marshal were involved in their frantic search, Roz was combing the town with a much different purpose in mind—locating a shop front within her budget on a street with the right sort of traffic. The "Nemesis Manifesto" had been the final straw, Nick's insistence on going through with something she considered morally wrong and his utter disregard for her feelings and opinions in the matter. Flying in the face of convention—which required that a good wife solicit her husband's opinion and attain his approval—Roz had informed her husband over dinner the previous evening that she was moving her seamstress operation from the spare bedroom on the second floor to a shop in town. When Nick started to object, she cut him off with a supplication that if he truly loved her and cherished their union, he would revert to being the husband he once was, stop all of his nonsense post haste. His acute silence was all the answer that Roz needed. If she backed down now, Nick would continue to ride roughshod over their marriage. She had to make a statement, had to shock him into realizing that she had finally reached the tipping point in the relationship.

It took the better part of a day, but Roz eventually found the perfect spot, a vacant shop a couple of blocks down Fourth Street from the plaza. The space was huge compared to her sewing room at home, enough for a boutique with window displays, her own small office, and a "factory floor" in the back where the garments would be made. After forking over the deposit and rent for the first three months, Roz marched over to Marston's Emporium and spent the remainder of her savings on four heavy-duty sewing machines similar to the one Nick had given her. Eventually she would get around to hiring a few more seamstresses, but for the time being she was content with Lupe. Her operation was still small fry compared to dressmakers in, say, San Francisco or New York. But the business would produce enough cash flow to grant Roz at least a modicum of financial independence from Nick.

Not a lot of money, mind you. But enough to give her an important psychological boost, one more step towards liberation.

And what if Nick didn't come around? What if even this bold move didn't compel him to place their marriage ahead of his career? As a good Irish Catholic, divorce remained out of the question. That left two alternatives, neither of them optimal. She could stay with Nick and live out the rest of their days with a charade of a marriage, pretending they were still a couple. If that be the case, she would certainly sleep in a separate room. They might share the same roof, but they most certainly would not share a bed. Or she could simply say to hell with it—move out, get her own place, damn what people thought. As long as she wasn't offending God, in the great scheme of things, it didn't really matter.

No matter which path she chose, Roz was staring down the barrel of a solitary life. No male companionship. No children of her own. No sexual relations of any kind. Her lips, indeed her entire body, would never feel the touch of a man again. But Roz had always been pragmatic. If that was her lot in life, so be it. There were worse things. And the upside would more than compensate for a dearth of romance. Given Nick's inattention over the past six months, she had already abated her salacious cravings to the point where they barely existed. If nuns could live such a life, so could she.

†

Cradoc stumbled back into the Oyster Bar around midafternoon, looking as glum as could be. Josie didn't have to ask; it was written all over his face. He had not found Emma Lee. And neither had she.

"I tried all the places I thought she might go," Josie told him. "Where a lot of my other girls board. But nothing. Not even a trace."

"Did any of the other girls know anything?"

Josie shook her head woefully. "It looks like she didn't tell anyone she was quitting, let alone what she was doing after."

Reading the marshal's mind, Josie reached for his favorite tequila, set the bottle on the counter with a couple of shot glasses. Like her husband, Josie normally didn't drink. But what the hell—this was no ordinary day.

They clinked glasses and downed their shots.

"There's an awful lot of things I could tell you Cradoc Bradshaw about how and how not to treat a lady. But I imagine it's nothing you don't already know and aren't feeling at this very moment. And it certainly won't help bring her back."

"She's gotta be somewhere," Cradoc insisted.

"Yeah, but there's an awful lot of somewhere to search." She gave him a strange look, wondering if she should even broach the next topic. But it would have to be addressed at some point. "We haven't checked the cribs yet. Nor the proper houses."

Cradoc ran his hands down his face in anguish. "She wouldn't do that, Josie." And then after a short pause. "Would she?"

"For an awful lot of women, it's the only way to survive."

The marshal thought back to the first time he'd met Emma Lee—the kitchen at Cliff House on the morning after Zebulon Archer's murder. She had been quick to explain that she was *not* one of the sporting girls that Archer had hired to service his poker-playing guests. Yet desperate times call for desperate measures.

"Where do we even start?" Cradoc asked dejectedly. San Diego flaunted more than a thousand whores spread across a hundred different places of business.

"It may not be easy," Josie answered. "They don't like to talk. And if she uses a different name…."

"You've got better connections in that world than I do."

"I'll put out the word," Josie promised. "See what I can find."

33

NEMESIS HELD THE copper-colored bottle in his hand, carefully tipping it sideways so as not to distress the liquid contents. Only if you held it up to the light could you discern the line that divided fluid and air inside the opaque container. *It looks so benign*, he thought to himself. And so would anyone who came across the bottle. But in the same breath he knew the opposite to be true. Ounce per ounce, there might not be a more powerful substance on the planet.

He had considered many other weapons. A firearm seemed the most obvious. The means by which Booth had dispatched Lincoln and Guiteau had slain Garfield just a few years prior. Many others had also died by the gun. But there were obvious drawbacks. You had to be a sharpshooter or extremely close to assure yourself a reasonable chance of hitting the target. He could handle a rifle, but only at close range. And while he had become fairly proficient with a sidearm, there was considerable doubt that he could work his way close enough to this particular prey. With a long list of enemies and others who might do him harm, the man surrounded himself with hired guns both night and day. Unlike those he had previously dispatched, Nemesis would never get this man alone, not for a second. So guns were out.

Poison offered another possibility. But that was very tricky business—determining the right dosage, as well as a means to deliver the deadly matter. And it required the unwitting cooperation of other people—cooks, barmen, housekeepers, etc.—without their knowledge, of course, and without any assurance that these unsuspecting proxies would succeed in delivering a fatal amount. And innocents might inadvertently fall victim: a friend or family member, or perhaps those very same servants. A course of events that would shatter his cardinal rule—that only the guilty must be harmed in his pursuit of justice.

Then came a brilliant stroke of luck. Like so many things in life, the solution arose by happenstance. Not long after re-reading the fabled *Iliad* and *Odyssey* and thinking of the legend of the Trojan Horse, he'd come across a newspaper story about Irish rebels and the fiendish means by which they dispatched so many of their British occupiers.

In keeping with their poetic mien, the Irish called it "Fenian Fire". The name derived from an ancient Celtic warrior clan, but the weapon was dreadfully modern: white phosphorus blended with a volatile liquid called carbon disulfide. The rebels had bottled the mixture and used it to deadly effect during the Irish Republican Brotherhood bombings of the early 1880s in England. Some of those freedom fighters had later fled to America. By tracking down and corresponding with one of them—anonymously of course—he obtained the formula and method for making his own incandescent Trojan Horse.

It was an exacting task, one that could have very well taken his own life simply to produce a single bottle of the volatile liquid. After acquiring the raw materials, he found a place where he could blend them in secret. After that, he located yet another spot—far from prying eyes and ears—where he could experiment with small amounts of the substance poured into snuff bottles and thrown against a brick wall. Reasonably assured that a whiskey-sized bottle was enough to kill the man, Nemesis was ready to strike one final time, the last phase of his long-overdue revenge. The only name that remained on his list was the man who most deserved to die.

Legal scholars would have deemed it a classic criminal conspiracy. A group of men brought together for the express purpose of committing illegal or immoral acts for their own advancement. This individual, this final target, had been the brains behind it all. Unlike the others, he had not been present for the actual crime. But no matter. He had hatched the plot and set in motion the chain of events that indelibly changed the course of his own life, and by extension the lives of so many others in San Diego.

The conspirators had all prospered from their actions that night, but none so much as their de facto leader, a man who now grasped for even more power. Nemesis welcomed his entry into the public arena, because it provided an ideal venue to launch his final attack. This has nothing to do with political parties, partisans, or philosophies. It's about unmitigated greed and unconscionable cruelty, reckless disregard for human life, and total lack of remorse for the lives extinguished and the families destroyed. After the fact, he would strive to make that perfectly clear—this quest was personal, not political.

Everything was falling into place nicely. His would-be victim had already handed him the perfect time and place to strike with such a modern weapon. His popularity with the masses had been revived by the recent manifesto. And it appeared that local law enforcement still had no clue as to his real identity, not even the slightest hint who might have taken the lives of Archer, Ingraham, and Figueroa.

He regretted killing Figueroa. Not because the padre didn't deserve it, but rather because of his reckless behavior in the rectory that night. He'd at least had the presence of mind to conceal his face. But even then, the attack had been dangerously spontaneous, not a part of his long-term plan, and carried out in front of a witness. Not accomplished by his normal self, but a new and unbridled force taking shape within his soul. Better to end this whole thing now than have the rage reemerge in the future in ways that even he could not imagine or control.

34

IT WAS A MONDAY, the first week of August, and Nick was lingering late at the office, trying to get his head around the half a dozen stories that Clive had thrown his way. The boss was pressing him to write about Fabian Kendall's pending run for Congress. In days gone by, Nick would have been all over this story. Yet he was still deeply distracted by the tumult in his marital life. Staring into empty space wasn't doing him or the newspaper any good. So he quietly slipped out of the back and across the alley to the stables.

In no mood to engage in small talk, Nick gave the livery manager a cursory nod and ambled to his big chestnut gelding about halfway down the barn. He removed the feedbag from around the animal's neck, gave the horse a good scratch beneath the chin. And as he always did before mounting up after a day at the office, Nick flipped back the cover of his saddlebag to deposit a copy of that day's edition of the *Times*.

The newspaper bumped against something in the bottom of the satchel. Reaching deep into the bag, Nick discovered a familiar white envelope. An equally familiar chill ran through his bones. The barn was too dark to read the letter at once, but he had no doubts whatsoever what it contained.

Nick whirled around, almost as if he expected to see someone watching him from a dark corner. There was no one, of course. Only the livery manager, sitting on a stool near the entrance, and the hands who mucked out the stalls, kept the horses fed and watered.

"Anyone strange hanging out around the livery today?" he asked the manager.

"No sir, Mr. Pinder," the manager claimed. "Not that I noticed. Someone trouble your animal?"

"The horse is fine. But someone left an item in my saddlebag. I was hoping you might be able to tell me who?"

The manager shrugged. "Sorry, Mr. Pinder."

Nick got the same answer from the stable hands. Nobody had seen anything or anyone unusual.

Rather than open the envelope on the spot, Nick hurried back to the *Times*, marching across the now-empty newsroom to Clive's office. The boss was ensconced behind his desk, editing last-minute copy for tomorrow's paper and no doubt anticipating whatever debauchery he planned for later. He casually glanced over his spectacles. "Thought you went home?"

Without a word, Nick flicked the envelope onto his desk. Clive considered the packet and frowned. "Bloody hell," was all the boss could bring himself to say at first, shaking his head in a blend of wonder and dismay.

"I found it in my saddle bag at the livery."

"Have you read it?" Clive grunted, trying to catch his breath.

"I was waiting for you."

Clive reached for his letter opener, slit the envelope up one side and tapped it on the edge of his desk to dislodge the contents—a single typewritten page. He picked it up with two hands, began to read out loud.

Dear Mr. Pinder:

I hope this finds you well. First, I would like to express my deepest gratitude for publishing my manifesto, in total I might add, without edits or comments. You have no idea how much this means to both myself and the cause of justice in San Diego. My thanks also to Mr. Bennett and his courageous statement on behalf of freedom of the press. The journalistic fraternity owes you no small amount of gratitude ..."

Nick glanced up at Clive, who bowed and rolled his hand with a flourish like an Ottoman potentate.

Meanwhile, I have chosen another matter to resolve, a very special case this time, extremely vital to both myself and the future of this fine city. In keeping with my core principles, I believe it vital to convey both the proof and grounds for my next deed to the general public. After all, education is the only means by which a society can advance ..."

Consumed by the letter and its content, neither man heard the front door swing open. Wendell Smith had gone to dinner at the chophouse down the street, and with no social life and little else to occupy his time on any given evening, he was returning to the office to pen a letter to his dear old ma. Wendell had expected the newsroom to be empty—he didn't like anyone around while writing Mother. So he was surprised to see light streaming from Clive's office.

Bending around a corner, Wendell could see Nick and Clive hunched over the boss's desk, staring at a document.

His curiosity piqued, Wendell decided on a closer look. Setting his valise on the front counter, the young reporter quietly moved across the newsroom. He slid behind the desk nearest the boss's office and listened through the open door. He could hear Clive reading from the document on his desk.

"With that in mind, you will be granted unprecedented access to the course of justice. I would like you to be there when the punishment is administered. With a photographer of your choice. Afterward, during an interview to be conducted by you and you alone, I will offer a full explanation of that person's crimes against mankind. I'm sure you won't be disappointed.

There is no gain in divulging more details at present. For reasons of security, I feel it best to keep the accused anonymous for a short while longer. I will dispatch another message shortly with details of the when, where, and who.

–Your Humble Servant, Nemesis

Clive looked up with a wild mix of emotions. He was angry and delighted and more than a tad bit leery about going through with an act the authorities were sure to deem accessory to crime at the very least. They had been given foreknowledge of a crime that had yet to be committed. Any other instance—prior to a bank heist, a train robbery, a rustling operation—Clive would have gone straight to the sheriff in an effort to stonewall the crime. But this was different. This was journalistic history in the making. And a windfall of further fame and fortune.

Nick licked his lips and scratched at the back of his neck, trying to hide his own angst. He noticed Clive staring at him, but Nick just shrugged. What was he supposed to say?

Outside, still quiet as a mouse, Wendell bent low beneath the desk. Barely able to control his breathing, he could feel a throat seizure coming on, something that hadn't happened since childhood.

Nick and Clive continued talking amongst themselves. Wendell could only hear snippets of the conversation, but even that shocked him. Clive—even without Nick's prodding—had decided they should consider the killer's extraordinary offer. But the most shocking revelation, at least from Wendell's point of view, had yet to come.

"If we do decide to go through with this," Nick stipulated, "it's me and me alone. No sharing, no partner, no double byline. Wendell doesn't get his gilded little mitts anywhere near the story this time."

"The lad's going to be sadly disappointed. Might even bid us adieu."

"All the better."

Nick had always been a pompous ass, but he had never been vicious. Not until now. Within a split second, whatever respect and regard Wendell still harbored for Pinder vanished. Pride kept him from rushing into the office and giving them both a piece of his mind. But one thing was certain: Nick would pay for his treachery. And Wendell knew at once how to accomplish that.

"Mum's the word," Clive warned as he rose from his desk. "No one should know but you and I. And I mean no one." Switching off the office light, Clive locked his door and headed across the newsroom with Nick in tow.

That's when Wendell remembered his valise. Nick and Clive would walk right past it as they headed out the front door. Wendell held his breath and peered around the side of the desk as they approached the front counter.

Nick stopped abruptly, reached for the valise. "Who's this belong to?" He didn't recall seeing it when he'd returned from the livery. Then again, he was in a hurry to find Clive and might not have even noticed. Craning his neck around, Nick scanned the dark newsroom, eyes flicking from desk to desk.

Wendell ducked as low as he could, body flush with the floor behind the desk.

"I believe it's Wendell's," Clive said glibly, not the least bit concerned. "Looks like he forgot it—again. Boy would lose his head if it wasn't screwed on."

Nick exuded an audible sigh of relief, and the two of them continued out the front door.

Wendell kept still until he could no longer hear footsteps on the stairs outside. Then he went to his own desk and sat in the dark, wondering how to employ the astonishing information that had just come his way.

35

MIDDAY AT THE *TIMES* and most everyone had gone for lunch. A young receptionist at the front desk looked almost comatose from the afternoon heat, her head on the counter and her eyes closed. The electric ceiling fans buzzed but otherwise the office had fallen into a deathly silence.

Wendell Smith sat at his desk, fidgeting even more than usual, more nervous than ever before. Several staffers had asked Wendell to join them at the beer garden, but he'd begged off with the excuse of an urgent deadline for tomorrow's paper. He had a deadline all right, but it had nothing to do with some pissant story. He needed to find the latest Nemesis letter. And find it fast.

Figuring the coast was finally clear, Wendell moved quietly across the newsroom into the boss's office. The letter wasn't amongst the documents scattered across the top of Clive's almost-always cluttered desk. The next step presented considerable risk—searching the desk drawers. That would have been impossible with Nick, because he always locked his desk, even during short trips to the water closet. But Clive had no such compulsion or paranoia.

Wendell opened the slender middle drawer and scanned the contents—nothing that even resembled a letter. In the top drawer he found a half-empty whiskey bottle and two glasses that looked as if they hadn't been washed in years. But the bottom drawer contained a metal box large enough to hold documents. It was locked—Clive wasn't quite as negligent as Wendell assumed. But then the young reporter remembered something. He pulled back the slender middle drawer again and grabbed the ring of keys sitting in a wooden tray.

Peering through the open office door, Wendell made sure the receptionist was still asleep and no one had returned from lunch before plunking himself onto Clive's chair. He removed the lockbox from the drawer and sat it on his lap. On the third key, the box opened. Wendell flipped up the lid and there it sat—the latest Nemesis letter.

He slipped the letter into his valise, closed the lockbox, placed it back into the drawer, and casually departed Clive's office. The receptionist didn't stir as he glided past the counter and down the stairs. In anticipation of his heist, Wendell had left his horse tied to a hitching post outside the *Times* rather than around the corner at the livery. He boosted himself into the saddle and took off.

†

Speed was of the essence. Wendell had to have the letter back in the lockbox by the end of lunch, before the newsroom filled up again, and especially before Clive and Nick returned to work. Moments later he was dismounting in front of the jailhouse and stumbling down the stairs into the lockup lobby.

Cradoc Bradshaw was nowhere in sight. "Is the marshal around?" he asked the deputy at the duty desk.

Big George Dow was about as vague as a man can be. "I'm not sure."

"He either is or he isn't," Wendell insisted.

"Then I guess he ain't," was the deputy's brusque reply. And while that may have been an honest answer, it was of no help to the increasingly anxious reporter.

If not at the county jail, Wendell figured the best place to find the marshal was at his home on the waterfront. Nobody answered Cradoc's front door. After five minutes of furious knocks and increasingly desperate supplications, the young reporter decided the marshal must not be home. Wracking his brain, Wendell tried to figure where he might be.

Leaving the waterfront behind, Wendell made his way to the cook wagon in front of the County Courthouse where Cradoc often dined. Not there either. Quickly running out of time and options, he could think of just one last place to look—the Oyster Bar. No longer caring if anyone spotted him, Wendell rode as fast as he could to the saloon. Through the big picture windows Wendell could see Cradoc at the bar, talking to a beautiful dark-haired lady he presumed to be Josie Earp.

Wendell couldn't just walk into the joint and announced that another Nemesis letter had arrived, and the brute was about to kill again. Not without drawing unwanted notice from other patrons and perhaps putting an end to his whole plan before it even got off the ground.

An idea occurred. Wendell galloped to the nearest cross street, hung a quick left and then another into the alley that split the block. Reaching the rear end of the Oyster, Wendell hitched his mount around a rubbish can and slipped through the saloon's rear door, where the kitchen and washroom flanked either side of a hallway. He still hadn't figured a plan, but one came together quickly. He reached into a jacket pocket, removed his reporter's notebook, and scribbled a short note which he handed to one of the scullery girls making her way toward the main room with a tray full of glasses. "Would you be kind enough to hand this to the gentleman at the bar?" he asked, including a silver dollar in the deal.

Moments later, the scullery girl placed the note on the counter in front of Cradoc Bradshaw. His heart raced with the thought that it might be a message from Emma Lee. That she had returned from wherever it was she had fled and wanted to rendezvous. Flush with anticipation and hope, he slowly unfolded the piece of paper.

Marshal Bradshaw,
If you would be kind enough to meet me in the washroom.
Yours truly,
W. Smith

"Dammit to hell." Cradoc mumbled to himself. The little turd was back. What the hell did he want now? The marshal downed the remainder of a tequila shot and slipped off his stool.

†

The door flew open and Cradoc stepped into the washroom at the back of the Oyster. The place looked vacant. "Smith, are you in here?"

One of the wooden stalls creaked open and Wendell Smith emerged, looking rather awkward. But then again, when didn't he look ungainly and out of place?

"What the hell do you want, kid?" the marshal barked.

"I thought you might like a peek at this," Wendell answered, withdrawing a white envelope from his jacket.

Cradoc gave him a dubious look. He snatched the letter from the reporter's hand, flicked it open with a snap of his wrist, and began to read. Immediately his face changed, morphing from blatant skepticism to something more like astonishment. "When did this arrive?"

"Day before yesterday," Wendell told him. "And I need to get it back—into Clive's desk—by the end of lunch."

"You stole this from Clive's office?"

"More like borrowed."

Cradoc shook his head in wonder. Maybe the kid had more balls than previously thought.

Wendell's anxiety continued to spike. "We made a deal, remember? When I came into the jailhouse with the first typing sample."

"We didn't have a deal. You made an offer," Cradoc reminded him. "Which I declined in no uncertain terms."

"No matter. You're the only one capable of doing something about this, Marshal."

True enough, Cradoc thought to himself. Still, could he trust the kid? Was this new letter the real deal or an elaborate hoax to draw him out, play him for a fool in front of the whole town? He wouldn't put it past Clive to concoct something so deviously clever.

Even more troubling was the lack of time. Smith was pressing him for an answer now, which meant that Cradoc wouldn't have a chance to double-check the letter's authenticity against the older Nemesis letters and typing machine samples. He could tell just by sight that the latest missive bore the same sort of wording and the same typeface as the others. But it could have been counterfeited by Nick or Clive, and Smith could be a partner in the hoax or perhaps getting duped himself.

He needed to know more before committing. "Did they share this with you?"

"No, I came upon them discussing it in Mr. Bennett's office late at night. Neither one of them realized that I was outside, listening to them discuss the details: Nemesis is back. He's going to strike again, and he wants to make a deal with Nick."

"And Clive agreed to this?"

Wendell scrunched up his face. "Not in so many words," he sighed. "But he did say they should seriously consider it."

"Did they make any sort of plan for proceeding?"

The young reporter sighed again. "Not that I could clearly hear."

Cradoc rolled his eyes towards heaven. "You don't know much, do you?"

But Wendell wasn't ready to capitulate. He stabbed a finger at the letter. "As you can see, Nemesis pledged to write again with the details of 'when, where, and who.' At that point, Nick and Mr. Bennett will have to decide if they are game or not. If they accede to the killer's request, they'll have to plot a strategy for going forward—what they are going to do with the information and when they are going to do it."

"And you're a fly on the wall again?"

"Precisely. When the next correspondence arrives, I ascertain the particulars and report them to you. Assuming we have all the facts we need, you can set a trap and catch the killer. Simple as that."

Only it wasn't so simple. Cradoc ran the various scenarios through his mind. Even if they knew the location and target ahead of time, that was no guarantee they could stop the killer from taking another life. And there remained the possibility that Clive might get cold feet, nix the whole affair. Or that Nick might decide to go it alone. "What makes you think Nick will continue to keep Clive in the loop?"

"You of all people must know that Nick doesn't make a move without Mr. Bennett's blessing. And he's no fool. He's not going to run off and have a chat with the killer without telling at least one person where's he going and when he should be expected back. That's been the case with every move on the Nemesis stories—Mr. Bennett has been kept informed. Given that Nick has already shared this latest message, I wouldn't expect anything different going forward."

"Fair enough," said Cradoc, who for the first time thought that Smith's grand plan might work. He still didn't know if he could implicitly trust the reporter, yet at the same time he recognized this as their long-awaited opportunity to catch the killer. Possibly the best chance they would ever have. The marshal couldn't pass it up. He would have to let Coyne in on the plan, and by extension several deputies. Best to bring in Wyatt, too. A small group of people he could trust not to blab beforehand and who would perform to the utmost of their ability when it came time to close the trap.

Cradoc handed the letter back. "Better get going."

But Wendell wasn't finished. "I want exclusive rights to the story. And I insist on being there when the arrest is made."

"The first one's fine," the marshal told him. "But I don't know about the second. The guy's way too dangerous."

"Then no deal," Wendell said. "I've got a lot more on the line than you. With me, you've got them licked. Without me, you're back to square one."

Cradoc grudgingly agreed. No harm in making that pledge now. They could always give Smith the slip when it came down to the crunch, when there was nothing the reporter would be able to do about it.

Yet something still nagged at Cradoc. "There's one thing I still don't understand: why are you doing this?"

"Can you think of a better way to advance my career?"

"I'm not so sure that's your primary reason."

"Why does it matter to you?" Wendell snapped.

"Because I wanna know what sort of person I'm going into business with, what your motives are. Call it a matter of trust. Why are you so keen to stab Nick in the back? He'll never forgive or forget. You'll make an enemy for life."

Wendell's face went flush, the anger rising inside. "From the moment I arrived, Nick has never taken me seriously. He's always treated me like a rich fop whose father got him the job."

Cradoc wanted to say: Well, isn't that the truth? But he held his tongue.

"If there's one thing I've learned from Nick," Wendell added, "it's that you'll never get anywhere in this world unless you're ambitious, maybe even ruthless, and willing to take chances. That's how he got where he is, and that's how I'm going to get where I want to be."

36

CRADOC QUIETLY FINISHED his lunch at the Oyster, chewing not so much on his grub but the incredible offer extended by Wendell Smith. Paramount in his mind was the issue of whether or not he could trust the reporter. You could never be sure—not just with Smith, but with any newsman—if they were being genuine or trying to pull a fast one to create a headline at your expense. Yet the young man's bile seemed genuine. If Smith despised Nick as much as it seemed, maybe he was willing to commit journalistic high treason and face whatever consequences lie beyond.

Back at the jailhouse, Cradoc made straight for the sheriff's office. "Got a minute?" he asked Coyne.

"For what?"

"A conversation best done in private."

They climbed three flights of stairs to the courthouse roof, a spot in the southwest corner where you could gaze down on Broadway and the bay. Cradoc had always enjoyed this vista—the silhouette of masts and canvas along the waterfront—and now he found himself admiring it again.

"We didn't climb up here for the view," Coyne reminded him.

Cradoc looked around at his boss. "I don't wanna put the cart before the horse, but I think we finally got the bastard."

"And which bastard might that be?" There were an awful lot to choose from.

"Who do you think? Nemesis."

"Balderdash," the sheriff responded. "If he killed someone else, we'd surely know by now."

Cradoc shook his head. "It hasn't happened yet. But that's the whole point."

Coyne cocked his head like a befuddled dog. Cradoc quickly elucidated. "I've come across a means to determine the identity of his next victim beforehand."

But the sheriff wasn't biting. "You been hitting the hooch?"

"On the contrary. I've just had a very interesting conversation with Wendell Smith."

"That milksop from the *Times*?"

"He may not be as much of a runt as previously suspected. Mr. Smith has agreed to assist our attempts to catch the aforementioned killer."

But Coyne remained unconvinced. "And how's he gonna do that?"

"They just got another letter from Nemesis, which Smith was kind enough to 'borrow' from Clive's desk and show me. He had to take it right back—lest Clive discover his treachery. So I couldn't match it to my typewriter samples. But it looks like the real deal."

Cradoc recounted the contents of the latest letter, how Nemesis had invited Nick to be there for his next kill. Cover the crime as it happens rather than write about it after the fact.

"And Bennett agreed to this insanity?"

"Not exactly, says Smith. But he did agree to consider it. And apparently leave Smith out of the loop. Nick wants it all for himself this time. And Smith, being the ambitious little bugger that he is, would like to screw him in return. He has this hair-brained plan to eavesdrop on Clive and Nick, feed us the details we need to lay a trap. I thought he was batty at first. But I gave it some thought, and it just might work."

A tiny smile twitched at the corner of Coyne's mustache. "Sounds too easy."

"I know. But sometimes the simplest solutions are best."

"Can we trust him?"

"You mean Smith? Truth be told, I'm not a hundred percent sure. My first reaction was that it was some kind of a set-up. Catching me out—making me look like a complete ass—would make a great story. Sell lots of papers. Maybe even ruin my peacekeeping career forever. But look at the alternative: if we call it bullshit, give Smith the brush off, and it turns out to be true…."

"You and I are done for."

"No shit. We'd never be able to live this down. Both of us would probably be run out of town. Not to mention the fact that someone else would be dead and the killer still at large. My gut tells me this is real, that Smith is legit, and his plan could work. And all the pieces fit. He's been working in Nick's shadow ever since he got to the *Times*. Smith wants to be the Golden Boy. But the only way to do that is—"

Coyne cut him off. "Catch Nemesis."

"Exactly! Prove that he can hook an even bigger fish than Nick. But it runs deeper than professional ambition.

Apparently Nick has treated him like a toad since Smith walked in the door. So this is retribution, too."

Coyne shook his head in amazement. "I can't believe Pinder is willing to crawl this far into bed with a brutal killer. Sure as shit, he'll go to jail. Bennett, too. They'll likely both go down for this one if they don't inform us beforehand."

"There's no guarantee they'll go through with it. Clive could weigh the consequences and change his mind. Nick on the other hand ... if there's a chance to boost his fortunes even higher, he'll jump on it. If this thing pans out the way Smith figures, Nick won't be able to walk away—even if Clive decides to stand down. He's like a chronic gambler, can't resist that one last hand."

†

Cradoc met up again with Wendell Smith the following morning, this time in a back room at the Oyster, to seal their deal and sketch out a plan for how the sting would play out. Wendell would keep an eye and ear out for anything that transpired between Nick and Clive, and then report that information back to the marshal with as much haste as possible.

The quickest means seemed to be using the telephone in the lobby of the Horton House, just across the plaza from the *Times*. Smith would call the jailhouse as soon as the details were revealed and Cradoc would set a trap to coincide with the supposed time and place of the imminent attack.

"I suspect it's going to happen any day now," Wendell told the marshal. "I hope you're ready. And don't bungle it."

Cradoc thought it brash of the kid to be offering him advice. All of a sudden the kid was cocky, a condition that always seemed to lead to no good. "It's not me I'm worried about."

"What's that supposed to mean?" Wendell shot back.

"I'm assuming you've never done anything like this before." When Smith didn't contest the statement, Cradoc knew it for a fact. "It's not gonna be as easy as you think. There's not much margin for error on your part either. And if there's one thing I know from my own bitter experience, it's that people don't take kindly to treason. You might recall a fellow named Benedict Arnold and what happened to him."

Wendell put on his bravest face. "I want this like nothing I have ever wanted before. And no one is going to stop me." At that, the young man spun on his heel and walked out without another word.

Cradoc watched as Smith barged out of the back door of the Oyster and down the alley, disappearing around the corner onto Broadway and the short walk back to the newspaper. The marshal still had his doubts that Smith could pull it off without getting caught by Nick or Clive. But there was no alternative. He had to trust in the young man's determination—and quest for revenge.

†

Returning to the *Times*, Wendell asked around for Nick and Clive and discovered that both of them were out. Once again, he waited patiently for the newsroom to empty for lunch and moved nonchalantly into Bennett's office, scanning the desktop for anything that might be useful.

Finding none, he moved onto the desk drawers and the lockbox, but again came up empty.

Admittedly it was a long shot. He had not seen Nick and Clive huddled conspiratorially in the boss's office like the other day. They had not changed their routines in any perceptible fashion and were not acting any different than normal. Given that it had been less than forty-eight hours since the arrival of the last letter, there was little reason to believe that another had already appeared. Still, it had been worth a shot, if only to distract from the gnawing anxiety eating through Wendell's gut.

He heard footsteps in the newsroom, somebody coming towards the editor's office, and coming fast. There wasn't time to exit. He had to act now. Wendell whirled around to face the bookshelf, reached up as if to extract a volume.

Moments later, the footsteps shuffled into the room. His arm still poised in midair, Wendell craned his neck round to see Clive making a beeline for his desk.

"Forgot my smokes," Clive said distractedly, reaching for the tobacco pouch and rolling papers on the desktop. He didn't seem the least bit fazed by Wendell's presence in his office. "Looking for something?" he asked helpfully.

"One of your reference books," Wendell blurted out.

Clive filled a rolling paper with a line of fresh tobacco and looked up at the young reporter. "Which one?"

Wendell had to think fast. "Father Serra's diary."

"The English translation, I presume. Unless your Spanish has improved markedly without me noticing."

"Yes … yes. The translation. Of course. I would have asked, but you weren't around."

Clive was amused that Smith would spend his lunch hour bucking up on local history and wondered if it meant the lad planned on staying in San Diego. Scooting around the desk, Clive retrieved the book from the far end of the shelf. "This the one?"

"I believe so," Wendell said. He began flipping through the pages.

"Feel free to borrow any of my books. Doesn't matter if I'm here or not," Clive told him. He lit his cigarette with a wooden match and departed.

Wendell kept his face buried in the book until Clive had made his way back across the newsroom and disappeared out the front door. Feeling his stomach erupt, he reached the washroom just in time to vomit into a toilet.

37

BIDING HIS TIME while they waited for Wendell Smith to come through, Cradoc returned to the St Joseph's rectory in search of any shred of evidence they might have overlooked the first time they searched the place. They had already carted off the typewriter, now under lock and key at the jailhouse. But everything else remained much as they had found it on the night of the murder—blood and brain splattered across the bedroom, the bindings still attached to the dead priest's bed.

Entering the rectory office, the marshal pondered the desk where the typing machine had once rested. He's been here, Cradoc thought to himself. Nemesis has been in this very room. And not for the first time during this long and drawn-out case, Cradoc found himself wishing that finger furrow identification was a peacekeeping tool of the present rather than the future. Undoubtedly the killer had touched this desk. And presumably other parts of the house—doorknobs, furniture, light switches, and certainly the rectory telephone that Nemesis had used to alert authorities to Figueroa's murder.

Back out in the sunshine, Cradoc pulled himself into the saddle and headed for the jailhouse, only a few blocks away. Hanging out at the jail and waiting for Wendell Smith to call had become his daily routine over the past week. The deputies kept giving him looks, wondering why the marshal sat there hour after hour without doing the slightest bit of police work. And why he jumped every time the telephone rang. Joe Coyne knew, of course. But the others were much too intimidated by Cradoc to ask.

A lot of that time was spent thinking about Emma Lee and what had become of her. Like everything else in Cradoc's life, he tried to approach the issue with as much logic as possible. There were countless business establishments in the Stingaree—boarding houses and bars, maritime stores and sawmills. But especially sporting houses. Dozens of places of ill repute, most of them eager for fresh quim to keep the old patrons coming around and attract new business. None of them would have turned away a female as luscious (and sexually experienced) as Emma Lee. But would she have gone down that road? He refused to believe that possibility and wouldn't until he saw it with his own eyes. And thus far, no such thing had happened. Rumors to the contrary, Cradoc had not come across a single person who could tell him with any authority that Emma Lee was working on her back.

He had made several forays below Market Street to quiz the locals. If he'd only had her photograph, something they had talked about but never got around to doing before she disappeared. But at least Cradoc had eliminated the most dreaded possibility. He had gone door-to-door (or rather curtain to curtain) in the notorious "cribs" between Fifth and Third streets—tiny wood-framed rooms without windows, running water, or electric lights—where the lowest echelon of hookers worked and lived in astonishing squalor. Hundreds of them crammed along an alley and around trash-strewn courtyards called bullpens. Most of these cribs contained nothing more than a bed, sometimes only a filthy mattress. Cradoc had scoured every single crib and questioned their tenants one by one until he was absolutely certain that Emma Lee was not amongst them.

So if she remained in San Diego and had found new employment, it was at a level above the very worst. That knowledge offered small but at least some consolation until Cradoc could devote all of his time to finding her. Time that would have been sooner rather than later if he didn't have to spend so much damn time waiting around for Smith.

†

Wendell Smith spent a good deal of his time over the next few days in the newspaper washroom, breaking out in cold sweats and generally trying to calm his nerves. Feeling the need for an explanation, he told workmates that he'd caught some kind of bug that wouldn't go away. Several staffers (including Clive) urged him to take a few days leave, stay in bed, and recuperate. But Wendell declined their kind advice with the excuse that he was behind on his work and not quite that ill.

Much to his chagrin, Wendell had discovered that he didn't have nerves of steel and was not cut out for clandestine work. For reassurance, he would make his way across the plaza to Horton House every few hours and telephone Bradshaw, ostensibly to report on the lack of progress, but more to listen to Cradoc's soothing voice as the marshal implored him to stay calm.

It seemed like an eternity to Wendell, but it took less than a week to reap the desired harvest. He was in the washroom again, on the verge of expelling another load of bile when he heard voices out the open window. Creeping to the ledge and cocking an ear, he heard Clive and Nick in the alley below, talking in a low and barely audible tone. Wendell could only make out bits and pieces of their conversation.

"August twenty-sixth," Nick was saying. Just over a week hence.

"What time?" asked Clive, exhaling out a cloud of cigar smoke.

"Four o'clock in the afternoon. At the Santa Fe Depot...."

A gust of wind blew away the rest of the sentence. By the time the gust was gone, the conversation had moved beyond details of the impending attack into a discussion about whether or not the *Times* should even handle the story. If the intended victim's name had come up, Wendell had missed it.

"What's your call?" Nick asked.

"I suggest we be good little boys and forget about this whole nasty business."

They pondered that point through a long moment of silence. And then almost in unison both of them said "Naw."

"Temptation is an awful beast," quipped Clive. "Nemesis is going to assassinate a major public figure. We know the place and time. We are there when it happens. We become part of the event. That's what real power feels like, lad."

"Don't you think we should tell someone?" Nick suggested. He meant law enforcement, of course. Not necessarily Cradoc Bradshaw, but someone else in a position of authority who might be able to stop the attack.

"Give me one good reason," was Clive's ice-cold reply. "By choosing to do nothing, we influence the outcome. It merely depends on how you want history to be written."

"Or headlines," Nick retorted.

"One and the same in this case. I'm serious when I say we have it within our grasp to change the course of human events. This is a moment we should cherish. Not many men are privy to this sort of influence. And it normally doesn't endure. We should take advantage of this opportunity while we can."

There was still a question of legality. Covering the would-be crime after the fact was not an issue. Every paper in California would splash the killing across their front pages. But pre-knowledge of the event and a post-assassination interview with the culprit would place them on very shaky legal ground and likely land them in hot water with the law.

"I suppose we could always leave town," Clive mused out loud.

"Is that even a possibility?" Nick wanted to know.

"You don't think any paper in America would have us after this? This story is gold. And so is the future. Yours in particular."

Wendell was busy scribbling notes, trying to get as much down on paper as he could, when someone knocked on the washroom door. If he could hear Clive and Nick in the alley below, they could certainly hear anything said through the open window above. Creeping to the door, Wendell unlatched the chain and slowly pulled it open. One of the German printers gaped through the crack. Holding his stomach, Wendell pretended to be ill. The German flared his nostrils and turned away. Wendell quickly re-latched the door and jumped back towards the window.

"… better idea," said Nick. "I think there could be a way for us to interview Nemesis and not get tossed in the hoosegow for thirty years."

"And what would that be?" Clive asked skeptically.

"What if we were to capture him? Make a citizen's arrest."

The proposal astounded even Clive. "Have you lost your bloody mind?"

"It goes back to your original precept, when this Nemesis business first started: the journalist as hero and society's watchdog. Wasn't that the moral justification for our initial coverage?"

"Yes, but I never intended my words to extend into actual derring-do. I was speaking more in a metaphorical sense. The pen is mightier than the sword and all that."

"But this is the ultimate, Clive."

"War is the ultimate," the editor countered.

"This is damn close."

"It's too dangerous. We're dealing with a lunatic."

"Which is why I can't pull it off on my own. I'm going to need help this time—from you."

If Wendell had been in the alley at that point, he would have seen Clive's jaw go slack and the cigar tumble from his lips. "You really have lost your mind."

"There's no other way," Nick said.

"There's always another way," Clive snapped back. "Like simply not doing what you seem to be suggesting."

But Nick wasn't dissuaded. "In for a penny, in for a pound—isn't that one of your quaint British sayings?"

Clive never got a chance for further rebuttal. A group of men rounded the corner, making their way up the alley toward the side entrance of the livery. Their covert conference interrupted, Nick and Clive ducked back into the *Times*.

†

Wendell dashed across to Horton House and telephoned the marshal. He could feel his breath increasing as he waited for the exchange operator to connect the call. Once again, he was on the verge of expelling the contents of his stomach. Breathe deep and slow, he kept telling himself. And then he heard Bradshaw on the line.

"It's incredible!" Wendell screamed into the phone. Heads in the hotel lobby whipped around at him. He turned toward the wall, shielding his mouth with a cupped hand.

"What?" Cradoc asked, knowing the moment had finally arrived.

Wendell's voice fell to a seditious whisper. "August twenty-sixth. Four in the afternoon. The railway station. That's when and where it's going to take place. And before you ask, I have no clue who the intended victim is. His name was never uttered or even hinted at, at least not during the part of the conversation I was privy to."

"You're sure about the other details?"

"Absolutely. I overheard the two of them talking—Mr. B and Mr. P," he said furtively, in case anyone in the hotel lobby should overhear. "Discussing the time and place, and whether or not they should become actively involved."

"Are they?"

"Not only are they going to interview the perpetrator in the aftermath of his next murder, they have concocted a scheme by which they will attempt to detain the fiend. Turn him over to authorities and in so doing launch themselves into everlasting hero-hood."

Cradoc couldn't believe his ears. Nick wants to capture Nemesis himself? "Impossible," he muttered into the phone.

"Without doubt," said Wendell at the other end of the line. "But that's exactly what they're planning."

†

Replacing the telephone earpiece, Cradoc went straight into Coyne's office and shut the door. "What's happening at the Santa Fe Depot on August twenty-sixth?"

"Kendall's launching his Congressional campaign," the sheriff said casually.

"Of course," said Cradoc, slapping himself on the forehead with an open palm. Kendall was giving a big speech, leaving on a special train that would convey him across California in the months leading up to the November election.

Coyne's face went dark. "Don't tell me...."

The marshal slowly nodded. "That's the scoop from Smith. He overheard Clive and Nick discussing the details."

"Nemesis is going after Kendall?" Coyne seemed un-characteristically shocked. Knocking off shady business-men was one thing, going after one of the most powerful men in the state quite another.

"Either him or someone else in the crowd. Smith didn't catch the name of the intended victim. But I'm thinking it's gotta be Kendall. He fits the profile of the sort of person Nemesis has been targeting."

"Everyone who's anyone in San Diego is going to be there, whether they support Kendall's bid or not. The mayor, the city council, every goddamn judge in town. And I would imagine every major businessman, too. There's no way we can protect all those people. We've gotta tell Kendall," Coyne declared. "Get him to call off the whole thing."

"You know what he's like. Even if we can convince him the threat is real, he won't give a damn. He's got his bodyguards and to hell with everyone else."

Coyne shook his head emphatically. "Doesn't matter. It's our duty to inform him. If he chooses to ignore our advice and shun our protection, there's nothing we can do. But at least we've done our duty. "

†

"What did you say?" Fabian Kendall looked more than a bit rankled. He had a stack of paperwork to get through before the end of the day and wasn't in a mood to be bothered by anything—even the prospect of death.

"We got an anonymous tip," Coyne repeated. "There's apparently going to be trouble at your campaign launch next Sunday."

The three of them were in Kendall's headquarters on Fifth Street, a second-floor office above a bank that the property, newspaper, and railroad magnate also owned. The room was flush with small American flags, campaign posters, and red, white, and blue bunting for the election drive that would shortly kick off.

"Nobody in their right mind would dare interrupt my campaign launch," Kendall said arrogantly. The man's hubris seemed to have no limit.

Coyne and Bradshaw exchanged an edgy glance. That was enough for Kendall to pick up their vibe. He laughed out loud. "Nemesis? Gentleman, give me a break." He looked far more amused than troubled.

"We don't know for sure it's Nemesis," Coyne lied.

"But this secret informant of yours must think so. And you believe him, because otherwise you wouldn't be wasting my valuable time."

"Sir, we take all threats seriously."

"Assuming this Nemesis fellow actually does exist, why would he want to kill me? What have I done to incur his wrath?"

Cradoc could name half a dozen things off the top of his head. But he wasn't going to, of course. No doubt Archer and Ingraham would have claimed the same if they had been forewarned about their own deaths.

By now, Kendall was on his feet, reaching for a bottle of scotch on a sideboard over to one side of his office. "A dram, gentlemen," he offered, holding up a bottle of Laphroaig single malt.

Both of the lawmen begged off. They had come for serious discussion, not social hour. Although it was tempting, especially to Cradoc, who knew good hooch when he saw it.

Kendall poured himself a shot, downed it in a single gulp, and exuded a satisfying aaaaaah as his two visitors watched. "World's best," he gushed. "Sure you won't join me?"

Coyne and Bradshaw gave each other a look. They were used to Kendall being a braggart when it came to his wealth and triumphs. But they couldn't believe how cavalier the man was being about a possible threat on his life.

Yet the sheriff persisted in trying to warn him, far more than Cradoc thought necessary. "Mr. Kendall, we would like you to consider the possibility of canceling or postponing your campaign launch ... or commencing your trip without a rally at the Santa Fe Depot."

Kendall's amused grin faded into a grimace. "No way—hell or high water—is that going to happen. I've been planning this for months. We have similar events in place all along the length and breadth of California. People expect me to speak at certain places at certain times. Not just voters, but the press and my political allies."

"Nobody's gonna vote for a dead man," Cradoc quipped.

Coyne shot him a disapproving glance. But Kendall took it seriously.

"I'm well aware of that, Marshal. And that is why I will have my own security men in place, here in San Diego and everywhere else I will venture on this trip and other journeys right through to the general election. I don't need the two of you traipsing in here to inform me that I have enemies. And I'm not talking about some phantom killer who may or may not be real. I'm talking about political and financial foes who would stop at nothing—even violence—to make sure that I do not represent this great state of ours in Washington."

Kendall did have a point. He was running as the underdog Democratic candidate in District 6 against Republican incumbent William Vandever. It was a huge district, stretching all the way from Fresno to San Diego, from the San Luis Obispo coast to the Colorado River—the entire southern half of the state. Kendall had one heck of a lot of territory to cover, and less than three months in which to do so before Election Day. It was just a stepping stone. If Kendall won this round, he would cast his eye on the Senate. And if he should achieve that status, he would no doubt lust after the highest office in the land. He was that sort of man, someone who saw no limits to his own power and advancement. And why should he? Kendall had conquered San Diego without raising much of a sweat. Now he was intent on doing the same with California.

"While I appreciate your concern about my well-being," Kendall said smugly. "I do not judge the level of threat significant enough to revise plans already in place. Now if you will excuse me, I have work to attend to."

†

Their consciences clean, the next task for Bradshaw and Coyne was figuring out how to police the rally, not so much to protect Kendall, but lay a trap to capture Nemesis and put an end to the bloody saga that had dogged them for so many months. If Kendall should perish in the process, that was no longer their concern. The visit to warn him was a courtesy call. Capturing the killer—dead or alive—had always been their primary goal. And now they could get down to the nitty-gritty of planning without distraction.

First and foremost, everyone on the sheriff's payroll would have to work the event. Screw the rest of the town. For a brief time on a Sunday afternoon, all of San Diego law enforcement would be concentrated in a small area around the train station.

Kendall's event would take place in the plaza on the south side of the year-old Santa Fe Depot. Rather than speak from the open-air deck at the rear of the caboose like other politicians, Kendall (being a railroad man) would climb onto the front of a locomotive to deliver his final words to a crowd expected to number in the thousands. After that, Kendall would officially launch his campaign train in much the same way as a newly built ship—by smashing a bottle of booze over the cattle catcher as the crowd cheered and photographers snapped his picture. And off they would roll, to whistle stops in Escondido, Temecula, and scores of other California towns.

As their primary goal was capture rather than prevention, Cradoc suggested they position a couple of deputies at high vantage points atop and around the station. They would also place armed men at the main exit points from the plaza including Broadway, the railroad tracks running north and south, and the muddy bay shore on the western side of the tracks. Even then, they had to assume Nemesis would stand a good chance of escape, especially if the crowd stampeded in the wake of a violent incident. If that was the case, they needed a backup plan, another way of apprehending the killer if he evaded their dragnet and fled the scene.

Coyne carved out that piece of their plan. Perhaps Nemesis never left a trail, but those who followed him surely would. If Smith's information proved correct, Nick would interview the killer after the fact. And Clive Bennett would be along rather than Nick going solo. Together, they would attempt to capture Nemesis. Extrapolating on that information, the logical move for law enforcement was keeping a close eye on both Nick and Clive before, during, and immediately after the event. Observe their movements at a sufficient enough distance not to raise suspicion and then follow as they made their way to the rendezvous with the killer.

Yet both of them knew such a task was much easier said than done. They had to assume Nick would take measures to make sure he wasn't tailed. Still, what other choice did they have? Like a marathon poker session that comes down to the final hand, they would go all-in and see how the cards fell.

38

ROZ HAD TAKEN TO WORKING six days a week, partly to avoid Nick and partly because the wealthy matrons of San Diego had already overwhelmed her new business with fashion orders. She normally left home well before Nick arose. But on one particular morning in mid-August he caught her on the way out the door. He requested lunch with her on the forthcoming Saturday. He had something he needed to discuss, something that concerned both their lives and could wait no longer. Roz accepted the invitation, out of curiosity and because it provided as good a time as any to confess her pending departure from their marriage.

They met in the ground floor restaurant in Horton House. Wearing black boots and a scarlet silk riding dress of her own design, Roz arrived early and asked for a table in the corner, where they would be away from prying eyes and ears. After ordering a pot of tea, she checked her face in a compact and powdered her cheeks. It seemed peculiar but at the same time quite human that she wanted to look her best for this crucial encounter.

From the moment he arrived, Nick was in an agitated state, fidgeting with the silverware, twisting the linen napkin around his finger. He smiled shyly, asked how she was doing.

Roz decided to get right to the point. "Nick, there's something I want to tell you—"

But he cut her short. "There is something I need to tell you first," Nick interrupted. "I know things haven't been very good between us lately. I admit that I haven't exactly been the ideal companion."

Roz sat back, hands folded on the table, eyes fixed on her husband, wondering what he was about to say.

"I've been spending far too much time on my work and not enough time on you. This is something I've only recently realized. You've been unhappy—it's not difficult to tell. And it's my fault, I know." Nick took a deep breath. "But I've made some decisions. This Nemesis business will end tomorrow."

"Tomorrow?" she asked. How could he place a date on such a thing?

"To be more precise, tomorrow afternoon or perhaps early evening, depending on how events play out. Clive and I are going to catch Nemesis."

"*What?*" she asked, leaning closer to the table.

"We're going to make a citizen's arrest and turn him over to Sheriff Coyne," Nick continued, in a tone that made it sound like a piece of cake.

"Have you lost your bloody mind—again?"

Nick's eyes lit up. "I knew you were going to say that! And while it certainly may sound that way, I am absolutely serious. We have it all sketched out. A brilliant plan, if I may say so myself. I've made an arrangement to interview the killer at his secret hideout"—he purposely did not mention the threat against Fabian Kendall—"and Clive is going to help me lay the trap."

Roz was truly stunned. "Neither one of you knows the faintest about how to go about arresting someone let alone a vicious killer."

"That's why I've got this." Nick pulled back his jacket to reveal a miniature pistol tucked into his waistband. An Iver Johnson revolver with a much shorter barrel than the Colts common among those who normally packed a weapon and thus much easier to conceal.

Roz's eyes flicked around the room, hoping no one had noticed. "Where in God's name did you get that?" she whispered.

"I've had it for years. In my desk at work. I actually found it at a crime scene—a brawl on the waterfront. One of the combatants was either too drunk or too hasty to notice that his gun had gone missing. Can you believe it?"

"Have you ever used it?"

"Enough to know it works," Nick told her. "Several times on my way to appointments in the backcountry, I stopped and shot at trees, rocks, and whatnot. Quite a handy little piece."

"That doesn't make you an expert," Roz snapped back. "Or your plan any less dangerous."

"No more discussion," Nick ordered. "There's one more thing I need to tell you."

What more could there be? she wondered in silence.

"As soon as this business is finished …" Nick pulled a pair of train tickets from his coat pocket. "I've booked us a holiday back east. St Louis. Chicago. New York. I figured we could both use the time away, a chance to get to know one another again." He sat up straight, grinning like a schoolboy. "I've gotta run now," he said hastily, pulling back from the table. "As you might imagine, Clive and I have numerous details to work out." He tossed his napkin on the table and was gone before she could open her mouth to protest.

†

Roz fetched her horse from the valet in front of the hotel and rode straight down Broadway. She could think of only one course of action: explain the situation to Cradoc Bradshaw and pray that he would help.

Bursting into the jailhouse, she found Cradoc and Wyatt sitting on either side of the marshal's desk, deep in conversation. Both of them stood at once to greet the lady.

"Nick's gone mad," she blurted out, the Irish in her voice more prominent than usual. "He's going to get himself killed."

"What in blazes are you talking about?" the marshal asked. Although he already had a good idea what must have set her off.

"He's going to interview Nemesis in person and try to capture him!"

"We know," Cradoc said calmly.

Her eyes went wide. "You do? How?"

"Doesn't matter. All you need to know is that we are planning appropriate action."

"To stop their rendezvous, I hope. Before Nick gets hurt."

Cradoc shook his head. "Nick's not the one we're worried about. We believe Nemesis will attempt to kill someone else tomorrow afternoon and that Nick is planning to interview him afterward."

"Oh my god," Roz muttered. "He didn't mention anything about another murder."

He gave her a quick lowdown. "We already know the time and place. We'll have men out in force. We don't know precisely who the target is or what sort of weapon Nemesis will use this time. But given the nature of where and when the attack will take place, we figure it's gotta be a firearm."

Roz looked up at him. "Nick's also got a gun. A tiny pistol he's taking to the interview. He doesn't seem the least bit worried that his crazy plan could backfire."

The marshal rolled his eyes. "He wouldn't."

"You've gotta help. Get him out of harm's way."

"He doesn't want my help," Cradoc said bitterly. "He wants to be the hero. If you couldn't dissuade him, I sure as hell can't."

"If the shoe was on the other foot, he'd do it for you. You wouldn't have to ask. I wouldn't have to beg you." Roz paused a moment, giving him time to mull that over. "The least you can do is try."

But Cradoc still wasn't convinced. "He'll accuse me of trying to derail his story, won't appreciate my help in the least bit."

"But I will," Roz pleaded. "Doesn't that count for something?"

Cradoc ran both hands across his scalp. There was no way he could win this battle. "All right," he said without much conviction. "I'll do what I can. But you've gotta understand that Nick is determined and unpredictable. And so is this killer. Anything can happen out there."

†

Nick and Clive met at the *Times* office on Saturday evening to run through final procedures. Where they should be and what their respective tasks were on Sunday afternoon. Where they would go directly after Kendall's rally and what they would do immediately following the interview. Clive had already decided to hold the presses, summon everyone back to the paper late on Sunday night and ram through a special edition focused on both the grisly crime and their heroic capture of the killer in the aftermath.

Nick removed a handkerchief from his coat and placed it on the desk in front of Clive. "I thought you might need this," he told his boss, peeling back the edges to reveal a small pistol similar to his own. "Know how to use one of these?"

"More or less," said Clive. "I carried one during the war—in case I was mistaken for a Yankee and needed to defend myself. I know the basics."

"If it comes down to the crunch, be prepared to fire."

"And what do you consider the crunch?"

"If either of our lives is in danger," Nick responded.

"You're quite serious about this."

"It's serious business. Isn't that what you told me?"

"Yes, but I didn't think it required armament."

"Clive, if you're getting cold feet ..." The comment nothing short of a dare.

"Far from it," was the editor's fraudulent response. He knew he would never use the gun. But he wasn't about to tell Nick that. Not at this late date. "You can count on me."

They shook hands, wished each other luck, and set out for their respective homes. Nick to his house on Golden Hill, Clive to his motor yacht along the waterfront, both of them fully aware that their lives would change drastically during the next twenty-four hours.

A pair of Wyatt's men, muscle from his saloons in the Stingaree, tailed Nick all the way home with instructions to watch from a safe distance and follow him back into the town on Sunday. Jose Cota and Fatty Rice, in civilian duds rather than their navy blue uniforms, had a similar task— keeping tabs on Clive Bennett until the campaign rally.

A trap within a trap within a trap, everyone certain they had the upper hand.

39

SUNDAY BROKE HOT AND MEAN, the front end
of a Santa Ana blowing in from the desert, whipping up
dust devils on the unpaved streets and whitecaps on the
bay. Some people loved the searing winds and others
hated them, yet nearly all agreed they'd drive you crazy if
you stayed out in the blow too long. But that didn't keep
thousands of citizens from heading down to the waterfront.
Damned if a little wind was going to spoil the show.

A massive crowd had already gathered around the train
station, even larger than the hordes that assembled for the
annual Fourth of July parade. Hundreds more poured down
Broadway and other streets leading to the depot. It wasn't
every day that one of their own ran for national office.
And when they did, it was never with this much pomp
and circumstance. Everyone who was anyone and even
those who were practically no one wanted to behold the
spectacle of Fabian Kendall launching his Congressional
campaign with a rousing speech and dramatic departure on
one of his own locomotives. Smothered in red, white, and
blue bunting, the train lingered beside the station awaiting

departure on a tour that would whisk Kendall across California's Sixth Congressional District.

A wooden stage had been erected in front of the station, with a cordoned-off area where the bigwigs would witness Kendall's oration. Many were already in attendance, ladies and gentlemen in their Sunday best who had come straight from church, everyone struggling to keep their hats and bonnets steady in the Santa Ana wind. Another roped-off area near the stage held members of the press, Wendell Smith among them, seated in the front row. Elliot Patterson and his massive Empire State camera perched on a wooden scaffold that gave the photographer an unencumbered view of the proceedings.

Below Patterson's platform stood the volunteer fire department marching band, instruments and music at the ready, as well as a list of the songs that Kendall had mandated for his grand entry, the completion of his speech, and finally the rail departure. The crowd also swelled with ordinary folks, all and sundry who made San Diego their home these days—longshoremen and fishermen, carpenters and washerwomen, ranch hands and school teachers, small business owners and shop assistants. Such was the level of hoopla that even those who normally took no interest in politics of any sort—Mexican peons, ladies of the evening, and even local Indians—were also present in no small numbers.

At around the same time the throng was settling in at the train station, Jose Cota and Fatty Rice arrived at the bottom end of Fifth Street. Deputies had been stationed there through the night, rotating three hours on and three hours off as they kept an eye on Clive Bennett's steam yacht, tied up to a live-aboard wharf adjacent to the hulking steamship pier. Surprisingly, the editor had forgone his usual Saturday night round of Stingaree saloons and cathouses in favor of a quiet night aboard *Medusa*. That alone was enough to alert the deputies that something was brewing.

Clive emerged from below deck at about nine o'clock on Sunday morning. He came ashore briefly for breakfast at one of the waterfront dives and then scampered back aboard. Almost immediately he began preparing the boat for departure: stoking the coal-fired engine, building up a head of steam, and finally casting off from the wharf. Cota and Rice had no idea how to respond; this had not been one of the eventualities that Cradoc Bradshaw and Joe Coyne had prepared them for. But neither did they panic, which is precisely why their bosses had chosen them for a task of such importance. Seeing their mark pulling away from the dock, the deputies crawled onto their mounts and followed at a safe distance along the shoreline. When they ascertained Clive's destination they would report back to Coyne.

As they watched from their horses, Clive's yacht looped around the deep-water end of the steamship pier. Rather than head into the middle of the bay and around the north shore of Coronado to the open ocean, the boat stuck close to shore around Dead Man's Point and into the northeast corner of the bay—towards the cluster of waterfront shanties where Marshal Bradshaw lived. Cota and Rice couldn't figure where the hell Bennett was heading. Another ten minutes and they had their answer: the yacht pulled up to a rickety old wooden pier on the opposite side of the tracks from the Santa Fe Depot, the closest place you could dock a boat to where the trains came in. Cota volunteered to continue the surveillance while Rice made haste for the county jail.

Tumbling downstairs into the jailhouse, Fatty Rice found the sheriff giving final instructions to a posse that would shortly attempt what they had been unable to accomplish in months of trying—catch or kill Nemesis. The group comprised around two dozen men, a mixture of actual deputies and a motley crew of Wyatt Earp's bouncers, dealers, barmen, and cooks deputized for the day. Those best with rifles would assume strategic positions in the train station clock tower and on the roofs of buildings around the depot. Others would wade into the crowd and spread out, on alert for any sort of trouble caused by Nemesis or anyone else. Kendall's own bully men would be guarding the inner sanctum, so they were at least spared from having to protect the candidate. None of Coyne's men or Earp's lackeys would be taking a bullet for the would-be congressman.

Rice waited for the posse to disburse before approaching Cradoc, Coyne, and Earp with the news that Clive Bennett had docked nearby.

"That's an odd move," Coyne mused. Didn't make a lick of sense.

"Get back there straight away,' Cradoc told the deputy. "And don't take your eye off Clive until this whole thing is over. I wanna know if he so much as sneezes. You got that?"

"Sure thing, Marshal. But where can we find you once the whole thing starts?"

"Inside the train station," Coyne explained. "We will be posted there throughout."

As Fatty disappeared up the stairs, one of Wyatt's bouncers came rumbling down into the lobby with a report on Nick's whereabouts since yesterday. Much like the owner and editor of the *Times*, Nick had spent a quiet Saturday night at home. Not that unusual in his case; Nick had never been much of a carouser. The only out-of-the-ordinary thing the bouncer noticed was a late-night confrontation between Nick and Roz.

Cradoc had begged her to check into a hotel, at least temporarily. The marshal didn't want her going anywhere near Nick until this whole thing played out. First and foremost because he valued her personal safety, but also because he didn't want Roz revealing—even accidentally—that they were onto Nick's scheme and laying a trap. In her typical obstinate way, Roz had rebuffed Cradoc's advice. She must have wanted one last chance to convince Nick not to go through with this madness.

While the bouncer couldn't hear the exact words being exchanged, Cradoc figured that's what had sparked their late-night quarrel. Apparently to no avail on Roz's part, because by midmorning, Nick had departed his house on horseback and headed down the hill. Tailing him had been a breeze because so many people were already making their way into town from outlying areas, headed for the station and Kendall's extravagant send-off.

Nick had gone straight to the *Times* and was still there as far as the bouncer could tell. The reporter had left his horse tied to a hitching post in the plaza rather than leave it in the livery. So it had to be assumed that Nick would be moving again soon, either down to the station to watch the latest Nemesis plan unfold or directly to his rendezvous with the killer.

The three lawmen had debated this ad infinitum since uncovering the plot and had not come to any unanimous prediction about what Nick's movements might be during and after the presumptive attack. In theory, Nick didn't have to attend Kendall's send-off at the foot of Broadway. Wendell Smith had been assigned to cover the actual event; Nick's task was meeting-up with the killer afterward. And catching him, of course, assuming he and Clive were still going through with that foolishness.

Coyne checked his pocket watch. Twenty to noon. "About time we hit the road, gentlemen." The three of them mounted up and moved down a side street to the train station, where they would take up watch just inside the front doors, directly behind the stage but with a clear view of the massive crowd.

†

Nick Pinder sat at his desk on the second floor of the *Times*, staring out the window at the plaza and the hordes of people heading toward the train station to witness Kendall's grand departure. He thought one last time: What am I doing? If he was going to abandon this insane plan, now was the time. It wasn't too late. He could just walk away. Let events unfold however they might and not get personally involved. There really was no need for a final interview. Nobody would be the wiser if he didn't catch Nemesis, because nobody—other than Roz and Clive—would know there had ever been the plan to do so.

Yes, he could view from afar like everyone else, watch what transpired and write the story. To hell with all of the other crap! He had earned more than enough repute from the other Nemesis stories to secure a big-time book deal and lecture tour. The foundation for his financial success and nationwide fame was already solid. When you thought about it, there was actually more to lose if he went through with his capture-the-killer plot. Especially if something went wrong. And there was a huge unknown and uncontrollable factor to consider: Cradoc Bradshaw. If everything played out as expected today, Cradoc would be out to take scalps—starting with Nick's.

"I don't need this," Nick shouted out loud, sitting in the newsroom by himself, pondering the pros and cons of a plan that would permanently alter his future. He was already a hero, already on his way. Kendall's fate had already been decided, and to a large extent, his own. Because no matter how many times Nick warned himself not to go through with this, no matter how long he sat there and stared out the window, he knew he wouldn't be able to resist the lure—and the necessity—of bringing all of this to an end on his own terms.

†

Along with Coyne and Wyatt, Cradoc had taken up vigil inside the train station lobby. Through the big picture windows, they could see most everything they needed to keep an eye on. The temporary stage loomed directly in front of them, as did the marching band and the roped-off areas for local press and power brokers, and beyond that, a mass of ordinary folk that Coyne estimated at four or five thousand. This might not be the largest-ever crowd in San Diego, but it certainly ranked as the biggest political event in the town's one-hundred-and-twenty-year history.

They watched as Nick arrived, exchanged a few words with Wendell Smith who was covering the rally, and then crawled up onto the scaffold platform with Elliot Patterson and his camera. Once again, Nick began to orchestrate the whole affair, pointing here and there, raising his hands in the air like imaginary picture frames, showing Patterson exactly which photographs he wanted for the paper.

Cradoc wondered how much Nick knew, whether his instructions to Patterson were being dictated by specific knowledge of what Nemesis was going to attempt or merely speculation on Nick's part of where the crime would take place. Either way, Nick didn't seem the least bit rattled by the prospect of watching a man's life extinguished before his very eyes.

If the attempt actually took place. Cradoc's doubts were growing by the minute. Who in their right mind would endeavor to slay someone in front of this many people? It wasn't just the size of the crowd. The weather was another wildcard. Even a skilled marksman would be hard pressed to hit a far target in this sort of wind. You would have to be very close to get off a good shot. And in doing so, you would run into Kendall's private army, arrayed all around the stage and his fancied-up election train. His own deputies were equally conspicuous amidst the crowd and on nearby rooftops. Sure, you could take a shot at Kendall. Maybe even more than one before the deputies or one of Kendall's men took you down. Otherwise, Cradoc couldn't see how the killer could pull this off. Then again, Nemesis had surprised them before and they had to assume the rogue might do it again.

Out of the blue, the band struck up "The Battle Hymn of the Republic" and Kendall came trundling into the depot plaza in an open-topped carriage pulled by four white stallions.

What a jackass, Cradoc thought to himself. He had never liked the railroad man and liked him even less now that he craved government office. If big-time business didn't bring out the worst in human beings, then politicking certainly did. And now Kendall was guilty of both.

His glad-handing completed, Kendall mounted the stage and began his speech. Cradoc moved closer to the window, his nose touching the glass as he scanned the crowd for any sign of trouble. If it was going to happen, now was the time.

Wyatt stood beside him, staring at the crowd. "You figure one of those people out there is Nemesis?"

"No goddamn clue," was Cradoc's surly reply.

"Not like the guy is gonna hang a sign around his neck," Coyne quipped.

"Gotta have a tell," said Wyatt. "Everyone does." He'd run gambling halls long enough to know that even the best card players gave it up eventually. You just had to look long and hard enough.

"He's too good," Cradoc whispered, more to himself than his companions. Amazing how you could loathe someone and still respect them. But Nemesis deserved his due. Never let his guard down. Always one step ahead of the law. In order to catch him you had to be there when he struck and be fully prepared. Cradoc hoped today—finally—was that day.

†

You had to give it to Fabian Kendall, too. If nothing else, the man knew how to put on a show. Stepping down from the carriage, Kendall waded through the dignitaries in the cordoned-off area, shaking hands and exchanging small talk with Mayor Hunsaker, Alonzo Horton, George Marston, and other luminaries, before ascending the stage to the cheer of thousands. Befitting an event of this stature, Kendall had clad himself in an expensive, three-piece suit trimmed in black satin, with a high-collared white shirt and matching white gloves. Black coattails and top hat completed the ensemble of a man who very much looked the part of a successful tycoon and ambitious politician.

Taking in the crowd and all those eager faces, Kendall cleared his throat and began to speak. He welcomed everyone to the gathering and singled out several of the VIPs seated in the special section, asking them to stand and be acknowledged by the throng. By extension—whether they intended to back him or not—they were endorsing Kendall's run for Congress by their very presence in the audience.

Kendall then got down to the meat of his speech, his reasons for seeking public office. "We have seen our metropolis—the finest in America if I may say so myself—grow by leaps and bounds over the past few years. An unprecedented boom in both population and commerce that has showered prosperity on those of us who have dwelt in San Diego for many years and even those who are new amongst us. While progress is achieved by hard work and determination, it is also stoked by audacious ideas and bold actions. Of particular importance was the daring decision to relocate the community from its original, landlocked Spanish location to this bayside 'New Town' that has grown with such vigor in recent years. Without that move, San Diego would have stagnated, become a backwater, fallen even further behind San Francisco as the most valuable nugget of the Golden State."

Kendall didn't have to mention his own name. Anyone who had been around in the old days knew he'd been one of the prime forces behind the town's controversial migration.

"And when it became apparent that San Diego could not thrive merely on the merits of its incredible natural harbor," Kendall continued, "we remade ourselves from merely a seaport into a railroad hub with few rivals on the Pacific shore. An iron horse that now connects us not just with our neighbors to the north and the rest of California, but to the entire nation. Trains rush our products to eastern markets in a matter of days rather than months and, in return, bring the necessities of modern life and luxuries that were previously unknown in these parts. Not just a new and modern means of transport, but an entirely new way of thinking that has revolutionized our lives."

Once again, no need to inject his own name into the monologue. Kendall was "Mr. Railroad" in San Diego and everyone knew it.

"Now we find ourselves at another crossroads, in need of big thinking and bold action once again. Not just as a city, mind you, but as a region and a state. And while I am not one to exalt my own qualifications, I cannot think of anyone with better credentials to take us there."

A loud cheer went up from the crowd. Kendall had them hooked. Not just as a native son, whom many of them would vote for automatically, but as the person who could envision the future and make it happen.

"Like the Caesars of old, we must not rest on our laurels. Progress is not just a word but a way of life. And to attain it, all of us must keep moving forward. I'm not going to stand up here today and lie to you—trying to achieve dreams and ambitions is never an easy prospect.

"I know more than anyone that government can often be a hindrance. Sometimes by accident and sometimes by design, but a hindrance nonetheless. And that more than anything else, my friends and fellow Americans, is why I have decided to seek public office.

"We need laws and lawmakers that encourage rather than stifle progress. Men in Washington who spark rather than strangle growth. Leaders dedicated to abolishing the unjust taxes and tariffs that threaten our economic future. Politicians willing to take the necessary steps to seal the border and thwart the ruffians who continue to threaten us from Mexico. Individuals who will not be tempted to line their own pockets from the public coffers.

"And while it may be possible to find these qualities in any number of men, I submit to you that I am the only one running to represent the glorious Sixth District of California who possesses all of these traits and more. With that, I hereby declare my candidacy for the United States Congress!"

Even before the crowd could strike into another rousing cheer, the band broke into "The Gladiator March," a brand-new tune by John Philip Sousa, and Kendall's favorite song at present. And march is exactly what Kendall did now, from the temporary stage over to his locomotive, a colossal Baldwin engine. Coal black with a stovepipe stack and steam dome, it had only recently been delivered from the Baldwin factory in Philadelphia and proclaimed the new queen of Kendall's iron horse armada. The Santa Ana breeze ruffled its red-white-and-blue bunting, black smoke wafting up and over the bay as the locomotive built up a head of steam. That only served to make the scene even more dramatic, as if Zephyr himself had endorsed

Kendall's candidacy and was urging him on with a stiff wind.

As a precaution—just in case the sheriff and that wayward marshal were correct about an attempt on his life—Kendall had instructed his bodyguards to keep the crowd at bay. Nobody should get close enough to take a pot shot or otherwise harm the boss. But that didn't mean he wasn't to be seen. Quite the opposite. Mugging for the crowd and the camera, Kendall swung himself up onto the narrow metal ledge between the cowcatcher and the cylindrical smokebox. His smile seemed a mile wide as he soaked up the adoration that would hopefully be replicated in Los Angeles, Fresno, Monterrey, Santa Barbara, and other stops on his campaign tour.

One of Kendall's minions pushed his way to the front of the throng and passed a rectangular wooden box to the boss. Lifting the lid, Kendall extracted a bottle of his favorite beverage—a bottle of Laphroaig. The very scotch that Cradoc and Coyne had been offered during their visit to Kendall's office just a few days before and that Nick Pinder had shared with him at the Cuyamaca Club, what now seemed like ages ago.

In the same manner in which he might hoist a mighty sword, Kendall thrust the bottle into the air with a single hand. The crowd roared its approval above the groan of the marching band. Taking the bottle by the neck, Kendall cocked his arm about as far back as it would go and launched into a mighty swing. As he smashed the scotch bottle onto the front of the smokebox, Kendall burst into flames.

40

NICK SAW THE BOTTLE SHATTER against the coal-black metal and Kendall consumed by a ball of fire. There wasn't so much a blast as the whoosh you hear when a piece of wood or paper instantly ignites, followed by Kendall's bloodcurdling screams. The railroad baron tumbled off the locomotive and onto the tracks below, immersed in the inferno. Those rushing to help were driven back by the intense heat and flames.

Awed by the hideous spectacle, Nick just stood there at first, watching. But now he broke from his daze. "Did you get that?" he asked Patterson.

"I think so," the photographer mumbled, as stunned as everyone else.

"Get the plates to the Times as quickly as possible," Nick instructed, leaping down from the platform.

Bedlam erupted in front of the train station, people shouting, pushing and shoving, running every which way, some of them trying to get a closer look at the burning man, but most just wanting to get the hell away. Nick plunged into the crowd, using his elbows and shoulders to knock people aside, desperate to reach Clive's yacht and get onto the water before anyone could stop him.

†

By the time Cradoc reached the scene of the explosion, the flames had been extinguished. Kendall was apparently still alive, surrounded by people trying to give him aid and comfort. If he did somehow survive, the marshal could see that his life would never be the same. Kendall was burned over most of his body, his face horribly disfigured, and his hands more or less melted.

Cradoc looked around at the locomotive. At first he thought the Baldwin had exploded, that it had to be some sort of industrial accident. But the giant engine was still intact, wicked scorch marks on the front of the smokebox, but otherwise undamaged. Cradoc couldn't figure out what the hell had happened. Had the bottle of scotch exploded? All he knew for sure was that something had transformed Kendall into a fireball.

Suddenly the marshal remembered what he was supposed to be doing—watching Nick. During the minute or so that Cradoc had taken his eyes off the mark, Nick had absconded from the photographic platform and disappeared into the crowd. The marshal scanned the chaos all around, thousands of people running and shouting, impossible to tell where the reporter might have gone. And now panic rose through Cradoc. If he lost track of Nick, they wouldn't be able to follow him to the interview. Wouldn't be able to corner and apprehend the killer. This whole day, all of the careful planning, would be for shit.

Wyatt came rushing up, face grim. "Nemesis?"

"Don't know for sure. But we've gotta assume so."

"Wily bastard."

"You're telling me. You seen Nick?"

Wyatt shook his head. "What about you?"

"Don't even ask," Cradoc sighed. But they couldn't just stand there. "You take his horse, I'll take the boat." And so they split up, headed in opposite directions, hoping they could at least catch a whiff of which way Nick was headed. If not, their opportunity truly had slipped away.

Leaping across the railroad tracks, Cradoc lunged into the panicked masses. It wasn't that far to the shoreline, a hundred yards at most, but hundreds of frantic people blocked the way, impeding his drive to reach the pier and Clive's motor yacht. "Out of the way! Out the way!" he kept shouting, but without much effect. He thought about raising his gun, shooting into the air. That would have moved cattle out of his way, but with people you just didn't know.

Finally he caught a glimpse of water through the blockade of bodies. But then fate intervened again. Out of the corner of his eye he spotted a familiar face—Emma Lee Dawes—fleeing the scene with everyone else. And at that precise moment she saw him, too. She tripped, went down hard on the gravel causeway. Without hesitation, Cradoc rushed to her side. Roughly pushing people away, he pulled her back to her feet.

There was no time to talk, to ask why or how or anything else. "Come with me," he cried, taking Emma Lee by the hand and pulling her towards the water.

Reaching the pier, he saw that Clive's boat had pulled away. Already a hundred yards into the bay, puffing on a full head of steam, pointed due west toward Point Loma and the ocean.

JOE YOGERST

Jose Cota and Fatty Rice came sprinting up the shore. "Nick's onboard!" Fatty screamed.

Once again, Cradoc had to think fast. He looked around at Emma Lee, back at *Medusa*. He had to get her out of harm's way, but not at the risk of losing Nick. "Goddamit!" he said to no one in particular.

"Fatty, take Miss Dawes to wherever it is she now stays." He spun around at her. "And stay there!" he ordered. "Until this shit is over."

"All right," she muttered as Fatty led her away. Like everyone else, Emma Lee was dumbstruck by the turn of events. She and Cradoc could sort themselves out later.

Still thinking on his feet, the marshal turned to Cota and said, "We gotta find a boat. Now! Something fast enough to catch them."

Both of them scanned the shore. The only craft close at hand were small sailboats that wouldn't have the speed to keep up with *Medusa* nor the power to cut through the ever-building swell caused by the Santa Ana winds. But a quarter mile down the waterfront floated something that might do the trick—a motor launch called *Della* that ferried folks back and forth across the bay. Cradoc and Cota looked at one another, shrugged, and took off running down the shore.

By the time they reached the ferry pier, *Della* was standing room only with spooked passengers trying to get back to Coronado. Cradoc flashed his star at the ferryman and passengers. "Everyone off. Now!" he shouted above the rumble of the boiler.

"You can't do this!" the ferryman yelled back.

Cradoc was in no mood for any kind of shit. "Oh yes, I can," he answered, leveling his sawed-off shotgun at the man. "In case you didn't hear me the first time—Everyone! Off! Now!"

The lady passengers squealed and the men grumbled, but they quickly fled the boat and gun-wielding lawman. When the ferryman tried to follow his passengers ashore, Cradoc grabbed him by the collar and said, "Not you! You're driving. You either," he told the stoker, a freckle-faced teenage boy.

All of the passengers safely ashore, Cota untied the dock lines and was just about to leap aboard when someone came running down the dock. "Wait!" Wendell Smith screamed at the top of his lungs.

"Push off now!" Cradoc told the deputy.

Cota kicked the side of the ferry with a boot and jumped aboard. But Wendell remained hell bent on joining them. Running at full speed, the young reporter took a flying leap across ten feet of water and landed on the bow. Momentum sent him tumbling into the first row of seats. His jacket and trousers torn and blood dripping from a cut on his chin, Wendell crawled back to his feet and glowered at the marshal. "You were going to leave me behind!"

"You saw what happened to Kendall. What more do you want?"

"Every reporter in town saw him go up in flames. Everyone's going to write about that. We had a deal!"

"I don't need anyone getting in the way."

"I only want to watch," Wendell said.

"I'll talk to you after, give you all the details, exclusive and all that," Cradoc said. "But I'm not going to let you or anyone else cock this up."

Wendell started to protest again, but the marshal cut

him short. "Take it or leave it. And by 'leave it,' I mean going overboard right now."

The marshal nodded at Cota, who took a hold of Wendell's arm and began dragging him toward the port side. The reporter snatched his arm back. "I'll take it," he spat. "But you better not cross me again."

"Or what?" said Cradoc, turning around to scan the water. The ferry seemed to be going so slow. They were never going to catch Nick at this rate. "Are we up to a full head of steam yet?"

"Almost," the ferryman answered. "And you might wanna tell me where we're headed."

"There!" said Cradoc, pointing towards where the sun hovered low above Point Loma.

"It's dark soon," the ferryman felt obliged to point out.

"Then the faster we go, the better,"

†

It appeared they had made a clean getaway. Both Nick and Clive came to that same impression as they steamed westward across San Diego Bay. Since pulling away from the dock, Nick had used Clive's field glasses to scan the waterfront behind. The incessant chop and unrelenting wind made it difficult to hold them steady for more than a few seconds at a time, but that was enough to determine that no boats were charging after them or anyone following by horse along the shore. Off to the right, he could see *Della*—one of the few craft that might be able to catch them—pulling away from the ferry dock. But Nick knew it was bound for Coronado rather than where they were headed.

The wind continued to grow in strength, as did the

whitecaps out in front of them. But it was nothing Clive couldn't handle; the man had long been an expert skipper, even better than himself. Like Nick, he'd grown up around boats, braved squalls and other troubles off the English coast. So this was nothing, this Santa Ana. If anything, the zephyr would aid their efforts by persuading less experienced sailors not to follow them.

Now that they were safely on their way, Clive's thoughts returned to the events in front of the train station. Through the binoculars, he had witnessed the explosion and subsequent fireball. But at that distance, it was impossible to see who or what might have been blown to smithereens. "What happened back there?" he asked urgently.

"Kendall is dead or close to it," Nick said. "A bomb exploded as he leapt onto the front of his train. Saw it with my own eyes. So did Wendell. Patterson has photographs."

"God almighty," said Clive, realizing that Nemesis had indeed struck again, killed another man ... another very important man. He would have never guessed the target was Kendall. For God's sake, the most powerful man in San Diego, perhaps all of California.

"All we need now is the interview," Nick continued.

"Should we even go through with it?"

"Why wouldn't we?"

"It just seems so brazen. So cold."

"Hell of a time to lose your nerve, Clive."

"I'm not losing my bloody nerve. But if Nemesis is willing to kill someone of Kendall's stature ..."

Nick picked up on his drift. "Then why not us? Because he gave me his word, that's why. And he's never let me down before."

Turning around, Nick checked aft again, gazing through

the field glasses. He could see *Della* steaming away from its pier into the open water between New Town and Coronado Island. It appeared to be slightly off course. But given the wind blowing in from the desert, that wasn't surprising and Nick wasn't the least bit troubled. Even if they weren't being followed, time was still critical. If they were going to publish the stories tomorrow morning, they had to wrap things up as quickly as possible and rush back to the office. Otherwise, their big news would have to wait until Tuesday. And neither Nick nor Clive relished that prospect.

As agreed beforehand, Clive would take the wheel while Nick stoked the yacht's boiler, keeping up a full head of steam by feeding wood into *Medusa*'s furnace. Not easy work, but exactly what Nick needed at this juncture. A repetitive act that served to both calm his nerves and give him time to double-check his plan for the next few hours.

He thought back to what he had just witnessed. Kendall's demise was much more gruesome than he had expected. But then again, fire did that to people. Nick knew all too well from his own life. He had also been surprised by the crowd's reaction to Kendall's arrival and speech, their enthusiastic applause and cheers. As if they really did adore the man, despite the brutal means by which Kendall wielded his wealth and authority. Were people naturally drawn to power no matter what its base? One also had to wonder if such a gut-wrenching demise would transform Kendall into some sort of martyr. At least temporarily, until Nick's interview ran and the public discovered the reason Kendall had been dispatched with such brutal authority. As with the previous victims, truth would eventually outweigh sentiment.

Up on deck, Clive kept a steady course across the northern sweep of San Diego Bay. Glancing over his shoulder every so often, he continued to scan the water behind for boats that might be following. So far so good. But he remained very concerned about what lay ahead. They would reach Ballast Point right around dusk. And depending on how long it took Nick to complete the interview, they would have to navigate back into town after nightfall. Not a welcome prospect even in the best of weather no matter how good a skipper you were. Clive harbored severe doubts about his ability to handle *Medusa* after dark in such vigorous and unpredictable winds.

The actual interview also troubled Clive. Where at Ballast Point would it take place? And how did Nick plan to apprehend the fiend? Nick had never explained the scheme in whole, no more than a terse mention that once the interview concluded, he would draw his weapon and make a citizen's arrest. "And if Nemesis resists?" Clive had asked. Nick had boasted that he wasn't afraid to use his sidearm. Dead or alive—didn't matter how they brought the killer in.

With *Medusa* up to full throttle, it wasn't long before they had passed both Roseville and La Playa, the twin seaports for San Diego in the days when the town sat inland, as well as the place where Nick had stowed the sailboat he used to get back and forth to school. Off to the left, Clive could make out the red tower of the Hotel Del across the sandy flats of Coronado. Dead ahead lay Ballast Point, a thumb-shaped spit that jutted off the port side of Point Loma. Covered in stones used as ballast by a hundred years of shipping, the little spit was also the last place to dock or anchor before the bay burst into the open ocean.

With their destination approaching, Nick came back on deck. He did a last check of his saddlebag, making sure that everything he needed—paper and writing implements, candles and matches—was stowed inside and in good working order. Nick also double checked his miniature pistol, spun the barrel, and slid it back into his waistband. Everything seemed ready; there wasn't much else he could do until the moment arrived.

Nearing the dock, Clive throttled down to reduce power. With such a strong wind blowing from the east, he thought it better to approach on the leeward side of the dock rather than risk having his beloved yacht blown into the old wooden pier. *Medusa* having completed that maneuver, Nick leapt onto the dock with a line attached to the front of the vessel and then ran back along the rickety wooden planks to secure the stern.

Clive cut the engine and clambered onto the dock. "Where's the rendezvous?" he asked nervously.

"Up there," said Nick, nodding his chin at the old lighthouse atop Point Loma.

"Where you used to live?"

"Perfect, don't you think? Nobody ever goes there. Complete privacy."

"What are we waiting for," said Clive, putting on a brave face and taking a tentative step forward.

But Nick held him back. "I'm going alone."

"Whattaya mean?"

"You were right. It's much too dangerous, Clive. And he's not expecting anyone else but me. We don't want to spook him. Don't want to run him off."

Clive tried to look terribly disappointed, but in reality, he was much relieved that he wouldn't have to confront the killer himself. But that didn't mean he wasn't concerned about Nick's safety. "What if events don't go as planned?"

"I've got this," said Nick, brandishing his revolver. "And the element of surprise. He's never going to expect what's coming."

"Even the best-laid plans of mice and men . . ."

Nick thought for a moment. "If I'm not back in two hours, sail without me."

"And—"

"I don't know!" Nick said distractedly, like he hadn't thought about the possibility of failing at this mission. "Tell Coyne or Cradoc to form a posse. But that won't be necessary, Clive. Because everything's going to go like clockwork."

And with that Nick departed, his boots clacking along the old wooden pier and then grinding through the stones that covered the spit. He made his way quickly through a cluster of wooden shanties erected by Yankee whalers and Chinese fishermen who had once lived at Ballast Point, onto a dirt path that rose to the old lighthouse.

"Good luck, lad!" Clive shouted into the wind. For once, the editor figured Nick was going to need it.

41

THE WIND WHISTLED through a broken window pane and rustled the papers on the table in front of him. Lunging forward, he anchored the sheets with both arms before they could fly onto the floor. Then the candle blew out and the room plunged into darkness. As much as the Santa Ana winds had abetted his voyage across the bay, they were now proving a major nuisance as he tried to get the interview underway.

Nick knew the room by heart and had no problem in the dark pushing a chair and the old wooden table—the same ones he had used as a child to do his school work— to a corner shielded from the wind howling through the broken window. He relit the candle and rearranged the blank pieces of paper on which he would carefully transcribe the interview. One last time, he ran through the questions in his head, in the order he would ask them. And then he was ready.

He took a long, deep breath, closed his eyes and summoned the killer. It didn't take long for Nemesis to emerge.

Nick opened his eyes and began to write, reading the words out loud as they appeared on the paper. "One question looms above all others: Why Fabian Kendall?"

After a pause to collect his thoughts, the killer spoke.

"Let me preface my answer by saying that Mr. Kendall is different than the others. To my knowledge, he has never personally taken the life of another person and never laid hands on a fellow human being. But that said, he is the crux to this entire affair. Without Kendall's direction, the event that prompted my quest for justice may have never taken place, and the others—except perhaps the priest—would still be alive. Or at least not slain by my hand."

"You've given an impression all along that Ingraham and Archer were guilty of individual transgressions committed long ago rather than a common incident. Now it sounds like that may not be the case. Were all of these other crimes bogus?"

"Not by any means. Archer did drown the Chinese merchant and Ingraham did shoot the squatters. And both escaped justice. If they had not been who they were—wealthy and powerful—they would have undoubtedly been hanged for their crimes. But I could say the same of dozens of other people in San Diego, hundreds or even thousands if one extrapolated across the entire state or nation. That's not my mission and was never my intention."

"So why did they have to die? What is this common sin you're alluding to? And how was Kendall involved?"

"You are far too eager to reach the denouement."

"Shouldn't I be? Isn't that why we're here?"

"It's a complicated tale. Have you got enough time?"

Nick glanced at his watch, very much aware there was little time if the story was going to make tomorrow's paper.

†

San Diego Bay curved in a broad arc before pouring into the Pacific, the sandy flats of Coronado on one side, and the rugged hump of Point Loma on the other. With its mudflats and shoals, the Coronado shore offered almost nowhere to safely anchor or beach a vessel, especially with a Santa Ana blowing. You had to figure that Clive wouldn't risk scuttling his live-aboard yacht even for another Nemesis interview. So Cradoc instructed the ferryman to hug the north shore, passing close to the old fishing villages and small coves where it would be much easier to put a man ashore.

The marshal already had Jose Cota scanning the water for the 60-foot *Medusa*. Even in the fading light, a vessel of that size and shape would be hard to miss. But when they didn't come across it in either Roseville or La Playa, Cradoc had no choice but to assume that Nick and Clive were headed out to sea.

With the Santa Ana winds rising from behind and whitecaps dead ahead, the ferryman quite naturally balked at taking *Della* into the open ocean. Not to mention that it would soon be dark with nothing to guide them in and out of the bay but the new lighthouse at the end of Point Loma and the sound of waves crashing against the shore. But that's exactly where Cradoc now told him to venture, the Colt in his holster and the shotgun in his hand as silent reminders that he would use force if necessary to impose his orders.

Wendell Smith hadn't said a word since pushing off from the ferry pier. Clinging to the gunwale, doing his best to keep from throwing up, he looked pale and lightheaded.

Cradoc was not surprised the young reporter had no sea legs. He looked even more out of sorts on the boat than in the saddle. Then again, the bay was much rougher than normal, the ferry getting tossed about by the swell and the persistent wind.

Cradoc wasn't thrilled about the weather either. Nothing to do with feeling seasick—having grown up in boats it rarely afflicted him—but rather because the tempest slowed their progress. Although the bluster would dampen the sound of *Della*'s persistent chugging when (and if) they came across Clive's boat.

"We've gotta slow down!" the pilot shouted above the roar of the engine and the wind.

"No way!" the marshal yelled back. "We'll fall too far behind." Swell breaking over the bow, the ferry was approaching the outer limits of its endurance. But they had to take the chance. To do otherwise meant failure—Cradoc wouldn't be able to catch the killer and put an end to this long-running nightmare, nor rescue Nick from whatever dire straits he had thrust himself into.

It was Cota who finally spotted the sleek white yacht. Cradoc rushed down the ferry's starboard side and squinted into the gloom. Sharp prow. Double masts. Seven portholes along the hull. Clive's boat all right, tied up to the old Ballast Point whaling pier. What the hell were they doing there?

Cradoc shouted for the ferryman to pull around, suggested they make the same maritime maneuver that Clive had done about half an hour prior—approach on the leeward side, use the pier and Clive's boat as a windbreak. Their arrival would not go unannounced to anyone still aboard *Medusa*. But the location gave them at least one distinct advantage: short of swimming across the bay to Coronado or trekking over the top of Point Loma, there weren't an awful lot of ways to exit Ballast Point. They pretty much had Nick—and whoever he was meeting—trapped.

The ferryman's deft navigation now came into play. He wheeled around with his hand on the throttle, forcing *Della* forward through the swell until it floated parallel with Clive's boat and close enough for Cota to attach a line to the motor yacht. The deputy scrambled onto the larger craft, followed by the marshal. Still feeling woozy, Wendell lagged far behind the others, stumbling across the ferry and face-planting on the wooden deck.

Aboard *Medusa*, the two lawmen fanned out to search the boat, Cota to the engine room and Cradoc down into the saloon that doubled as Clive's stateroom. At first glance, the marshal spotted no one and almost left. But on second thought, he decided to check the head at the opposite end of the cabin. Shotgun cocked and ready, Cradoc gently kicked open the door. Moonlight pouring through the porthole, Cradoc could see the silhouette of someone inside the washroom.

"Drop it!" he screamed, not knowing who it was or whether they were armed.

"Don't shoot!" yelped a familiar voice. And Clive Bennett stepped from the shadow, arms raised in surrender.

"What the hell, Clive," the marshal growled. "I could have shot you."

Using the barrel of the shotgun as a pointer, the marshal motioned for Clive to climb the stairs to the main deck.

"Look what I found," Cradoc announced to Cota. "Pat him down."

Cota found the pistol tucked into Clive's waistband, held it up for the marshal to see.

"You've gotta be kidding me. A gun, Clive?"

The editor shrugged. "These are dangerous times."

"And I thought Nick was the only fool."

Just then, Wendell tumbled over the yacht's port-side railing.

"What in the blazes are you doing here?" Clive growled at the young reporter.

Smith's silence said it all.

"You bloody traitor!" yelled Clive, forcing Wendell back against the railing and almost overboard. It took both Cradoc and Cota to pull him off and restore order.

"Cuff him!" Cradoc told the deputy.

Cota slapped the metal restrainers around the editor's wrists, but Clive continued to howl. "You're done!" he shrieked. "You are so finished. You're never going to work in this town again. Anywhere on this coast. Daddy can't save you this time."

"You think I care?" Wendell retorted. "I've got the big story now. Not you or Nick or anyone else. And if you won't publish it, I'm sure there are papers in New York and San Francisco who will."

"Kiss my ass!" Clive lunged at Wendell again, head-butting him in the chin before Cota could pull him off. The deputy slammed Clive into the nearest deck chair.

"Enough of this shit!" Cradoc yelled. They were wasting time, squandering the opportunity. "Where's Nick? Where are they doing the interview?"

Clive answered with a blank stare.

"I'm dead serious, Clive. Answer me. Where the hell are they?"

When the editor once again failed to respond, Cradoc drew his Colt.

"You'd never shoot me," Clive said self-assuredly.

The flash of the muzzle told him differently, a bullet that zinged between the Englishman's legs into the wooden deck. "Jesus Christ!"

"Tell me!"

Clive pointed his chin to the crest of Point Loma. "Up there! The bloody lighthouse where Nick used to live."

†

It took Cradoc and Cota about twenty minutes to reach the top of Point Loma via the same zigzag trail that Nick had taken not long before. Smith would have been with them, if not for the fact that Cradoc had cuffed him too, left the reporter and his boss behind with the ferryman and stoker at guard. The marshal didn't want anyone getting between him and the killer. It would be hard enough making sure that Nick didn't meddle—or come to harm.

Reaching the summit, the marshal and deputy checked their weapons one last time. They really had no idea what they were walking into. Nemesis could be gun free or armed to the teeth. Best be ready for anything. The old lighthouse lurked about a hundred yards north of where the trail topped out, its whitewashed walls shimmering in the moonlight, but its glass-enclosed lantern room now completely dark. After thirty odd years of showing the way into San Diego Bay, the structure had been recently abandoned in favor of a modern light station down at water level that could more effectively shepherd maritime traffic in and out of the bay. Cradoc hadn't been out here for years.

But he knew the brick edifice almost as well as the house where he'd grown up in Old Town. Nick's boyhood home, a place where he'd spent many a summer day and night. Until the war came and everything changed. Strange how it had all come 'round to here—him and Nick and Nemesis.

Their footsteps muffled by the relentless wind, the two lawmen crept closer. Soon they could see a horse tied up to the hitching post on the building's north side, near the start of a trail that rambled across the crest of Point Loma and eventually down to the northern shore of the bay— the only other way off this mount other than leaping into the sea.

Cota nodded at the horse. "Nemesis?" he whispered.

The marshal shrugged. Hell if he knew. But it was a reasonable assumption. He must have ridden out from town after attacking Kendall.

Angling around the white picket fence that surrounded the lighthouse, Cradoc approached the horse in a way that wouldn't spook it. The animal was fully tacked out, ready to ride. Yet when he stroked the animal's neck, it wasn't sweaty. It had not been ridden recently. Which didn't make sense. Then again, little about Nemesis did. Cradoc's intrinsic caution told him to check the animal for a rifle scabbard or other weapons that needed to be secured before they moved in. That's when he noticed the saddle was covered in something wet and sticky. Smelling the metallic aroma on his fingertips, the marshal knew at once it was blood. What the hell?

More cautious than ever, Cradoc sent his deputy around the lighthouse in one direction, while he slowly and silently moved in the other, on the lookout for movement or voices from inside the structure. The parlor, the kitchen, and the

ground-floor bedrooms were all dark and apparently empty.
Not a single sign of life.

Coming face-to-face with Cota again, Cradoc lifted both
hands in the air as if to say "Where the hell are they?"

Cota beckoned with a finger for the marshal to follow
around to the front of the lighthouse. To the right of the
main door, down at ground level, the deputy pointed out
a small rectangular window with a missing pane of glass.
Anyone else might have thought it a basement, but Cradoc
knew the sunken chamber had been Nick's bedroom in
days gone by. If you looked close enough you could see a
smidgen of light escaping from a corner of that window.
Artificial light. And that could only mean one thing:
somebody was in there.

Having slipped in and out of the aperture as a kid—
when he and Nick went on secret nighttime forays—
Cradoc knew exactly how to approach in complete silence.
Holstering his sidearm and laying the shotgun aside, the
marshal crept up to the window and got down flat on
his stomach to peer inside. Putting an ear to the broken
pane, he could hear Nick's voice, but not quite what the
reporter was saying. He could see Nick too, sitting at an old
wooden table, his back to the window, unaware that he was
being watched from behind. Hastily scribbling notes, Nick
appeared to be engaged in an intense dialogue. Yet Cradoc's
view of the person being interviewed was blocked by a wall.
If he could just crane his neck a little further to the right …

†

Nick momentarily looked up from his notes. "So Horton
wasn't a part of this?"

"Without doubt, Alonzo Horton originated the campaign to move San Diego from its original Spanish position to his new 'Horton's Addition' beside the bay. As the addition's primary property owner, he stood to make millions if the town relocated. It's also clear Mr. Horton masterminded the secret midnight transfer of the county records from Whaley House in Old Town to the Express Building in New Town on the third of April, 1871, thus shifting the county seat to bayside. Mr. Horton was reasonably sure that his bloodless coup d'état was irreversible. But others who stood to benefit handsomely from the town's relocation were not so confident. They feared that a flurry of lawsuits would reverse the move and ruin their covetous plans. Unlike Mr. Horton, they were of the opinion that a more final solution was needed—one that could not be reversed."

"You're saying the Old Town fire was deliberately set?"

"What better way to ensure the county seat would never be moved back and that New Town would forever thrive?"

"But it started in a kitchen," Nick shot back. "The stove at the back of Schiller's store."

"Indeed it did. But that doesn't mean it was accidental."

"What's your proof?" Nick demanded.

"Father Figueroa," the killer said cryptically. "Around a year ago, I caught him, quite by accident, defiling a young Mexican girl who was cooking and cleaning the rectory. I threatened to reveal his depravity, but Figueroa offered me information in exchange. Breaking one of his most sacred vows, he related what someone had confessed to him on their death bed—Juanita Ingraham."

"Yankee Jim's wife?" Nick blurted out.

"For many years she carried the guilt of knowing that her husband was a killer, that he was responsible for igniting the fire and the deaths that occurred during the arson that destroyed Old Town on the twentieth of April 1872. Given her own greed and, I suppose, loyalty to her husband, Mrs. Ingraham failed to report her knowledge of the event to the authorities. She kept it bottled up inside, eating away at her soul, a fact that no doubt contributed to her premature death. She also revealed in her last confession that Zebulon Archer was equally culpable in setting the blaze. But the arson was not their idea. They were merely following orders from a much more sinister personage...."

†

Cradoc nearly gasped outloud, shocked not so much by revelations from the interview but the utterly astounding fact that Nick was talking to himself. Having craned his neck as far to the right as possible, the marshal could clearly see there was no one sitting on the other side of the table. There was no one else in the entire room. Nick would ask a question out loud, ponder a moment, and then recite the answer as he wrote it down.

Still not quite believing his own eyes, Cradoc considered possible explanations. If Nick was both asking and answering his own questions, if there was no one else present, that could mean only one of two things. The previous interview and all the letters were frauds concocted by Nick in order to boost his own journalist fortunes. Or Nemesis had never existed. Which meant the killer had to be—

All of a sudden Nick shoved his papers aside, pushed back from the table, and headed for the door, his boots clanking on the short flight of stairs leading up to the main floor.

Placing a finger to his lips in a sign to stay quiet, Cradoc waved for Cota to move away from the front door. The marshal then scurried back around to the north side of the lighthouse, where the fully saddled horse waited. He heard the front door swing open, someone make their way down the front steps and across the gravel yard, the footsteps getting closer and closer. Cradoc retreated again, around the west side of the building this time, where he would be out of sight to anyone approaching the animal.

Peeking around the corner, the marshal saw Nick step into the moonlight and move toward the horse. The reporter untied the reins, pulled the horse around so the animal was facing the trail into town, pulled out a pistol, and fired once into the air. The startled beast took off like a shot. Nick fired again, waited a few seconds, and fired a third shot into the air.

That's when Cradoc stepped from the shadows. Nick whirled around at him, the gun drawn, pointed at the marshal's chest.

"What's this all about?" the marshal asked.

"Cradoc?" Nick said with genuine surprise. "What are you doing here?"

"I could ask you the same."

"Following up on Kendall's death," Nick said, his tone wary. He had no clue when Cradoc had arrived on the scene, what he might have witnessed. He was staggered, straining his brain, trying to figure out how the marshal had uncovered his plan. How much did he see? How much does he know? And who told him?

"So, where is he?" Cradoc asked. "Where's Nemesis?"

"He got away," was Nick's quick response.

"I heard shots."

"I think I winged him as he rode off."

"Aaaaaah," said Cradoc, as if all was suddenly illuminated. "That's why there's blood on the saddle. It's supposed to make me—and everyone else—think you shot Nemesis as he made his getaway. Am I right?"

Nick's silence confirmed the theory quickly taking shape in Cradoc's mind. "But you got your interview, right? I heard you through the window, chatting up a storm … with yourself."

Now it was certain. Cradoc knew everything. Or at least enough to figure what was really going down. Nick could hear his heart pounding, feel the sweat forming on his brow. He tightened his grip on the pistol, realigned his aim. Insane notions raced through his mind: He could shoot Cradoc. Blame it on the killer. Get away scot-free if he acted now, if he could just bring himself to pull the damn trigger. Instead, he let out a deep sigh. "You don't think Kendall deserved to die?"

"I wouldn't know. I haven't read your story yet."

"He was the worst of all of them."

"How's that?"

"It was his idea. The fire that killed my mother! They all deserved to die—for what they did to her, what they did to so many others. Justice was done."

"I'm supposed to just turn a blind eye to your vengeance, go along with this farce?"

"It's not like you never bent the law," Nick countered.

"True enough. But I never killed anyone. Not in cold blood. And the only way you're gonna stop me from taking you in right now is pulling that trigger."

Nick glanced down at the gun in his hand, still pointed at Cradoc.

"What's it gonna be, Nick?"

Nick pulled back the hammer.

"You gonna kill me, too?"

Nick raised the gun to Cradoc's face.

"Whatever good you've accomplished, whatever state-ment you think you've made in the name of justice or the common man, it all goes up in flames if you shoot me dead."

Nick's hand broke into a tremble, shaking so bad it would be a miracle if he got off a clean, straight shot.

"Put the gun down, Nick. Put that damn thing down."

Nick's arm fell like a dead weight. He dropped the revolver, slumped to his knees.

Jose Cota rushed from his hiding place around the corner of the lighthouse, gazed back and forth between the marshal and Pinder.

Cradoc looked at Nick and then back at his deputy. "He got away! Nick winged him, but he was able to ride off."

Cota started to dash down the trail that cut north from the old lighthouse, but the marshal quickly called him back. "We'll never catch him that way. Back to the boat! We've gotta get back into town double time! You go on while I help Nick down to the pier."

Once Cota was gone, the two old friends faced each other again, a tense moment of silence as they considered the next move.

Both mystified and relieved, Nick shook his head in wonder. "Cradoc, I don't know what to say."

"Nothing," the marshal shot back. "You keep your damn trap shut. This ain't over. Far from it. Both of us sure as hell better hope that Cota didn't see what I saw inside that room."

"So you agree that—"

"I don't agree to anything yet. Other than the fact that I need more time to think."

42

BY THE FOLLOWING afternoon, the Santa Ana winds had faded into a warm, summer calm. But San Diego was still reeling from the shock of Fabian Kendall's assassination in front of thousands of people. Clinging to life, his aides had carried him up Broadway to a hotel opposite the courthouse. Horribly burnt, the man expired less than an hour later, at around the same time Cradoc Bradshaw and company were docking at Ballast Point.

The marshal sat in Joe Coyne's office, slumped in a wooden chair, his face showing the strain of the previous evening. He'd been home for a couple of hours, caught a few winks, and changed into clean clothes before heading back to the jailhouse. But the physical and mental fatigue he felt was going to take much longer to sort out.

Wyatt sat next to him, equally dazed by the events of the past twenty-four hours. Both of them waited in silence as Coyne read through the marshal's detailed account of events at the Santa Fe Depot, Ballast Point, and the old Point Loma lighthouse. Cradoc had been at his desk since the crack of dawn, scribbling everything down, every detail he could remember about the killing and its aftermath, knowing the more time that passed, the vaguer his recollections would be. The sheriff scratched at his bald spot and grunted whenever he came to an interesting passage.

Coyne finally looked up. "You found the horse?"

"Yep. Wondering down Broadway this morning," the marshal answered.

"And it's definitely the one that Nemesis rode away on?"

"Blood all over the animal and saddle. Gotta assume it's the same steed. Not like we get blood-covered horses trotting into town every day."

"But no body yet—dead or alive?"

Cradoc let out a deep sigh. "Not that any of my men can locate. We've been searching Point Loma and Dutch Flats since daybreak and no sign of anyone, least of all our phantom killer."

"I think he got clean away," Wyatt interjected. "Probably had a second, maybe even a third horse, stashed at a remote location. He changed mounts and lickety-split he's gone."

"Is that even possible?" asked Coyne.

Cradoc shrugged. "If there's one thing I've learned over the last six months, it's that anything is possible in this town, in this day and age."

The sheriff hocked a wad of chew into the spittoon beside his desk, dug into his tobacco pouch for another clump. He tucked it carefully between his upper molars and inside cheek before resuming his inquiry. "What about Nick?"

"What about him?" Cradoc asked.

"Isn't there something we can charge him with … obstruction of justice … aiding and abetting a crime?"

"I looked into that months ago," the marshal explained. "Had a long talk with the district attorney. There's not a lot of precedent, at least not when it comes to charging or convicting journalists who fraternize with criminals. It really is a gray area of the law. And I suppose an argument could be made that Nick was merely exercising his First Amendment rights."

"We wouldn't be going after him for what he's written in the paper," Coyne pointed out. "That's not the issue. It's his failure to inform us beforehand that he was going to meet the killer at a specific time and place."

"Even so, I can see them trying to make that case. Especially Bennett, who I would imagine is quite well versed in this sort of thing. And to make those charges stick, we would need to gather far more evidence of Nick's collusion with the killer than we currently have in hand."

"How about accessory before the fact?" asked Wyatt.

"Once again, we need indisputable proof that Nick had prior knowledge of the attack on Kendall. Unless more evidence comes to light, it appears that Nemesis struck before his rendezvous with Nick rather than afterward. So technically speaking, Nick did not have prior knowledge. The bottom line is that we would need something more substantial— and legally sound—to make a case."

"There must be something!" barked Coyne. "Do we really care if the charges are trumped up or not? The objective isn't putting Pinder behind bars, it's forcing him to reveal the killer's identity. He sure as shit must know by now. For God's sake, he met the bastard. Spoke with him in person. How can he not know?"

"I'm not even sure he ever even saw him. Said he had to conduct the interview in the dark. And even if he did see him," Cradoc declared, "he still might not know his name. And even then, Nick wouldn't give up the killer's name in a million years. Protecting his sources and all that journalistic First Amendment stuff. He tried to bring the man in, but if he couldn't do it in print—"

"Besides," Wyatt interrupted, "we gotta look at the larger picture."

Coyne groaned and turned to Wyatt. "And what might that be, Mr. Earp?"

"That Nick Pinder is an even bigger hero today than he was twenty-four hours ago. Championed by the masses. Admired by the great unwashed. The man who finally brought down Nemesis. Doesn't matter if we never find the body. It's what the hoi polloi wanna believe."

Coyne sneered at the very thought. "Do you agree with this hokum?" he asked the marshal.

Choosing his words carefully, Cradoc said, "As much as I think Nick deserves some sort of punishment for what he's done, I don't think you'd find a jury anywhere in California that would convict him of anything at this point in time."

"So he goes Scot free?"

Cradoc took another deep breath. "As long as the killing is over—and Nemesis never reappears—I don't see that we have any other choice."

43

December 1888

CRADOC BRADSHAW TIED his horse to the hitching post outside the Pinder home on Golden Hill, gazed around at the town spread out below, and disappeared inside.

Nick was sitting at the kitchen table, his fingers gliding across the same Sholes & Glidden he had used to compose the now-famous Nemesis letters. Only the two of them were aware of that truth, and that's how it would stay. The reporter now used it every day, pounding out his words for Frank Bliss and the American Publishing Company in Hartford—Mark Twain's original publisher and one of the most eminent literary houses in America. Several publishers had offered book deals based on the Nemesis saga, but Nick had held out for one that would let him spin his own life story, starting with the lighthouse and his youth with Cradoc, his apprenticeship in Old Town under Clive Bennett, and the run-up to recent events that would prove his crowning glory.

The book royalties were likely to be sizable given how much publicity the Nemesis case had garnered around the nation. Anyone who read newspapers from Boston to

Bakersfield knew the name Nick Pinder by now—and if they didn't, they would know it when the book came out.

They had a strange kind of relationship now—Nick and Cradoc. No longer mortal enemies, but not really friends again either. Yet inevitably bound together by their childhood, their years of professional collaboration, their love for the same woman, and the vast, dark secret both now shared.

"My goodness," said Nick, looking up from the machine. "Marshal Bradshaw visits again."

"How's the book coming along?" Cradoc asked, taking a seat on the opposite side of the table. Out the window, he caught a glimpse of Lupe in the backyard, tending to the vegetable patch Roz had planted with such optimism about the future.

"I'm about halfway through the final chapter—the most recent events. So everything is fresh in the mind. I suspect I'll finish sometime tomorrow."

"You got the horse in there, the blood on the saddle, the body we never found?"

"Of course. All of that's vital to the climax."

"But hopefully not the part where you persuade me to go along with your cockamamie story."

Nick allowed himself a subtle laugh. "Didn't take much convincing. "

"I could still rat you out."

"Yeah right," said Nick, like it was the most unlikely thing he had ever heard.

"You don't believe me?"

"Besides you looking the fool—and probably losing your badge for lying to your boss, the mayor, the papers and everyone else—there's the fact that justice was done. Finally."

"I've never said anything of that sort. To you or anyone else."

"You don't have to. You've always been much bigger on getting justice than sticking to the rules or doing exactly what the uppity-ups want. Isn't that why you quit the army, why you left Dodge? Armed with all the facts, you know the only way to get justice for the murder of my mother was doing it my way. And don't you tell me you wouldn't have done the same if someone you dearly loved had died in the same manner."

Cradoc shrugged. "I still haven't killed anyone who wasn't in the process of trying to kill me at that very moment."

"And I had never even come close to taking a life until earlier this year. Thought about it, for sure. But things happen—like finding out who caused the fire that killed your mother. And that makes people change." Nick thought a moment and then continued. "Do you think I did a wrong thing for a right reason? Did the means justify the ends in this case? Those are the questions we have to ask ourselves. Both of us, Cradoc. We're the only ones who know the whole truth."

With a sigh, he took his hat off and laid it on the table. "I don't know, Nick."

Rather than press the matter, Nick changed the subject. "I hear you got yourself a lodger," he blurted. "Someone to share that seaside shack you call a home. Is this Emma Lee a keeper?"

Cradoc shrugged. "I suppose you could say that. She gave up her own place, moved in with me a couple of weeks ago."

"Do I hear wedding bells?"

"We're a long ways from that. Both of us relish our freedom. Reminds me, have you heard from Roz since last we spoke?"

"I got another letter just the other day. San Francisco seems to be working out fine. Her shop is going great guns and she's already thinking of starting another."

Cradoc nodded. "It's where she belongs. She was never at home here, never settled. San Diego will never be sophisticated enough to hold a woman like that."

"Still, I do wish ..." Nick's voice trailed off, a sentence that didn't need to be completed.

The awkward pause was enough to get Cradoc back on his feet. "I was just checking in," he said. "See how things are coming along."

But Nick had something else to get off his chest. "Cradoc, I'm sorry," he said. "About you and me and Roz. If I had it to do over again ... let's just say that all of our lives would be substantially different today. Other than my mother's death, it's the one thing I would change about the past. We really did both believe you were, you know. Anyway, what I'm trying to say is that if there was some way we could ever work together again ... well, what I wouldn't give for that. Do you think that could ever happen?"

"I don't know," said Cradoc, bowing his head and kneading the brim of his hat in his hands. "That's an awful big hill to climb."

"But not impossible," Nick said with a hopeful lilt.

"It was my fault as much as yours. I suppose neither of us really thought about the consequences. Roz didn't either, for that matter. It's just one of those things."

"Yeah. One of those things."

Nick stood and held out his hand. "Coming around again?"

Cradoc took the proffered hand and gave it a brisk shake. "Of course." He nodded at the manuscript. "And you better have that damn book finished by the next time I'm here."

"Don't worry. It'll be waiting for you."

Outside, Cradoc pulled himself back into the saddle, pulled his horse around and trotted down the hill. He squinted into the December sun and thought about the man he'd left inside and the woman he was headed home to, both people he loved—yeah, might as well admit it—and both people who'd had to find justice their own way. He pulled down the brim of his hat and looked out at the sparkling bay. What was wrong and what was right these days? It was getting awful hard to tell in California.

THE END

HISTORICAL POSTSCRIPT
NEMESIS: TRUTH VS. FICTION

As is the case with much historical fiction, *Nemesis* is a blend of characters who really did walk the earth and others that took shape in my imagination.

Cradoc Bradshaw, Nick Pinder, Roz Hanna, Emma Lee Dawes, Clive Bennett and Wendell Smith are fictional characters, based on no one who ever lived (other than possibly myself). However, a number of other characters in Nemesis are based on historical figures who lived in San Diego in the late 1880s. All of the crimes for which Nemesis seeks revenge are inspired by true events that occurred in southern California during the 19th-century Wild West era. Among these were:

- The racism-driven hanging of 18 Chinese men and boys in Los Angeles in 1871 (largest mass lynching in American history);
- The Moosa Canyon Massacre of 1888 near present-day Escondido, CA, during which three squatters and one vigilante were killed.
- The mysterious Fire of 1872 that destroyed much of Old Town's commercial district.

- A long history of abuse against the local Native Americans—including rape, murder, hard labor and false imprisonment—stretching back to Spanish colonial times.

REAL PEOPLE

- **Jose Cota (1850-1902):** His law enforcement career in San Diego spanned four decades (1874-1902) including a stint in the late 1880s as one of Joe Coyne's deputies. Later he was San Diego's first Hispanic police officer and the department's first Hispanic supervisor.
- **Joe Coyne (1837-1916):** Drawn to California as a teenager by the Gold Rush, Coyne apparently made and lost several fortunes. He drifted into law enforcement after one of those fortunes was stolen by armed bandits who nearly killed him. Elected sheriff of San Diego in 1876, Coyne oversaw the transformation of the local constabulary from a ragtag gang of deputies into a proper police force with himself as chief of police.
- **Josephine Marcus "Josie" Earp (1860-1944):** Wyatt Earp's common law wife was born in New York City to German-Jewish parents who later moved the family to San Francisco. Leaving home at 14, she worked as a dancer and actress (and most probably a sporting lady) in the Arizona Territory. After meeting Wyatt in Tombstone—shortly before the fabled shootout at the OK Corral—the two of them spent 46 years together roaming from boomtown to boomtown across the West, including several years in San Diego. She often used the stage name "Sadie" rather than her given name.
- **Wyatt Earp (1848-1929):** One of the iconic figures of the American West, Earp called San Diego his home from the mid 1880s to early 1890s. In addition to

investing in local real estate, the legendary lawman ran three saloons and gambling halls (including the Oyster Bar on Fifth Avenue), refereed boxing matches and raced horses. After San Diego's real estate boom went bust, the Earps moved to San Francisco and from there to the Klondike Gold Rush.

- **Alonzo Horton (1813-1909):** Often called the "Father of San Diego," Horton was an ambitious and visionary real-estate developer who moved from San Francisco to San Diego in 1867 with the dream of creating magnificent new city beside one of the best natural harbors on the West Coast. He purchased 960 acres of waterfront land (most of present-day downtown San Diego) and christened it New Town to distinguish from Old Town in Mission Valley. Horton funded the steamship pier at the bottom of Fifth Street (1869), built the posh Horton House hotel (1870) and was one of the movers and shakers behind establishing Balboa Park—first city park west of the Mississippi. Although he didn't directly take part, Horton was one of those who engineered the 1871 "bloodless coup" during which the county archives were clandestinely transferred from Old Town to New Town in the middle of the night. Whether or not he was part of the plot to burn Old Town to the ground in 1872 is still open to debate; but Horton and his New Town certainly benefited from the demise of their only commercial rival.

- **William Hunsaker (1855-1933):** Born and raised in northern California, Hunsaker served as San Diego's duly elected mayor for just 10 months—January to November 1888. Disgusted with the way politics was run in San Diego, Hunsaker resigned and eventually moved to Los Angeles, where he practiced law.

- **Dr. Joe LeFevre:** San Diego County Physician and chief administrator of the County Hospital & Poor Farm from 1888-1891.

- **George Marston (1850-1946):** A natural-born entrepreneur, Marston arrived in San Diego in 1870 and worked as a clerk at the Horton House hotel and several local mercantiles before starting his own business. His department store at the corner of Fifth Avenue and C Street remained a thriving family business until 1961. Marston served as president of the San Diego Chamber of Commerce and founded the San Diego Historical Society. A very active philanthropist, he used his own money to save the old Spanish Presidio site in Old Town. Marston's Arts & Crafts-style mansion on Banker's Hill is now a museum.

- **Elliot Patterson:** The *San Diego Times* shooter is based on Frances Elliott Patterson, a professional photographer who ran a camera store in Fifth Avenue and later lived in a Victorian-style home at the corner of 22nd Street and Broadway on Golden Hill. The historic Hayward-Patterson House is still there, on the northwest corner of the intersection.

- **Fatty Rice:** Served as a deputy in San Diego from 1885 to 1889, before moving to Seattle where he lived for the rest of his life.

- **Kate Sessions:** The woman who recruited Roz Pinder to move from Boston to San Diego, really was vice principal at Russ School (now San Diego High School) before becoming a noted horticulturalist, landscape architect and the beloved "Mother of Balboa Park."

- **Ida Bailey:** Starting in the 1880s, San Diego's most notorious madame ran several houses of ill repute in the

Stingaree. Her most famous place of business was the legendary Canary Cottage (opened in 1903), allegedly frequented by many of the city's movers and shakers.

CHARACTERS BASED ON HISTORICAL FIGURES

- **Zebulon Archer:** San Diego's "lumber king" blends aspects of two historical figures—land developer Billy Carlson (who with partner Frank Higgins founded Ocean Beach in 1887) and fortune-hunter Asbury Harpending (a Rebel-sympathizing Copperhead who hatched an unsuccessful plan to have California secede from the Union and join the Confederate States of America during the Civil War). In addition to rendering all of the street names that still exist in Ocean Beach, Carlson and Higgins built a huge seaside resort hotel called the Cliff House that burned down in 1898.

- **"Yankee" Jim Ingraham:** The second Nemesis victim also blends two historical figures: homesteader Levi Stone (who led the Moosa Canyon Massacre of 1888 during which several squatters were murdered in cold blood) and North County rancher Cave Johnson Couts (who shot and killed rival Juan Mendoza in Old Town in 1865). Both men were charged with homicide and later acquitted despite overwhelming evidence that both were guilty of murder. Couts' longtime home—the Rancho Guajome Adobe ranch house—has been preserved as a museum in Vista, CA.

- **Fabian Kendall:** His fictional persona is based on Frank Kimball, who along with his brothers founded present-day National City on San Diego Bay and established the California Southern Railroad. Kimball's home at 932 Avenue A in National City is now a small museum.

Along with Alonso Horton, Kimball was a major bene-
ficiary of the 1872 fire that destroyed much of Old
Town and permanently shifted the balance of San
Diego's political and economic power to New Town.

LOCATIONS IN THE BOOK

- **Ballast Point:** Mentioned several times in *Nemesis*—
  including the across-the-bay chase at the end—this small
  peninsula protects San Diego Bay from the open ocean.
  Called Punta Guijarros by the Spanish who settled the
  area in 1769, the name gradually changed to reflect the
  fact that Yankee ship captains dumped their ballast there.
  During the 1850s and 60s, the point provided a venue
  for whalers to boil blubber inside 150-gallon cauldrons.
  Nowadays the peninsula is part of U.S. Naval Base Point
  Loma.

- **Balboa Park:** Cradoc Bradshaw and Wyatt Earp venture
  twice into the wild lands that later became Balboa Park.
  On their way to the County Hospital & Poor Farm, they
  ride up Presidio Canyon along the same route as present-
  day Highway 163. Later in the story, the two of them
  venture to Switzer Canyon on the park's eastern edge
  to evict a band of Kumeyaay Indians. The City of San
  Diego declared the area an open-space preserve in the
  1860s—one of the nation's first and largest city parks.
  Kate Session planting the park's first ornamental trees
  in 1892.

- **Baldwin locomotive:** The train engine that Fabian
  Kendall christens with a bottle of explosives is of the
  exact type that the California Southern Railroad used
  between San Diego and the Inland Empire in the late
  1880s.

- **Clive Bennett's motor yacht *Medusa*:** Is based on the real-life *Medea*, a vintage steam yacht built in Scotland and now part of the substantial collection of the San Diego Maritime Museum.

- **County Hospital and Poor Farm:** Established in 1880, the medical and welfare facility was located in Mission Valley, on the south side of the San Diego River. The hospital buildings are long gone, replaced in modern times by Fashion Valley Mall, the San Diego Union-Tribune office, several hotels, and the interchange of Interstate-8 and Highway 163.

- **Cuyamaca Club:** The oldest chartered private club in California was founded in 1887 and patronized by many of San Diego's movers and shakers; women were not admitted to the club until 1923.

- **Dutch Flats:** San Diego International Airport, Liberty Station and the Marine Corp Recruit Depot (MCRD) now occupy the tidal plain that was once called Dutch Flats. Prior to the diversion of the San Diego River in 1877, the river curled around Old Town and flowed across Dutch Flats into San Diego Bay.

- **Golden Hill:** The slightly elevated area where Nick and Roz Pinder built their home became popular in the 1880s as a cheaper alternative for those who couldn't afford to live on Banker's Hill. Nowadays the Golden Hill neighborhood is bounded by Interstate-5, Highway 94 and Balboa Park. Villa Montezuma at 1925 K Street is a surviving example of the sort of elaborate mansions that arose on Golden Hill in the late 1800s.

- **Old Point Loma Lighthouse:** The hilltop lighthouse where Nick Pinder was raised—and where the climax to *Nemesis* plays out—was erected in 1855 and protected the entrance to San Diego Bay for 36 years. Perched at 400 feet above sea level, the light was often shrouded in low clouds or fog, in other words useless to ships trying to enter or leave the bay. In Nemesis, the old light has been abandoned and fallen into disrepair by 1888. In reality, it was replaced by a more modern lighthouse at water level slightly later, in 1891. The lighthouse received federal protection in 1913 as part of Cabrillo National Monument. The Bayside Trail roughly traces the route that Nick Pinder and Cradoc Bradshaw would have taken from Ballast Point to the lighthouse on that fateful night in 1888.

- **Old Town:** Founded in 1769 by Spanish conquistador Gaspar de Portolà, Old Town was the military and civilian hub of San Diego through the Spanish, Mexican and early American periods. In the early 1870s, the municipal government, much of the commercial activity and most of the residents relocated to Alonzo Horton's New Town on San Diego Bay. Many of the buildings destroyed by fire of 1872 have been faithfully reconstructed and form part of Old Town State Historic Park.

- **Oyster Bar:** Wyatt Earp's saloon and gambling establishment was located on the ground floor of the Louis Bank of Commerce Building at 835 Fifth. The elaborate Baroque Revival-style structure (San Diego's first granite building) still stands, rising four stories above Fifth Avenue and its rowdy modern-day nightlife scene.

- **The Plaza:** Later called Horton's Plaza after the "Father of San Diego," the plaza has served as a major focal point and gathering spot in downtown San Diego since the

1870s. The U.S. Grant Hotel now sits on the block-long plot where the Horton House once stood. The fictional San Diego Times building was on the western side of the plaza, where a 23-story, black-glass skyscraper called 225 Broadway now rises.

- **San Diego Chinatown:** Many of city's early Chinese residents lived and ran businesses in the southwest portion of the Stingaree district. Their story is illuminated at the San Diego Chinese Historical Museum at 404 Third Avenue and J Street.

- **San Diego County Courthouse:** Erected in the late 1880s, the stout brick building served municipal functions until 1959 when it was torn down. The jailhouse was located at the rear of the courthouse with public hangings carried out in the livery across the street.

- *San Diego Times:* Clive Bennett's newspaper is pure fiction; however Fabian Kendall's *San Diego Union* was a real paper. Now called the *Union-Tribune*, the publication was founded in 1868 and has been the city's leading newspaper for more than a hundred and fifty years.

- **San Diego Train Station:** The original station—the venue for Fabian Kendall's fiery demise—was constructed in 1887 by the California Southern Railroad to handle the thousands of migrants pouring into San Diego. Demolished in 1915, it was replaced by the present-day Santa Fe Depot with its distinctive Spanish Revival architecture.

- **Sunset Cliffs:** The lofty sandstone palisades define the San Diego coast between Ocean Beach and Point Loma. A narrow, water-filled chasm called Devil's Pot—pounded by incoming tides—was a landmark in Victorian times before it partially collapsed. The Cliff

House was located near the northern end of the cliffs, around the spot where Ocean Beach Pier juts into the Pacific Ocean. The beach where Cradoc Bradshaw and Emma Lee Dawes venture on the Fourth of July is located at present-day Sunset Cliffs Natural Park, below Point Loma Nazarene University.

- **Steamer *Santa Rosa*:** Launched in 1883 in a Philadelphia shipyard, the *Santa Rosa* ferried passengers and cargo along the California coast until 1911, when she wrecked at Point Arguello on the grounds of what is now Vandenberg Air Force Base. State-of-the-art for the time, the iron-hulled ship was 326 feet long,

- **Stingaree:** San Diego's notorious red light district sprawled across a dozen blocks between present-day Market Street and the waterfront. At one point it was estimated the neighborhood harbored more than 120 saloons and brothels. Depending on their place in the prostitution hierarchy, sporting ladies worked out of respectable bordellos like Ida Bailey's Canary House (behind 536 4th Avenue) or rented space in tenement-like "cribs" with nothing more than canvas or cloth walls. In 1912, the city began a successful crackdown on illicit activities in the Stingaree. The First & Last Chance Saloon stood on the intersection of Firth and K, a block up from the Pacific Coast Steamship Company wharf, which stretched out into the bay on what is now reclaimed land occupied by the San Diego Convention Center and Embarcadero Marina Park.

- **St. Joseph's Church:** Now the cathedral of the San Diego Archdiocese, the old Catholic Church was originally constructed in 1875 on a plot of land at the corner of Third and Beech streets donated by Alonzo Horton.

- **Waterfront shanties:** Cradoc Bradshaw's home—
located roughly where the San Diego Maritime Museum
and historic *Star of India* clipper ship are located today—
is among the many "stilt houses" that arose along San
Diego Bay during the latter half of the 19th century. As
bay wasn't owned by anyone, people could construct an
over-the-water house wherever they wanted without the
need for homesteading or property purchase. The City of
San Diego eventually outlawed the flimsy structures as
health hazards.

ACKNOWLEDGMENTS

There are many, many people to thank for NEMESIS coming to fruition, starting with my wife Julia Clerk, who proofread every version of the manuscript as it grew and shrank and evolved. And kudos to my youngest daughter Shannon Yogerst, for her computer skills and steady hand when it came to drawing the maps.

Thanks also to Fauzia Burke, who immediately saw the value of a book that illuminated the rich history of Wild West San Diego when others wavered, and for introducing me to agent Evan Marshall, who undertook this project without hesitation. Evan put me on the trail to Lisa Miller at Amphorae Publishing Group who was intrigued by the plight of Cradoc Bradshaw and Nick Pinder. Thanks also to Amphorae interns Mina Bozeman and Catherine O'Mara. And finally a huge round of applause for Kristina Blank Makansi, my editor at Blank Slate Press, who was an absolute joy to work with in shaping NEMESIS into its final form and finally getting it out the door.

History has always been close to my heart, and I have many to thank for my interest in the past including the Pacific Beach Branch of San Diego Public Library (where I spent so much of my youth). In more recent times, I lingered for hours at the San Diego History Center in Balboa Park, poring over old maps and copies of the

San Diego Union from the 1880s in order to get a flavor for the everyday events that shaped life along the Southern California coast at that time.

My parents, Henry and Marjorie Yogerst, were instrumental in exposing me to various aspects of San Diego history at a very early age through the simple process of taking me to many of the places that appear in NEMESIS—the Embarcadero waterfront, the Sunset Cliffs in Ocean Beach, Horton Plaza and the Santa Fe Depot, Old Town in Mission Valley, and the Old Point Loma Lighthouse at Cabrillo National Monument.

Teachers also played a role. Dennis C. Hart, my long-time history teacher at the University of San Diego High School, taught me that studying the past provides valuable insight into who we are today. While Danny Wilson—who was both my math teacher and moderator of the *El Cid* student newspaper—encouraged all of us young scribes to reach for our dreams.

ABOUT THE AUTHOR

Born and raised in southern California, Joe Yogerst's articles on travel, business, culture and sports have appeared in the *Washington Post, Los Angeles Times, San Francisco Examiner, International Herald Tribune* (Paris), *Conde Nast Traveler, CNN Travel, USA Today, BBC Travel, TIME, Newsweek and Travel & Leisure* and 32 National Geographic books. *Land of Nine Dragons*, his account of a modern-day journey through Vietnam, was named America's Best Travel Book in the Lowell Thomas Awards competition. *The Long Road South* about his four-month journey along the Pan American Highway between Texas and Argentina was named one of America's top travel books by the Society of American Travel Writers. His latest National Geographic book, *50 States, 5,000 Ideas*, soared to No. 1 at Amazon Travel Books.

As a staff writer at MTM and Steven J. Cannell productions, he developed television movies and wrote episodes of TV shows like *Two* and the long-running *Silk Stalkings* mystery series. He has an ongoing relationship with Craig Anderson Production in Hollywood and Creative Street Entertainment in Indianapolis, developing action adventures and sci-fi series and reality shows for network and cable TV.

Nemesis is his first novel published in the United States.